UNDONE

JOHN COLAPINTO

UNDONE

a novel

SOFT SKULL PRESS
an imprint of COUNTERPOINT

Soft Skull Press Edition 2016

Library of Congress Cataloging-in-Publication Data
Names: Colapinto, John, 1958- author.
Title: Undone : a novel / John Colapinto.
Description: Berkeley : Soft Skull Press, 2016.
Identifiers: LCCN 2015045987 | ISBN 978-1-59376-642-9 (softcover)
Subjects: LCSH: Authors--Fiction. | Celebrity--Fiction. | Swindlers and swindling—Fiction. | Fathers and daughters—Fiction. | Impersonation--Fiction. | BISAC: FICTION / Literary. | GSAFD: Black humor (Literature)
Classification: LCC PS3553.O4369 U53 2016 | DDC 813/.54—dc23
LC record available at http://lccn.loc.gov/2015045987

Cover design by Kelly Winton
Interior design by Patrick Crean

Soft Skull Press
An imprint of Counterpoint
2560 Ninth Street, Suite 318
Berkeley, CA 94710
www.softskull.com

Printed in the United States of America
Distributed by Publishers Group West

10 9 8 7 6 5 4 3 2 1

To Donna and Johnny,
and to my mother

And the LORD said unto Satan,
Hast thou considered my servant Job,
that there is none like him in the Earth,
a perfect and an upright man, one that
feareth God, and escheweth evil?

—Job 1:8

Satan Trismegistus subtly rocks
Our ravished spirits on his wicked bed
Until the precious metal of our will
Is leached out by this cunning alchemist:

The Devil's hand directs our every move—
The things we loathed become the things we love . . .

—Baudelaire, *Les Fleurs du Mal*
(tr. Richard Howard)

PART ONE

1

For two days the girl did nothing but lie in bed and cry. It was driving Dez crazy. The sobs, the shuddering intakes of breath, the sudden wails of "Why, God? *Why?*" before the diminuendo of sniffles and nose blows; then the whole process repeating itself. True, she had just lost her mother—abruptly, violently—in a car crash. But how much was a man expected to take? He was on the point of yelling at her to *Get a grip* when, on the afternoon of the third day, she lifted her head from the pillow and said, in a blurry, tear-muffled voice, "I'm hungry." Dez found this an improvement over her blubbering, but he wished she could have chosen a better moment to start talking to him. His show was about to start.

He was slouched on the sofa—really just a narrow padded bench—that ran along one wall of the trailer where he had been holed up, like a fugitive, for almost two months, ever since losing his job (or, rather, fleeing from it). The trailer, a three-decades-old Tartarus model, sat among other sagging relics much like it in a clearing in the woods of northern Vermont. With its cracked concrete parking areas, ill-tended grass and communal bathroom hut, the trailer park made a sharp contrast to the privileged neighborhood in Raleigh, North Carolina, where Dez had grown up, to say nothing of the ivied quadrangles of Duke University where he got his BA, or the mellow Gothic spires of Boston College where he earned his legal degree. But there were compensations. His neighbors were mostly retirees on a tight budget, a low-key community ignored by the local authorities, and thus the perfect place for Dez to be sojourning until he figured out his next move.

The day was hot and humid, the trailer stifling. He was dressed in a pair of jeans, no shirt or shoes. His skinny torso might have been that of an underfed eighteen-year-old, but Dez was, in reality, thirty-one, a fact betrayed chiefly by the triangular areas of balding above his temples, and the deeply carved smile lines (pentimenti of more carefree days) bracketing his lipless, downturning mouth.

"Come and make me feel better," Chloe whimpered from the sleeping nook at the end of the trailer.

"Can't," he said. "Show's started."

He kept his eyes on the television's small, static-riddled screen. He'd bought the set for eight dollars at a swap meet in

Sayer's Cliff and was running it on a pair of bent rabbit ears (couldn't afford satellite, if such a luxury were even available in these godforsaken woods). Despite the abysmal reception, he never missed *Tovah in the Afternoon*, the top-rated daytime talk show that specialized in true tales of human fortitude, the endurance of the human spirit, the likely existence of Angels, and the healing powers of love. Dez considered Tovah's show the crystallization of all that was pitiable in the American character: the sentimentality, the infantilism, the dithery-headed optimism, the lust for success disguised as a quest for the spiritual. (He particularly loved those episodes devoted to the perils of material desires, which ended with each member of the studio audience practically wetting herself with joy over receiving a *100% genuine Rolex watch!*) The show always buoyed him; it was living proof that his own dramatic fall from a life of comfort and respectability (a fall precipitated by the most natural and insistent of all human impulses) was anyone's fault but his own: it was the fault of a sick, silly, hypocritical society, a society in its death throes.

To the sound of the show's raucous theme music—a blend of balalaikas and soft rock guitars—Tovah burst from the wings, a short, heavyset woman with a mannish, square face and tear-misty brown eyes behind her trademark pink-framed glasses. She strode to the lip of the stage and threw her arms wide, as if to embrace the studio audience, which unleashed a storm of cheers and clapping. When this died down, she swept her gaze over the crowd and said, in an accent flavored by her native Queens, "Welcome all! Today, we bring you a story of inspiration. A tale of hope and courage and survival; of choices made,

of hurdles crossed, of deep loss and terrible sacrifice, and—*always*—the power of Love."

Dez's favorite guests—the ones who best lent themselves to his sardonic ridicule—were the spirit mediums, the life coaches and ghost-whisperers, the angel-summoners and "relationship experts." Alas, today's show featured a mere memoirist, author of the book *Lessons from My Daughter*, the true story of the catastrophic stroke suffered by the writer's wife while she was giving birth to their only child, the titular daughter, now almost five years old. The episode promised to be a dreary bore.

"Please," Chloe said, drawing out the word. "Come."

Dez did not budge. He felt an uncharacteristic pang of self-reproach at his disinclination to console the child in her grief. But he was at a loss for how to do so. Partly this was owing to that simple lack of human empathy which Dez freely and unapologetically acknowledged in himself. Then there was his *own* experience of parental loss, clearly so different from Chloe's. (When his despised father, a judge, died last year, Dez was ecstatic—not because the old man had left him any of his considerable fortune; he hadn't, not a penny, which explained in part, but only in part, Dez's current reduced circumstances.) Finally, there was Dez's fear that any tenderness he might display toward the girl would be mistaken for an overture toward a different kind of intimacy—the sexual intimacy that had been his reason for pursuing her in the first place but which, lately, had become a physiological impossibility, ever since his job loss and the subsequent depression that had settled over him, rendering him, humiliatingly and for the first time ever, impotent.

"Well, then, I'm getting up," Chloe said.

He turned toward the sleeping nook and watched as she threw back the sheet and climbed from the bed. Dressed only in a pair of white Y-front underpants and a shrunken T-shirt, she stood in profile to him, lifting her elbows high as she swirled her hair into a ponytail, the gawkiness of her elongated limbs contrasting with the roundness and resilience of her womanly curves. At seventeen, she had not fully left childhood, but neither had she fully entered adulthood, and it was the teasing, teetering balance between the two states that so stirred Dez—or used to, before this gloom killed all desire.

She tiptoed into the living space and curled up beside him, pulling her feet onto the sofa and cushioning her head in his lap. He kept his eyes on the television.

"Look at me," she softly admonished him.

He glanced down into her upturned face—a round, pertly pretty face that still retained a cushioning layer of baby fat but through which the angled cut of her cheekbones was just beginning to show. There was some puffiness under her wide-set green eyes, patches of pink raw skin around her delicate nostrils, and her lips had a more swollen quality than usual, from all that crying. But none of this could mar the overall impression of youth and freshness in her face. She was peering up at him, Dez noted, with an expression of unsettling emotional ardency and need.

"Feeling happier?" he said, turning his eyes back to the TV.

"I guess," she said. "But know what I was thinking, just now? Before I got up?" Dez made no response. She went on,

undaunted: "Now that my mom is gone, you're the only person I have left in the world."

This was, unfortunately, quite true. She had told him, when they first met, of how her father had drowned when she was an infant: slipped below the ice on frozen Lake Sylvan during some bibulous antics with friends. Dez had expressed the conventional condolences over her loss, but had secretly applauded it: he knew from bitter experience that when courting a girl as young as Chloe it was best there be no potentially enraged father in the picture. But now, with her mother having contrived to join her father in violent, untimely death, she was officially an orphan, Dez her sole protector. He did not relish responsibility even at the best of times, and these were hardly that, with his bank balance fast dipping toward zero and no plans for how to replenish it.

He had thought more than once about ditching her—packing his few possessions into a bag and slipping out while she slept, lighting out for California, Florida, Mexico—anywhere but here. But he had somehow not been able to do that. There was something about this one that had gotten under his skin. The same thing, apparently, that had made him risk everything by seducing her in the first place, despite the warnings, the legal threats, the second chances, the therapeutic interventions, the sober promises to reform.

"See what I mean?" Chloe said.

"Hmmm?"

The television show, despite its dismal guest, had started to interest him. With her usual breathtaking invasiveness, Tovah had

just asked the hapless memoirist about his sex life—inquiring how he "managed," given that his wife was confined to a wheelchair, unable to speak or to move any body part, save for her eyelids. The guest, a tall, sandy-haired man of around forty with bulging blue eyes and a diffident smile, was staring at Tovah in apparent shock, evidently having failed to anticipate her question.

"I'm saying," Chloe repeated, "all we've got is each other."

"Absolutely," Dez said, his eyes on the screen. He was straining now to catch the answer produced by Tovah's guest, who had begun mouthing some platitudinous euphemisms about how he missed "physical closeness of that kind" with his wife. "But," the man went on, "having resolved to take my marriage vows seriously, I've been forced to accept that love is about more than the purely physical act, an act that partly—but only partly—defines marriage."

"Dez?" Chloe said.

He grunted dismissively.

"Oh, forget it," she said, giving up and rising from the sofa.

She stepped across to the kitchenette—an arrangement of camp stove, icebox and sink beneath an overhang of shallow cabinets—and began to hunt for something to eat.

Dez sat up now and leaned toward the television screen, where Tovah continued to badger her guest about the demands of his frustrated libido. "You're only forty-one years old," she said, "still in the prime. Yet you're saying that you remain *faithful* to Pauline?"

"Well," the man replied, "those vows did say 'in sickness or

in health' and 'for better or for worse.' I was granted the worst, from which I must try to extract the best."

"But it must be so difficult," Tovah pressed, "to commit, at your age, to a life of celibacy?"

"Perhaps not as difficult as we men would have you believe," he replied, glancing up into the studio audience with what Dez perceived as a self-satisfied little smile. "We plead biological necessity when caught straying. But that's often just a convenient rationalization to explain away a moment of moral failure—of weakness. We *can* control ourselves."

In the moment of stunned silence that greeted this utterance, the director cut to a wide shot of Tovah's studio audience, a crowd of some 350 mostly middle-aged women. They were staring at Tovah's guest with mouths agape, as if (Dez thought, with an inward spasm of delighted contempt) the man were a member of some alien species—a species that produced creatures who looked identical to human males but whose souls were blessedly free of all the worst male characteristics: the selfishness, the obliviousness, the immaturity, the grotesque, ungovernable lusts.

"Ladies?" Tovah said. "What did I tell you? A *mensch*. Are we talking to a *mensch* or what?" An avalanche of answering applause crashed down from the seats. The man on the screen dipped his head, as if too shy to accept this outpouring of adulation.

Dez snorted. The exchange epitomized why he never missed the show; it was what he called a Pure Tovah Moment—a mixture of mendacity, sentimentality, self-congratulation and

self-promotion. "That's right, buddy," he muttered. "Sell them books."

Chloe, finding nothing in the cupboards, had excavated a canister of ice cream from the frosted-over freezer and plucked a spoon from the sink. She stepped back to the sofa and settled in beside Dez, sucking the ice cream off the spoon like a lollipop. Tovah had gone to commercial—an elaborate Busby Berkeley–style production about the joys of a wonder mop that used only static electricity to clean up dust and crumbs. Dez muted the TV. Chloe seized her opportunity.

"Want some?" she said, digging out a fresh bite of ice cream and holding the spoon toward him. "Mom always said that it's good for you, because it has milk in it."

"Not hungry," he said. Nor did he particularly care to listen to her prattle on about her suddenly sainted mother's theories about nutrition. *Ice cream, for God's sake! Good for you!* He tuned out her further babbling—she was discoursing now on her late mother's favorite recipes culled from the menu of the Snak Shak diner where the poor woman had toiled as a waitress. He shushed her violently when his show resumed.

"Welcome back," Tovah cried. "My guest is the author of the magnificent new memoir *Lessons from My Daughter*—Mr. Jasper Ulrickson."

Chloe looked up sharply. She could not believe her ears. And she could not stop herself. "*Jasper Ulrickson?*" she said. She swung around on the sofa and stared at Dez. "Mom knew a guy called that!"

His first thought was that this was some new manifestation

of the child's inexplicable sorrow over her mother's death, a grief-induced delusion. But she looked in earnest; her eyes popped wide, her lips ajar. He again hit the mute button.

"What are you talking about?"

"Before I was born," Chloe said excitedly. "When Mom was working as kitchen girl at the New Halcyon Country Club. He was the tennis teacher! They had a fling. Wait—let me see if it's him!" When the camera cut to a shot of Tovah's guest, Chloe pointed with her spoon and screamed, "That's the guy!"

The man on the screen was heavier than the handsome, sun-reddened youth in white T-shirt and shorts in her mom's old photographs of that summer, but he was the same person. Definitely. Those slightly bulgy blue eyes, that high brow and forehead, that sandy hair and nice, shy smile.

"That's him!" she repeated. "When I get Mom's stuff from her house, I can show you! That's him! I swear!"

Dez had never met Chloe's late mother—had, indeed, taken some pains to avoid such an encounter—but he'd glimpsed her often enough when he drove through New Halcyon: framed like a three-quarter-length portrait in the Snak Shak's takeout window (*Portrait of Dejection*), or humping up the steep sidewalk to the VistaVue Motel where she had a second job as a chambermaid; a woman well past her prime at thirty-five, with over-dyed blond hair, a barrel-shaped body and a drinker's flushed face ringed in cigarette smoke. He'd often wondered if the woman had, when young, possessed any of her daughter's fanatic allure. Probably—if this Ulrickson had bothered to take a run at her.

"When, exactly, was this?" Dez rapped out.

"Sumavore eyes bore," Chloe said, speaking around a bolus of ice cream that she was trying to keep off a sensitive molar. She swallowed, giggled and repeated, "The summer before I was born." Then she dropped her voice, as if to impart an off-color secret. "Actually, it's kind of funny. Mom told me that when she found out she was pregnant with me, she wondered if I might even be his kid."

Dez was not sure he had heard her properly. "*His* kid?" he said, pointing at the screen. "She thought you might be *his* kid?"

"Well, for like two secs," Chloe explained. "See, she did it once with him—at the very end of the summer, at the closing dance. So when she found out she was pregnant, at first she didn't know who did it. But then she realized it could only be Hughie, her boyfriend, my real dad."

"How?" Dez said sharply. "How could she be so sure?"

Startled by his harsh tone—he spoke as if his life depended on her answer—she said, with exaggerated calm, "It was easy, silly. She realized she got her period right *after* this Jasper guy went back to school. So it couldn't've been him. Plus, I look just like Hughie. Mom showed me a picture. We have the same sexy mouth!"

She pursed her lips into a moue to make Dez laugh. But Dez didn't laugh. He simply turned back to the television—although now (she noticed) he had a strange look on his face, his eyes wide, fixed and staring, as if he were watching the approach of something huge from beyond the flickering screen. And, strangely, he had not turned the sound back on.

"Anyway," she said, digging around for a final bite and speaking more to herself than to Dez, who was hurting her feelings by ignoring her that way, "looks like this Ulrickson guy got rich. I could've used a rich daddy."

"Yes," Dez said in a soft, faraway voice. "Yes, you certainly could."

And it was from that innocent exchange that he hatched the plan. Of course, in matters of creativity, an artist often conveniently forgets the anguished hours that go into honing an idea, sanding away its rough edges, solving its internal problems. Still, its basic shape, its *gestalt*, came into being on that morning of the first day of April, in that flash of inspiration which Dez would later think of as the moment at which he began to claw his way out from the pit of poverty, squalor and despair into which he had allowed himself to sink.

Not that his motives were purely, or even primarily, mercenary. For the scheme, if he could make it work, offered something more lasting, more satisfying, than mere money. As a man who had fallen so far in life—all due, he believed, to the hypocrisy of a society that punished men like him, men who had the courage to live out their animal nature, and exalted men like this Ulrickson, who could so convincingly masquerade as a dutiful, disciplined, decent male—Dez felt he had something to prove: namely, that when you stripped men to their primal essence, they were all the same, all equally prey to the ferocious, feral appetites that roiled, secretly, behind even the most saintly exterior. What had Ulrickson said in reply to Tovah's question about his enforced celibacy? *We* can *control ourselves.* The sanctimoniousness of that boast! The

self-congratulation! That was the gauntlet thrown down; that was the challenge which fired Dez's determination to test Ulrickson's smug resolve, to prove that, for all his success and wealth and fame, he was no better than Dez, no better than any other man (as Dez understood all men to be)—and, perhaps, given the right conditions, a good deal worse.

A movement in his peripheral vision made him look up. Chloe had risen from the sofa. Seeing his sharp glance, she said, on a note of apology, "I'm just going to take a shower."

She turned her back and peeled her T-shirt over her head, then slid the Y-fronts down her legs. She was stepping toward the flimsy accordion door of the bathroom when she heard Dez say, in an oddly thickened voice, "Actually . . ."

She stopped and turned. She saw a look on his face—a look she hadn't seen in weeks and which she had despaired of ever seeing again. All things being equal, she might have preferred to see softness and sympathy on his features, an understanding smile, as if he cared about her sadness over her mother—rather than this leer of wolfish appetite. But she was ready to settle for any kind of attention from him, just so long as she could be sure that he still loved her. And that's what this ravening animal grin meant—didn't it?

With an upward flick of his chin, he beckoned her.

"I just remembered," he said as she moved obediently toward him, "that no one can resist you. No one. And that has given me a naughty—a *very* naughty—idea."

Plus, of course (Dez reasoned), there was bound to be money in it.

2

The paternity complaint, sent from the Department of Children and Families of Vermont, was delivered to Jasper's house in the town of Clay Cross, Connecticut, on an afternoon at the beginning of May, four weeks after his appearance on Tovah's show. He did not recognize the missive as a legal summons, arriving, as it did, with the usual avalanche of letters and packages sent by fans of *Lessons from My Daughter*. It was unusual for a letter (in an eight-by-ten-inch manila envelope) to be delivered by hand (he hastily signed for it), but by now nothing could truly surprise him: over the last month he had received, by UPS delivery, a crate containing a life-sized pastel portrait of

him and Pauline rendered by a septuagenarian fan in Dallas; he had fended off, from his doorstep, a pair of Swedish fans wheeling a carry-on packed with first editions of his memoir for signing (and obvious resale on eBay); just two days ago, a local farmer had appeared bearing a truckload of spring asparagus for Jasper and his family. So a hand-delivered business envelope from an unfamiliar address raised no immediate alarms, its bulk suggestive of, perhaps, a brochure outlining the activities of one of the hundreds of stroke or head injury charities that continually approached him for endorsement, cash or speaking engagements.

At forty-one years old, Jasper had been a professional writer all his adult life, producing, at a rate of one book every two years, a series of mystery novels featuring his blind private eye, Geoffrey Bannister. The books had never put him in the first rank of mystery writers, but they had won him a small, dedicated following. He had never imagined, for himself, anything like the success of *Lessons from My Daughter.* The memoir was already in its sixth printing, and had, to date, earned more than all his novels combined and multiplied by a factor of twenty.

Although he had always known that a single book could make a writer wealthy—*In Cold Blood* helping to fund Capote's decades of drinking and dissipation; *Catcher in the Rye* buying Salinger fifty years of publishing silence—Jasper had never seriously pondered such a fate for himself, or even longed for it. He had not needed to. With the death of his parents in a private plane crash when he was twenty-three, he had come into the inheritance that put him beyond financial worries.

His father, a mild, sweet-tempered man, had been heir to the frozen fish fortune amassed by Jasper's enterprising immigrant grandfather from Oslo. His mother, an accomplished triathlete in her youth, had enjoyed a vigorous middle age as a devoted kayaker on nearby Long Island Sound. Raised in a happy and loving home in the tenets of his parents' devout Lutheranism, Jasper decided early in life to eschew the family business and become a writer, an ambition touched off in him, at age fourteen, when he first read *The Adventures of Sherlock Holmes*. Whereas stories of the famous sleuth were, for some aspiring writers, a springboard to more sophisticated reading (and writing) in later life, something perennially boyish, not to say naïvely innocent, in Jasper inclined him to see the Baker Street polymath as a permanent hero and inspiration, and apart from a short-lived phase directly after earning his postgraduate degree, when he flirted (unconvincingly) with growing his beard stubble, smoking unfiltered Gitanes and writing abstract poetry in an East Village garret, he had never had literary ambitions greater than to invent a detective modeled, without apology, on Conan Doyle's great creation.

Most critics dismissed his Bannister series as a pale imitation of Sir Arthur's masterworks, and sales were decidedly mid-list, but large royalty statements, important awards and critical bouquets were not necessary prods to Jasper's muse. Materially secure, after his parents' passing, he was able to write his detective novels simply because he loved writing, and because he relished the difficulty of showing how a sightless man, with the aid only of his sharpened senses and his faithful Seeing Eye dog, Smokey,

could ferret out, through Holmesian feats of deduction, criminals. (Never one to cheat, Jasper took it as a point of pride and honor always to lay before the attentive reader the necessary clues for solving the mystery one step ahead of blind Bannister.) He had written his memoir of Pauline's stroke with a similar lack of commercial ambition—had written it, in fact, with no other motive than to exorcise his grief and horror over his wife's incapacitation, to celebrate her strength and endurance, and to tell the world about the inspiration he drew from the example of Maddy, their only child.

The invitation to appear on Tovah's show had arrived quite out of the blue, without Jasper's either hoping for or expecting it. Any slight reluctance he might have felt about appearing on a program infamous for its lachrymose wallowing in tragedy, its tabloid-like exploitation of others' suffering, was outweighed by what he understood to be Tovah's unique power to publicize a book, and thus to spread more widely the message of hope and inspiration that was his main reason for publishing the memoir in the first place. And so he had agreed to go on the program. To date, the only truly regrettable fallout from that decision was the massive increase in his mail, which he felt obliged to sift through, and answer, each day.

Stooping, he gathered up the fifty or so letters that lay on the carpet below the mail slot and, with the mystery envelope tucked among them, walked from the foyer into the large, sun-filled open-plan kitchen at the front of the house. He sat at the table and began going through the mail. He had opened and

read only one letter when he heard a car pull up in the drive: Pauline, arriving home from her daily physiotherapy.

He walked back out to the foyer and opened the door on a fresh, flower-scented May afternoon. Standing on the front step, he saw, through the play of confetti-like light and shadow cast by the maple tree that grew from the front lawn, Deepti, Pauline's live-in caregiver. She was standing by the back of the car, operating the hydraulic lift that lowered Pauline's wheelchair from the retrofitted SUV onto the gravel driveway.

"Need help?" he called.

"No, no, Mr. Jasper," Deepti sang out in a lilting Indian accent. "I am fine."

Maddy, whom Deepti picked up from preschool every day on the way home from the hospital, unclasped her seat belt, clambered from the backseat and ran up the flagstone path through the mobile green-filtered light. "Daddy!" she cried, throwing herself into Jasper's arms.

"Hey, Muffin!" he said, swinging her up off the ground. She was almost five now and, as the twinge in his lower back told him, getting too big for him to lift in this way. He nuzzled her neck, then pulled his head back and studied her face, the soft bow-shaped lips, the near-transparent skin glowing as if lit from within. Her dark bangs and the dimple in her right cheek were exact replicas of Pauline's. From Jasper she had inherited only his blue eyes and the suggestion of a cleft, really just a shallow dent, in her chin. "How was House of Wee Folk?" he asked.

"Great! I can sing the whole ABC song!"

"Wonderful," he said. "I'd love to hear it." He lowered her, gingerly, to the floor. "But right now, I want you to go wash all that preschool off your hands."

"Kay!" she said, and ran off into the house.

Deepti, in the meantime, had wheeled Pauline up to the front door.

She looked strikingly as she had before the stroke: smooth-skinned, large-eyed, dark-haired, her almond-shaped face as beautiful as ever, save for the slight droop of the right side of her mouth and her right eyelid. Her once-animated hands, through disuse, were curled permanently into fists in her lap. But there was no doubt, in her alert gaze, of her undiminished awareness and intelligence. She returned Jasper's greeting and kiss with a blink and a kind of twinkle that Jasper, who had known her for over fifteen years, recognized as true contentment.

When first told by Pauline's neurologist that her locked-in status did not necessarily mean a shortened lifespan—"Indeed, with good care, she can live as long as you or me," Dr. Carlucci told him—Jasper had been assailed with horror. He thought of Pauline trapped, indefinitely, within her isolating paralysis. Might not death be a welcome escape? Dr. Carlucci had quickly reassured him, saying that recent long-term studies showed that locked-in patients who were well cared for and encouraged to communicate, to be engaged with their world, reported levels of contentment *equal* to those of healthy people—stunning results that, frankly, called into question the most basic assumptions about human happiness. "Of course, the patients who do

best are those who feel that there is something to live *for,*" the doctor added. "A great many are parents of young children, like your Maddy."

Pauline was proof of all that Carlucci had said. She had, since coming home twenty-two months ago, made remarkable strides. Increased diaphragm strength meant that she no longer breathed with a ventilator; she no longer fed through a gastrointestinal tube, and was able to swallow smooth purees and thickened liquids; improved bladder control meant that she no longer relied on a catheter—all advances that had resulted in a marked uplift in her mood, which in turn gave her doctors hope for continued improvements. So, despite what was undeniably a difficult circumstance, Jasper refused to surrender to despair. Pauline would not have allowed that, in any case.

Deepti pushed the wheelchair through the foyer and into the kitchen, parking it by the table where the pile of mail lay. She went to fill the kettle, and Jasper sat down beside Pauline. "Today's haul," he said, gesturing at the stack of letters. He liked going through the fan mail each day with Pauline, soliciting her opinion on which letters to answer, which to discard. "Shall I?" he said, lifting one. She blinked.

These blinks (once for yes, twice for no) were her sole means of communication. Pauline had tried to master the art of dictating messages to Jasper by blinking at the appropriate time as he recited the alphabet to her, picking out sentences letter by letter—some locked-in patients managed to write entire books with this method—but deficits in her short-term memory (an

effect of the stroke, Carlucci surmised) so far made it impossible for her to hold a phrase of any length or complexity in her mind while laboriously spelling it out. A retina scanner to aid her in choosing letters from a computer tablet with movements of her iris had proved little better, since this too required holding an utterance in the mind for extended periods. Much of her current physiotherapy was aimed at improving her memory and overall mental and physical stamina so that she might, one day, accomplish the task of writing by dictation. Her therapists, lately, had noted some improvements. But for the time being, she relied solely on the binary, yes-no responses of blinking. Jasper had been duly trained in how to avoid asking open-ended questions, how to start and stop conversations, and how to recognize when Pauline wished to "speak." For all its initial cumbersomeness, the method had proved surprisingly effective.

"I was looking at this letter when you arrived," he went on, smiling, to signal that it belonged to that category bound instantly for the trash. "It struck me as amusing—in an end-of-the-American-Empire kind of way."

Pauline's eyes twinkled in anticipation.

"It's from a man, Scooter Reece, in Atlanta. A so-called marketing entrepreneur. He suggests I travel around the country preaching what he calls the gospel of Daughter. Ten thousand per speech—guaranteed. As a nondenominational lay minister, I won't pay taxes on any monies brought in through my ministry. Scooter will get this house listed as our parish—no more pesky property taxes. We'd have to cough up 60 percent to Scooter,

but he's a man with ideas, including a special limited edition American Girl Maddy doll. Do we go for it?"

Pauline's eyes sparkled with mirth. Just to be sure, she blinked twice, in quick succession.

"Thought so," he said with mock disappointment. He tossed the letter onto the pile reserved for the trash. "I knew your integrity would ruin everything!"

Maddy ran into the kitchen and climbed onto Jasper's lap.

"Hey, don't get too comfy," he warned. "Nap time in five minutes."

Deepti brought over to the table a tray laden with a teapot and cup for Jasper. He pushed the pile of letters aside. "So," he asked Pauline, "did you have a good day?"

She blinked once. She waited a beat, then blinked again, asking the question back to him.

"Not bad," he said. "I'm still trying to start this new Bannister. But I'm not getting anywhere. By now I should have an entire outline."

"Mr. Jasper," said Deepti sternly as she poured him a cup of tea. "It is too soon for a new book, with all the excitement over your memoir. The *Tovah* show. All this mail to answer. You must take a break."

Jasper smiled across the table at Pauline, whose eyes glinted in response. "You're right, Deepti—very sage advice," he said. "But you know the saying about the devil and idle hands."

"What kind of hands?" Maddy piped up.

Jasper explained that unless you keep busy, you start doing

bad things. "For instance, not getting ready for your nap." He lowered her to the floor and playfully swatted her bottom. "Go forth," he said.

She ran off down the adjoining hallway, shouting, "Come and tuck me in! And bring Mom!"

"In a minute," he called after her. He turned to Deepti, who was fussily laying out cookies on a small plate. "Please, Deepti," he said. "Take your break."

She thanked him, finished with the cookies and then repaired, as she did every day at this time, to the guesthouse out back to phone her daughter, an undergraduate at Brown University.

Jasper again took up the subject of his stalled Bannister mystery with Pauline. "I've actually drawn up a list of possible crimes and solutions and characters," he said. "But everything feels so familiar." Serial killers, rapists, forgers, counterfeiters, kidnappers—he'd done it all before, sometimes more than once. He needed a fresh crime, something that would stretch Bannister's powers of detection, and Jasper's powers of invention. "Maybe we could talk about this tonight, after dinner?"

Pauline blinked.

It was amazing to Jasper how helpful Pauline could still be with his writing. They had met, fifteen years ago, when she was an assistant to Maxwell Smythe, his first editor at Crucible. She had been one of the earliest and most enthusiastic champions of his Bannister series, and after four years, with the unexpected death, by heart attack, of Smythe, she had taken it over, vastly improving it in all aspects. They had, as a natural outgrowth

of their work together (her desk at Crucible strewn with marked-up manuscript pages and half-full Chinese food cartons, or having a post-work drink in one of the old-fashioned bars on Third Avenue), fallen in love and, in their fifth year together as editor and writer, married. Pauline remained a crucial collaborator. During his composition of *Lessons from My Daughter*, he read every new draft passage to her at the end of each working day, pausing often to ask: "Is that too sentimental?" or "Is that too private?" or "Is that how you remember it?" Her advice was indispensable, and it was only because of her strenuous refusal that he agreed to leave her name off the book as coauthor.

"With this new Bannister, just to shake things up, I'd like to try something new," he said. "I'm thinking of writing alternate chapters from the perspective of the bad guy." Every previous Bannister had been written solely from the blind detective's point of view.

Pauline blinked, to signal that she liked the sound of this.

"I'm thinking of making him *really* bad," he continued. "A total sociopath. Let's face it, the bad guys are always more interesting—at least in fiction. Give me Iago over Othello any day."

As he spoke, he absently dug around in the pile of mail in front of him, dislodging a lingerie catalog that slid into view on the tabletop. It featured, on its cover, a trio of nearly naked models, all bronzed, blemish-free skin and cascading locks. Demonstrating the latest in lacy bras and thongs, they looked boldly out at him with just a hint of a smile and an expression of dulcet invitation. He felt an involuntary jolt through his

nervous system, a reaction wholly divorced from his rational mind. Almost simultaneously, he felt a spasm of regretful frustration, of self-castigation, at this bodily reflex—a reminder of that one aspect of his marriage missing ever since the stroke. A reminder that, for all the love, fellow feeling, regard, respect and closeness that he still shared with Pauline, gone was that central element: the physical.

He pushed the catalog under the pile, pushed it from his mind.

"Dad!" Maddy's voice reached him from her bedroom down the hall. "I'm ready! Bring Mom!"

"Coming," he called.

When Jasper's father built the house, forty years ago, he did so with the foresight typical of a man obsessed with long-range planning, instructing the architect to put all the rooms on a single story, in anticipation of the day (decades off, it was hoped and assumed) when he and Jasper's mother would be too old to manage stairs. Thus Jasper had been able to bring Pauline home from the hospital to an already wheelchair-accessible house.

He rolled the wheelchair out of the kitchen and down the hall to Maddy's room and parked Pauline by the foot of the bed. Maddy was already under the covers. He kissed the child's forehead and whispered, "See you in half an hour." He turned off the bedside and kissed Pauline on the cheek. She blinked in response, and he slipped out.

3

Back in the kitchen, he stood over the pile of mail on the table and struggled with himself. Perhaps it would be best after all if he were simply to surrender to biology, grab the cursed catalog and slink off to the bathroom to deal with what was becoming an increasingly disruptive urge. He reached under the pile and in doing so uncovered the mystery envelope—the one he'd signed for. Perhaps it contained some information (an offer, an invitation) that would provide a distraction from the silly lust stirred in him by those Photoshopped models. Or at least briefly delay the inevitable.

The return address read: "Department of Children and

Families, Office of Child Support, Newport, Vermont." An appeal for a donation, he assumed. He almost put it aside for later consideration, but the letter's origin in Vermont sparked his curiosity. He had spent a summer teaching tennis there, in the lakeside town of New Halcyon, almost twenty years ago, after graduating with his BA from Columbia and before starting his master's at Yale. That was four years before he met Pauline and six months before his parents' deaths. He had felt an affinity for the state ever since, a sentimental attachment that derived from his sense of Vermont as belonging to a prelapsarian world, a time when his family was still intact and he was, as yet, innocent of tragedy.

Standing there, envelope in hand, he was visited by a visual memory of New Halcyon, of undulating green hills and narrow, blue Lake Sylvan, at whose northern tip was clustered the handful of buildings (general store, post office, diner) that made up the town. On the eastern shore was the country club, with its big, barnlike main building, where Jasper would, between tennis lessons, play the battered piano or rig up an informal round robin ping-pong tournament for the kids. Some hundred yards down the beach were the two red clay courts bounded by windbreak cedar hedges, where he patiently ladled balls to the six- and seven- and eight-year-olds ranged along the service line; and behind the courts, the drooping stand of weeping willows sprouting from a secluded section of beach where, on his final night in New Halcyon, Jasper had allowed himself to be dragged by the pretty and flirtatious kitchen girl, Holly, whose advances

he had successfully parried all summer. (At just eighteen, she had seemed too young for an almost twenty-three-year-old graduate student like himself; besides which, he did not believe in romantic entanglements with coworkers.)

This last reminiscence formed his only discordant memory of New Halcyon. For he had permitted things to go further than intended with Holly, a bout of innocent kissing and caresses devolving, under the combined impetus of the broken moonlight on the water, the two or three glasses of wine he had drunk and the melancholy sense of summer coming to an end, into a session of increasingly fierce and passionate making-out. Their grapplings had culminated in a muddled moment of arrested intercourse when Holly, after zipping open his fly and pulling off her underwear, clambered up his body, arms around his neck, legs around his waist, and briefly impaled herself upon him. He still wondered at the presence of mind that had compelled him almost immediately to withdraw, to fight free of her octopus embrace long before the threat of climax. Embarrassed, he had hastened back to the clubhouse, saying that he had to dispense the tennis trophies. She failed to return to the party, and he left early the next morning for Yale and never saw or spoke to her again. But he had always felt an obscure, lingering sense of shame over the episode—as if there had been something ungallant in his quick retreat from the beach, where he had left her searching in the sand, with a sweeping, balletically pointed toe, for the flat-soled, strappy silver sandals that had fallen off during their exertions.

He shook off the memory, and absentmindedly drew his thumb under the envelope's top flap. Inside were half a dozen pages held together at one corner by a small bulldog clip. The top sheet carried yesterday's date (April 30, 2007). In place of a salutation were the meaningless words, "In re: Paternity." Below were a few curt sentences:

> Be advised: you have been named as defendant in a parentage complaint involving the daughter of Holly Elizabeth Dwight (deceased). Please consult the attached summons and accompanying documentation and reply to the Office of Child Support of Vermont within twenty days of receipt. If you have questions for this department, please contact Mr. Nathan Stubbs, Family Service Division Officer. [A phone number followed.]

He had to read the letter two or three times before its meaning sunk in. When it did, he was deeply shocked. Not by the paternity claim—he had not seen Holly in—what?—almost twenty years. That he could be the father of any *baby* of hers was patently ridiculous, the result of some bureaucratic snafu, some misunderstanding that he could quickly clear up with this (he looked again at the letter), this Nathan Stubbs. What had shaken him was to learn that Holly was dead. She would have been only, what?, thirty-eight—no, thirty-*six* years old. So young. And to have left behind an infant child!

He flipped through the attached pages—various forms

snarled with legalese and an affidavit by someone identified only as "CD." He did not bother to read the attachments. Eager to clear up the misunderstanding without delay, he carried the complaint with him down the hallway to his office, treading lightly past Maddy's room so as not to wake her. He eased closed his office door, went to the desk and punched in the number at the bottom of the letter. When he got Stubbs on the line, Jasper explained that the summons had been sent to him in error: he had not seen Holly in almost two decades, and it was thus impossible for him to be the father of her baby. But he was curious to know how poor Holly had died. Could Mr. Stubbs share any details?

"Ms. Dwight died in an automobile accident," the man said, with just enough waspish haughtiness to communicate his impatience at having to dispense this detail. "The child in question, however, is not a baby," he went on. "We have a female minor making the claim of paternity. A seventeen-year-old girl."

Jasper, who had been pacing the carpet in front of his desk, stopped dead. He opened his mouth to say something, but nothing came out.

The man went on: "When interviewed by Family Services, the child informed us that her mother on several occasions told her that her father was Jasper Ulrickson, author, residing in Clay Cross, Connecticut. Hence your receiving a summons from this office. If you do not dispute the claim, then—"

"Hold on," Jasper said, finally finding his tongue. "You're saying this child is *seventeen*?"

He heard clicking computer keys on the other end of the

line. Then Stubbs said, "Date of birth is thirty-first May, 1989, which would make her seventeen. End of the month she turns eighteen. That information was supplied in the documents sent to you."

Jasper's mind was racing now as he was plunged back into that distant summer, that moment at the Labor Day dance with Holly. He had pulled out of her almost immediately, long before orgasm—although he knew that in rare instances even so short a contact could result in pregnancy. But could he have been so unlucky?

He did a rapid calculation, counting forward nine months from that Labor Day of 1988. If he had made her pregnant, she would have had the baby at the end of May 1989. The child's precise birthday!

He groped with one hand, like a sightless person—like his blind Geoffrey Bannister—for the back of his office chair. He sat.

"Mr. Ulrickson?" said a voice in his ear. "Are you still there?"

"Yes," Jasper managed to say. He had forgotten that he was on the phone.

"You will see, in the documents, a Voluntary Acknowledgment of Paternity Form. If you do not dispute the claim, please fill that out and return it to the Department of Children and Families within twenty days."

Holding the phone between his shoulder and ear, Jasper paged through the documents and found the form. Below a block of legal language was a place for him to sign, pledging that the child was his. Despite the clinching evidence of the dates, and a certain doomful certainty that had established itself in his

heart, he knew that he could not sign the form without first speaking to a lawyer, and said so.

"If you are disputing the claim," Stubbs resumed, in the robotic tones of someone reciting a familiar speech, "please have your lawyer contact this office so that we may arrange for a DNA test." He asked if Jasper had any questions. Jasper had nothing but questions yet somehow could bring none of them to mind right then. "Well, feel free to call back," Stubbs said. He rang off.

Jasper holstered the receiver and rested his elbows on the desk. He rubbed his face for almost a full minute. Could this be a dream? He actually pinched at the skin on his forehead to check that he was truly awake. Then, with trembling fingers, he took up the complaint. He leafed through to a page labeled "Affidavit of CD." This, he now realized, was the sworn statement of his alleged daughter. The *D* must be for *Dwight*. But what did the *C* stand for? *Christine? Cynthia? Catherine?* He knew, from a Bannister mystery he had written about a child kidnapping, that minors were identified, in court documents, by initials, to preserve their anonymity—but still, it struck him as strange beyond reckoning that he did not know what his alleged child's given name was.

The affidavit read:

> When I was small, my mother always said that my father was Hughie Soames, manager of Soames's Bait and Tackle, and that he died when I was two years old.

> But when I was about eleven, she admitted that my real dad might be a man named Jasper Ulrickson, a writer in Connecticut. They met when they were working at the New Halcyon Country Club, nine months before I was born. My mother worked in the kitchen and Jasper Ulrickson was the tennis pro. I said that she should try to find out for sure if he was my dad, because then he could help to pay child support. (Even though my mom worked two jobs, we were always short.) My mother said no, she didn't want to tell anyone and she didn't want me to contact him. She had had some run-ins with the law, mostly DUIs and one for shoplifting, and some bill payment problems, and she said that the state would take me away and put me with my father because he was rich, and that was not fair, because she had done everything to raise me. So I did not tell anyone. But when my mother died, I was frightened. I did not want to go into foster care and be with strangers. And that is why I could not keep the secret any longer, and why I have come forward to try to see if Mr. Ulrickson is my father.

Below were her initials in a looping, girlish hand: *CD.*

Jasper had always had an acute sense of his good fortune and privilege, had understood that he belonged to a tiny minority free from the material concerns that plagued most of humanity. To assuage his sense of inequity—his guilt—he had donated

liberally to charities, volunteered at homeless shelters, dispensed medicines to underprivileged neighborhoods. Those actions now struck him as not so much futile as misplaced: he had been blind to the need that resided at his *own* doorstep, within his *own* family, his *own* bloodline.

That is, if the girl was truly his.

He glanced at his watch. Three-seventeen—still almost a quarter of an hour before he had to wake Maddy. He snatched up the phone and called Omar Mohyeldin, a lawyer who handled his publishing contracts. Jasper often turned to him for advice about legal procedures in his Bannister novels. Struggling to sound calm, he told Mohyeldin that he needed to speak to a good family lawyer. "For a new Bannister," he added, permitting himself this small white lie. (The fewer people who knew, at this point, about the paternity claim, the better.) Mohyeldin (after some thought, and some audible clicking on his computer) gave Jasper the name and number of Murray Pollock of Pollock, Munson and Kline, in Hartford. Jasper thanked him, hung up and immediately called the number.

After the usual struggle with spectral receptionists and phantom assistants, interspersed with would-be "calming" interludes of classic rock hits played on synthesizers, Jasper finally got Pollock on the line. He poured out his story in a torrent: his moment on the beach with Holly, the letter informing him of her death and the claim, by her surviving teenaged daughter, that he might be her father. When Jasper finally fell silent, Pollock, in an unhurried, leathery-grained

voice, said, "Are you the Jasper Ulrickson who just came out with that memoir on *Tovah*—the one my wife can't stop talking about?"

Jasper was brought up short. "I suppose so," he said. "Yes." The last thing he expected was to have to field questions about *Lessons from My Daughter.* "But my concern at the moment—"

"Because phony paternity claims," Pollock went on implacably, "do have a habit of cropping up when someone wins the lottery—or goes on *Tovah* and has a best seller."

"Oh, I see—"

"Mind you," Pollock went on, "such scams are usually pretty easy to spot. A drunken phone call in the middle of the night. A handwritten letter sent regular mail. How were you served?"

Jasper described how a man had come to his door and requested that he sign for the envelope. "I assumed he was from FedEx. But I suppose he could have been a process server. I wasn't really paying attention. In any case, the summons certainly looks real."

"Any guess," Pollock said, "as to why she never told you about the child?"

Jasper recited the girl's claim that Holly, a struggling single mother, had feared that the child would be placed with him.

"Smart woman," Pollock muttered. "Well," he went on in a businesslike tone, "I'd like to get a gander at that complaint. I'll also have a word with the folks at Child Services in Vermont. It's their job to contract with a lab for the DNA test. Results are reliable to a statistical certainty of one in six billion, so if it

comes back positive, she's your kid. No amount of lawyering can change that."

"I understand," Jasper said.

"And don't worry," Pollock said. "We'll get to the bottom of this."

4

Dr. Carlucci, in agreeing to discharge Pauline from the hospital into Jasper's care, had told him to avoid subjecting her to any undue shock or upset. "A strong jolt could trigger a new stroke," the doctor had warned. As Jasper went down the hall to Maddy's room to wake her from her nap, he wondered if the paternity claim was not precisely the kind of development from which Carlucci would have advised him to shield Pauline. Certainly, if a DNA test were to come back negative, she need never know of the whole business. But if their lives together since the stroke had taught him anything, it was the impossibility of keeping even the smallest secret from Pauline, whose compensatory powers of observation made her awareness of his inner

life almost telepathic. Nor did he wish to keep the secret from her. Openness, honesty, transparency were the foundation upon which their marriage was built, and he could not, in any case, have imagined facing something as momentous, as potentially life-changing, as this paternity claim without the support and advice of his life partner.

He stepped into Maddy's darkened room. Pauline looked up with the usual smile in her eyes—but her gaze instantly darkened. She had detected something in his face. He made an expression meant to calm her, then stepped to the bed and kissed Maddy's forehead, his usual method of waking her. She stirred and sat up. "I had a dream about something scary," she said, screwing her fists into her eyes. "Someone was *coming* here."

"You can tell us about that later," he said. "Right now, I want you to go to the kitchen and be with Deepti—I just heard her come back in. I have to talk with Mommy about grown-up things."

"What grown-up things?"

"They wouldn't *be* grown-up if I told you," Jasper said. "We'll be out in a couple of minutes."

Maddy climbed from the bed and ran off.

Jasper then smoothed Maddy's covers and sat on the end of the bed, facing Pauline. He took her warm, motionless hands in his own. He inhaled a steadying breath and then asked if Pauline recalled the name Holly Dwight. Her eyes kindled—and Jasper knew she remembered. Years ago, when they first began dating, he had, in a bid to remove ghosts of former loves, insisted on

trading with Pauline a list of their past romantic partners. His had not been particularly extensive—he had always been somewhat timid in affairs of the heart—and included only a rather low-key and passionless romance with a fellow English major that dragged on through his undergraduate years; a short-lived adventure with an older woman, a divorced professor, during his postgraduate studies; and an ill-advised affair with a manic-depressive magazine fact-checker during that period of six months when Jasper tried out the louche life of a would-be poet in the East Village, before his parents' deaths, which soon brought him back home to Connecticut (where, temperamentally, he had always really belonged). He had not omitted from the list of past romances Holly, despite the brevity, and seeming inconsequence, of their liaison.

"Well," he went on, "I've just opened a letter saying that Holly has died."

Pauline's eyes widened.

"She left a teenaged daughter. An orphan."

The expression in Pauline's eyes melted into one of sympathy for the girl left all alone after her mother's death.

"But this letter—from child welfare in Vermont—well, it suggests that she might *not* be an orphan." He looked at Pauline meaningfully and, after a moment, saw a stirring in her dark pupils, a looming surmise. "Yes," he said at length. "Seventeen years old. Turns eighteen at the end of the month. The dates work out perfectly."

He was relieved to see none of the emotions he had feared he might read in her eyes: recrimination, anger, retroactive

jealousy. Instead, Pauline's gaze continued to register piteous concern for an abandoned, grieving child, with a clear admixture of concern about *him*, about how he was coping with the news.

"I'm fine," he said. "A little shaken up, of course. But fine. Are you?"

She blinked once, firmly. Then a new look came into her eyes, a quizzical look that asked him how they should proceed.

"Of course, we have to be sure," he said. "I've already called a lawyer to arrange for a DNA test. There's a chance—a slim one, but a chance—that she isn't mine. But if she is—well, I don't see any option but to have her come and live with us." He spoke this last utterance as a statement, but the slight upward inflection at the end of the sentence betrayed that he was, indeed, asking a question, seeking Pauline's blessing for the plan.

Without hesitation, she blinked in the affirmative.

"Oh God, honey," he said. "Thanks for being so understanding." He rose from the bed, leaned forward and embraced her.

But then, he thought, he should not be surprised at her ready agreement to take the child in. Pauline, who had faced the possibility of living out her days in a chronic care ward, would know better than anyone the horrors of being abandoned to the care of paid strangers. Was it any wonder that she was unwilling to consign the child to such a fate, in foster care? In that respect, he thought, Pauline and his possible—what had the lawyer called her?—his *reputed* daughter—were not so different.

5

Pollock called at noon the next day. He had spoken with Stubbs at Vermont Child Services and had learned the details concerning the paternity test. "They use DDS Diagnostics in Ohio—excellent place," he told Jasper. "They've got licensed donation sites everywhere. Couple right near you. They offered some times when you might go in and give a sample."

Jasper chose the first available option: three o'clock that afternoon, at Clay Cross Pediatrics, half a mile from his house.

"Very good," said Pollock. "Ask for Cochrane."

At two-thirty, Jasper set out, on foot, for the clinic. It was a bright spring afternoon and, on Cherry Tree Lane (where he lived at number ten), fragrant lilac blossoms glowed here

and there above flowerbeds thick with tulips and drooping peonies. In the rustling green canopy overhead, birds set up a mellifluous chatter. Jasper had grown up here, knew every crack in the sidewalks, every gnarled root and paving stone, but now, with the consciousness of his possible fatherhood—a fatherhood which, if real, had run parallel to his life for the last seventeen years without his knowledge—he felt as if he were seeing everything for the first time. That he could be the father of a child he had never known—Holly's child—meant that, on some fundamental level, he had never fully known *himself.* The sensation was, to his surprise, not altogether unwelcome, and he was furthermore conscious of a stirring, within, of an unexpected paternal pride, and even excitement, at the prospect of getting to know this daughter (should she prove, truly, to be his); of taking her in and raising her. With that came an acknowledgment of the slight weariness that had settled over him lately, in the routine of caring for a small child and an invalided wife, a numbing regimen interrupted only by long bouts at the computer, where even his Bannister mysteries had begun to seem a little overfamiliar. On some level, he realized (with a queer inward shock), he had been longing for some kind of change in his routine—a longing so deeply buried he had not even been aware of it until now.

The Clay Cross clinic was housed in a former blacksmithing shop on a lane off the town's main street. Cochrane, a smiling African-American man in a medical smock and jeans, invited Jasper back into an examining room, where he quickly disabused Jasper of the impression that he was a doctor ("I'm a

mere phlebotomist—which means I'm trained to take blood and swab cheeks"). He asked for a government-issued ID (Jasper handed over his driver's license) and he wrote Jasper's address and phone number on a business-sized envelope with a preprinted case number. Then he took out an inkpad of the type Jasper had seen at the local police precinct when researching an early Bannister, blackened Jasper's thumb and rolled the print onto the collection envelope. He then donned rubber gloves and said, "Okay, let's take some DNA." Brandishing what appeared to be a Q-tip, but with a longer stem and only one end terminating in white matter, he scraped several times on the inside of Jasper's left cheek, placed the swab into the envelope, then took a fresh one and repeated the procedure. He did this four times in all, swabbing both the right and left cheeks twice. He sealed the swabs in the envelope, then asked Jasper to sign his name along the tamperproof tape.

"Now, I need you to hold the envelope up, with the case number and thumbprint facing me," Cochrane said. Wielding a disposable camera, he snapped two pictures, then put the camera and the envelope containing the swabs into a paper pouch and sealed it with a fresh piece of tape, which he also had Jasper sign.

"Wow, that's quite a rigmarole," Jasper said. He had done extensive research into DNA testing of crime-scene blood for several Bannisters over the years, but had never had occasion to look into the procedure for paternity testing.

"That's how we maintain chain of custody of the sample," Cochrane said. "Otherwise, the results are no good in court." He put the pouch into a FedEx box addressed to DDS Diagnostics,

then buzzed the front desk and asked the receptionist to call for a pickup.

Jasper asked how long he would have to wait for the results.

"Varies," Cochrane said. "Three, four weeks. Sometimes six or seven."

"*That* long?" Jasper cried. "I don't know if I can stand the suspense!" He realized, to his surprise, that, if asked, he would not in that moment have been able to say which outcome he was hoping for: a positive result or a negative one.

But Cochrane did not ask. Instead, he said in a kindly tone: "We always tell our clients to forget about it. Try to relax. Lose yourself in your work."

6

In the days that followed, Jasper stuck to his usual routine, rising each morning at seven-thirty, showering, helping Deepti to dress and feed Pauline, serving breakfast to Maddy, then standing on the front stoop and waving as Deepti drove them off to physiotherapy and preschool respectively. He then repaired to his office to work on his Bannister. Still in search of a fresh crime on which to hang the tale, he sifted old notebooks, visited news Web sites, checked police blotters. To no avail. With the paternity test preying on his mind, he found it impossible to focus. That is, until the morning when he stopped trying to force his thoughts away from the test results. Instead,

he surrendered to obsessing about the outcome—and it was only then that he had his creative breakthrough: why not *write* about these uncertainties? Why not address, head-on, what was uppermost in his mind?

He opened a fresh Word file and began to tap out a scene that showed a family—some half dozen adults and a scattering of children—all of them dressed in black and standing by the graveside of a beloved patriarch. Jasper described balled Kleenexes raised to red, raw noses, downcast, tearful eyes and the priest murmuring the familiar psalm ("he leadeth me in the paths of righteousness for his name's sake . . ."). He described the creak of the winch as the casket was lowered into the ground. Then he began a new paragraph, describing a stranger, a gaunt, hollow-cheeked young man, also dressed in black, standing some way in the distance, beneath a rain-dripping willow. The young man came forward and, to the family's shock and surprise, identified himself as the illegitimate son of the dearly departed—a child, he claimed, born out of wedlock to a now-deceased chambermaid at a hotel where the father had once stayed, twenty years earlier; and thus an heir to the old man's fortune.

"He is, of course, an impostor," Jasper typed, in a note to himself. "A psychopath bent upon removing his rival 'siblings' one by one, and appropriating the full fortune for himself—a scheme in which he will be foiled only by the timely intervention of Detective Bannister, an old friend of the family. B's suspicions are aroused by a certain false note in the young man's voice—and a tendency on the part of Smokey to growl in his presence."

Typing fast, he began to sketch in the villain's background, tracing his motivations to a childhood of deprivation and cruelty in an orphanage; he started to write notes on the grieving family, conceiving of them as a wealthy clan with deep New England roots. Freed from the agonizing writer's block that had stalled him for weeks, Jasper wrote rapturously, without pause, stopping only when he heard the ringing of the doorbell.

Fingers poised above the keyboard, he waited for Deepti to answer it. But he heard no footsteps hurrying out to the foyer, and after a moment the bell sounded again. He glanced at the clock. Seven minutes past three. He realized that he had been working, without pause, for more than five hours! Maddy and Pauline must have arrived home, with Deepti, and be napping; Deepti must be in the guesthouse talking on the phone to her daughter. He furthermore realized why he had been able to keep writing, undisturbed: Pauline, hearing the fusillade of typing from his office, must have known that he had conquered his writer's block; she must have forbidden anyone from interrupting him. Still his invaluable collaborator!

He jumped to his feet and hurried to the front foyer, where he paused and looked through the peephole. On the stoop was a man in white coveralls carrying a toolbox and wearing a white painter's cap with the logo "ACE" above the brim. "Can I help you?" said Jasper, upon opening the door.

The man, his eyes obscured by a pair of mirrored aviators, said, "Furnace inspection."

"Furnace?" Jasper said. "There's nothing wrong with my furnace."

"Let's hope not," the man said. "Governor has mandated that every furnace in the state be checked for carbon monoxide leaks. Letter went out last week."

Jasper had seen no such letter. He must have overlooked it in the mountains of correspondence that arrived every day from fans of his memoir. "How long will this take?" he asked.

"Tops, ten minutes."

Jasper ushered him in and led him to the back of the house, where he opened a door off the boot room and flicked a light switch, illuminating a descending staircase. "It's down there," he said. The man touched the beak of his ACE cap and set off down the stairs.

There was no hope of Jasper's continuing to write with a stranger in the house. He retreated to the living room, dropped onto the sofa and picked up a magazine from the coffee table. He paged through it impatiently. Perhaps five minutes later, he heard footsteps coming up from the basement. He threw the magazine aside and went out to the kitchen. "Looks fine," the man said, ascending the final stairs. "But hey, mind if I use your bathroom?"

Inwardly cursing at the prolonging of this interruption, Jasper led him out to the hallway, pointed at the bathroom and then repaired again to the living room. Less than two minutes later, he heard the toilet flush. He went out to the hall. The man emerged from the bathroom and Jasper escorted him to the foyer.

"Hey," the man said, pausing at the open front door. "Aren't you that writer?"

Jasper debated with himself whether to admit it. "Yes," he

said finally, and with some reluctance. The last thing he wanted to do right now was discuss *Lessons from My Daughter.*

"Yeah, I love those Bannisters," the man said. "I've read 'em all."

"Oh," Jasper said, surprised. "Thank you."

"Read some two, three times."

"Well," Jasper said, "I'm delighted." He rarely met a Bannister fan face to face and had lately begun to despair that the success of his memoir would eclipse his work as a novelist. "I've actually just started a new one," he offered.

"Lucky me," the man said. He pulled his sunglasses down to the tip of his nose and regarded Jasper with pale eyes. "I always root for the bad guys."

Jasper smiled. "Well, don't we all—in a way? But we like seeing them caught in the end."

"Not me," the man said, grinning. He poked his glasses up his nose and stepped out the door.

Jasper watched him walk down the flagstone path to his car at the curb. Slightly odd parting, he thought. He closed the door, then glanced at his watch. Alas, not even a minute to spare for rushing back to his computer and getting down a few more thoughts. It was time to wake Maddy.

On her bed, she lay, as usual, sprawled starfish-wise, her mouth a small black O as she snored gently at the ceiling. Pauline, however, was awake and greeted Jasper with a strangely fixed and unwavering stare. He crouched in front of her wheelchair and asked, "Are you all right?" She blinked twice: *No.* He asked a series of rapid-fire questions—"Are you in pain?" "Is

it your breathing?" "Do you need to go to the hospital?" To each, she answered *No*. "Is it something with Maddy?" he asked, glancing at the bed, where the child continued to snore serenely. Pauline blinked once, *Yes.* "Did she wake up?" *No.* "Was she frightened—a nightmare?" *No.*

He kissed Maddy awake and, as she sat stretching and yawning, asked her if anything bad had happened during her nap. She said no. He sent her to go and see Deepti in the kitchen.

Jasper then spent the next ten minutes asking Pauline questions, trying to hit on the right prompt that would elicit the reasons behind her strange upset. But her answers only seemed to carry him further from any understanding. He realized that, for the first time since the stroke, they had run up against the limits of their communication. He simply could not understand what she was trying to tell him. The expression in Pauline's eyes, meanwhile, grew only more distressed. It was heartbreaking—that look of shock, mixed somehow with urgency and alarm. And something else, something wild and frightened. Almost as if she were trying to impart to him a warning.

PART TWO

1

The scheme, when you got right down to it, was really nothing more than an elaborate practical joke—and Dez had always loved practical jokes. His decision, after college, to become a lawyer had been motivated not by any love for the profession or, still less, a desire to aid his fellow man, but as a kind of prank on his grim old widower of a father, Judge Dezollet. Known throughout North Carolina as "The Hanging Judge" for the serene lack of mercy he demonstrated toward those convicted murderers unlucky enough to come before him for sentencing, the Judge had, in his forty years on the bench, put on death row some eighty people ("or hardly enough," as he liked to quip).

Dez knew how ardently his father wished him to follow his footsteps onto the bench—the old man had made it clear enough in his stentorian hectoring and shouted demands. Dez (considerably more obedient at age twenty-two) duly enrolled at Boston College Law School, graduating in the top third of his class. How his father smiled upon him that day! But that's when Dez put his special ironical twist on things—the practical joke aspect. Instead of his coming home, as Judge Dezollet expected, to take a job with the North Carolina prosecutor's office (so that he could begin his ascent to the bench), Dez joined the New England branch of the Innocence Project, the group of crusading defense lawyers dedicated to freeing wrongly convicted murderers from death row. Again, he felt no special drive to exonerate the falsely accused. Instead, it was his ambition to return to his home state and save someone sentenced in his father's own courtroom—oh, the delicious irony of seeing one of the unfortunates whom the Judge had marked for death walk free! Sadly, he never got the chance. Shortly after joining the Innocence Project, Dez ran into a problem in his personal life, his extremely personal life.

Dez was then twenty-six, and it was not the first time he experienced trouble over his sexual nature. He had long known that his tastes differed subtly from those of his male peers—or, at least, the tastes his peers would admit to. Teenaged girls, anywhere from fifteen to eighteen—but strictly confined to those age limits—were his sole erotic interest; and it was an interest that amounted to obsession. This was not a problem when he was, himself, younger; certainly not in eleventh grade, when he,

at seventeen, had his first serious girlfriend, a lissome ninth-grader. Back then, his male peers admired him for his sexual success; they exalted him as a "player," a ladies' man. As a college senior, he took as a girlfriend a seventeen-year-old from a local girls' private school. Except for his friends' jocular (and, as Dez saw it, secretly envious) cries of "Baby snatcher!" and "Cradle robber!" he suffered no stigma.

But as a professional man, an adult of twenty-six, a practicing lawyer whose colleagues had already started to marry and even, in some instances, have children, Dez found that he could not openly date a girl of sixteen, or even voice an interest in such females, without drawing puzzled (or worse) looks from his coworkers. This was especially true in a state—Massachusetts—where the age of consent was eighteen. (Back home in North Carolina, it was two years younger—a difference Dez found out too late).

The problem was that normal, attractive, sexually available and demonstratively interested young women of twenty-two or twenty-four or (God forbid) *thirty*-four simply awoke no sexual thrill in him. They lacked what Dez saw as the exquisite fragility of limb and grace of movement in females of the middle teenaged years, a combination of innocence and womanliness that vanishes by the time they cross into their buxom, matter-of-fact twenties. He was not a pervert, a pedophile. Dez had no interest whatsoever in prepubertal girls—in children. Such men were, indisputably, criminals, creeps. Like any normal male, he thrilled to the sight of womanly secondary sexual characteristics: the fullness of a pair of breasts under a

cotton T-shirt; the swell of buttocks in second-skin denim. But he liked these manifestations of femininity not in their fullest flower, but rather in the act of blossoming, of *becoming*.

His first significant scrape had actually occurred when Dez was just twenty-three and newly arrived in Boston to study law. He committed the gaffe of approaching a girl at a bus stop. Mistaking her shy glances as an invitation, he was frank in his proposals to her. She turned out to be the fifteen-year-old daughter of a local doctor who had told her to wait for him on that street corner, where he would pick her up in his car after her piano lesson. That car happened to pull up to the curb at the moment when the girl was recoiling from Dez's eager, sharklike smile and pointed proposition. He tried to flee on foot, but the doctor—a jogging enthusiast—caught up to him in a few strides, collared him and began yelling for the police. (Hence the special care Dez took ever after to learn the whereabouts of fathers.)

Dez managed, somehow, to convince the authorities that this bus stop contretemps was all a misunderstanding—he was new in town and merely inquiring about the transit schedule—but he was less lucky a year later, when he invited to his room a seventeen-year-old visiting her older brother in the building where Dez had an apartment. She was a milk-pale redhead with eager green eyes and a dusting of what looked like cinnamon across the tops of her breasts (exposed by the V-shaped opening of her much-too-low-cut sweater). She threw a blushing look at Dez in the elevator and he intercepted her before they reached her sibling's floor. After several glasses of rum-spiked Coke in Dez's living room, the girl energetically succumbed

to his importuning and the next day she returned to his apartment, this time in much more conservative attire, and with two police officers and her brother in tow. The cops informed him that the age of consent in that state was eighteen and that he had, in completing an act of "penetrative intercourse" with the complainant, committed a Class B1 felony.

Judge Dezollet, in that instance, came in handy. Pulling God knows what interstate strings, he got all charges dropped on what lawyers call the "Romeo and Juliet laws," which provide for dismissal of statutory rape charges in cases where the victim, although a minor, is not more than six years younger than the perpetrator. In this instance, she was *seven* years younger, but owing to her relatively advanced age (her birthday was in two months) and whatever favors Judge Dezollet was able to call in from whatever legal cronies, Dez got off with nothing more than a stern reprimand and a court-ordered year of therapy with a sexologist, Dr. Cyril Geld, a reputedly brilliant British implant famous in psychological circles for his work on the so-called paraphilias, or sexual disorders.

Dez met with Geld once a week in the doctor's home office, a dark, oak-paneled room at the back of a narrow Victorian row house in a surprisingly down-at-heels neighborhood in Boston, next to the tenderloin district. Geld had a lean aristocratic face, an upper-class accent and mobile blue eyes that moved restlessly behind the lenses of his wire-rimmed spectacles, like some form of transparent sea creature in dual aquariums—until such time as his patients began truly to open up about their most private sexual peccadilloes, at which point his pupils would dilate

and his roving irises would train themselves on his interlocutor unwaveringly, like twinned predators stalking what nourished them. After close-questioning Dez about his erotic leanings, Geld informed the patient that he, in sexological terms, belonged to a "perfectly identifiable classification."

Dez was an *ephebophile*—in plain English, someone whose sexual preference is restricted to partners in mid- to late adolescence. ("Tell me something I don't know," Dez inwardly remarked.) This was not a passing condition, Geld warned, not something that would "clear up" or "go away" when Dez reached some magical stage in life when age-appropriate females would suddenly hold an allure for him.

"Increasingly, we are coming to see such quirks as genetically based," Geld said, "as inextricably in-wound with the DNA, and thus as a matter of microscopic differences in the makeup of the prenatally organized brain." Furthermore, it was a curious complication that the sufferer's erotic response to girls of the mid- to late teen years often coincided with his demonstrating a more than ordinary degree of attractiveness to the young female—"a phenomenon we, in sexology, have not readily been able to account for in hormonal or pheromonal terms," Geld said. "But the effect is pronounced and can much complicate the life of the ephebophile who, despite aging into his forties, fifties and even sixties and seventies, often retains what we call a 'Peter Pan quality' that is perceived and responded to, erotically, by the teenaged love object. You can imagine the tragic difficulties this inter-echoing of libidinal call-and-response can cause to the aging ephebophile who

seeks to master and control his condition but who is, constantly, made the object of shy, flirtatious glances and sometimes playfully bold 'come-ons' from the pretty teenagers he so ardently seeks *not* to desire." (Dez could indeed.)

"But that's the bad news," Geld hastened to say. "The good news is that ephebophilia is not classified, by science, as a disease as defined in the *Diagnostic and Statistical Manual of Mental Disorders*; and in the vast majority of cases, even severe ephebophilia can be managed, controlled—and not with drugs, but with simple, open, frank conversation."

Dez, for the next year, engaged in that simple, open, frank conversation with Dr. Geld, describing in detail his torments of lust, his masturbation fantasies, his little slips; and Geld counseled him on how to curb and control his impulses. In a year's time, the doctor pronounced Dez, if not cured, then at least properly conditioned to manage his compulsion. And all credit to Geld, Dez briefly tried to be good; he really did. Shortly after being released from therapy, he (now freshly graduated from law school) joined the local branch of the Innocence Project and threw himself into the work with gusto. He garnered glowing assessments from his bosses and was told that he had a fine future with the outfit. But at the end of his first year—a year that had seen a sharp increase in the responsibilities conferred upon him by his superiors—he once again slipped; this time with the young niece of one of the partners in the law firm: a raven-haired, black-eyed beauty of no small experience who, her antennae quivering at the Peter Pan waves Dez helplessly (innocently!) emitted, boldly propositioned him one day when she dropped by the office to see Uncle on

some family matter. Dez disappeared with her into a stationery supply closet. He might have gotten away with this moment of stolen pleasure had he and his now quite disheveled paramour not elected to slide from their hiding place at the precise moment when Uncle was hurrying past clutching a "While You Were Out" memo and asking, "Has anyone seen Emily?"

This time Judge Dezollet declined to use any influence to soften the hand of justice. Dez pled guilty to two counts of statutory rape. He was fired from the Innocence Project, disbarred and sentenced to five years' parole, placed on the state's registry of sexual offenders and enrolled in yet another course of sex counseling, this one far more rigorous, as it entailed daily hour-long sessions of talk therapy as well as a course of experimental "aversion therapy" of Geld's own devising—a course Dez agreed to undergo on the promise that, if successfully completed, Geld would see to it that his name was expunged from the register after five years.

After filling out the mountain of paperwork that absolved Geld of all legal liability, Dez had his chest and loins shaved, then hooked up to a set of electrodes. Geld sat, his delicately tapering fingers on a small switch. Dez was shown photographs and film clips of teenaged females and was administered electric shocks every time his humiliatingly exposed manhood betrayed him. At the end of three weeks of treatment, Geld pronounced himself "stunned" at the tenacity of Dez's fixations—his erections seemed to be growing *more* powerful under the combined stimulus of the imagery and the electric jolts. "I cannot say that the prognosis is good," Geld told him.

Dez, however, insisted that the treatment be continued and, over time, learned to counteract the imagery through a meditative technique that involved imagining scenes of sickness and torture as the teen beauties were projected before him. In time he achieved, through this act of "self-blinding," the flaccidity Geld was seeking. When the doctor switched to showing him "therapeutically positive" images of age-appropriate women—female business executives climbing out of taxicabs in tight pencil skirts; an aproned mother bending at the waist to remove a well-browned turkey from the oven—Dez brought up from the storehouse of memory, and superimposed on the projected pictures, visions of adolescents bending in skirts to pick up tennis balls, or pale girls in private school uniforms retrieving heavy books, on tippy-toe, from a high shelf. Thus did he induce the hearty erectile response his doctor was looking for.

Geld's long, complicated paper on Dez's case was published as a lead article in the *New England Journal of Medicine* and was covered by *Time* and *Newsweek*. In a *Dateline* TV documentary, Dez (shown in darkened silhouette and identified only as Patient X) was described as being among the world's very rare examples of a successful sex aversion therapy, his case reviving the debate over whether it was, after all, possible to "cure" homosexuality (the Holy Grail of all sexological research in America). Dez's name was duly removed from the state's sex registry. He was, however, barred from working in any profession in which he had authority over young females. For instance, teaching.

But it so happened that Dez had always been drawn to pedagogy and the opportunities it offered for expanding the horizons

of young people, and after some six months working as a clerk in a shoe store (Men's Department only—Dez, again, was trying to be good), he enrolled in a teacher's training program and earned his certificate as an instructor of high school–level English. Not long after that, he came across an advertisement for a position in rural Vermont and on a whim sent off a fanciful résumé. (Dez had seen the many news reports over the years of convicted sex offenders slipping through the cracks and figured, "Nothing ventured, nothing gained.") He was granted an interview, which was conducted by a panel of three teachers, two of whom were pretty, thirtyish, unmarried women of precisely the kind who always warmed to Dez's sly, cruel good looks (and who left him utterly cold). Dez got the job (by a vote of two to one) and that September took up duties at New Halcyon High, a coed institution housed in a brick one-story building of sixties vintage perched on the brow of a hillside that overlooked the town's post office, tiny bank, grocery store and log cabin–themed diner. The school catered to the sons and daughters of the local farmers and the year-round workers of the small lakeside town—a pretty hamlet that, Dez was told, became a vibrant summer cottage resort area for the moneyed clans of the Northeast during July and August.

2

Dez had his extra-professional reasons for being overjoyed about his new position. But he also needed the job. Judge Dezollet had died the previous year, of a fast-moving cancer, leaving his son (a deep disappointment to him) nothing in his will. Penniless and in debt, Dez had undertaken his teaching duties with every intention of obeying the law. His paycheck was not princely, but it would serve until a new opportunity arose. In the meantime, he had no compunction about a little surreptitious voyeurism, some window-shopping. He was human, after all. But he vowed to himself that he would never, ever touch. He was determined to be strong.

That was before the start of his third class, on his first day at the school—an eleventh-grade class that began in the period just after lunch. Dez was standing at the blackboard, in his adult guise of black jeans, white button-down shirt and dark sports jacket, watching the group of twenty or so bored teenagers straggling into the room. Suddenly the air went thick and his body began to tingle with that special sensation so familiar to him. At the back of the group was a slender girl with two curtains of glossy, streaky-blond hair framing a round, baby-like face. Dressed in a white halter top and short denim skirt, she hugged a stack of notebooks to her breasts and moved slowly, in a maddening drag-toed gait, her pink-painted toenails exposed in a pair of grubby flip-flops (also pink)—a girl herself disguised in the everyday costume of the female adolescent but whom Dez, a connoisseur in these matters if ever there was one, recognized instantly, with every sense available to him, as a rare and exceptional specimen.

Chloe, for her part, immediately felt the teacher's eyes upon her. At seventeen, she was hardly a stranger to the attentions of men; as early as thirteen, when she lost all that baby fat and shot up four inches in height, she had been fending off their exploratory glances, or worse, but never had she been visually devoured as was now happening as she moved across the classroom (she could practically feel the exposed skin of her legs and arms tingle under the pressure of his gaze)—and never by a man at once so boyish yet worldly-looking, so sweetly attentive yet so rakishly handsome, as Mr. Dezollet.

As seductions go, Chloe proved to be one of his more delicate

conquests. After administering to the class a test devised to determine their relative knowledge of books and writing, he placed her in a program of after-school tutoring (her grasp of basic spelling and grammar was, to be fair, atrocious). There, over the course of a few weeks, he casually drew out her story: he heard about the early loss of her father, and about her single, overworked, underpaid waitress-cum-chambermaid mother—a pathetic creature who, Chloe said, relieved the boredom, drudgery and disappointment of her existence with regular weekend visits to the dive bars strewn along the highway between Shelburne and Charlotte, and from which she brought home a steady stream of one-night stands: beery farmers, sad-sack seed salesmen, tractor mechanics. To Dez's concerned questioning about whether or not these men ever interfered with *her*, Chloe sorrowfully admitted that, lately, they had started trying to, but that she had, so far, managed to fight them off. Nevertheless, the experience, Dez discerned, had imbued Chloe with a deep suspicion of, and even dislike for, the attentions of men and boys. This would have been more discouraging for Dez had she not, almost in the same breath, admitted to a deep yearning after a father-figure protector, a man unlike the sloppy would-be seducers her mother brought home: a strong, warm, handsome, witty, intelligent older man to guide and shape her. Such inchoate desires, coupled with a loathing for life in New Halcyon and unformed dreams of a career as a model or actress in a vaguely imagined New York, Paris or London, inclined her to see in Dez (he easily divined) not only an attentive and caring teacher but a man of thrilling worldliness, of a poise and sophistication

that spoke of worlds beyond the oppressive and confining hills of New Halcyon.

In early November, Dez announced to Chloe his conviction that, for her own academic good, she should attend extra tutorial sessions, on weekends, at his home. At the time, Dez was living in an apartment above a local restaurant, the Mill, conveniently tucked away from the prying eyes of the town's busybodies and tattletales behind the general store on a blighted plot of sandy ground between the gas station and the marina. The Mill's appropriateness as an illicit trysting spot was further enhanced by its operating hours: it closed every evening at ten, after which the building was inhabited by no one but Dez, whose attic apartment ran the length of the building's peaked roof, the walls on either side of his rooms slanting steeply upward to a high point in the center. With its brown shag broadloom, zebra-striped foam couches and woozy water bed, the place was a time capsule from the seventies, a sybarite's ironic paradise.

Chloe's first weekend tutorial was on an evening when a cold snap had rimed the windowpanes with delicate patterns of frost and made the ancient radiators groan and clank like monsters. Dez chased away the chill with hot cocoa spiked with Kahlúa ("This tastes so nice and chocolaty," Chloe innocently observed). They were an hour and a half into the session, and on their third refill, when Dez lowered his hand onto Chloe's, which lay, so invitingly, beside the foolscap page filled with examples of subject–verb agreements. She started, blushed and looked up at him through her lashes. He confessed, haltingly, to how very, very lonely he was in New Halcyon, how he had

failed to find, among the farmers and day laborers, or indeed his fellow teachers, any soul mates—except for Chloe herself. He felt such a special kinship with her, a connection that went beyond that of teacher and student, like friends, like equals. Dez quickly withdrew his hand and said, No—no, it was worse than that. He was not being entirely honest with her—or with himself. He jumped to his feet and began to pace. He confessed that his feelings for her had crossed into a region of emotion strictly forbidden to any pedagogue—a region so unprofessional as to be criminal. His feelings were especially unforgivable given what she had confided to him about the men her mother brought back from the bars, those drunken louts who attempted to seduce her. He was really no better than them. Actually, he was worse—given the position of authority he held over her! But truth be told, lately, he had not been able to keep from his mind dreams of touching her, of kissing her, of holding her so very, very close. And it was for that reason, he said, turning to face her, that she must go. Go away! Right now.

Chloe, who (incredibly!) had been having so many of the same feelings, the same reservations and the same fears, emitted a strangled sob. She got to her feet and rushed over to Mr. Dezollet, throwing her arms around him and pouring out her confession of reciprocated adoration and desire. Somehow, she had managed to remain, despite every effort of nature to militate against it, a virgin—a happenstance she was now ready, desperately ready, to rectify. "Please," she cried, "please make love to me."

Dez, after a great show of inner struggle, obliged her.

3

Even in his most polluted fantasies, Dez had never dared to imagine a girl like Chloe (and this was saying something)—a girl whose very inexperience paradoxically made her so wanton and free, so without inhibition or shame, so pliant and passionate. She came to him every night after dark, sneaking from her mother's small house down the River Road, riding her bike to his apartment above the Mill.

He knew that it was madness to have her come to him every night, this way, for five or six hours of undreamed-of exertions on those sofas, on that shag rug, on the kitchen counters, in the bath, on that lurching water bed. He was risking not only his job but his freedom. (He had been expressly warned that another

transgression would result in a long incarceration.) But it was a measure of the spell she had cast over him that he was willing to risk everything to be with her, to experience those hours of savage bliss—before he sent her home, in the wee hours of the morning, and they met up again a few hours later at the school, in the blameless roles of teacher and student, his fingers and face still redolent of her musk and sweetness—a subterfuge whose practical joke aspect only further fueled his lust.

And something more than lust. He was surprised, mystified, by the depth of his feelings for her. His desire seemed to go beyond his insatiable appetite for her flesh. He felt an unfamiliar possessiveness, a desire to have her wholly to himself and under his control. She was something new in his experience. Certainly he could be contemptuous and cutting about her ill-informed opinions; he could be brutally derisive about the thoughts she set down in the essays she wrote for him in class ("In *Catcher in the Rye* J. Slinger has a great writing style of sounding like a teenage boy . . ."). He was annoyed by the regimen of diet and exercise, culled from *Glamour* and *Seventeen* magazines, that she used to tone her already lean and graceful body; he mocked her for her fascination with the celebrities she had been trained, by her television shows, to be enraptured by. But on a deeper level, shielded, hidden, he recognized some profound connection between them. He felt an almost frightening reliance on her, an emotional dependence. The feeling was unprecedented for him and brought him a form of happiness.

If Dez could not bring himself to use the word *love* in connection with Chloe, she had no problem whatever applying the

term to her feelings for him. In her diary, she described herself as "totally and completely head over heels in LOVE with Dez"—a feeling that went beyond the sexual. She had developed a pure, unswerving devotion to his soul. She idolized him as a "genius." She lived to please him.

By this time, she was barely speaking to her mother. Holly had long since noticed the painful shift in interest on the part of her "boyfriends" from herself to her blossoming daughter, and this had given rise to that oldest of familial rivalries, one no less real for being a cliché. As the mortifying awareness of her own vanished charms was borne home to her, Holly, who had once confined her drinking to weekends, now sat guzzling wine or beer in front of the television every night, while at the same time discoursing, in an increasing slur, about how she had wasted her life by staying in New Halcyon, by failing to go to college, by having a *kid*, especially such an ungrateful, lazy, scheming little kid as Chloe. Chloe hated listening to these monologues, which modulated seamlessly from self-pity to castigation. But at the same time, she welcomed them as a prelude to the moment when Holly would drop into alcoholic unconsciousness, allowing Chloe to slip out, undetected, to see Dez. Indeed, so low had Holly sunk, by mid-March of that year, that she failed even to respond with any surprise or outrage when Chloe's principal telephoned, one afternoon, to notify her of the scandal.

Principal Heinrichs explained, in an urgent murmur, that one of Chloe's teachers—"a Mr. Dezollet, who teaches English"—had been witnessed, by a fellow faculty member, behaving toward Chloe in an "inappropriate manner." The incident had occurred

when the two were alone in a classroom—or thought themselves alone. Miss Simmons, the art teacher, had entered Mr. Dezollet's room, between periods, with the intention of asking him if her art students might paint a mural depicting the literary history of Vermont on his wall (and, it might be added, with the shy hope that Mr. Dezollet might notice, and comment upon, the new dress Miss Simmons, who had been so taken with Mr. Dezollet at his job interview, was debuting that very day). She had slipped in just as Mr. Dezollet, standing behind the girl, was removing his pursed lips from her swan-like young neck. It was, to be sure, just a peck, a quick pressing of the lips to an area where her shoulder met the turn in her clavicle. But it was done with a familiarity that left no doubt in Miss Simmons's mind that she had seen something worthy of severe sanction. Dez, who had seen Simmons flee the room, soon heard himself being summoned to the principal's office over the school's PA system. He elected not to obey the invitation, and instead quit the school with a haste that suggested the building was in flames or in imminent danger of exploding. When Dez failed to appear in the principal's office, Miss Simmons, her breast heaving with indignation and hurt, demanded Principal Heinrichs notify the authorities of his flight. But Heinrichs, assured by Chloe that Mr. Dezollet had simply been innocently demonstrating a scene in a book (*The Scarlet Letter*), and eager to avoid a scandal, declined to call the police. However, when he recounted all of this over the phone to Holly, he did add: "This does not preclude *you*, as Chloe's mother, from pressing charges, if you so choose."

Holly had already begun her afternoon cocktail hour. Drink

always made her belligerent. Her response was blunt. "If anyone should be locked up," she said, "it's that little slut of mine." She did, however, attempt to question her daughter when Chloe returned from school that afternoon. But the child simply ran past her and vanished into her room, slamming the door behind her.

Chloe threw herself on the bed. Her heart and mind were in turmoil. After her last class, she had rushed to Dez's apartment above the Mill—but found it empty, his belongings cleared out. He was gone. She would never see him again. She wept inconsolably. Then, shortly before midnight, the phone rang. It was Dez! He told her, in a hurried whisper (he was speaking from a pay phone at a pizza parlor ten miles down the lake, in Sayer's Cliff), that he had moved to a trailer park, where he had rented a single-wide motor home. The location was secluded and would suit their needs for now. He told her how to get to him—"just follow the main road around the lake until you come to the sign for Black Point; take the next right, and then follow the narrow dirt path that leads into the woods and terminates at the grounds of the trailer park. I'm in a white and blue Tartarus."

She went to him, pedaling furiously through the icy dark, past jagged, leafless black trees, with a sliver of silvery March moon keeping pace with her both above, in the sky, and below, in trembling reflection, in the thawing lake. And it was from Dez's new location—the scrubby clearing in the woods, with the ramshackle collection of trailers and RVs parked in rows amid the surrounding black pines and maples—that they resumed their romance. Dez insisted that she continue to live at home, continue attending school ("You've got to act like nothing happened—let

them forget"); but he also insisted that she come to him, every night, without fail. And he vowed that he would think of a way to better their lot.

So matters rested for the next two weeks, until that morning at the end of March when Chloe arrived home from Dez's trailer, at dawn, to discover a police cruiser in front of the house. Her mother's car was not out front, in its usual spot. Dropping her bicycle, she ran up to the policeman, who was standing on the porch ringing the doorbell. She asked what was going on. Where was her mother? The cop, a young man with strangely lush, feminine-looking eyelashes, removed his hat. The cruiser's red light kept spinning, intermittently bathing Chloe's stricken, uncomprehending face in its harsh, hellish glow.

The cop asked if she had any relatives with whom she could stay. She said that she had no one—her father was dead; both sets of grandparents likewise; and she had no aunts or uncles. The policeman informed her that it was against the law for a minor to live alone, so he would be delivering her to the Department of Children and Families, in Newport. He told her to go and wait in the back of the cruiser while he finished his paperwork.

Chloe walked to the curb, but instead of getting into the squad car, she bent, slowly, never taking her eyes off the policeman, who remained on the porch, scribbling in his pad. She righted her bicycle, mounted it, then glided off, glancing behind her every few seconds to see if he was following. He was not. She rounded the corner, then stood up on the pedals and pumped hard, racing back to the trailer park in the woods at the far end of the lake, back to Dez.

4

She was surprised at the keenness of her grief. Long-buried memories of her mother—young, slim, sober, beautiful, smiling down at her in a garden somewhere, tickling her on a sofa long ago in some forgotten room in a slant of sunlight, a smell of talc and lilies of the valley . . . the nubbly texture of a white cotton bedspread at nap time with Mommy . . . These vague, jumbled impressions were joined by memories from a few years later, when she was a shy, melancholy preteen—fat, freckled and docile—and her mother, not yet addled by booze, was Chloe's best, her only, friend. They would sit together on the sofa, in the evening, and Holly would reminisce about her various boyfriends, including Hughie Soames and Jasper Ulrickson, about

the original confusion over which one of them was Chloe's father. She loved to hear these stories of her mother's life, stories that took on the coloration of high Romance and that sharpened Chloe's appetite for the days when she would be the object of rival males' affections. "Tell me again about when you were young," she would say as she lay with her head in Holly's lap, her mother's soft hand absently stroking the hair at Chloe's temple. These were the memories that haunted her after Holly died, when Chloe, having taken refuge with Dez in the Tartarus, buried herself under the sheets and blankets on his bed and cried and cried and cried.

True, she wished that Dez could be more sympathetic toward her in her grief. But she knew that he was dealing with his own problems. After losing his teaching job, he had sunk into a dangerous lassitude, unable most days to get out of bed until noon and only then to sit, unshaven, unwashed, in front of the television. He had even lost all interest in sex, pushing Chloe away when she made an advance or, on those rare occasions when he had tried to make love to her, rolling off with a muttered curse, sweat-slicked and shame-faced, but offering no excuses, no explanations for his failure. She had even begun to worry, after her mom died, that he had fallen out of love with her. But then came that *Tovah* show. And the moment when Chloe heard the name Jasper Ulrickson and told Dez, in all innocence, that her mother had been with a man of that name. The words had acted on Dez like a spell from a fairy tale, woke him from his slumber, brought him back from the dead. For weeks, he had barely budged from the sofa. Now, he barely slept.

In fevered bouts of pacing the tiny trailer, he thought aloud, talking out the plan, throwing out his hands, and laughing when he found his way around some blockage that threatened to ruin the scheme.

So glad and relieved was she to see him alive and happy again, she would have been willing to go along with any plan he dreamed up. But this scheme in particular, the plan for her to seduce, then expose, Jasper Ulrickson, struck her as right and just—especially after Dez patiently explained to her *why* Ulrickson deserved to have the trick played on him. Dez had made her see how Ulrickson had cruelly *used* her mother, taken *advantage* of her, then tossed her aside to go and pursue his education, his career, his fame and wealth, while poor Holly, in the years and decades that followed, sank into poverty and despair and drink. Had Ulrickson ever called to ask how Holly was? Had he ever offered to help her out a little financially? Think of the difference that would have made to Holly—and to Chloe! And what if Ulrickson had ever deigned to return to New Halcyon to visit the woman he so casually seduced and then shunted aside? "Do you think for a minute that your mother would have become a desperate alcoholic?" Dez asked. "Do you think she would have been trawling the singles bars every weekend? Chloe, do you think she'd be *dead*?"

All of this strengthened her resolve to play her part in the scheme. But her motivation was less about punishing Ulrickson than it was about making Dez happy. And he *was* happy! Suddenly, he was voracious—alternating his bouts of planning with absolutely brutal attacks upon her body. Sometimes, he continued to

plot and plan even during their lovemaking. Thrusting into her, he would grunt into her ear that she was his "secret weapon," his "equalizer." Sometimes it frightened Chloe to know that the fulfillment of all his dreams rested on *her*. One night, after a particularly fierce session—which Dez had punctuated, at climax, with a triumphant shout about how the plan was going to "change everything!"—she began to cry.

"What if I mess it *up* somehow?" she asked tearfully, in the panting aftermath. "I don't want to wreck all your dreams."

She was lying on her back on the trailer's narrow bed, her wheat- and honey- and rope-hued hair fanned out around her flushed face. Dez, sitting cross-legged beside her in a stupor of sexual satisfaction, simply laughed as he looked down at her Eden-naked body. He dreamily swept his hand from her collarbones over her improbably full breasts (she was otherwise so slender), down the incurved bare belly, which still rose and fell rapidly, to the poignant points of her pelvic bones, down her legs until he cradled one of her delicate feet in his hands. "I assure you," he said, kissing the tips of her pink toes. "You are the one element of the plan about which I have no doubts. No doubts whatsoever."

5

On a Friday morning seven days after her mother's death, Chloe rode her bike into Sayer's Cliff, bought a ticket at the greasy spoon–cum–bus terminal, then boarded a Greyhound bound for the city of Newport. She was dressed in the sober ensemble that Dez had picked out for her at the local mall the day before: white blouse, black blazer and matching slacks. Her hair was in a no-nonsense ponytail, her face free of makeup.

She arrived in Newport (a down-at-heels resort city perched on a peninsula at the southern end of Lake Memphremagog, on the Canada-US border) just before noon. As Dez had instructed, she walked six blocks east to the Division of Family Services district office, a large gray government building at 100 Main Street,

across from a block-long dollar store. On the second floor, she spoke to a receptionist, and a minute later a heavy, pear-shaped man in shirtsleeves, crumpled tie and brown slacks appeared and identified himself as Mr. Stubbs, Family Services Division Officer. He invited her back into the rat's maze of work cubicles, to a small corner office. There, he invited her to sit in a chair facing a desk heaped with papers and file folders from which a brownish-gray computer sprouted like a mushroom.

"You are classified, by the Vermont state police, as a runaway," Mr. Stubbs said, peering at the computer screen. "You fled the custody of a police officer."

"Yes, sir," she said. "I did run away, but there was a reason."

("You're going to tell them about your mother's history with Jasper Ulrickson," Dez had told her when he coached her about this meeting. "You're going to say that she told you never to tell anyone that he is your father." He warned her that the agency people would doubt her—at first. "So you're going to tell them that the proof is in your mother's house—the diary and photos.")

Chloe did as Dez instructed. She even drew on the acting skills she had honed in her role as a fairy in a middle-school play, and pretended to weep. Stubbs listened, impassively, then tapped at his computer. He said that a police officer would be dispatched to her mother's house to collect the diary and photos. In the meantime, Chloe would be kept in Department of Children and Families custody. "Which means," he said, "we will place you in short-term foster care while we work to resolve the paternity issue." (Dez had told her, in advance, not to panic; that her time in foster care would be brief.)

Stubbs was able immediately to place Chloe with an elderly, childless, Christian couple, the Gaitskills, on the Capeville Road in a house filled with lace doily–draped furniture, porcelain Nativity scenes, crucifixes and a baby grand piano with keys the color of yellowing teeth and upon which old Mr. Gaitskill played hymns from a songbook while Mrs. Gaitskill sang along in a quavery voice. They did not own a television, but they did listen, after dinner, to the "wireless," an ancient radio on which they tuned in a religious program broadcast from Burlington. At bedtime, Chloe would retreat to her room and, under the gaze of various framed saints, call Dez in the trailer—their sole form of contact for the time being, since it was, he said, far too dangerous for them to see each other while the plan was in its early, delicate, stages of development.

Shortly after she began her imprisonment with the Gaitskills, Chloe learned, in a call from Mr. Stubbs, that both she and her reputed father, Jasper Ulrickson, would have to submit to DNA testing. Stubbs and a lawyer, Mrs. Barnes, would drive her to the appointment in Newport. Before he could hang up, Chloe asked the name of the clinic, the time of her appointment and the name of the contact. (Dez had drummed into her head, over and over and over again, that it was *crucial* to the success of the entire enterprise that Chloe learn these details.) Stubbs said that the appointment was for Thursday (the day after tomorrow) at the G-Tek Clinic in Newport, at 255 Main Street, at 10 a.m. with a man called Ames. Chloe jotted the words on the back of an envelope, then dashed up to her room and phoned Dez.

He had been awaiting her call.

6

He wasted no time—had no time to waste. First hastily assuring her, in cooing tones, that she had done "wonderfully," and that "everything was going to work out fine," and that they would "soon be back together," he hung up and then burst into frantic motion, peeling off his jeans and T-shirt and donning the pair of white coveralls he had purchased a few days earlier at Home Depot. He grabbed his pre-packed travel bag (which contained a quite different disguise) and slung it over his shoulder. Then, toting the (empty) toolbox he had excavated from the trailer's storage space, he biked into Sayer's Cliff. There, he caught a bus for Burlington airport and used his credit card to buy a round trip to JFK, departing 11 a.m. Dez loathed flying, hated being

thirty-five thousand feet in the empyrean where only God and angels—or those about to *become* angels after double engine failure or a terrorist bombing—belonged. Fortunately, the flight was smooth, with only a single colossal bouncing bump upon landing. At the Hertz counter, he rented a subcompact, then drove thirty minutes north to Clay Cross. He felt increasingly at home as his rental car was enveloped by the surroundings of the wealthy enclave: sweeping lawns, stone mansions, and century-old trees; indeed, he might have been back in affluent Hayes Barton, in Raleigh, where he had grown up. (Thank God he was not!) With the help of the rental car's mellifluously voiced GPS, he easily found his way to Cherry Tree Lane and to the house near the end of the street, a long, low, single-story dwelling with a great spreading maple shading its white clapboard front. Number ten. Dez pulled up to the curb, parked, then glanced at his watch. It was six minutes past three. He was right on time.

He had, by then, completed several close readings of *Lessons from My Daughter*, a book that offered a cornucopia of personal information highly useful to any man setting out to perpetrate a hoax upon its unwary author. For instance, it was from Ulrickson's book that Dez learned that Maddy took a nap at three each afternoon ("a pattern so regular you could set your clock by it," Ulrickson helpfully wrote), and that her bedroom lay one door beyond the bathroom in a hallway off the living room (a fact Ulrickson unwittingly divulged by describing his daily ritual of waking Maddy at three-thirty by tiptoeing "down the front hall, past the bathroom," then entering the room and kissing her, "like Prince Charming," on the forehead).

Before climbing from the car, Dez donned the ACE Hardware cap he'd found in the trailer, slipped on a pair of mirrored aviators and grabbed the toolbox.

His cover story about testing furnaces gained him easy entry, and after a five-minute sojourn in Ulrickson's pleasantly cool, if cobwebby, basement (where he flipped through a few *National Geographics* he found on a dusty shelf), he went back upstairs, stated his need for a bathroom and was duly pointed down the hall. From there, it was child's play (literally) for him to dodge into Maddy's bedroom, where the girl lay sleeping on her back, a soft snore coming through her parted lips.

During his time on the Innocence Project, Dez had seen countless sample-takers perform DNA swabs on prisoners. He moved with practiced ease, pulling on a pair of rubber gloves (hidden in his capacious coverall pockets), then easing open a package of regulation swabs. He extracted one, inserted it carefully into the child's open mouth and scraped lightly the inside of her cheek. He collected four specimens, which he deposited, one after another, into a paper envelope (always paper, never plastic, since moisture builds up in plastic and destroys the sample). As he worked, Dez marveled at Ulrickson's accuracy in describing his daughter as an unusually heavy sleeper. Only in the most halfhearted way did Maddy, at one point, snuffle, groggily open her eyes, bat weakly at Dez's hand, then subside back into thick oblivion.

His task completed, Dez slipped into the adjacent bathroom and flushed the toilet (for aural verisimilitude). Unable to resist the opportunity for a little gratuitous fun, he had thought to

compliment Ulrickson on his preposterous Bannister mysteries—a series that dutiful Dez (for research into his victim's habits of mind) had forced himself to read. Ulrickson's blushing delight at this praise nearly caused Dez to burst out laughing, but he mastered himself. A delightful coda to a most successful mission!

Indeed, the only element of the plan that failed to go precisely as Dez had visualized it in advance was the unexpected presence in the girl's bedroom of Ulrickson's wife, whom Dez had discovered sitting in her wheelchair beside the sleeping child. Her staring eyes and the soft susurration of her breathing gave him quite a turn at first. But he knew that the unfortunate creature was unable to speak, cry out, move or otherwise communicate, and thus she posed no threat to him. Indeed, as a kind of joke, he even took the time, during his ministrations over Maddy, to raise a gloved index finger to his lips and whisper, "Shhh!" A dangerous little jape, to be sure, but one too good to pass up.

7

From Ulrickson's house, Dez drove straight back to JFK and caught a return flight to Vermont. There, he picked up a new rental car and drove, through a sudden downpour, to nearby Newport. Arriving at nine in the evening, he checked into the Jack Pot, a casino-themed motel with small but tidy rooms arranged around a central cement courtyard. The "adult" offerings on the SpectraVision were, alas, precisely that, so Dez had to content himself with an hour or two of teen sitcoms on Nickelodeon before turning in. At eight the next morning, after an unexpectedly solid and refreshing sleep, he rose, showered, donned a freshly laundered shirt, then took from his overnight bag the one good suit he still possessed from his days as a lawyer: a black wool

number that was, truth to tell, a little out of date now—jackets and pants had narrowed considerably in the last few years, and no one was doing three buttons anymore; but it would have to do. Skipping breakfast (he couldn't have choked down a single bite), he set out, on foot, through a crystalline, storm-polished May morning, for the G-Tek Clinic, three blocks away.

It proved to be a narrow storefront sandwiched between a nail salon and a check-cashing establishment. Before entering, he flipped open the satchel that hung from a strap over his shoulder and peered inside. Everything was in readiness. He stood for a moment, breathing deeply, steadying his nerves for the task ahead. Then he pushed in through the clinic's glass doors.

Beyond a set of armchairs grouped around a low table piled with dog-eared magazines was a reception desk—a long counter shielded by a sliding glass window—behind which a heavyset African-American woman was trying, surreptitiously, to consume a tuna sandwich. She looked at him quizzically as he approached, then held up an index finger, bidding him to wait until she had swallowed her food. She did this, then wiped her lips with a paper napkin.

"Innocence Project, right?" she said. "How long has it been?"

Dez began to think that perhaps Providence was on his side. He had no memory of ever having set foot in this particular clinic. But then, he'd visited a lot of DNA testing centers, four years ago, when working with the Project. "Ages," he said. "I moved out of state for a while, but now I'm back."

She screwed up her face. "Rizzoli—or *Diz*oli?" she said. "Am I close?"

"Amazingly close," Dez said. "Dezollet—Russell. Everyone calls me Dez."

"That's it—Dez!" she said. She looked at the appointment calendar on her desk. "I don't know if I've got you down for today . . ."

Dez said that he did not have an appointment. But could he see Mr. Ames?

"Coming right up," the woman said, grabbing her phone and punching the intercom button. "Dunc?" she said. "Lawyer from Innocence to see you." She released the button and said, "You can take a seat if you like."

Dez, feeling considerably more relaxed, sat at the table and dug through the magazines, selecting a *Teen Vogue*. He studied an advertisement for a retro hippy-themed clothing company that featured a photograph of a girl of early high school age dressed in a tiny lace dress, thigh-high white knit socks and cork-soled platform sandals. A mass of teased blond hair framed her sullenly pouting face. He thought about sneakily ripping out the page for inclusion in his "files," but just then a tall, muscular man in a medical smock, jeans and white running shoes stepped out from behind the reception desk. Dez rose, using the magazine as a fig leaf to conceal the accident of physiology that made standing to his full height difficult. The man, who seemed to notice nothing of Dez's momentary discomfiture, introduced himself as Mr. Ames. Dez stared, puzzled, at the man's beefy face and weight lifter's neck upon which the tendril of a spiky tattoo was just visible, peeking up from the collar of his smock. The man was peering at Dez with similar puzzlement. Then he smiled.

"Hold it," Ames said. "Don't tell me. Dex. No—Dez! Right?"

Dez told him that he was correct.

It was all coming back. Four years ago, Dez had spent a day driving around from prison to prison, halfway house to halfway house, in Vermont's northeast kingdom with Ames, taking samples from potentially innocent inmates and ex-cons. Back then, Ames had been the new man on the job at G-Tek. An amiable if not too bright guy, a motorcycle enthusiast who had, grudgingly, switched from a footloose life as a part-time house painter (which paid just enough to keep him in gas money for his secondhand Triumph) to a nine-to-five gig as a phlebotomist when he got married and had twins. Yes, Dez remembered Ames quite clearly now, the hulking, henpecked husband who, by his early thirties, had already felt the last dregs of his youth draining out of him.

"Promotion?" Dez asked, pointing to the Supervisor badge on Ames's smock.

Ames shrugged. "If you want to call it that," he said.

Dez asked if they might speak for a moment in private.

"Hell, yeah," Ames said. He gestured, beckoning Dez behind the reception desk. They went down a short hall and into an empty examining room. Ames looked a little surprised when Dez stepped around him and closed the door behind them.

Dez decided to dispense with the small talk. There was really no point. Ames would either go for it or not. Everything depended on the next few seconds.

"I'm not here as a representative of the Innocence Project," Dez began. "I'm strictly on my own. I've got a proposition for

you. It doesn't involve a death row case; no one's life will be jeopardized, no murderer or rapist will go free. It's not even a criminal matter. It's nothing to trouble your conscience over—just the opposite. If you're willing to help out, you'll actually make one young woman's life a good deal better."

Ames looked at Dez expectantly, as if Dez were about to burst out laughing and announce that he was kidding. From what Ames could remember, the lawyer was a bit of a joker. But whatever he saw in Dez's expression convinced him otherwise. "Sorry," Ames said, "I don't think I'm following."

"Look," Dez said, "you've got two kids, right?"

"Three now," Ames said joylessly.

"Congratulations!" Dez said. "But that must get expensive?"

"Listen," Ames said, his tone now edged with some bitterness and impatience, "what's this about?"

"I need a favor," Dez said. "And I bet you could use some extra money."

Dez was at a clear advantage. He had met a lot of phlebotomists during his time with the Innocence Project, and he'd talked with them about the job; the rest of his knowledge he had filled in, recently, on a Sayer's Cliff Public Library computer, on the Internet. He knew, for instance, that certification in the field required only a high school education, forty classroom hours of instruction in basic anatomy at a community college or vocational school, and three weeks' training and practice in drawing blood and taking cheek swabs. Current starting salary: twenty-four thousand a year. After ten years, the ambitious phlebotomist could hope to command the top pay in the

field: thirty-two thousand—thirty-five if you rose to supervisor, like Ames. Dez believed that every man had his price. A phlebotomist's could not, he reasoned, be especially high. Especially when the man, like Ames, was trying to support a family of five on thirty-five grand a year. In the otherwise ironclad chain-of-custody safeguards, phlebotomists were the weak link. Dez had always known this and, with his penchant for practical jokes and schemes and scams, had stowed that knowledge away in some secret recess of his brain, in case it came in handy one day. It was coming in handy now. Or so he hoped.

He reached into his satchel and pulled out a pile of cash bound with a rubber band—five thousand dollars in twenties, which made a not-unimpressive stack. He dropped it on the examination table. It was everything Dez had had left in the bank.

"That's five grand," he said. "That's more than the extra money you get paid for being supervisor. Except you don't have to pay taxes on this, and it'll take you five minutes to earn. Instead of a year."

Ames looked at the money, then back at Dez. "Um," he said. "Go on."

"Tomorrow," Dez said, "a young woman will come here to give a DNA sample. A representative of Vermont Family Services will be with her, a man named Stubbs, and a female lawyer, Barnes. You will swab the girl in the normal fashion, but instead of sending the swabs to the lab, you'll switch them with these." Dez pulled from his bag the paper envelope containing the four swabs he had taken from Maddy. He put them back in the bag. He looked at Ames. "What do you say?"

Ames stared at the money and licked his lips. Dez saw an idea wink to life in the other man's mind, stirring glinting points of greed in Ames's pupils. "If you want to make it ten grand," Ames said, "you got a deal."

Dez scooped up the money, put it in his bag and turned to leave. Ames saw disappearing from his life forever the 2004 secondhand Ducati Monster 620 Dark motorcycle that he had fancifully, daydreamily, bookmarked on eBay last week.

He grabbed Dez by the arm. "Hold up," he said.

8

The next morning, at five minutes to ten, the G-Tek receptionist heard the light jingling of a bell that signaled someone coming through the front door. She saw, approaching, a short, stocky man in an ill-fitting and not especially clean-looking shirt, and a plump middle-aged woman with a salt-and-pepper bob and steel spectacles, dressed in a knee-length blue skirt and jacket. With them was a being that could not have provided a more dramatic example of how the expression of human DNA could differ from individual to individual: a sylph-like young woman in narrow dark jeans and a sleeveless white T-shirt, with waist-length wheat-colored hair framing a serenely pretty, softly rounded face. The pale, pudgy man introduced himself as Mr. Stubbs, and said

that the young woman had an appointment with Mr. Ames. The receptionist picked up her phone intercom and said, "Dunc?" A minute later, a well-muscled man with a Supervisor badge on his smock came from a back room.

Ames's eyes lit, then lingered for a few seconds, on Chloe, as men's eyes tended to do, before he recovered and invited the trio back to an examining room. There, he performed the well-oiled ritual: he examined Chloe's ID, wrote her name and address, the date and the clinic's details on the DDS collection envelope, put on gloves, then peeled open a package of swabs and—with Stubbs and Barnes looking on—took four samples from Chloe's mouth, placing each swab in the collection envelope. "Okay," he said in a slightly louder than normal voice, "that's all there is to it."

This was the prearranged signal for Dez, who had been loitering outside in the hall. He burst into the room on a dead run. "Sorry I'm late!" he cried. "Traffic!"

Chloe and Ames made a great show of surprise. Stubbs and Barnes's shock was genuine. In unison, they turned and glared at the intruder, thus giving Ames ample time to slide the envelope of swabs into the inside pocket of his smock and extract an identical-looking envelope from the same pocket.

"Hold it," Dez said, looking around the group. "Is this the Hollenbeck case?"

Ames informed him that it was not.

"I thought they said ten!" Dez exclaimed. He apologized, bowed, then dodged out.

"Can we finish up, then?" Stubbs said, irritably.

Ames inked Chloe's thumb and pressed it to the corner of the envelope. He photographed her, sealed the camera and samples in a pouch, and had her sign the safety tape. He called the receptionist to summon a courier.

Thirty minutes later, the swabs (labeled "Donor B") were en route to DDS Diagnostics in Fairfield, Ohio, where they arrived the next morning, then languished for four weeks in a temperature- and moisture-controlled room awaiting analysis among the backlog of cases, until an afternoon near the end of May when a technician collected the swabs, then used a pair of sterilized scissors to snip off the Dacron tips. These were placed in a test tube containing a solution that released the skin molecules scraped from the inside of the donor's cheek. The sample was dye-tagged, heated to ninety-five degrees Celsius in a thermal cycler, and then lowered to sixty degrees and finally heated back up to seventy-two degrees, to elongate the DNA strand. This strand, with its arrangement of bases and pairs laid out along the chromosome, was injected into a capillary electrophoresis genetic analyzer—a tube the circumference of a hair—and subjected to a laser scan that revealed a picture of the DNA profile, including those short genetic sequences, called alleles, shared by parents and their biological offspring. Had Chloe's actual sample been sent, the lab workers would have readily seen that there was no match. But as things stood, the sample, when compared with alleles from Donor A (submitted by Jasper Ulrickson of 10 Cherry Tree Lane, Clay Cross, Connecticut), revealed that Donor A was, to a 99.9 percent degree of certainty, the father of Donor B.

Informed of this result, Stubbs, at the Department of Children

and Families, notified Mrs. Barnes, who in turn telephoned Chloe at the home of her foster family. Mrs. Gaitskill, hearing the news, clapped her hands excitedly and chanted, "You're going to know your father! You're going to know your father!" Her husband began playing a plunging, triumphal rendition of "O Sons and Daughters, Let Us Sing!" on the piano, and Mrs. Gaitskill lifted her voice in song:

> On this most holy day of days
> Our hearts and voices, Lord, we raise
> To Thee, in jubilee and praise.
> Alleluia! Alleluia!

When the last ringing chord died away, Chloe excused herself—saying she "just needed to be alone for a minute to process everything"—and ran up to her room. There, she called Dez and told him the tidings. He was, to understate the case considerably, relieved. A slight chance had existed of Maddy's sample being contaminated or damaged in transit, thus yielding a result known, in DNA testing, as an "exclusion," which required a second test—a do-over. This had seemed cold comfort to Dez, who doubted he would ever again be able to talk his way into Ulrickson's home to collect a new sample from Maddy. How much sleep had he lost lately, tossing and turning on the Tartarus's narrow bed, trying to dream up alternate methods of collecting a new sample in case of an exclusion (enroll, briefly, as a teacher at the brat's preschool?). But he could forget about all that now and concentrate on the plan's next phase—a phase to which he had devoted several even more stubborn insomnias.

9

It was an unpleasant detail, a dangling loose end the removal of which he had deliberately not focused on in advance, lest the enormity of the act prevent him from undertaking the entire project in the first place.

Whatever faults of character Dez possessed, he was not a violent man. He had not, for instance, been able to fight back against that father who collared him at the bus stop all those years ago. In those episodes of "self-blinding" during Geld's aversion therapy, no imagery could more reliably dampen desire than imagined scenes of torture, maiming and murder. And at the heart of his contempt for his father had always been the cavalier way Judge Dezollet consigned those sad killers, mental

defectives and abuse victims to the gas chamber, electric chair and lethal injection—where death (Dez knew, from an ill-advised glimpse into one of the execution reports prepared for his father) came not with the clinical efficiency fondly imagined by proponents of capital punishment, but with writhing and cries, whimpers and pleadings, tears, vomit, blood, smoking scalps and pitiful loosened bowels.

Yet for the plan to go forward from this point, he must rise above that physical and moral squeamishness; he must behave like a good soldier; he must commit the act whose name he could not even pronounce to himself. No use pretending that Ames could remain forever a silent partner; once apprised of the crime he had been inveigled in (and a splashily public denouement was virtually the scheme's main *point*), that silence was something Dez would have to pay for dearly, in blackmail payments. No, no. No point trying to delude himself that a cash-strapped father of three would fail to return to the money well. Not that money was the problem. Dez would happily pay off forever, if it meant avoiding the act he was now obliged to commit. It was the inevitable, ongoing contact between blackmailer and blackmailee that had to be avoided. Such contact would perforce open up dangers of accidental exposure—an unacceptable risk.

God knew, he had tried to avoid this—tried to devise a plan that involved no one but himself and Chloe. In the early stages of planning, he had considered taking the six months' training necessary to earn his own phlebotomy credentials—a scheme he soon discarded, since the requisite background check would as a matter of course turn up his compromised legal

past. He toyed, mentally, with enrolling in classes on sleight-of-hand magic so that he might, while posing as Chloe's lawyer, accompany her to the clinic and somehow accomplish an act of sample switching. But Dez, for all his mental agility, was notoriously fumble-fingered. The notion of him performing a Ricky Jay–like bait and switch under the eye of a watchful trained professional . . . well, that was clearly hopeless, and Dez abandoned that plan too.

There were other imagined strategies (Chloe feigning a seizure so that Dez might gingerly remove the sample envelope from the phlebotomist's distracted grip and switch it for Maddy's; or Dez himself mimicking an exploded appendix while Chloe accomplished the switch). But he had, eventually, reluctantly, faced the fact that there was one way, and one way only, to beat the chain-of-custody safeguards—and that was to enlist a short-term accomplice, a paid pawn who, owing precisely to his very ignorance of the larger chess game, must, once his role in the combination was complete, be removed from the board. How precisely that "removal" was to be accomplished, Dez had not allowed himself to look at squarely. There were so many nearly insuperable obstacles that he was first obliged to clear—that risky masquerade as the furnace repairman chief among them—that this later erasure had seemed comfortably hypothetical. Now, it was anything but.

For weeks, he had imagined that a timed-release poison (slipped into a Coke or a beer?) was the best method, allowing Dez time to get away before the retching and coughing and convulsions. But a little Internet research on toxic compounds

had brought up a news story from the St. Louis *Dispatch* about a female murderer undone by investigators who combed her computer and found Web searches for "instant poisons," "undetectable poisons" and "fatal digoxin dose." Dez instantly shut down his search and abandoned all further thought of poison.

He ruminated on luring his prey to the top of one of the blue-misted mountains that loomed over Sayer's Cliff, and using an almost accidental elbow nudge to send his man sailing into the void—but abandoned this dream upon recalling the sheer size of his would-be victim (Dez would have to take a run at him, like a defensive tackle—and even at that, he might fail to topple him, the man turning, windmilling his arms, reaching out to grasp Dez, pulling him down too). Only after wasting time over these, and countless other, unworkable plots had he finally gotten serious and arrived at the sole strategy that could conceivably have a chance of success: that of the violent surprise attack during the man's routine, daily rounds. For some days now, Dez had been planning to bus into Newport to make a visit of inspection at the future scene of the crime, and to gather some necessary intel in order to implement it. He could delay no longer.

On the bus ride into Newport, on a dull gray morning the day after receiving the DNA result, he tried to empty his mind of the violent visions that were trying to breed there. Best not to visualize, too clearly, the act in advance.

At noon, he found himself standing outside the G-Tek Clinic. He kept his face averted as he strolled past the big plate glass window (so as not to draw premature attention from the weirdly

observant receptionist), then ducked down the alley that separated the building from the adjacent nail parlor. At the end was a weedy lane bounded on one side by the backs of the buildings and on the other by a wooden fence. Ames had mentioned the other day that he always parked "out back." There was no way of knowing which of the four automobiles stowed there now was his victim's, but he could settle that in a minute. The main thing was to establish whether there was a suitable place for Dez to lie in wait, lug wrench or baseball bat at the ready.

Running vertically up the wall of the building, a few feet from the back door, was an immense duct, chipped and over-painted many times. Dez experimentally fitted himself into the nook formed where the pipe met the wall. Yes. Yes, this would do admirably. He would hide here this evening, then creep out, on tiptoe, as his unsuspecting prey emerged from the clinic's back door and took the five or six paces over to his car. Shimmer out from the shadows, weapon raised.

He could see and feel how that first blow would stove in the back of the head with a sensation of heavy iron sinking into soft watermelon. He must be careful to land the blow squarely lest he simply graze the head, cleaving away an ear or opening a sanguineously spurting, but not fatal, scalp wound, allowing his victim to swing around and begin to fight back. He would take the time to aim that first blow at the place where Ames's hair whorled in a spiral from the thinning crown, he would smack that sweet spot in a two-handed downward chopping motion, felling the man. Then he would deliver a series of added blows, to ensure that his victim was well and truly dead,

pound the brain and face and eyeballs and tongue and hair to a consistency resembling steak tartare. At the thought, he grew light-headed, and nausea fluttered his guts. He bent at the waist, dry-retching briefly.

Still woozy, he walked back up the alley to the sidewalk in front of the building. He was now obliged to enter the establishment, to drop in, unannounced, on Ames, invite him out to lunch and, under the pretext of friendly conversation, draw him out on the make of his car and what time he left work each day. A difficult task, especially given that his victim might, for good reason, be suspicious of such attentions from Dez. Still, there was nothing for it. He needed this information and, short of trying to pry it casually out of the receptionist (could he *do* that?), Dez could not figure out how else to get it. He squared his shoulders, pasted on his face what he hoped looked like a friendly, innocent smile, then pushed in through the glass door.

Advancing toward the desk, and seeing the odd expression on the receptionist's face at the sight of him, Dez instantly knew something was wrong. Had Ames already blabbed about his sample-switching exploit to his coworkers? But no, that did not seem to be it. For when Dez stepped up to the desk and boldly asked to see Mr. Ames, the woman, instead of looking at him with suspicion or accusation, gave him a melting look of commiseration.

"Oh—then you haven't heard," she said.

And that is when she told him, between sniffles and dabbings at her eyes with a crumpled napkin, about the accident. Just a week ago now. So terrible. On that Italian-made motorcycle that

Duncan was so proud of, that he saved so carefully for. And on his debut outing! Simply lost control—apparently those things are so much more powerful than the American-made bikes Dunc was familiar with. The cops later estimated that the poor man was doing about eighty when he hit the bridge abutment. He was wearing a helmet, for all the good it did him. Split the plastic like a nutshell. Killed instantly—which was, she guessed, a blessing of sorts. "He didn't suffer."

Disbelief was the primary sensation that assailed him, disbelief that gave rise to a floating, hovering sensation of hushed, eerie, cosmic solemnity and then to a widening, spreading sense of expanding incredulity that fate or luck or destiny or Providence was so allied with him as to effect the necessary removal in so timely a manner and entirely without his agency. For Dez had no way of knowing that the motorcycle in question, a Ducati Monster 620 Dark, had been purchased with the money Dez himself had paid to the deceased. Nevertheless, he did feel sufficiently spooked by the synchronous happenstance as to wonder if his visions, seconds ago, about splitting open the man's head had, through some infolding of the space-time continuum, retroactively catalyzed the accident.

Dez said how sorry he was, that he had dropped in to see if old Duncan wanted to grab some lunch, that it was a dreadful tragedy—think of those three kids and his widow; he must send them some money! It was all so horrible, so incomprehensible, the fragility of life, how everything just hung by a thread. Backing toward the door, Dez cast an eye over the table where, not so

long ago, he had studied that fascinating teen fashion magazine and that ever-so-stimulating advertisement. He thought about pausing to dig through the strewn periodicals and discreetly rip out the page for inclusion in his "files," but decided, under the circumstances, to let it pass.

10

"Dad?" Maddy said. "What's a Ella Menno?"

She was sitting on the living room floor, a few feet across the carpet from Jasper, at the foot of Pauline's wheelchair, paging through a book made of felt, with Velcro-backed, removable bits of cloth that depicted various items—a violin, a lion, a cat—each item to be matched with the corresponding letter of the alphabet sewn onto each page.

Jasper was on the sofa, laptop open on his knees, working on his Bannister mystery. In the weeks since first conceiving of his plot concerning a villainous psychopath posing as the illegitimate son of a dead patriarch, Jasper had made great strides. He had honed the backstory of deprivation and abuse that had

warped his villain's mind. He had further fleshed out in vivid scenes the wealthy, noble Gutterson family and its ancestral home in the leafy reaches of Princeton, New Jersey. All had gone with surprising smoothness.

The thorniest problem, as Jasper had foreseen, was that of the DNA test that his villain would be obliged to undergo to convince the Guttersons that he was the illegitimate son of Lemuel Gutterson. How to get around the chain-of-custody safeguards?

It seemed obvious that the only way for an impostor to pass a paternity test would be to use a sample taken from someone who was the biological offspring of the father. Jasper had, accordingly, created for these purposes a child—youngest scion of the late lamented Lemuel—from whom his antihero could steal some cheek cells. Because Jasper's criminal was male, and would have an XY chromosome makeup, the child had to be male too, but young enough so that the sample could believably be stolen from him without his awareness. This suggested a preschooler, a kid Maddy's age, or younger. He had duly written such a character into the story—which had required him (in the infernally difficult business of composing fiction) to backtrack and weave seamlessly into the story a second wife for the octogenarian Lemuel, a woman young enough to bear a child but not so young as to suggest that Lemuel (who was meant to be an admirable character) was a predatory old cradle robber. Jasper had created a forty-one-year-old female nurse (modeled in no small part on Deepti) who had faithfully seen Gutterson's first wife through a long, fatal bout of cancer, and to whom Lemuel, alone and grieving, had turned for support after his wife's death.

In an act applauded by his older children, Lemuel had married his wife's former nurse and sired the little DNA provider so crucial to Jasper's plot.

But now he was wrestling with the problem of how, exactly, his villain could extract a cheek sample without anyone being the wiser. He had been struggling with the conundrum for days and at the moment was asking himself if his villain might not pose as a dentist who visits the boy's preschool to give the children a lesson about dental hygiene, thereby managing to collect a cheek sample while pretending to inspect the boy's teeth. But even as he began, excitedly, to tap this into his laptop, he felt that the plan could never be made to seem believable; the teachers would surely notice his villain poking the swabs into the child's mouth. Besides which, the reader would inevitably wonder why the child would not speak up, asking why the dentist was scraping away at the inside of his cheeks. Which raised the question: could the child somehow be *unconscious*? Perhaps asleep! Napping! His villain need only dream up a ruse, an imposture, to infiltrate the home—pose as a repairman or contractor? Jasper began to type this inspiration, when Maddy's indignant voice drew him back to the here and now.

"Dad?" she said. "What does it *mean*?"

"Sorry, honey," he said, looking up from his screen and blinking away the fictional visions that clouded his eyes. "What does what mean?"

"Ella *Men*no."

"Ellamenno?" he said. "Not a clue. Where did you hear that word?"

"At preschool. We were singing the ABCs."

"Oh, I see!" He chuckled. "Ellamenno. It's not a word. It's part of the alphabet. The letters *L-M-N-O*. It's funny, because when *I* was a kid, I also used to think exactly the same—"

The phone, on the table beside the sofa, rang. Jasper checked the caller ID. It read: "Law Offices, Pollock."

His heart jumped in his chest. It had been several weeks since he donated his sample. This *must* be Pollock, finally, with the results.

Deepti called from the kitchen: "Do you want me to get that?"

"No, no," Jasper said. "I've got it."

He glanced at Pauline. She was staring at him. Her eyes had a hooded, haunted look, the same look they had had for weeks—a look he had, until her recent change in mood, never seen before.

Dr. Carlucci had warned Jasper that many locked-in patients suffered "emotional lability"—marked mood swings—and at first Jasper had tried to convince himself that the sudden change in Pauline, a few weeks ago, could be chalked up to that. But the dramatic shift in Pauline's emotions, he was finally obliged to admit to himself, was no temporary thing: it was part and parcel of a dramatic reversal on the subject of the paternity claim. From her earlier ready acceptance, Pauline had, overnight, adopted a stance of rigid opposition to, and disapproval of, anything touching on Holly and the child. She refused even to respond to Jasper's efforts at engaging her on the subject. His attempt, the other day, to talk about what room they would put the child in, should she turn out to be his, had made Pauline shut down completely—closing her eyes to indicate her refusal even to consider the subject.

He was, at first, mystified by this abrupt reversal. But upon reflection, he understood its origins. Pauline's opposition must derive from the retroactive sexual jealousy she felt about his long-ago liaison with Holly—a jealousy that could only be heartbreakingly magnified by Pauline's physical incapacity, which made it impossible for her to assert her sexual "ownership" of Jasper, through intercourse—to stake her claim against what she clearly suspected were his reawakened memories of Holly, of that moment on the beach. Having arrived at this insight, he inwardly cursed himself for the lack of empathy, the blindness, that had prevented him from realizing it earlier. For days, he had blundered on, trying to force Pauline to engage on the subject of the girl, to acknowledge the very real possibility that the child would be coming to live with them. Having finally seen his error, he had ceased trying to talk about the situation. But, obviously, the subject could not be avoided forever—as the ringing phone now attested.

Pauline's stare sharpened. She had obviously divined that it was Pollock calling.

He lifted the phone to his ear and said a cautious hello.

"Results are in," the lawyer said without preamble.

"Hold on," Jasper said. He put his hand over the receiver. "Pollock," he confirmed to Pauline. He shot a glance at Maddy, who knew nothing, as yet, about her prospective half-sister. "I'd better take this in my office," he added, simultaneously feeling a stab of guilt at using their child as an excuse to quit the room; for Jasper's true motivation was to escape the searing heat of Pauline's gaze, which awoke in him a vague and inexplicable

feeling of guilt. "I'll be right back," he added, getting to his feet. He carried the cordless phone down the hall to his office, shut the door behind him and sat at his desk. "Okay," he told Pollock. "I'm ready."

"She's your daughter."

Scalding blood bounded into his face. His heart began to tom-tom. He had tried to acclimate himself to this result in advance, to internalize it, make it real for himself, so as to blunt the shock when it came. Those efforts had been in vain. He was reeling. "My daughter," he repeated tonelessly.

"That's correct," said Pollock. "Which means that I can now, legally, divulge to you her name. She is Chloe. Chloe Dwight."

"Chloe," he said softly. His daughter. *Chloe.* Of all the many *C*-names he had imagined, this lovely one had never come to him. Had Holly known the derivation? From the Greek: "to bloom, to blossom." Is that why she had chosen it, or had she merely liked the sound? In any case, she *was* Holly's bloom—and, of course, his own. He felt a surge of that paternal pride, that excitement, that had surprised him during his walk to the clinic to donate his DNA sample a few weeks ago. He immediately thought of Pauline, and a terrible apprehension overcame him.

"Mr. Ulrickson?" Pollock said. "You still there?"

"I am," he said. "I'm just trying to absorb it."

"I'm sure it'll take a while. And you'll have some time." He explained that Jasper should not expect immediately to bring Chloe down from Vermont to live with him. "She is currently a ward of the state," he said. "So you've got to make a formal petition for custody—same as if you were adopting. Government's

got to be satisfied you can support and educate the child; that you've got a stable home, that you're not crazy, that you don't have a criminal record. So there will be some background checks, interviews, that kind of thing. She'll undergo something similar in Vermont, social workers and shrinks making sure she's strong enough, emotionally, to leave her friends and school and start living with a father she never knew. They never actually deny custody—not unless she's a basket case or you're a raving drug addict or living on the streets or a convicted sex offender. Still, it takes time."

"How much time?" Jasper asked. To his surprise, he was disappointed to hear of the delay.

"It's the judicial system, so don't expect things to happen overnight. But if I light a fire under them, we might have this done in—what is it now? End of May? Say, two months. Early August. If you're lucky. Now," he added in a lighter tone, "I'm sure you'd like to have a word about all this with your daughter."

"Maddy?" Jasper said. "I don't see what—" Then he realized his mistake.

"I've got the number for her at her foster parents' place," Pollock went on. "She's waiting for your call. Got a pen?" He recited the number and Jasper wrote it down. "Okay," Pollock said, "we'll talk. And congratulations." He rang off.

Jasper sat there, trying to imagine what to say to the girl. To Chloe. His *daughter*. There seemed, at once, far too much to say (how do you catch someone up on seventeen years of life in a phone call?) and not nearly enough (apart from the little he had been able to glean of her life from the affidavit, he knew almost

nothing about her). But there was no point in trying to prepare speeches, to script a conversation. He would trust to emotion, let his heart speak. Wasn't that always the best way?

With a shaking index finger, he punched the number into the phone. It had scarcely begun to ring when he heard a click, then came an elderly-sounding woman's voice. She said, with a certain coy expectancy, "Gaitskill residence . . . ?"

He cleared his throat—a hot, hard obstruction had taken up sudden residence there. "I'm calling for Chloe—" His voice hung for a moment. Did he need to supply a surname? And if so, which one? Dwight? Ulrickson? "From Connecticut," he offered instead.

"Just a moment." Through a muffling palm, he heard the woman say urgently, "It's for you. *Connecticut*." There followed a rustling sound. Then he heard, through the thrumming cataract of blood in his ears, a featherlight voice: tentative, shy, hopeful.

". . . Dad?"

"Yes, it's me," Jasper said, on a gust of breath that burst from him like a sob. Then he *was* sobbing. Something about that soft, vulnerable, childlike voice—his *daughter's* voice—coming through the phone line, from so far away, the girl he never knew, *his* girl, living among strangers, until now an orphan, or believing herself to be, and thus all alone in the world. He struggled to master himself.

"Sorry, sorry," he managed to say, gulping down the sobs that convulsed his throat and lungs. "Yes, it's—it's your dad." And then he was doing what he had told himself he must not do, since it might sound like an indictment of Holly for failing to tell him

of Chloe's existence: he was apologizing—apologizing for not having been in her life, not having raised her, not having been there for her at the important moments, birthdays, graduations, her mother's death. "But I didn't know about you, honey," he said, "otherwise everything would have been different—everything."

"Don't worry, Dad," came that soft, light voice, sweetly melodic. "It's okay. I don't blame you. I know Mom didn't tell you about me. I know it's not your fault."

Her readiness to forgive also made him cry, and he was some time getting control of himself. "Well, the main thing is, we've found each other," he said at length, mopping at his eyes and cheeks and nose with a Kleenex he had snatched from a box in his desk. "That's what's important now. We have the future."

"That's what I'm excited about," Chloe said, her voice brightening, quickening. "I can't wait to see you."

"Well, I was hoping that you would come and live with us," he said. "Do you want to do that? I know it would mean leaving all your friends and the places you know—"

"I can't wait!" she cried. "That's my biggest dream! But I guess it's going to take a long time. I've got to talk to psychiatrists and everything."

"Yes," he said. "And I have to talk to all sorts of official people too. But we'll both come through with flying colors, and then you'll be here. I would come to see you right away, but I've got a small daughter—your half-sister, Maddy; and my wife, your step-mother, Pauline, is an invalid. It's very difficult for me to get away."

"Oh, I understand," Chloe said. "I've still got *school* too. But can you tell me about Connecticut? I want to be able to picture it."

Jasper described Clay Cross, its location near the Sound, and told her about the house, the spreading maple out front, the patio out back with the view, over the lawn, of the water and the distant twinkling skyscrapers of New York visible like a mirage on clear days. He told her the layout of the rooms, and was about to explain where Chloe would be sleeping when his office door flew open and Maddy ran in.

"Mommy wants you," she announced. "I can tell." She turned and ran out.

Pauline! He had left her waiting all this time to hear the results of the DNA test! How could he have forgotten her? It had never happened before. "I'm sorry, Chloe," he said, "but I've got to get off the phone. It's my wife—Pauline. Your stepmom. She needs me. But we'll talk again soon. And I'll *see* you soon."

"Okay," Chloe said. "I love you, Dad," she added before he could hang up.

"I love you too," he said and, in saying it, felt the strangeness of it: professing love—no, *feeling* love—for someone he had never met, never seen. How wonderful that the bond between parent and child could be felt, over a phone line, after less than five minutes' acquaintance! Could anything speak more eloquently of the mystical connections of family? He surrendered to a fresh storm of sobs—then hurriedly mopped his face and blew his nose. He stood, and brought his breathing under control. Then he went down the hall to face the difficult task of breaking the news to Pauline.

11

She was staring at the carpet when Jasper returned to the living room. As he approached, she raised her gaze to his. He saw in her eyes a light of hope, which instantly died when she read his expression.

Maddy was sitting on the sofa, coloring. "Please be a good girl," he told her, "and go see Deepti in the kitchen. Mommy and I have to talk about grown-up things."

"*Again?*" Maddy said. But she picked up her pad and crayons and trooped off.

He pulled up a footrest, placed it in front of Pauline and sat. He took her hands in his own. She would not look at him, her eyes cast down.

"Honey," he said softly. "You have to face this. *We* have to face this. We can't—I don't know—*wish* it away. The good news is that I just spoke with her. She sounds like a wonderful child. Not angry or sullen or blaming. She sounds very sweet, and she very much wants to come and live with us and be a part of this family."

At this, Pauline looked up, and stared meaningfully at him.

"Yes," he said, misreading that look, "I know that having her here will be disruptive of our routine. At least, at first. But we'll get used to it, and there will be benefits to having her here. I'm sure of it. She can help with Maddy. She can lend a hand to Deepti. I can give her chores—Xeroxing, opening mail, buying printer ink—any number of things. Having her here will actually free up *more* time for us. Do you see what I mean? Do you see the positive side?"

She blinked twice. *No.*

He felt a flare of exasperation but tried not to show it. "Darling," he said calmly, soothingly, "she's my *daughter*. Surely you're not saying, 'Don't take her in'?"

She blinked once.

"Oh, honey," he said, risking a smile. "You don't expect me to believe that? That you think I should leave my own flesh and blood to be raised by strangers? By a foster family?"

Yes.

"So you're saying a father shouldn't take responsibility for his own child?"

No.

"Yet I should abandon Chloe?"

Yes.

"Well, that makes no *sense,* honey," he said. "You've just flatly contradicted yourself. The point is, I could no sooner leave Chloe to foster care than I could have left *you* in the chronic care ward." This struck Jasper as an emotional equivalency that Pauline could not fail to acknowledge with an affirmative blink. But she only dropped her eyes, in a gesture of helpless surrender, and stared at the carpet.

He understood about retroactive sexual jealousy. If the roles were reversed, Jasper, who suffered acutely when he thought of Pauline's old boyfriends, would have had a mighty struggle to accept into their home a child she had engendered with an ex-lover. But he would have done it, because he trusted her, trusted in her love. He knew that, deep down, she trusted him the same way. She just needed some reassurance. How to reassure her? He told her that Holly was a long, long time in the past, that he had never thought of her in the intervening years, and that he loved Pauline and Pauline only. "Isn't that obvious?" he asked.

She considered him with a woeful gaze. A tear squeezed up from the lower lid of her right eye, trembled there for a moment, expanding, then ran in a rapid rill down her cheek. He reached up and, with his index finger, wiped it away.

"It's going to be okay, honey," he said. "I promise."

Deeply unsettled by this exchange, he wondered if he was, after all, wrong in thinking that he must bring Chloe to live with them. Perhaps a family with their challenges could not reasonably be expected to take on the disruptions a teenager would inevitably bring. But when he discussed this later that evening

with Deepti, she assured him that he was doing the right thing, the only thing, by taking Chloe in. "She is your flesh and blood," Deepti said. "She is family."

Jasper's sister, Laura, two years his junior and married to a successful software developer in San Francisco, gave him similar advice when he called her that evening. "Of *course* Pauline is going to feel strange about *any* change in the household," Laura told him. "Think of how vulnerable she feels. How powerless. But when she meets the girl—and you're saying she sounds like a terrific kid—everything will change. Honestly, Jaz, it's going to be fine. And you really don't have a choice. She's your daughter. Trust me, Pauline will come round."

Laura's words became a mantra to him; he repeated them to himself whenever he felt his doubts rise again. *She'll come round. She'll come round. She'll come round.*

Because, of course, she had to.

PART THREE

1

Interstate 91, the six-lane superhighway that runs on a near-perfect vertical from New Haven, Connecticut, to the town of Derby Line, Vermont, on the American-Canadian border, cuts past lush, cow-dotted pastures, rounded mountains fleeced in green forests, and twinkling New England towns nestled in valleys where white church steeples, pointing skyward, make explicit the implied connection between the paradisiacal surroundings and the supernatural being who seems their only possible creator. But on the afternoon in early August when Jasper steered his car off Exit 48, at Stamford, onto I-91 to begin the long haul through Connecticut, Massachusetts and Vermont, he was not conscious of scenery. He was thinking only about his impending meeting with Chloe.

He had spent the previous weeks being investigated by government accountants who pawed through his tax returns and royalty statements; by social workers who quizzed his family, friends and neighbors; by psychologists who delved into his attitudes to family, adoption and teenaged girls. He was questioned by an FBI agent who checked his fingerprints against international crime databases. Chloe, meanwhile, had undergone a similar vetting in Vermont, with special emphasis on her psychosocial and emotional functioning. On a morning at the end of July, Murray Pollock called Jasper to say that the family court judge in Newport had read the dossiers on both parties and had ruled that Jasper would be awarded custody. Formal transfer would occur at a hearing in Judge Gerald Howard's courtroom at noon on August 3—tomorrow.

He had considered flying (there was a direct from JFK to Burlington) but decided to drive. It was a five-and-a-half-hour trip each way. He thought that the return journey would offer an ideal opportunity for him and Chloe to get to know each other—to *bond*—before she met the rest of the family.

They had spoken several more times on the phone but had not progressed much beyond cooed avowals about how much they looked forward to seeing each other. He had, however, had a series of mandatory telephone "sessions" with Chloe's transitioning social worker, Dr. Doreen Edwards, whose job it was (as she put it) "to smooth out any little wrinkles in Chloe's adjustment from one life to another"—and from whom he had been able to glean some much-wanted background on the girl he believed to be his daughter.

Edwards had made a point of reminding Jasper that Chloe had recently lost her mother—"the only parent or parental-figure the child has ever known"—and that for all Chloe's superficial cheerfulness, she *was* grieving and might be harboring "several unresolved issues." Thus, he should not be surprised if she became rebellious, argumentative, limit-testing. She might bear subconscious resentments toward Jasper, whom she could perceive as having "abandoned" her and her mother—"even if such ideas do not fit the facts." Chloe was, furthermore, a child of addiction (Holly had, Edwards said, "suffered from the disease of alcoholism"), and this might bring forth, in Chloe, "an array of negative behaviors"—anything from shoplifting to lying and fighting, to sexual promiscuity, exhibitionism and "inappropriate relationships." And although Chloe had yet to display any such self-destructive tendencies, everyone in a position to guide her must stay alert to their possible appearance.

He had spoken, too, with Chloe's school guidance counselor, a Miss Shelley, who said that IQ testing in elementary school had suggested a child of slightly *above* average intelligence, but who demonstrated a marked lack of intellectual curiosity—although this might result from the home environment where the mother was often absent and the child was given few opportunities to develop interests outside of television. She demonstrated a "pacific, even passive, temperament," and tended to cling to those she perceived as vital to her welfare. No disciplinary problems had been reported in school—and indeed the only incident ever to have raised any alarms dated to mid-March of this year, when a teacher was observed to initiate inappropriate physical contact

with Chloe (a kiss on her neck). It was determined that she had done nothing to provoke or encourage the act—"apart from being a singularly attractive child," Miss Shelley added, "for which she can hardly be blamed!" Chloe's mother had declined to press charges, the offending teacher left the school, and the child had demonstrated no ill effects from the incident. All told, she was well behaved, given somewhat to daydreaming and fantasy, athletic though not much driven to compete, well groomed, punctual and with a stated interest in acting and modeling, although she had not participated in any of the school's extracurricular activities geared to those pursuits.

Thinking of all this now, Jasper (as he flicked on his headlights against the gathering dusk over northern Massachusetts) found much to be heartened by. Certainly, there were some problem areas to be conscious of (passivity; possible latent hostility), but things were far from as bad as they *might* have been, surely. No drug use, abortions, arrests, juvenile detention. Clearly, she was working below her academic potential, but Jasper believed that would change once she was in his family's supportive and nurturing environment.

He stopped at a diner near Brattleboro, ate a hamburger and then carried on north. At Exit 27, he followed the off-ramp onto a two-lane highway that cut through monotonous corn and wheat fields. Eventually, out his right passenger window, appeared the brooding profile of Mount Orford, over the Vermont border, in Quebec. He knew its shape from the summer he had spent in New Halcyon, all those years ago. He was getting close.

He reached Newport at midnight and drove along Main Street, turned left at School Street then right onto Prospect, where, a few doors down, he found the Little Gnesta, the Swiss chalet–styled bed-and-breakfast at which he had made a one-night reservation. He parked behind the building and then climbed, stiffly, out of his car.

He was almost overcome by the remembered aroma of honeysuckle and ragweed, mountain flowers and nearby Lake Memphremagog—a perfume that carried him back to that summer almost twenty years ago. Before moving toward the porch, where a flurry of moths swarmed the lit bulb over the door, he paused and marveled at the strangeness of his situation: that single moment of unguarded passion on a beach not ten miles away, a single moment from his youth that might have vanished like so many other lost instants, but which, owing to the vagaries of human reproduction, had reverberated down the years, to this moment, his return, and his standing on the brink of a momentous meeting. He turned his face up to the night sky, to the vast, heart-quaking star field so much larger and clearer here than back home, where light pollution from nearby New York City erased the evidence of the heavens. Facing that twinkling black expanse, he pondered the mystery of how a single sperm cell of the hundreds of millions he had produced found its way to the egg nestled in Holly's womb, there to set in motion a new life, a cosmos of thought and feeling. The randomness—the sheer statistical unlikelihood of that occurrence—seemed objectively reflected in the gasping array of stars and galaxies overhead, an infinity of cosmic accidents that had produced this beautiful

Earth. A rationalist (he had abandoned his parents' formal religion at age eighteen), Jasper nevertheless did, privately, retain the belief that there was a force for good shaping everyone's ends, that no occurrence, regardless of how dire, was without meaning in some larger plan—a faith that had survived even the calamities of his parents' deaths, and of Pauline's stroke, and which now buoyed him with the conviction that the advent of Chloe in their lives could only be a harbinger of good and joyful things.

He shouldered his overnight bag and went inside.

In the pine-paneled lobby, a crookbacked old woman behind the desk handed him his door key, and he shuffled down the hall to his room. Exhausted, he did not even bother to shower, and instead only hastily washed his face and brushed his teeth before falling into bed.

2

He was up with the alarm at eight the next morning. He took special care shaving (he did not want his daughter's first impression of him to include a bloody scab where he had nicked himself), got dressed in the light-colored summer-weight suit he had packed in his overnight bag, then went down the hall past the dining room, where a lively breakfast among strangers was in progress. He eschewed this—he was feeling far too nervous to sit and make small talk with people he did not know—and walked up to Main Street, where he found a health-food diner. He ordered, but was unable to eat, a bowl of granola. At eleven-thirty, with a half hour to spare, he paid the waitress and then set out.

Perched like a chess piece on its manicured square of green, the courthouse was a compact Federalist structure of red brick with green trim, a clock tower rising from a triangular pediment over three tall windows. At the sight of it, Jasper felt a new attack of nerves: his armpits, freshly deodorized, prickled hotly and he felt his heart begin to canter. He mounted the shallow stone steps to the entrance. Inside, it took a moment for his eyes to grow accustomed to the cool gloom of the wood and marble interior. A uniformed security guard seated at a table (no metal detectors here) asked his name, consulted a clipboard, then pointed him to a stairway that led to the second floor. "Courtroom Two," he said.

At the top of the stairs was a gallery off which a series of courtrooms was arranged. The hall was empty—save for a short, harried-looking man in a gray suit standing by a closed door marked *2*. The man looked up from his BlackBerry. "Mr. Ulrickson?" he said, pocketing the device. He held out a hand. "Farkiss, your daughter's attorney." They shook hands. "Is Mr. Pollock with you?"

"No," said Jasper, nervously glancing around. "He said he would catch an early morning flight from New York. But I haven't seen him."

"Well, airlines these days," Farkiss said. "This hearing is a mere formality anyway. At least, it should be. You never know with these judges. I mean—not that you should be worried. I'm sure it'll go like clockwork."

"Very good," Jasper said distractedly. "And . . . my daughter?"

"My God!" Farkiss cried. "I'm sorry! I'm crazy this morning."

He pointed toward a closed door a few feet down the hall. "She's with her social worker, who thought it would be good for you and your daughter to meet privately for a few minutes before the hearing. They're waiting for you."

Jasper thanked him, then moved down the hall. He stopped in front of the carved and polished wooden door Farkiss had indicated. Squared his shoulders and knocked. A chair scraped within. He heard the click of heels approaching. The door cracked open. A middle-aged woman's face appeared in the gap; pinched and suspicious, it suddenly lit up in a smile.

"Mr. Ulrickson!" she said, throwing open the door. "I know you from your book jacket. And of course the *Tovah* show! I'm Doreen Edwards. We've spoken on the phone!" She made a self-mocking face. "But it's not *me* you want to see!" She leaned in close and dropped a hand on his forearm. "Come." She took a step backward, allowing him to see into the room.

Ten feet away, sitting at a long wooden table, was a slender blond girl.

"Your daughter!" Edwards caroled. She added, in a hurried whisper, "I'll leave you two for a few minutes." She threw a smile at Chloe and then slipped around him and out into the corridor, closing the door behind her.

Chloe, without taking her eyes off him, pushed back her chair and stood.

He was rooted to the spot, frozen, unable to move. She came forward shyly, like a child edging toward a stranger, looking up at him through lowered lashes, a timid smile on her lips. But Jasper would have known her anywhere, stepping, as she did,

straight out of his past. She was dressed as he had never seen Holly dressed: in a smart ensemble of white blouse, dark pencil skirt and heels, in which she walked inexpertly, her slim ankles quivering with each step. But her wheat-blond hair, in a bun at the back of her head, with a few loose strands dangling, was Holly's hair, and her face was Holly's face, which, until now, he would not have been able to bring to mind but which was instantly restored in his memory: the long green eyes tilted up at the outer corners, the straight, delicate nose, the high cheekbones and tapering chin. The only obvious difference was in the mouth; Chloe's had rather more ample lips, the top one as if pulled up in the center in a pronounced triangle that revealed a glimpse of her two large front teeth, white as a baby's.

Chloe, for her part, was surprised by the look in Ulrickson's eyes. His expression—hopeful, shy, even a little frightened—was so at odds with the picture Dez had painted of the ruthless predator who seduced and abandoned her mother. It reminded her of how Ulrickson had looked on Tovah's show, gentle and kind, and it reminded her of those phone calls she had had with him, his voice seemingly filled with genuine interest in her. For a confused moment, she felt as if she were meeting her *real* father, and something rose up in her, a tide of yearning that she associated with being a small child. She caught herself, recalled Dez's stern admonishments, his lectures about Ulrickson's deviousness, coldness and disdain; he had warned her not to be fooled by the man's studied "nice guy" act—and, remembering this, she again steeled herself against him, vowing that she would (as Dez had put it) "avenge her mother." Thus resolved, she stepped forward on her

unsteady high heels and stood close, smiling up at him, tilting her head to the side in just that way that men, she knew from movies and television, found irresistible. "Daddy?" she said softly.

Jasper, in trying to imagine this moment, had seen himself overcome with emotion, sobbing as he had done on the phone, gathering her up in his arms. But he found himself seized by a strange reticence, as if an invisible arm were thrust out to hold her at a distance. Was this Pauline's influence? That look of warning in his wife's stricken eyes seemed to flash before him. Overriding this, he moved stiffly, awkwardly, to take her in his arms. He was flooded with Holly's until-this-moment-forgotten-but-now-instantly-remembered aroma of ginger and vanilla—not a perfume, but the actual smell of her skin and hair. He felt the warm pressure of her breasts against his shirtfront, the encirclement of her arms, and then he was stepping away, breaking contact, which had, like a shot of adrenaline, kicked his heart into galloping motion.

"My God!" he said, holding her by her shoulders. He was dazed, off-kilter. When trying to imagine her, he had conjured a hybrid of himself and what he could remember of Holly. But there was not even the most distant echo of his features in her small, perfectly formed face, with its lingering hint of baby fat. "You're just so—so much like your mother," he said.

"Am I?" she said, veiling her eyes as if too shy to accept his gaze. But when her lashes lifted again, she was staring straight at him, unwaveringly. She knew that men were always helpless against a show of shy bashfulness mixed with challenging boldness.

"And you're so much taller than I was expecting—taller than your mother," he babbled. "You're just much more . . . more . . ."

The correct word to complete this thought eluded him. His eyes played quickly over her figure, as if he might find there the term he was seeking. Noting the movement of his eyes, she shifted her weight onto one foot, swaying her balance so that one hip jutted out slightly. Jasper's eyes reflexively traced the contour of her torso in its fitted blouse, her narrow yet rounded hips, her long, naked, flower-stem legs. Until now she had somehow existed in his mind as a *child*, like Maddy—not as a near woman. He was reminded of the surprise he had felt at Maddy's birth, when she emerged from Pauline, at the C-section, not as a half-formed entity that would need time to "develop," like an old-fashioned photograph in its chemical bath (as he had vaguely imagined), but instead as a fully articulated, finished newborn, from the tips of her moist eyelashes to the pale moons in her minuscule cuticles.

From the flush that suffused his cheeks, Chloe thought that his scrutiny of her was having the desired effect, so she was surprised when he said, in an unexpectedly controlled and paternal tone, "You're just more grown-up than I thought you would be."

She smiled. "Well, I did turn eighteen." She shook a tendril of hair away from her face.

"That's right," Jasper said. "End of May. Two months ago . . ."

So she was the same age as Holly was that summer! She looked older, in her chic outfit, as if she were a young lawyer who had come to try a case.

"Should we sit?" she said, pulling him by the hand back to

the table. He lowered himself onto a seat, and she resumed the chair she had been sitting on. Their knees, he was aware, were almost touching. She leaned forward and grasped his hands. "So you're not disappointed?" she said.

"Disappointed?" he echoed.

"I guess we don't look much alike," she said, "except I'm taller than Mom. I must get that from you."

"No, no, no," he said. "I could never be disappointed. Not at all. I'm still just stunned. Overwhelmed. There's something about seeing you in person. It's not like talking on the phone."

"I know!" she said, smiling and revealing a glimpse of wet, pink gums. "It's crazy. You look just like you did on TV—only handsomer."

He stared at her, unable to form a response. He was distracted by the soft, somehow yielding look in her caressing eyes, a kind of beckoning vulnerability or submission, and by the flickering play of a smile around her lips, a knowing little grin, as if some secret existed between the two of them. She dropped her eyes shyly, then raised them again and looked up at him through her lowered lashes. She spoke as if confiding a shameful secret, even though her words carried no such message. "So," she said, "I guess it's supposed to be a short hearing?"

"Yes, very short," Jasper said woodenly. "About five minutes."

"And then I'm yours!" She brought one of his hands to her face, resting the palm against her cheek. She kissed it. "All yours!" She wondered if this was too much, if she was moving too fast—Dez had instructed her to play out the early stages of the seduction slowly, teasing him along gently. She returned his

hand to his lap, but continued to smile at him in just that way that made men weak.

There was a sharp rapping at the door and a male voice said, "About to go in."

"Oh," Chloe said, on a note of disappointment. "That was fast."

They rose. She slid an arm around his waist, snuggling against his side. When he, still feeling that strange physical reticence, failed to respond, she reached around him and seized his free hand and snaked it around her. He felt her narrow, mobile waist under his moist palm. "Like that!" she said, smiling up at him. With her free hand, she reached for the small wheeled carry-on bag that sat beside her chair, and which Jasper, until that moment, had failed to notice. He realized, with a pang of obscure guilt, that it probably contained all her worldly belongings.

They moved together, linked, to the door, which he opened, and they stepped into the hall. He saw, across the polished marble floor, Farkiss and Doreen Edwards, but he did not recognize the older man, in an elegant dark suit, who had joined them. This man dropped whatever he had been saying and came toward Jasper, hand extended. "Murray Pollock," he said.

Despite their phone exchanges, they had never met in person. Tall, with a large head of frizzy salt-and-pepper hair, Pollock had one of those saggy, sagacious faces that exude a becoming melancholy.

"Congratulations," he said mournfully, shaking Jasper's hand. He turned to Chloe. His drooping eyelids widened and his lips pulled into a smile. "You must be Chloe!" he said, shaking her hand. "My goodness, you could pass for twenty-five!" He turned

to Jasper. "I'm not sure I would have realized, on the *physical* evidence, that she's your daughter—no insult intended."

"There isn't much resemblance, is there?" Farkiss chimed in. He had joined them and was moving his eyes up and down Chloe's figure.

"Perhaps the height . . . ?" Pollock said, like an art appraiser comparing notes with a fellow expert.

"Yes, the height . . ." Farkiss said.

Under this close scrutiny, Chloe flushed and shot a glance at Jasper, who realized, with sudden incredulity, that both men were coming alive under the catalyst of his daughter's beauty. Their roaming eyes and heightened color and eager smiles were manifestations of that atavistic male response that Jasper knew so well from publishing parties, editorial meetings—gatherings of any type where males and females mingled. He was obliged to admit to himself that his tall, glowingly beautiful daughter was precisely the kind of female to ignite such primitive responses, to turn ordinarily sensible men into babbling idiots. It was a phenomenon he could ordinarily forgive, except that the female, in this instance, was his *child*.

He cleared his throat. "So," he said pointedly, "this hearing should be *short*?"

Pollock dropped Chloe's hand as if it had scalded him. "Indeed," he said soberly, turning to Jasper. "Not more than ten minutes." He cut a sidelong glance at Chloe, who, hands folded innocently over her skirt, toes turned slightly inward, affected a great interest in the ornately carved ceiling overhead.

"Yes," Farkiss said, also sounding chastised. "And we ought

to be going in soon. Oh," he added, "I should warn you that Judge Howard is known for being a little—"

But at that moment the door to Courtroom Two opened and the bailiff, in beige court uniform, stepped into the hall and summoned them into the room. Not the grand, cathedral-like chamber Jasper had been expecting, it was a small room lit by fluorescent panels in a low ceiling. The lawyers led the way, followed by Edwards, then Jasper and Chloe. The social worker took a seat in the observers' gallery, which consisted of just two rows of wooden benches, like church pews, at the back of the room. Jasper was directed to sit at one end of a table facing the bench, Chloe, at the opposite end. The lawyers sat between them. Pollock pulled from his briefcase a sheaf of documents. Farkiss followed suit. As they waited for the judge, Jasper leaned back slightly in his chair and peered around the lawyers' heads at Chloe, who was staring straight ahead, apparently unaware that he was looking at her. Sensing his gaze, she waited a few beats, allowing him to drink in her doll-like profile, then she turned and beamed at him one of her most heart-stopping smiles. As if caught in the surreptitious act of spying on her, he felt a blush invade his face. He produced an answering smile, then turned away.

The bailiff stepped to the front of the room. "All rise," he said. They stood.

Judge Gerald Howard, a large man with white hair brushed back from a leonine face, emerged from behind a curtain-like wooden panel. He lowered himself into his chair. "Be seated," he rumbled. They sat.

The judge fussed with some papers, then looked up and

scanned the faces before him.

"Welcome," he said in a fruity baritone. "We're gathered here on an occasion happier than many that take place in these halls, where we sentence many a juvenile delinquent, finalize many a divorce, hear many an argument in custody battles. Right now, though, we're transferring guardianship of a young girl, currently a ward of the state of Vermont and living in foster care, to her biological father, who has only recently learned of her existence." Howard paused and looked at the people before him. "To be sure," he went on, "there is sadness in that the girl in question, Chloe Vanessa Dwight, recently lost her mother, but it is a graceful thing that in her time of mourning she displayed the courage to speak up and seek out the man she understood to be her biological father, and to begin proceedings to find out if that man, Mr. Jasper Ulrickson, could truly claim that honor and privilege." He held up a piece of paper. "I have before me the written findings of a DNA paternity test conducted on both individuals, and despite the presence of legal counsel in the room, I gather that neither party is here to contest these results?"

"Correct," said the lawyers.

"Well, then, we're really here to do the formalities," Howard said. "Let me read into the record that the samples, which were donated under conditions adhering to the criteria that govern admissibility of DNA evidence in all courts of the United States, and which were analyzed at one of the leading facilities in the country, reveal, to a 99.9 percent degree of certainty, that Miss Dwight is the biological offspring of Mr. Ulrickson. Is that the

understanding, as well, of both lawyers present?"

"It is, your Honor," they said.

"And of your respective clients?"

"Correct, your Honor," said Pollock.

"Yes," said Farkiss.

"Let's hear them say it," Howard intoned.

Jasper and Chloe said, simultaneously, "Yes, your Honor."

"Excellent," said the judge. "Now," he went on, looking over the tops of his glasses, "allow me to take just a moment to say why these recent events in the lives of Chloe and Jasper are of such import. Having a father is a vital element in everyone's life, not only because it promotes a child's emotional well-being but also because it protects her rights. It allows her access to legal benefits she would not otherwise enjoy. It helps establish an accurate medical history. God forbid Mr. Ulrickson discovers, tomorrow, that he suffers from a genetic anomaly that he might have passed down to his daughter; she would wish to have that checked out. On a happier note, Chloe automatically has the right to financial support from Jasper and she automatically possesses, along with his younger daughter—her half-sister, Madeline—inheritance rights to her father's fortune, which, I understand, is considerable." He peered owlishly at Jasper. "I saw you, sir, on the *Tovah* show. Condolences regarding your wife, but you have turned lemons into lemonade by sharing her story, and as I think we're all aware, Tovah sells books!"

The lawyers politely chuckled, as did Jasper, who was beginning to wonder what was going on. This extraordinary performance from the judge must have been what Farkiss had

been about to warn them of.

Still holding Jasper in his gaze, the judge went on. "Now, you obviously understand that Chloe is your actual flesh and blood, and though you have only just recently learned that fact, you will treat her as such, behave toward her as if you had raised her from birth, with as much love and care and affection and attention as I'm sure you lavish upon your younger daughter, providing education, food and shelter, travel, wisdom, religious instruction if you're a believer. In short, it is your duty, Jasper, to provide to your issue whatever it is within your means to provide, in order to make of her a productive, happy, healthy member of our society. How's that sound?"

"Very good, your Honor," Jasper said.

"You never changed her nappies," the judge went on. "You never gave her a bath, or tucked her up in bed; you never comforted her when she had a temperature or accepted her under your covers when she woke you in the wee hours with a nightmare, never kissed away the pain from a boo-boo. In short, you missed all those ineffable moments between father and child that secure the mystical bond of parent and issue, moments that can never be recaptured. But you can make up for that now, in other ways, can't you?"

Jasper, thinking that this was a purely rhetorical question in the judge's astounding peroration, sat silently listening, waiting for him to continue.

"Can't you?" Judge Howard repeated.

"Yes!" Jasper almost shouted.

"You, in turn," he said, looking at Chloe, "will honor and

obey your father. You're a teenager, and we all know what that means. But being a teen is not license for *unreasonable* rebellion. Don't sneak out and use the car without his permission. Don't smuggle boyfriends into the house when they come a-calling—and, if I may venture to say so, the evidence presented in this courtroom today would lead any judge and jury to the verdict that the boys will be a-calling." He cocked a comical glance at Jasper. "Do you keep your shotgun loaded?"

Polite, awkward chuckles from the lawyers and their clients.

Howard again leveled his gaze at Chloe, furrowing his brow. "Don't hold drinking parties in the house," he continued. "Don't raid your dad's home bar when he goes on an overnight business trip. Do your homework when he tells you to, and, *please*, clean your room. All that comes as an order of the court."

More lawyerly chuckles. Chloe nodded. "Yes, your Honor," she said.

"And remember," Howard went on, "even though your daddy, when you were small, never did change your nappies or tuck you up, or hold you on his knee, or take you into his bed, that doesn't mean he's any less your daddy, does it?"

"No, sir," she said.

"All right, then," Judge Howard said. "I think we can do this thing. Let the record show that custody of Chloe Vanessa Dwight is hereby relinquished by the state of Vermont and is transferred to that of Jasper Oivind Ulrickson of Clay Cross, Connecticut. Miss Dwight's birth certificate will be duly altered to reflect that Mr. Ulrickson is her biological father; and we've got some papers to sign, people!"

The bailiff brought down from the bench two stacks of

documents, which he placed in front of the lawyers and their clients. Pens were uncapped, and Jasper and Chloe affixed their signatures to the requisite places. The pages were borne off by the bailiff.

The judge hit his gavel against the table and said: "We are adjourned!" He gathered up his papers, stood and moved with a stately pace behind the curtain.

Jasper, dazed, got to his feet. Chloe threw herself on his neck. He almost drew back but recalled himself and accepted her flood of affection, and indeed returned it, holding her to him and kissing her cheek. The lawyers stood and shook hands like captains of industry upon closing a successful merger. Doreen Edwards rushed forward crying, "Congratulations! Congratulations!"

3

Having emerged into the sunlight in front of the building, Jasper and the others stood for a moment at the top of the stairs that led down to the sidewalk. Edwards, still gushing, apologized and announced that she was due at a meeting at Child Services but assured Chloe and Jasper that she would soon be sending someone to check on their progress in Connecticut. She hastened down to the sidewalk, then hurried off in the direction of the Department of Children and Families building. Pollock, too, had to go—to catch a flight back to Hartford. He followed Edwards down the steps, then disappeared into the airport limousine idling at the curb. "I'm afraid that I'm also due elsewhere," Farkiss said. "Divorce hearing." He congratu-

lated them, said something about how they no doubt wished to be alone, then turned and stepped back inside the courthouse.

Jasper was instantly seized by that same strange feeling of restraint in her presence, that diffidence which had hindered his movements earlier. He felt the need to make a momentous utterance to mark the occasion of their being united, but invention failed him and he was able to offer only the hackneyed: "Well, today is the first day of the rest of our lives."

Chloe smiled, raised herself on tiptoe, kissed his cheek and said, "I feel like people should be throwing *rice*!"

Arms around each other's waist, they descended to the sidewalk, then set off on foot to fetch his car. Conscious that he had never walked down a street in the company of a female quite as arresting as Chloe, Jasper quickly became aware of the attention that she drew from people. Pedestrians, passing in the opposite direction or overtaking them in the same direction, turned to stare quite frankly at her; drivers and their passengers craned around to look. Several people cast sourly disapproving glances, which puzzled Jasper at first—until it burst upon him that they must be mistaking him and Chloe for a May–December romance—the increasingly grizzled forty-something male with the petal-fresh teenaged girl! No wonder they scowled! Fortunately, Chloe, looking down at the uneven sidewalk to avoid tripping in her heels, seemed oblivious of this embarrassing misapprehension. (In reality, she was anything but oblivious, but she thought it best to feign innocent unawareness.)

When they reached the bed-and-breakfast, Jasper went in to settle his bill. The crone from last night had been replaced by a

tall youth with mousy, center-parted hair and pustules around his mouth. He glanced up from his computer and did a double take at Chloe, who had followed Jasper inside. His eyes glinted with conspiratorial admiration when he asked, "Room for two?"

Jasper was at first mystified by the note of insinuation in his voice. Then he realized what lay behind it. "No, no," he said, mortified. "I'm checking *out*—with my *daughter*," he added, with irritated emphasis.

The clerk, blushing, kept his attention glued to his computer as he prepared Jasper's bill. But as the receipt was printing, his eyes slid over helplessly to a corner of the lobby. Jasper followed his gaze. With her back to them, Chloe was bending at the waist, her legs straight, to inspect the lower tier of a rack of tourist brochures. The clerk smiled, shrugged and handed Jasper his receipt.

"You okay, Dad?" Chloe asked when they were outside.

"I'm fine," he said as he led her around to the back of the building. "It's just that boy at the desk. He was very rude."

"Was he?" she said. "I didn't notice."

He popped the trunk and placed Chloe's carry-on inside. She stood, like a date, waiting by the passenger door. He stepped over and opened it for her. She settled herself inside, primly pulling down on the hem of her skirt and throwing Jasper a shy smile as she did so. She saw him snatch his eyes away but could not tell if this was because he was resisting the impulse to stare or if he had truly been unmoved by the kind of leg show that ordinarily stopped men in their tracks. He slammed the door,

walked around to the driver's side and got behind the wheel. With a grunt, Chloe pulled off her pumps. "Those kill," she said, tossing the shoes into the backseat and wiggling her toes. She stretched her feet into the space under the dash, glancing sidelong to see if he was taking note. Alas, he seemed quite oblivious as he put the car in gear, executed a three-point turn and drove out of the lot.

He piloted the car along Main Street. When they came to a red light, he looked over at her. Her head lay sideways on the headrest. She was gazing at him dreamily. Her half-veiled irises, unnameable in color between gray and green, with tiny flecks of graphite and glints of copper, held him.

She said on a sigh, "I can't believe I found you."

"Yes," he said, with a sensation of dry mouth that made it oddly difficult to form words. "It does seem surreal."

The light turned green, he pressed the accelerator, and they drove off in search of the exit for the highway. He found it, and guided the car onto the curving on-ramp. They joined the stream of cars flowing south.

4

Traffic was still fairly thick near the city. Jasper readjusted his body, settling in for the long haul. He ransacked his mind for something to talk about. There were any number of topics they had not yet touched on in their phone conversations, but when he spoke, he was surprised to discover himself asking her about something the school's guidance counselor had mentioned, in passing, in their phone call of a few days ago, a detail from Chloe's life that, until he actually saw her, he might never have thought about again but which now loomed curiously large in his mind. He asked about the teacher who had kissed her. "What exactly happened?" he said. "Did this teacher actually . . ."—he paused in search of the word—"interfere with you?"

Chloe looked out the side window. Stunned by this unexpected, unimagined allusion to Dez—her heart had jumped into her throat and her head seemed to be expanding with heat—she nevertheless managed to speak calmly when she said, "Oh—it was nothing." She meant to leave it at that, but could not resist adding, "How did you hear about *that*?"

He explained about her guidance counselor.

"Oh," she said. "Yeah, well, that was all a big mix-up. He was just trying to comfort me—it was right after Mom died. It was taken the wrong way. Schools are super strict now: teachers aren't even allowed to *touch* students. He was fired right away."

She glanced over. He seemed to be buying this. But Jasper was confused. He thought the guidance counselor had said that this incident occurred in mid-March—some weeks *before* Holly's death. Hadn't she said something about Holly declining to press charges? He must have gotten that wrong. "And the teacher's name?" he asked, puzzled at his own determination to get to the bottom of the incident.

Chloe pretended not to understand. "Miss Simmons," she said, naming the teacher who had reported Dez's infraction. "She's sort of crazy."

"No, sorry," Jasper said. "The male teacher. The one who, um, who . . ." For some reason, he found it impossible to say the words *kissed you*. "The one who was fired."

"Oh!" she said. "Mr. . . ." She paused. There was no way she was going to utter Dez's real name. "It was this teacher—Mr. Butler."

Jasper could see by her hesitations that she did not feel

comfortable discussing the incident. Nor did he, particularly. He let it drop.

They drove for a time in silence—a perfectly comfortable silence, he thought, punctuated by frequent glances at one another and smiles. An easy accord seemed to be growing between them, Jasper decided—a harmony that lay beyond words. He attributed this, in part, to the illusion caused by her resemblance to Holly, but also perhaps to some silent signal, an emanation of pheromones, perhaps; some part of a biological fail-safe warning system that was bound to exist in humans, a subsensory alert that informed people when they were in the presence of their own kin. Wouldn't such an adaptation have evolved in the species if for no other reason than to minimize the risk of accidental inbreeding in parents and children long separated? *Did* such a thing exist? He must google this. And if it did exist, was he feeling something like that right now?

He turned and looked at Chloe. Her face was directed away from him as she watched the farmers' fields and the distant mountains stream by out her passenger window. He lightly inhaled through his nostrils, trying to detect that theoretical silent signal, or early warning system, of paternity. Instead, all he could discern was the aroma of ginger and vanilla that wafted from her—a fragrance so evocative of Holly, that scent which made the years disappear, carrying him back to that grove of willows at the edge of the club beach where he had held Holly in his arms. He remembered now how she had seized his hand from where he had been tentatively touching her breast, and guided it down her flank, over her hip and under the hem of

her flimsy party dress, onto the indescribably smooth skin of her inner thigh, and finally up to the hollow between her legs where she pressed his cupping palm against the cotton-covered mound, moaning into his open mouth as he kissed her.

His gaze, driven by youthful memory, unconsciously strayed up Chloe's legs to an area on the inside of her thigh. A slant of sunlight through the windshield brought out a gleam on the mirror-smooth, matte brown skin.

He raised his eyes and was startled to discover that she was looking at him. He felt his face scalded by a blush of embarrassment and confusion, but was surprised to see no corresponding discomfort in her; indeed, she simply smiled demurely and drooped her eyelashes. Aghast, he whipped his head around to look out the windshield. In his peripheral vision, he could see that she continued to gaze at him with that strange serenity. He furthermore could see that she did not shift position. He expected that she would, as an act of reflexive modesty, close her legs a little or pull down on that infernal skirt. But she continued, with an apparent lack of any self-consciousness, or awareness, to offer to his gaze the smooth expanse of inner thigh while looking with sober innocence and seeming unknowingness at the side of his face.

In fact, she was overjoyed finally to have caught him in what seemed an act of ogling her, but she was confused by how he had looked away and was now so easily keeping his eyes off her; had she misconstrued his reaction? Had he actually been looking at her quite innocently, with nothing more than a warm, paternal regard?

"I thought you might be asleep," he said, his eyes aimed strictly forward at the highway. His face was on fire.

"No," she said. "I was just wondering."

"Wondering," he echoed. "About what?"

"I don't know," she said, finally closing her legs and turning toward him. She drew her feet up on the seat so that her body formed a *Z*. "About what we're going to *do* in Connecticut."

"I've given that quite a bit of thought," Jasper said, taking up the subject energetically, to dispel his embarrassment. "I thought you should just take it easy. After all, it's only about four weeks until school. I think you should get to know your new family and your new home and your new town. I've got a membership at the country club. I thought you might like to take some tennis lessons and maybe hang out there at the club. You can swim, sail, and there are a lot of kids your age. You can make friends."

"I don't care about other kids—I just want to be with *you*. But I've never tried tennis. Can you teach me?"

Jasper chuckled. "I'm afraid my days as a tennis pro are behind me. Besides, I've got work to do. I'm writing a new novel. I don't have much time for tennis."

"So I won't ever *see* you?" she said on a note of real panic. She pictured him hidden away behind an office door day and night, writing. How would she enact the plan?

"Oh, you'll see far too much of me, I'm sure." He glanced over and smiled. "Every day at breakfast. At lunch, if you're around. Dinner. And in the evenings. You'll get your fill of your old dad."

"Never," she said, relieved. "I want to be with you every second!" She leaned across the seats and nuzzled Jasper's ear. "I'll sit on your lap when you're writing. Like a little cat—you won't even know I'm there." She made a purring sound, and then placed her arms around his neck. She rested her head on his shoulder. "Oh, Dad," she said, "I'm so happy we're together!"

Jasper murmured his assent. And he *was* happy; indeed, he felt his heart brimming with that paternal pride that had so surprised him a month ago. But he continued to feel a peculiar rigidity, a constraint and physical awkwardness at her touch. Why could he not relax? Why was it so difficult to return her physical affection? Was it that he'd fallen out of the habit of touching and being touched? Since Pauline's stroke, he had lived so much in his mind, as a writer, struggling with phantoms, locked away in his work cave down the hall, an ascetic. But no. He was not a complete stranger to physically expressed love. He hugged and kissed and touched Maddy every day. Why should Chloe be any different? Yes, Chloe was, of course, older—a woman, really. Or almost. But Jasper saw men cuddling their teenaged daughters all the time. Why could he not take one of his hands—which gripped the wheel with white-knuckled tightness—and slip it round her shoulders? Draw her face to his and give her a kiss on the cheek? The hell of it was that he could feel the yearning in her body, the sense of her straining to press herself against him, to express and receive physical affection—and no wonder, given her recent loss and the period of foster care she had endured. Yet here he sat, absurdly distant and cold, like a statue, with her warm, quiveringly alive body draped upon him.

He must get control of himself. He forced himself to remove his right hand from the steering wheel. He awkwardly snaked his arm around her shoulders. She moaned softly and snuggled still more closely to him. Yes, he thought. Yes, this is fine. He felt himself beginning to relax a little. Actually to enjoy the feel of her, the weight of her head against his shoulder, the feel of her breath on his neck, the sending aroma of her skin. He responded by giving her a quick peck on the forehead.

She murmured, "So, what's your new novel about?"

Jasper never talked about works in progress with anyone but Pauline, but he sensed an opportunity now to let Chloe know him better by taking her into his confidence about his writing. Besides which, he thought she might be amused to learn about how she had, inadvertently, inspired him. "Well, as a matter of fact," he said, "you had quite a bit to do with my new book."

"Me?" she said, lifting her head from his shoulder. Her forehead had puckered into soft wrinkles.

"Yup," he said, turning his eyes back to the highway. "I dreamed up the idea after I first learned about you. Writers often take a real situation—something from their own lives—and play with it; they ask, 'What if?' In this case, I asked myself, 'What if a person tried to *pretend* he was someone's child and faked a DNA test to prove it?'"

Chloe whipped her arms from around his neck.

Jasper, startled, turned and saw that she had retreated from him, actually pushing her body back against the passenger door. One of her hands was on the door handle—as if she were contemplating jumping out onto the highway. (She was

certainly prepared to do so—depending on where this conversation was going.)

"What's wrong?" he said, frightened. She was watching him, clearly terrified, as if she expected him to pounce at her, to attack her. He could not imagine what had gotten into her. "What's *wrong*?" he repeated.

"Why would you think something like that?" she said, her eyes on him, her fingers still on the door handle. "Why would I make you think of someone playing that kind of trick?"

He realized his terrible mistake. He was so used to discussing his working methods with Pauline—a former *editor*. Yet here he was, talking to a high schooler about the mysteries of literary creation and expecting her to understand. All he had succeeded in doing—by speaking of falsified DNA tests, impostors and lies—was to make her think he had entertained such suspicions about *her*! How could he have been so stupid, so insensitive?

He apologized, explaining that his novel had *nothing* to do with their situation, that he had merely used a kernel of information about DNA testing to play a game of make-believe.

Inexpressibly relieved—for a nightmare moment, she truly thought he had somehow learned of the plan—Chloe felt the tension drain from her body. She let go of the door handle and resettled herself in her seat. "Well, that's a crazy idea anyway," she said. "No one's going to believe it. It's impossible to fake a DNA test."

"Of course," Jasper said. "But it's pure fantasy. My books are just for fun. Like puzzles—they're not supposed to be real."

"Okay," she said, pouting. "But I still think it's stupid."

Jasper, duly chastised, sat in shamed silence. The relentless highway, cutting through featureless tracts of farmland, flowed past. After a few miles, Chloe edged toward him. She reached over and took his hand off the wheel and placed it around her. She leaned over and once again cushioned her head on his shoulder. "I forgive you," she whispered.

The aim of this long drive was to draw her out, to touch on subjects they had not discussed on the phone, to talk about things they might feel uncomfortable discussing in front of the rest of the family. There was one topic, in particular, he had wanted to be sure to bring up on this drive. There seemed no time like the present.

"So," he said, "we haven't really talked about your mother."

"What about her?" Chloe said, once more going on alert. She felt, instinctually, that it was best to keep him off all topics related to her life at home, in New Halcyon.

"Just how sorry I was to hear about what happened."

"I don't really like to talk about it," she said. "It makes me sad."

"I understand. But it can be good to talk about things that make you sad."

"Yeah, that's what all the social workers and shrinks keep telling me," she said, tipping her face up on his shoulder and looking at him with what she knew was one of her most ardent, knee-weakening expressions. "But I don't want to think about Mom right now. I don't want *you* to think about her either. I just want to be *your* daughter who you can kiss and hug and hold. I just want you to fill me up with love." This was pushing

it, she knew, but it felt imperative that she somehow deflect Ulrickson from this paternal line of inquiry.

He looked down at her face. She was staring up at him with a gaze so intensely beckoning that it took an effort for him to disentangle his eyes from hers. He looked back out onto the highway. He felt her wriggle against him, repositioning herself. For some reason, his heart was pounding so hard in his chest that he was sure Chloe could feel it.

She *could* feel it, like a trapped bird beating against the inside of his rib cage and sending its tremor against her hand, which lay on his chest. So she was surprised that when he next spoke, it was to voice the most banal of questions.

He asked if she was hungry.

In fact, she was. But determined to keep up the pressure, she snarled and took a playful bite at his neck—actually catching some of his flesh between her teeth and giving a painful little pull. She quickly kissed the spot, and said, "*Starving.*"

They stopped at the next fast-food place and went inside to stretch their legs. Jasper was again forced to endure the spectacle of males—seemingly of every age, ethnicity, social class and education level—staring hungrily at his daughter, looking up from their burgers and fries and milkshakes. As usual, Chloe seemed oblivious of the quiet chaos her presence caused. She simply swayed against him as they waited in line. Jasper could feel the envy that radiated from her admirers. In a gesture half protective, half defiant, he put his arm around her and pressed her against him.

Surprised and encouraged, she smiled up at him. "Oh," she said, giggling, "McDonald's makes you romantic, huh?" She

raised herself swiftly on tiptoe and kissed his chin. She dropped back onto her heels and continued to scrutinize the menu posted above the workers' heads.

Jasper looked around the room. Burgers were arrested in midair; straws, unsucked, lay against protruding tongues. He smiled blandly, and then stepped up to the register.

They ate in the car as Jasper drove. Chloe picked lightly at her Filet-O-Fish sandwich, left more than half of it for Jasper to finish, and took only a single bite from one of his fries. She did, however, greedily suck down all of her strawberry milkshake, and half of his chocolate one.

Feeling that they had, in the humble act of eating side by side in the car, fallen into a dangerous dynamic of actual parent-and-child intimacy, she decided that dramatic measures were called for. She stuffed the trash into the takeout bag and tossed it into the backseat. Then, in a single fluid motion, she lifted her legs, swiveled in her seat, ducked her head under his extended arms and laid the back of her head on his lap. She rested her bare feet on the passenger seat.

"Chloe!" Jasper cried, nearly losing control of the car. He gaped down at her upturned face in his lap. "What in God's name are you doing?"

"Resting," she said matter-of-factly. "I didn't sleep much last night, I was so nervous about meeting you."

"Well, I'll pull over and you can get into the backseat!"

"I don't *want* to lie in the backseat. I want to be here with you."

"This is insane," he cried. "It's dangerous. I can't drive like this."

"Why?" she said. "You're driving right now."

"Please sit up," he said. "You're not wearing a seat belt."

"You won't crash. You drive so slow."

"Nevertheless, a policeman might see us."

She batted her lashes at him. "Are we doing anything *wrong*?"

"Yes—it's illegal not to use your seat belt."

She ignored this and rolled toward him onto her side. She heaved a contented sigh, then joined her hands as if in prayer and slid them between her cheek and his thigh, pillowing her head. She felt, suddenly, quite genuinely tired; her claim about sleeplessness last night because of nerves had been true.

"Chloe?" he said. "Are you listening?" Her eyes were closed. "Chloe?"

"Mmmm?"

"Will you sit up?"

She merely nestled herself more snugly onto him. Then she got an inspiration. She took one of her hands from under her cheek, placed the thumb between her lips, and began to suck.

"Don't be silly, Chloe," he said. "That's not good for your teeth."

He grasped her wrist and pried her thumb from her mouth. Instinctively, she seized his hand and jammed his little finger into her mouth, sucking on it avidly. He felt a thrill like a stream of electricity pass through his hand, up his arm and into his body. For a moment he could not react. He was remembering how he had used precisely this method to pacify Maddy, as a newborn, between feedings in the middle of the night when she woke him with her squalling and he was too tired to fetch the bottle of milk expressed by pump, each day, from Pauline's breasts. He would simply roll over to the crib beside his bed and

stick his little finger, blind, into Maddy's mouth. She would suck for a minute or two on the tip and soon fall asleep—a practice his pediatrician had frowned on ("You don't want her to get *nipple confusion*") while admitting that every exhausted parent resorts to it. Then as now, Jasper felt the soft enveloping wetness sheathing his digit, the ridges in the curved upper palate, the ticklish workings of the velvety tongue and lips. Stunned, he could only gape down at Chloe for several seconds before pulling his finger from her mouth.

"That's enough," he said sternly. "You're being quite ridiculous!"

But she did not protest. Her lips had gone slack, her hands limp. Her breathing had taken on a smooth, deep, slow rhythm and her head felt heavier against his thighs. He said her name. She did not respond. Her fingers twitched. She was, in fact, deeply asleep, lulled by the slight rocking motion of the car, the warmth of his thighs and the strange, unexpected comfort she had taken in sucking on his finger, as if she truly were a small child, *his* child.

He looked down at her vulnerable, outlandishly pretty profile. Certainly, it was inappropriate for her to have sucked on his finger that way—but perhaps, he thought, this was a natural reaction to the strangeness of the situation she found herself in. Hadn't Doreen Edwards warned him that the child might display just such episodes of regression, of defensive slipping back into infantile states, as a coping mechanism? Thinking of this, he felt a surge of paternal love and protectiveness, but he was not tempted to slip his finger back into her softly working

mouth—or, rather, dismissed as ridiculous the obscure impulse to do so.

He looked out the windshield. Evening was coming on. They had entered the northern part of Connecticut. The lowering sun deepened to purple the green of the surrounding fields and lengthened the shadows of the trees and fences that bordered the farmhouses sliding past. He felt a flutter of nervousness, not the first, at the thought of their arrival home, of Pauline. He saw before his eyes that look she had given him as he left the house yesterday. A dark, almost accusing look. He pushed the thought from his mind. He told himself that everything would work out, that Pauline would come round. To calm himself, he looked down again at that impossibly pretty face and inhaled through his nose. Her bouquet acted on him like a calming drug, a tranquilizer.

He looked at his watch. They would be home in less than an hour! He let Chloe sleep for another thirty minutes, and then decided it was time to wake her. He reached down and stroked her hair. She snuffled, pawed at her face, and her eyelids quivered.

"We're getting close now," he said softly.

Her eyes flew open and she sat up. "Close?" She had been a million miles away, submerged in a dream that seemed to feature two other girls and a small apartment in some densely populated metropolis where she had never been. Jolted back to the perilous present, she looked around in panic at the unfamiliar landscape and was once again on high alert. She began to rearrange her hair, which had come loose from her bun and lay in messy

tangles around her face. "How close?" she asked, trying to keep the fear out of her voice.

"Maybe fifteen minutes," he said.

It was now dark outside. Gone were the mountains, pastures and farmhouses. They drove through a wasteland of widely spaced industrial parks twinkling with lights, dark highway under- and overpasses. A scattering of hangar-like big box stores appeared on either side of the road. These gave way to a denser grouping of garishly lit gas stations, fast-food restaurants, Cineplexes, strip malls. They arrived at a large intersection where eight lanes of traffic converged. Jasper turned right, took another turn and still another. Then they were skimming along a quiet road, semi-rural in its wooded seclusion, lit by widely spaced old-fashioned street lamps among the lit leaves of huge, massy black trees.

Chloe quickly touched up her face with the help of a compact drawn from the small purse over her shoulder—brushing some mascara onto her lashes, touching some color onto her pursed lips—then turned and retrieved her shoes from the backseat. She slipped the high heels on, then sat up alertly, her back straight, moving her head from side to side, looking at the large stone estates wheeling past. Her anxiety about soon meeting Jasper's family mingled with genuine excitement and fascination at seeing the lush and luxurious neighborhood where he lived—where *she* would now live. "I've never seen places like this," she said with awe. "Except in the movies."

They turned onto Cherry Tree Lane. "Your new home is coming up on the left," he said.

Chloe gaped at the long, low-slung structure behind the

maple on the front lawn. She leaned forward, almost pressing her face against the windshield. "Wow," she said, "it's huge."

Actually, it was one of the neighborhood's smaller houses. Jasper's father had deliberately built it to sane proportions—with just enough room to accommodate himself, his wife and his two children. Jasper, in his turn, had honored his father's, and his own, aesthetic by resisting the orgy of expansions and renovations even then being undertaken by his neighbors in the overheated housing and home equity–loan bubble soon to burst—the building on of extra wings and higher stories and additional outbuildings. But he knew that Chloe was comparing the house with where she had grown up, on New Halcyon's River Road, a stretch of houses quite literally on the wrong side of the tracks. On one of his days off from the club, that long-ago summer, he had paddled in a canoe under the disused railroad trestle bridge and down the stagnant, weed-choked river where ramshackle dwellings were clustered on the overgrown bank. One of those dilapidated shacks, he realized with a pang akin to the one he had felt when he saw her pathetic carry-on, was where Chloe had been raised. Well, all that was behind her now.

He pulled into the driveway, the wheels crunching on the gravel. He parked and cut the engine. Into the sudden aural vacuum flooded the muffled sound of crickets. He looked at Chloe, who was staring at him with a look now of frank, and unfeigned, terror.

When the plan had been nothing more than theoretical, a series of actions outlined by Dez in their trailer in the woods, Chloe had scarcely bothered to imagine what it would be like

to arrive, for the first time, at Ulrickson's house, and to meet his family. She had not *wanted* to imagine it. But now that this was about to happen, she found herself seized with a fear so acute it almost made her cry out to Ulrickson and confess the ruse. But, of course, she could not do that. Instead, she smiled at him with trembling lips, trying to mask her fear. With that strange ability he seemed to have to sense her anxiety and apprehensions—just as she imagined a real father might do—he smiled back at her, with warm reassurance, and said, "Don't worry, everyone's going to love you." Yet for all the steadiness in Jasper's tone, he too was in a state of high anxiety. For the last hour at least, he had felt a steadily rising stress at the prospect of Chloe's impending meeting with Pauline.

He got out of the car, went around to the trunk and popped it open. He pulled out the carry-on, lowered it onto the driveway and closed the trunk. Chloe had gotten out of the car and was standing on the driveway waiting for him. She was lit by the iridescent glow of a half-moon, and she was—he saw with a shock that made his guts jump—breathtaking, her hair, which she had tried to tuck up into the bun, falling around her face, her hands folded over the front of her abbreviated skirt as if she was afraid a stray breeze might lift it, one knee turned in slightly. This vision obscurely troubled him, in a manner he could not identify.

He approached her, rolling the bag bumpily over the gravel. She took a half step forward to meet him. He stopped and she stood close, and he felt, in the early August chill, the warmth of her body.

"I'm scared," she said, placing her hands on his chest and looking up at him.

"Scared?"

"To meet your family." She dropped her eyes and added: "Your wife."

"Just be yourself," he said. "She'll love you."

She leaned against him, in genuine search of physical comfort. He put his arms around her. The cicadas creaked deafeningly, like rhythmically laboring bedsprings. He could smell the salt and seaweed aroma of the nearby Sound mingled with her scent. When he tried to release her, she clutched at him and breathed, "Hold me!" He would not have been able to say how long they stood there, bodies pressed together as if for warmth, when suddenly he heard the crunch of the front-door lock. He stepped away from her almost guiltily and looked toward the house.

The door swung slowly on its hinges, a fan of light opening across the dark porch stone. In a moment of absurd anticlimax, a small barefoot figure in an ankle-length cotton nightgown with a high white collar stepped out from behind the door onto the stoop.

"Maddy!" Jasper said.

"We're waiting for you!" the little girl cried. "Why arnch'ya coming?"

"We *are* coming," he said.

Jasper led Chloe up the walk, his hand on the small of her incurved back. She moved with short, uncertain steps, hindered in part by the height of her unfamiliar heels but also by her

fear at approaching the house, which loomed before her like a haunted mansion in a horror movie.

Maddy's eyes grew ever wider at Chloe's approach. Jasper read in the little girl's expression her surprise (so similar to his own, this morning, in the anteroom at the courthouse) that the promised sister was no child after all, but a statuesque, almost fully grown young woman. Chloe, smiling, stopped in front of Maddy, who stared up at her, round-eyed.

"Maddy," Jasper said, "this is Chloe. Chloe, meet Maddy."

"But—but—" Maddy spluttered in a voice that rang with a sense of betrayal, her eyes going back and forth between the two of them. "She's all grown-up!"

Chloe, feeling some of her fear disperse in the presence of this unexpectedly adorable child, squatted on her haunches, bringing her face to the same level as Maddy's. "I'm not really so old," she whispered. "I'm still a kid. Like you. I'm just dressed up right now. And I have some makeup on." And indeed, in her apprehension about entering the house, and seeing Ulrickson's wife, and executing the plan, she really did not feel any different from a defenseless, inexperienced child, a child no older than Maddy.

Craving the comfort of the child's touch, Chloe now opened her arms and said, "Hug?" Maddy stepped into the older girl's embrace. Chloe held Maddy to her and felt the security of sheltering her small body.

After a moment, Maddy pulled away and said excitedly to Jasper, "She's warm and smells like *cake*!" She turned and ran into the house, yelling, "Chloe's here! Chloe's here!"

Chloe rose to her full height. Jasper noticed that she seemed to be avoiding his gaze, keeping her face down and turned away, as if something in her exchange with Maddy had unsettled her.

And indeed, that encounter had, for the first time, brought to Chloe's awareness how the successful execution of Dez's plan was going to tear this family apart, changing the little girl's life forever. Dez had sketchily addressed this, telling Chloe that the girl would suffer no deprivations worse than what Chloe herself had faced growing up—and, when it came to that, a good deal less harsh, given Ulrickson's indecent wealth, which would help to cushion the child's passage through life, a cushion denied to Chloe, especially after her mother's death, which was (in Dez's telling) directly traceable to Ulrickson's unconscionable abandonment. "No, no," Dez had said with finality, "I wouldn't lose a lot of sleep over Ulrickson's pampered little brat." This had seemed to make sense to Chloe at the time. Now, having actually seen the child, she was not so sure.

"Are you okay?" Jasper asked, breaking into her thoughts.

She started and looked at him. "She's so cute," Chloe said in an uncertain, wondering voice. "You didn't tell me how cute she was."

"Oh, she's cute,all right," he said cheerfully. "She can also be a handful. But come." He again touched her back, and escorted her into the foyer. The plan was in motion again, and she was powerless to stop it. Besides, she told herself, Dez was probably right about Maddy. He *must* be right. In any case, it was far too late, now, to second-guess him, or the plan.

He closed the door behind them and they were enveloped in the darkness of the unlit foyer. She turned to him. He put his arms around her and said in a steady voice, "Everything is going to be fine." Although Jasper, recalling Pauline's dark, baleful gaze at his departure yesterday, was not at all sure that this was true.

5

He abandoned the carry-on by the front door, then led her toward the light at the end of the short entry hall, to the wide door that looked onto the living room. There, they stopped. On their right were the sliding glass doors that, in daytime, gave a view onto the patio, lawn and Sound. But it was now night, and the windows were black mirrors that doubled the width of the room and twinned everything within it, including Maddy, who had taken up position behind the wheelchair where Pauline sat, facing them, halfway down the room.

"I'll bring her!" Maddy cried as she began trying to wrestle the unwieldy chair into motion.

"Just leave Mom," Jasper said. "We'll come over."

As they approached, Jasper saw Pauline's eyes boring into Chloe, her gaze cold, hostile. He had allowed himself to believe that Pauline might disguise her displeasure, soften it—if only to minimize social embarrassment. But apparently the threat she felt from Holly's ghost was so acute, she could do nothing to mask it. He suddenly understood the unnamed discomfort that had assailed him, on the driveway, at the sight of Chloe's beauty. He had been, unconsciously, anticipating Pauline's reaction to this vision of youthful loveliness, which could only exacerbate whatever miseries of jealousy and threat Pauline felt over the encroachment of dead Holly's ghost.

They halted a few paces in front of her and stood side by side, at attention, like soldiers on parade inspection. Jasper cleared his throat, licked his lips and pulled his facial muscles into a smile.

"Pauline," he said, "this is Chloe. Chloe, this is Pauline—your stepmother."

"She can hear everything you say!" Maddy shouted.

"She knows that," said Jasper. "And there's no need to yell."

Chloe made a tentative bow. "It's nice to meet you," she said in a voice barely audible.

She stood, in a state of agonized self-consciousness, as Pauline's eyes picked their way down her body, lingering on the short skirt and the long expanse of bare legs. How she longed, now, to be wearing a floor-length skirt—or sensible dress pants! Finally, Pauline's gaze moved back up to Chloe's face. Jasper, looking on breathlessly, noted how Pauline's eyes drilled into the girl, like lasers, and she did not blink in acknowledgment of

Chloe's shy pleasantry. This was worse than he had feared. He only hoped that Chloe did not realize it.

That hope was dashed when the girl turned to him, a look of wild panic on her face. Jasper pretended not to see it and—determined to fill the expanding silence—spoke up. "We had a good drive," he said, looking back and forth between the two women. "The traffic wasn't too bad."

Pauline made no reaction: no blink, no twinkle of curiosity in her eyes. Chloe, frozen in fear, remained silent.

"And the hearing itself," Jasper continued, "went without any problems—although the judge was quite pompous and eccentric, wasn't he, Chloe?" He turned to her, trying to draw her out. Chloe, however, declined to accept the conversation ball tossed to her, pressing her lips together and dropping her eyes.

Maddy spoke up. "What's a hearing?"

"Please, Maddy," he said. "The grown-ups are talking."

"Chloe isn't," Maddy observed. "Asides, she told me she's *not* a grown-up."

"Maddy—" he began, but just then Deepti emerged from the kitchen. She was wearing a black-and-white striped cooking apron and holding a stirring spoon.

"Hello! Hello!" she cried out. "I was in the basement, getting something from the freezer, when you came in!"

"I was about to bring Chloe to meet you," Jasper said. "Chloe, this is Deepti—I've told you about her."

Chloe turned and saw a short, middle-aged woman with dark, lovely skin and a warm smile beaming at her. She felt an absurd urge to throw herself into the woman's arms and start crying.

"It is a pleasure," said Deepti, shaking Chloe's hand. She looked at Jasper. "My goodness—so beautiful! No one told me! Like a model!"

"Deepti is a wonderful cook," he said, quickly changing the topic. "Wait until you taste her food."

"Do you like paella?" Deepti asked the girl.

Chloe looked at Jasper, her face registering terror. "I've never had it," she whispered.

"It's wonderful," he said. "I think you'll love it."

Once again, Chloe felt a gust of gratitude for the kindly way that Ulrickson spoke to her in that comforting tone, so attentive of her insecurity. He seemed able to read her thoughts and emotions, just as she used to dream that a real father might.

"Well," Deepti said, "it is ready now, if you are hungry."

Ordinarily, the family ate in the kitchen, informally, around the Saarinen tulip table. But for the special occasion of Chloe's arrival, Deepti had set the long mahogany table in the dining area at the far end of the large living space. Pauline's wheelchair was drawn up to a corner beside Jasper, who sat at the head of the table. Chloe was to his left, and Maddy beside her. Maddy ignored her own food in the interest of watching Chloe raise each bite of the paella to her mouth. She kept up a running commentary on the girl's actions: "Chloe isn't eating any of the shrimp!" "Chloe doesn't eat very much." "She eats so slow." "How come Chloe doesn't get any wine?" (Jasper had poured himself a glass of pinot grigio.)

"Please leave your sister to eat in peace," Jasper said. "She can't drink wine until she's twenty-one, and that's still a long way off."

"Daddy is going to be forty-*two* soon," Maddy stated.

Chloe, who had been keeping her face close to her plate, looked up at Jasper.

"Next month," he told her. "The tenth. Some of us are more excited at the prospect than others."

Chloe did not smile and only lowered her eyes back to her plate. But a few seconds later, she ventured a glance at Pauline and saw that she was staring at her with that same freezing hatred. It was uncanny, as if the poor woman had somehow divined the plan. But that, of course, was not possible.

With Maddy's commentary stanched, the table and room fell into a silence punctuated only by the sound of forks clinking against brittle china, a sound that accentuated the pall that had fallen. Jasper racked his exhausted brain for a topic of conversation that might draw Chloe out a little, and demonstrate to Pauline that she was a sweet child, not deserving of anyone's enmity.

"Maybe you'd like to tell Pauline—your stepmom—a little about today," Jasper said. "The courthouse was unexpectedly interesting, I thought. Architecturally."

Chloe glanced up at Pauline, then over at Jasper. "I guess so," she said timidly. "I never was in one before."

"No, of course not," Jasper said. They fell to eating again in silence.

Deepti came to collect the dinner plates. Chloe jumped up and began to help clear the table. Deepti said that she did not have to do that, but Chloe insisted. Anything to get away from the table.

"Isn't that great of her?" Jasper whispered eagerly to Pauline

when Chloe was in the kitchen putting a stack of plates on the counter. "I think she's going to be a *big* help around here."

Pauline answered with a look of such murderous hostility that he immediately fell silent.

Chloe came back into the room. She had taken her shoes off and was padding around in her bare feet. "Did we get everything?" she said, scanning the table.

"Yes, that's fine," Jasper said. "Let's move to the living room."

He steered Pauline over to one end of the sofa, parked her there and took a seat beside her. Chloe made one last trip from dining area to kitchen, carrying the salt and pepper shakers and two glasses, then came into the living room. Her eyes darted back and forth over the grouping of chairs and sofas around the glass coffee table, and after a moment she stepped over and carefully lowered herself onto the sofa beside Jasper—a spot she chose because it put him as a physical barrier between her and the terrifying Pauline.

Maddy, who had been sent to the bathroom to brush her teeth before bed, charged into the living room crying out, "I wanna sit beside Chloe!" She leapt onto the sofa, clambered onto the cushion between Jasper and Chloe, and then settled herself, legs outstretched.

"So," he said, smiling stiffly and rubbing his hands together as if to warm them, "what do you think of Connecticut so far, Chloe?" He was determined to get her talking.

Chloe, too, was determined to overcome her nervousness. She cleared her throat and said, "It's very nice," addressing herself to Pauline. "But I haven't seen very much of it yet," she added with

a shy smile. "Like, just the highway—and now this room. And they're—they're very nice." Chloe was mortified at the vapidity of this halting utterance but was surprised to see that the effort seemed to have brought a slight softening in Pauline's gaze. Jasper, thrilled, noticed it too.

"Will you play the alphabet game with me?" Maddy asked, tugging at Chloe's arm.

"Maddy," Jasper said, "Chloe just got here after a long, long drive. She's relaxing now. Maybe tomorrow."

"What's the alphabet game?" Chloe asked.

"Trust me," Jasper said, "you'll be hearing all about it from Maddy. Speaking of whom . . ." he added, throwing Maddy a loaded glance.

"I don't want to go to bed yet!" Maddy cried. "I wanna stay and talk!"

"You've got preschool tomorrow," he said, "besides which, you're already up a half hour past your bedtime. So it's off to slumber land now, my darling."

"I'll only go if you carry me," she announced flatly.

Sensing an opportunity, he quickly acceded. "Okay," he said, rising from the sofa. "But no story tonight. I'm going to put you in bed, tuck you in, and that's it."

She hopped up into a standing position on the sofa cushion and then jumped into Jasper's waiting arms. Chloe threw him a panicked look, clearly terrified at the prospect of being left alone with Pauline. Seeing that look of desperate entreaty, he almost took pity on Chloe and sent Maddy down the hall on her own, but he had resolved that Chloe and Pauline would

have to get to know each other sooner or later, and it might as well be sooner. But to give her something to do during his absence, he pointed out the stack of family photo albums on the shelf under the table at the end of the sofa. "You might want to take a look while I tuck Maddy in," he said. Chloe fairly dived at the albums.

He carried Maddy down the hall to her bedroom. She obediently scrambled under the covers.

"So, what do you think?" he asked, standing beside her bed. "Is Chloe nice?"

"Yes!" Maddy said. "Are you going to marry her?"

"*Marry* her?" he almost shouted. He dropped his voice to a hissing whisper. "Don't be silly. I explained to you: she's my daughter. Daddies don't marry their daughters! You know that."

"Yeah," Maddy said. "But Chloe is so pretty."

"Now listen," Jasper said, sitting on the edge of the bed. "Chloe is my daughter, same as you. That's why she's here. I want Mommy and me to finish raising her, just like we're raising you. Besides, I have Mommy. Marry Chloe! What a silly thing to say!"

"I'm glad," Maddy said. "Where will she sleep?"

"Sleep?" he said. "In the *bedroom* we made for her! In Mommy's old office. You remember!"

"Oh yeah," she said. Her jaws opened in a yawn. She was already bored with this topic. "Will you read to me?"

"You remember our deal," he said. "Sleep." He kissed her, stood and put out the light. *Marry Chloe!* If the idea weren't so strange, he would have to laugh. The misapprehensions of children!

He returned to the living room.

Chloe, her head bent low, was looking intently through a photograph album, her legs crossed demurely, high at the thighs. Pauline sat, silent and watchful, near the end of the sofa. Without lifting her head, Chloe asked, "You went to Mexico?"

"For our honeymoon," Jasper said, pausing at the dining table and pouring himself a fresh glass of wine. "One week in Ixtapa, on the west coast. This was before the drug cartels and beheadings. It was lovely."

He came over and sat next to her. She had the album open on a double-page spread that showed Jasper and Pauline lounging in swimsuits in front of their hotel, a five-star place on a private beach. The hotel was built by an indigenous architect who outlawed air-conditioning and used ancient principles of cooling devised by the Mayans: the adobe-style brown clay walls were six feet thick to keep out heat, and the glassless windows had been cut fore and aft in the structure to allow the constant breeze off the ocean to aerate and cool the rooms naturally. Though spartan in appearance—on arrival, they thought they'd made a terrible mistake choosing the place, with its unadorned walls and bare tile floors—the hotel proved to be the most comfortable and strangely luxurious that they had ever stayed in. He explained all this to Chloe, who nodded dutifully.

He turned to Pauline. "Remember, honey? I got so sunburned the first day on the beach. I turned into a lobster and had to spend our second day lying in our room covered in lotion. Remember that, Paul?"

Pauline, whose eyes were fixed on the photo album, glanced up at him and gave him a blink—a sign, perhaps, that she was coming out of her shell. The contrast between his memories of that week in Mexico and the sight of her now, a slightly hunched figure in a wheelchair, her balled fists and bent wrists in her lap, the right side of her face drooping slightly as if made of wax that was lightly melting, made him see her appalling debility with fresh eyes, and he felt a wave of sadness and horror he had not felt in some time, perhaps years.

Deepti came from the kitchen and said that it was time for Pauline to go to bed. Chloe got quickly up off the sofa. She bowed slightly to Pauline. This gesture too seemed to soften something in Pauline's gaze.

"Good night, Mom," Chloe said. "If I can call you that."

There was a weighty pause as Pauline considered the girl. Seconds passed. Then she blinked. Jasper, ecstatic at this turn of events, bent and kissed his wife on the forehead. "Night, honey," he whispered. "And thanks."

Deepti rolled Pauline out of the room. A minute later, they heard the back door close.

Jasper, who had poured another glass of wine, sat down again next to Chloe. "That was wonderful," he said.

"What was?" She had opened the album again on her lap.

"Calling Pauline 'Mom.' It means so much to her. And to me."

"Well," Chloe said, "she *is* my mom, now." She meant this, oddly enough. If the last few hours had shown Chloe anything, it was that she would not be able to live in this house, even for

as long as it took to complete the plan, if she did not at least try to act like a daughter to Ulrickson and Pauline, and a sister to Maddy. Besides which, against all expectations, Chloe had, over the course of the evening, begun to feel stirrings of real sympathy for Pauline, trapped as she was in that wheelchair, in her paralysis. Dez had described her to Chloe as a kind of monster, a grotesque being hardly human. But you only had to look into the woman's eyes to realize that that was far from true.

She turned the thick page to a photograph of Pauline standing on a beach. Jasper explained that he had taken the picture, near the end of their honeymoon, in the town of Zihuatanejo, a small fishing village some miles from their hotel. He remembered now how they had eaten scrambled-egg burritos at a tiny roadside restaurant and gotten terrible stomach cramps. Jasper later surmised that the cramps were from the water used to wash the lettuce in the burritos. But the picture was taken before their symptoms had set in, and Pauline was smiling broadly. She looked beautiful in her sleeveless linen T-shirt, her sun-bronzed arms exposed. She was gazing at the camera (and Jasper behind it) with a look of melting contentment, love and satiation. Looking now at her expression, Jasper remembered, suddenly, that they had made love in their hotel room that morning, gingerly, Pauline on top because of his burn, before setting out in a cab for the small seaside town. The memory pierced him like an arrow.

"It's so sad about Mom," Chloe said, as if reading his mind.

"Yes," Jasper murmured. He was remembering, viscerally

now, the sensation of lovemaking, the warmth of skin on skin, the sense of velvety, sheathing engulfment, a tactile memory that he usually strove to keep at bay; the memory almost made him gasp. It had been so long.

Chloe felt a mood of sadness about Pauline settling over both of them. An absurdly misplaced impulse to comfort Ulrickson, as if he were her actual father, arose in her, but she quickly tamped it down, remembering the plan, remembering Dez's imperative that she stay focused and detached, that she remember the injury Ulrickson had inflicted on her mother, the misery he had visited on Chloe. She closed the album and shifted it off her thighs onto the cushion beside her, exposing her long, bare, brown legs to view. Men, she had long noticed, could never ignore the sight. On Dez's orders, she had, on the eve of the hearing, submitted to a full-body waxing, legs included, and her private awareness of all-over silky smoothness enhanced her sense of desirability and emboldened her now in her efforts at entrancing her prey. She looked at him. "Are you all right?" she said.

Jasper nodded. He realized that he had probably had a glass or two more of the pinot grigio than was strictly advisable after such a tiring two days. All that driving. An eleven-hour round trip. Not to mention the stress of meeting Chloe for the first time, the emotions of the hearing and the racking tension of introducing her to Pauline. He was exhausted.

With the photo album gone, Chloe's legs stood fully revealed to his gaze, shining in the shaded lamplight. He must remem-

ber to insist, as a father, that she wear longer skirts in future, he thought. He remembered that dirty-minded hotel clerk. Not to mention the two lawyers and their slavering and gawking. And all those people on the sidewalk. And in the fast-food place. Even that insane judge had alluded to her beauty!

Chloe, humming lightly to herself and looking straight ahead, seemingly wholly unconscious of his gaze, abruptly raised her feet off the floor, bent her knees and rested her toes on the coffee table in front of her. Her toenails, he noticed, were like ten shiny little mirrors in the lamplight. The toes themselves were curiously childlike, smooth and without obvious knuckly joints. The baby toe curled slightly under. Were she actually a baby, or a toddler, it occurred to him blearily, he could seize one of those adorable feet and kiss the ticklish arch. But she was almost full-grown now, and although she was his daughter, there was no chance now, or ever, of his taking one of those appendages into his hands, of kissing it affectionately. The crazy judge, come to think of it, had said something about this.

A small bone twitched on the outside of her ankle.

"You know, I'm beat," Jasper said, snatching his gaze away and rubbing his eyes. He massaged his closed lids for almost half a minute, rubbing away the image on his retinas. "I think I'm going to turn in."

"Me too," Chloe said, but she made no move to get off the sofa. Neither did Jasper. She yawned and shifted on the cushion. For the first time, she thought she might be making some progress in the plan. She was convinced that Ulrickson was looking at

her legs—or, rather, trying *not* to look at them. Which amounted to the same thing. She decided to increase the pressure.

"I'm so stiff from the drive," she said. She lifted her right foot off the coffee table, straightened her leg and raised it slowly to a forty-five-degree angle toward the ceiling, pointing her toes like a ballet dancer. "I really need to stretch." She flexed her foot, pulling the toes back. She lowered it to the table and repeated the action with her left leg. Jasper, leaning back against the sofa cushions, watched mutely. This was good. She definitely had his attention now. She said, "Feels so good. Do you do yoga?"

"No, never," he said. He sipped his wine. "Never done yoga."

"It's the best," Chloe said. "This is a great one."

She placed the soles of her feet together, then reached forward and enclosed them with her two hands. She pulled toward herself, pressing her knees flat to both sides, her right thigh suddenly lying warm against Jasper's legs, pressing down on them. She arched her spine backward. She breathed in slowly, then sighed blissfully. She held the pose for several seconds, her eyes closed. She rolled her head forward, released her feet, extended her legs and placed her toes, once again, on the edge of the table. She smiled at Jasper. "Gets out all the kinks," she said. "You should try it."

"No, no," Jasper said. "I'd tear every muscle in my back."

"Actually, it gets you right here." She placed a hand flat against the inside of her thigh. She saw him close his eyes and breathe evenly through his nose for several seconds. Surely, he would now open his eyes and place his hand on her thigh in a

feigned "fatherly" caress—at which point she could torture him by jumping up from the sofa, skipping away and blithely saying that she needed to go to the bathroom.

But instead, he slapped his legs and rose from the sofa. "Yup," he said, "I'm going to hit the hay."

Nonplussed, she groped for a way to prevent the encounter from coming to an end. He had seemed so close to a slipup. But had he been? She could not say for sure. At the moment, he was looking at her with an expression indistinguishable from how she imagined any father might look at his daughter. And then he said, with a clipped paternal sternness, "You should get to bed too. You had a big day."

"Okay . . ." she said. A new inspiration had struck her. "But, Dad?"

He looked at her expectantly.

"Can you show me the house? I don't know where anything is."

"How stupid of me," he said. The anxiety of introducing her to Pauline had driven all such thoughts from his head. "I'll give you the grand tour. But quietly. We don't want to wake Maddy.

"You know the kitchen, of course," he went on, as he led her into the unlit hall. He pointed to the door on the right and whispered, "Bathroom." He advanced a few paces, Chloe following on her silent bare feet. "Maddy's bedroom." He indicated the rooms at the end of the passage. "My office and my bedroom," he whispered.

He stepped around her in the narrow space and began to

lead her back down the hall when, from behind him, he heard her say, "Can I see?" He turned and saw her pushing through the door of his bedroom.

"Hey!" he said. He hurried back up the hall and stepped in after her.

6

She had advanced several paces into his room, halting near the foot of the bed. She turned and looked at him. He glanced around and was relieved to see that he had tidied the place up, which meant that he had put away in his bedside table the dog-eared stack of *Vogue*s and the accursed lingerie catalog that had arrived on the day of the paternity claim. Two nights ago, he had thumbed through these periodicals, not in an effort to arouse himself but rather to see if he could, as a kind of test of his will, override the impulse that had flared up, badly, in him. He had succeeded.

Chloe stood looking at him, a peculiar, unreadable expression on her face. She was thinking it was essential that she move

the plan along. Over the course of the day with Ulrickson, she had continually felt herself slipping in her concentration, gliding into a confused state in which she saw in him, not a target for seduction, but an actual, longed-for father figure, a kindly and loving man deserving of nothing but her gratitude for taking her in. Remembering Dez's warnings about Ulrickson's charm and duplicity, she was now convinced that the absurd daughter-like feelings he had awakened in her were only part of a deliberate plan on his part to disarm her, to control and manipulate her, just as he had her mother. A memory of Holly—slumped on the sofa at home, overweight, drunk and railing against the direction her life had taken—flashed before Chloe's eyes, that vision of a life squandered and destroyed, and which Chloe had been convinced, by Dez, to believe was Ulrickson's doing. She scolded herself for her gullibility and, thinking how Dez would praise and love her if she could bring it off successfully, refocused herself on the seduction.

The chamber was illuminated only by a feeble trickle of light that fell through the venetian blinds. Jasper reached for the wall switch.

"*Don't!*" she cried. Then she added, softly, "My eyes. And it's so nice and peaceful in here."

He dropped his hand to his side.

She swept her gaze around the room, her eyes playing over the dresser, the small velvet-covered divan in one corner, the king-size bed, which she now stepped over to with a sinuous, silent, tiptoe gait. She stopped, turned and faced Jasper, her hands folded in front of her, as she had stood on the driveway when

she first got out of the car. "Mmmm," she said, "so nice and peaceful in here. Your bed is huge," she added, bending slightly and touching its surface with her fingertips. She straightened and looked levelly at Jasper. "Where does Mom sleep?"

He explained about the guesthouse. "It's a very nice little house, actually," he said. "And it makes more sense. Now."

She nodded. She looked at the bed, where the shadows of the blinds lay in diagonal stripes across the light cotton spread. "So sad," she said softly. "You must get so lonely."

Jasper was about to answer when Chloe, on a sudden diabolical impulse, dropped into a sitting position on the edge of the bed. She looked at him with a stricken expression. "Dad," she said woefully, "I hope you're not *mad* at me!"

"Mad at you?" Jasper said, mystified. "What do you mean?"

She was looking at him pleadingly, her hands clasped between her knees. "Mad that I told Child Services about you," she said. "That I made them look for you. I mean, I've come into your perfect life, here, and . . . and changed everything for you and Mom and Maddy—"

"My goodness, no," Jasper said. "No, no, no." He came forward and sat beside her. "No, I'm very glad you did that." He placed his arm around her shoulders.

"I was just so scared of being in foster care," she said, looking down at her hands. "I didn't want to mess up your life. I didn't want to wreck everything for you! But I was frightened! And sad about my mom, and just so . . . so . . ." She turned and looked at him; her features were contorted, as though she were about to start crying. "So confused and lonely."

"Oh, my dear," Jasper said, "I couldn't be happier that you're here with us! Couldn't be happier that you spoke up about me."

"Honest?"

"Of course," he said.

"Oh, Dad!" she cried, and she lifted her legs and swung them around so that they lay over Jasper's thighs. She put her arms around his neck then hiked herself up so that she was sitting athwart his lap, twisting her torso around and hugging him tightly. Jasper felt her crush her almost disconcertingly womanly-feeling upper body against his chest, nuzzling her face into his neck. "I promise to be a good girl," she said, her voice muffled, her lips moving against the ticklish flesh where his neck joined his shoulder. "I just want to make you happy. Happy and proud."

"You will," Jasper said into her soft hair. "You *do*." He rubbed her back.

"Oh, Dad," she said, "never let me go!"

They sat this way, silently breathing, for several minutes in the semidarkness. It felt so *good* to hold her. It must have been simply his natural shyness that had made it difficult earlier, when they first met at the courthouse, to obey the instinct to embrace her. He had felt the same constraint several times today. A hesitation. He hoped that she did not, in seeing that balkiness, think him standoffish, cold, remote. But now, all those worries were swept away as he unselfconsciously held her to him, gently rocking her, as when he lulled Maddy to sleep after a bout of tears. He could actually feel her heart beating against his chest, and he suspected that she could feel his. He breathed deep of her exquisite aroma, burying his face in her soft neck.

She lifted her head from his shoulder. He lifted his head too, and they peered into each other's eyes. She blinked a strange, slow, hypnotic blink that left her eyes dreamy, almost drugged-looking. Her mouth was not quite closed. He could feel her breath on his lips; smell the gentle, trembling exhalation, a sweet, transparent, clear scent. Her eyes, which held a crescent gleam from the weak light of the window, played over his face, darting down to look at his lips, then back to his eyes. There was a freighted quality to her gaze, a penetration, as if she were silently trying to tell him something. Something of urgency. But she said nothing, merely stared into his eyes, her lips parted, exposing a triangular glimpse of those two moist, slightly glinting front teeth.

She was absolutely sure that he would have to try to kiss her, that he would move his face toward hers in the semidarkness—at which point she would quickly pull back her head, eluding the touch of his lips, then hop from his lap and run gaily from the room as if nothing had happened, leaving him to boil and stew all night, until the morning, when she would resume the torture. But instead, she heard him say, huskily: "Well, it's late. I should show you your bedroom . . ."

She moved her face a millimeter closer in the darkness and whispered, "I wish you could carry me to my room, just like you carried Maddy to bed tonight."

He smiled. "You're very slender, but my back . . ."

"But if you carried me, I would feel even more like your daughter. Just like Maddy."

"You *are* my daughter," he said. "As much as Maddy is."

"I know," she whispered, "but I want you to *show* me." She

drooped her face close to his, as if to graze his lips with her own, but she simply lowered her head onto his shoulder again. He felt her moist mouth touch his neck. He really was so tired now and, despite what he believed to have been a relatively modest wine intake, could feel the effects of the alcohol. With his eyes closed, he felt her shift her body, her clothes releasing a fresh wave of warmth and bodily scent. The aroma filled him with a spreading sensation of well-being. She murmured into his ear, "*Will* you show me?"

Muzzy-headed, he could not recall what they had been talking about. "Show you what?" he said, his eyes shut against the world.

"That I'm your *daugh*ter, silly."

He chuckled and nuzzled her soft neck. "Aren't I showing you right now?"

"Mmm hmmm," she said, tightening her arms around him. Yes—she was getting somewhere, finally. Wasn't she? She shifted her buttocks on his lap, trying to detect the giveaway sign of his arousal, but failed, amazingly, confusingly, to feel anything except the tense muscles of his upper thighs. On the other hand, he did now embrace her more tightly, crushing her slim but cushioned body against him. "Oh!" she laughed. "Don't break me!" Then she whispered in a thunderous rush of hot breath, her lips against his ear: "Let's just go to sleep here!"

"Here?"

"Your bed is so big and I'll make myself very small. You won't even know I'm here."

Jasper laughed softly, assuming she was joking. "Can you

imagine?" he murmured. "I've only just trained Maddy to stay in her own room all night—and then to have to train *you*? A grown-up girl?"

"Not *so* grown-up," Chloe said in pretend baby talk, sticking out her lower lip. She continued in her normal voice: "And what if I have a nightmare? And don't know where I am?"

Intoxicated by the smell of her hair and skin, his judgment blurred by the wine, he asked himself what harm could there be in letting her share one side of his king-size bed? She was his daughter, after all. And she made an excellent point about having a bad dream and waking in a strange and unfamiliar place. But *no*, he immediately thought, through the thicknesses of his exhaustion and the confusions of the wine. No, no—that would be wrong. *Wouldn't* it?

He felt her arms around him, felt her shift her warm, mobile weight on his lap. The aroma of perfumed flesh breathed from within the interstices of her blouse, and he felt the resilient double cushions of her buttocks against his legs, the concomitant pressure of her breasts against his shirtfront. He swooned with physical love and tenderness for her, and he began to say, "Yes, yes, of course you can sleep here"—when he heard a small voice say, "Daddy?"

"Mmmm?" he said in reply, nuzzling her neck, opening his lips slightly to take a forbidden sip of her sweet skin. But why "forbidden"? Could a father not kiss his daughter? He pressed his lips against the flesh over her throbbing carotid artery. She moaned softly. The voice came again, more insistent this time, and on a note of whining complaint: "*Daaad*dy!"

He opened his eyes and looked at Chloe, whose eyes were closed, her head tipped back in a swoon. There was a movement in the edge of his vision.

He turned and saw Maddy.

She was standing by the bedroom door in her nightie, screwing one small fist into her eye and squinting at him and Chloe with the other.

He jumped to his feet—nearly throwing Chloe onto the rug. She caught herself awkwardly with one foot on the floor, an arm around his neck. She pulled herself up straight, retreated a few steps from him, then stood, staring wide-eyed at the little girl.

Maddy jutted out her chin. "You said Chloe was gonna sleep in her *own* room!"

"She is," he said. He turned and gaped at Chloe, who was hastily adjusting her skirt and tucking in her blouse. "See?" he said to Maddy. "She's getting ready right now."

"But she's putting her clothes *on*," Maddy said. "You take your clothes *off* for bed."

He rushed forward. "You've got to get to bed too," he said, taking her by the shoulders. He turned her around and steered her out of the room. "Chloe was just saying good night to me." He marched her across the hall. "She's going to her room, right after you get back in bed."

"Promise?" Maddy said, her head lolling as they entered her room. "Because it's naw . . . naaww . . ." —her mouth stretched in a yawn—"not fair."

"I promise," Jasper said.

Maddy climbed into bed and under the covers. She was immediately unconscious.

Jasper hurried out into the dark hall and nearly collided with Chloe. She smiled and reached up her arms, as if to continue their embrace. She was sure that he would resume hugging her, sure that she had set in motion the fateful sequence, and that he must lead her back into his bedroom, to continue the shadow play of wordless flirtation that must result, eventually—if not tonight, then a week or a month from now—in her joining him under the covers of his bed. But for Jasper a spell (that he had not consciously realized he was under) had been broken, and he stepped back from her. She looked at him quizzically. His earlier sense of warning restored, and for some reason magnified, he turned away, embarrassed, and said, pretending nothing had happened to interrupt their tour, ". . . and *your* bedroom is at the other end of the house. I thought that, as a teenager, you'd appreciate the privacy."

He strode off without looking back at her, down the hall, across the living room and dining area, through an arched doorway, to the suite of rooms at the far end of the house. These included the television room, a bathroom and a second bedroom where Jasper's sister had slept when they were children, and which Pauline had converted into a home office when they married. Last week, Jasper had finally rid the room of Pauline's desk and shelves, replacing them with a twin bed, black lacquered dresser, matching bedside table and modernistic white desk with hutch shelves. He had not put down a rug, hung curtains or put anything on the walls, thinking that a teenaged girl

would undoubtedly want to decorate the room according to her own taste. He explained all this as he pushed open the door, then stood back against the doorjamb to let her pass.

With slow steps, using both hands to hook her loose hair behind her ears, she came forward, almost cautiously, tiptoeing. She moved past Jasper to the center of the room and turned a slow circle. "It's so *big*," she said in an entranced voice. "Bigger than our whole house!"

Her eye fell on the desk, on the presents Jasper had assembled for her over the previous weeks: the sleek aluminum Mac laptop, the iPhone and audiophile headphones, the Xbox, the flat-screen TV monitor. She turned and looked at him in confusion.

"For you," he said, smiling. "And a few other things . . ." He turned his gaze to the bed. She followed the direction of his eyes.

That's when she saw the new clothes laid out in boxes on the white duvet—items chosen according to sizes he had collected, in a secret phone call with Mrs. Gaitskill last week, when Chloe was out. With the help of a salesgirl at Urban Outfitters (a store that his sister, Laura, had assured him would pass muster with a female teen), he had bought an array of summer and fall dresses; faded denim jeans and jackets; wispy linen and cotton and silk T-shirts; and a selection of shoes: Converse Chuck Taylors in three different colors (turquoise, pink and black), suede ankle booties, a pair of flat-soled, strappy silver sandals.

She picked up and inspected each item, lifting them to the light, sometimes holding a blouse up to her shoulders and peering down at herself, then reverently laying it down again. She looked at him. Her face registered not the happiness he

expected to see but a confused anguish. She did not run to him. Instead, she simply stood there. Her shoulders began to shake. Her features crumpled and she buried her face in her hands. "No one," she said through jerking sobs, "ever . . . I never had—anything . . . like . . . this."

Jasper went to her. He felt emboldened, once again, to put his arms around her. This time, it was Chloe who grew stiff, rigid, in his embrace.

"I don't deserve this," she said. "I don't deserve it."

He petted her hair and said soothingly, "You deserve everything—and more."

"No, *no*," she said, shaking her head. "I don't. I *don't*."

"Shhh," he said. He held her closer, and eventually she cautiously placed her arms around him. They stood, joined, for several minutes, until her crying subsided. Jasper kissed her hair, and then whispered softly, "Time for bed. Have a nice long sleep—lie in as late as you wish. You've had a big day." He bestowed a final kiss on her forehead, and then went off to his own end of the house.

7

In his bathroom, a few minutes later, Jasper inspected his naked torso in the mirror above the sink. He was startled to see how much weight he had put on lately. His pectorals were flabby and seemed to droop a little over his swollen belly. The area under his chin held a ridge of fat. And there were, he noticed, two symmetrical areas of shiny skin visible on his temples where his hair was receding. Maybe he should think about growing his hair out a bit—cover those bald spots. And he should definitely get out and do some running. To think of how his body had changed from those days when he had taught tennis at the New Halcyon Club, as a lean twenty-two-year-old with rocklike deltoids and sharply cut abdominal muscles. Funny, he hadn't until

now noticed *any* of these changes. Hadn't, perhaps, *cared* about them. Was it something about Chloe, about her youth and freshness, that had made him suddenly so conscious of how he had aged and of how quickly time was passing? Had her power to pull him back, in memory, to that summer almost twenty years ago underlined the toll that the years had already taken on him? Perhaps that's all it was. But then, he *was* going to be forty-two in a few weeks.

Forty-two. This struck him now with unexpected force. They called it middle age (he thought as he finished brushing his teeth and began to wash his face), but could anyone expect necessarily to make it to eighty? Or, rather, eighty-four? And if he was one of the lucky ones, what would that final decade and a half be like, with its infirmities and creeping fears of death? Reasonably, then, he could expect maybe twenty more good years, if that. He wondered if he had taken full advantage of his youth. All that scribbling, scribbling, scribbling. And then, of course, the last four years, shuttered away in the house, tending to Pauline and Maddy. He was visited by a wave of that weariness, or ennui, he had acknowledged in himself a few weeks ago on his way to the DNA clinic, now joined by a pang of something that felt almost like resentment, a qualm of self-pity. And now forty-two, he thought, as he toweled off his face. People said age was "only a number." But that was wrong. Forty-two felt like something. Something new and unexpectedly ominous. It felt like cresting the hill at the halfway point on a car journey and seeing, in the valley below, one's rumored destination, that terminal town which, up until then, had existed only as an unseen abstraction,

but was now a concrete reality toward which one was hurtling. Had he lived enough? Experienced enough?

In his bedroom, he donned boxers and a T-shirt, then climbed under the covers. He lay there, waiting for sleep to overtake him. But despite his earlier exhaustion, he found that his brain would not quiet itself. His thoughts, however, had taken a happier turn.

He was thinking now about Chloe, about the events of the evening, and specifically Pauline's reaction to the girl; and Maddy's too. All things considered, it had gone rather well, he thought. Pauline had shown definite signs of thaw and he assumed that this would only continue. Maddy was clearly mad for Chloe, and apart from that ridiculous misapprehension she voiced when he put her to bed—and that unfortunate incident a few minutes ago—she was clearly delighted to have her older sister living with them. Chloe, meanwhile, had been a perfect *angel*: wonderfully polite and well mannered—saying "please" and "thank you" at dinner, helping clear the dishes, exhibiting great patience with Maddy, standing when Deepti took Pauline off to bed—and, finally, calling Pauline "Mom." In his most optimistic dreams of how this day could have gone, he had not dared to imagine that she would, so quickly, accept Pauline as her mother! Say what the social workers might about Holly's shortcomings, Jasper had to give her credit: she had raised Chloe to have wonderful manners, and great poise. Thinking of all this, his earlier depressive thoughts about aging and death were swept away and he was flooded with a sense of excitement about tomorrow, when he would rise from bed and see Chloe again.

If he had any concerns at all about her, it was that she seemed excessively innocent sexually—hardly a worry in anyone less amply endowed with feminine allure. But, as matters stood, he could not help wishing that she, for her own protection, were inclined toward a greater awareness of men's impulses and intentions and would thus take care to demonstrate a higher degree of physical modesty. The blithe, uncalculating frankness with which she displayed, for instance, her legs suggested to Jasper someone with little or no understanding of the effect her physical being was having on others. Specifically men. He recalled how she had unconsciously exposed the gleaming backs of her naked thighs to that gawking desk clerk at the bed-and-breakfast. For that matter, how she had, just minutes ago, so trustingly undertaken her yoga stretches on the sofa, waving around her lovely long nether limbs in that minuscule band of fabric that passed for a skirt. He was her father and thus she could not be accused of "immodesty," in the abstract, but he was, still, a man, and he might have wished that she would instinctually feel inhibited from demonstrating quite so much naked flesh to *any* male's eyes.

But then, he thought, maybe he should be *glad* of Chloe's innocence, her apparent lack of awareness of, or interest in, the opposite sex. Maybe this meant that he would not have to face an endless stream of be-pimpled boys on the doorstep—to say nothing of the fears of teenaged pregnancy. And maybe he should, furthermore, be *glad* that Chloe was already so innately trusting of him that it would not even occur to her that there could be anything untoward about him seeing so very much of her bare legs. As, of course, there could not.

That slant on things helped to quiet his concerns. A delicious tingle overcame him, a fuzzy warmth that muddled his thoughts, and soon he was asleep.

It was sometime later, at a deep, uncharted hour of the night or very early morning, the weak stripes of illumination from the venetian blind swallowed by darkness and his bed seeming to float, like a raft, in the middle of an ink-black ocean beneath a moonless and starless sky, when Jasper swam up from a profound sleep and broke the surface of consciousness. Groggy, disoriented, he looked at the red digits that hovered just to the right of his head: 4:02. He closed his eyes again and cuddled still more closely to Pauline, who lay spooning with him, her back and buttocks and legs conforming to the protective curve of his sheltering body, his arm draped over her waist. He had been having a harrowing nightmare that she had suffered a stroke and been reduced to total silence and immobility. He was inexpressibly relieved to feel her in the bed beside him, to know that it had been only a dream.

He nestled his face into her hair and felt her stir. She turned her head on the crepitating pillow and kissed his mouth. "Mmmm," she murmured sleepily. Through the veils of his slumber, he realized how terribly long it had been since they last made love—it seemed like *years*—and he instinctively began to move his hands on the smooth skin of her thighs and hips, surprised to feel not her remembered womanly curves but narrow, boyish nates, no less arousing for their slender firmness.

She answered in the affirmative to his questing touch, emitting a soft moan and pushing her buttocks against his tumescence. His engorgement was total, but he wished to savor the moment, so instead of moving to slip her underwear down, he instead withdrew his body a little and lightly turned her around on her back. With his eyes still closed, he kissed her cheeks, her eyes, her open mouth. Eager, now, to drink in her beauty—it seemed so long since he had seen her face pillowed beside him—he lifted his heavy lids and saw: Chloe.

A noise reverberated in his ears and he realized that it was the lingering echo of his own startled, horrified shout bouncing off the walls of the bedchamber. He was sitting up, his chest heaving, his mouth gaping as he fought for breath. Slowly, flinchingly—horrified at what he knew he would find there—he turned and looked at the space beside him in bed.

It was empty, the sheets and blanket undisturbed. He was alone. He had been dreaming.

Heart hammering, body slicked with sweat, underwear disgustingly distended in a telltale tent-pole stretch, he stumbled to the bathroom, drank a draft of water from the toothbrush cup, then crept back into bed. But he did not try to sleep. He could not risk a return of that dream. Instead, he sat up rigidly against the headboard, staring in front of him, trying to master himself, trying to will his insurgent body to subside. He was still sitting that way, wide-eyed and staring, when dawn began to brighten the horizontal gaps between the slats of the venetian blind.

PART FOUR

1

Girls and boys. Some as young as fifteen, the oldest maybe eighteen—twenty at the most. Lined up five deep. Clamoring for Dez's attention, waving at him, calling his name. Shouting out orders. Actually, almost always the *same* order—for these were cash-strapped high school and college kids. They wanted beer, draft beer. Gallons of cheap draft beer. The odd rich-kid smart-ass asked for a martini or a manhattan. Whereupon Dez would give him a look, snatch up his cocktail shaker, then dust off the skills he'd learned back in his college days, when he had spent a summer tending bar.

He had been obliged to go back to work over a month ago, at the beginning of August, as the credit card bills for his recent

orgy of plane travel and car rentals began to arrive, on top of the usual expenses: rent, phone, food. He could have defaulted on some of these payments but was determined not to draw any undue attention to himself. Toe the line. Keep his nose clean. Fade into the background as he awaited the moment when the plan came fully to fruition. Then reap the payoff.

He had chosen this place, the Lantern—a dark tavern on a stretch of highway on the outskirts of Sayer's Cliff—not only because he could reach it by bicycle from the trailer park but because it was notorious for its leniency toward underage drinkers. He had no intention of jeopardizing his freedom, and thus the entire scheme, by indulging in an indiscretion, but as long as he was forced to join the ranks of the gainfully employed, there seemed no reason not to mitigate the horror with some voyeuristic pleasures. His vantage point from behind the Lantern's long, beer-stained wooden bar afforded him an ideal view of the nightly offerings, which had swelled lately with the arrival of September and the return of these high school and college kids from their summer vacations. Dimpled coed freshman girls. Tanned high school seniors. But Dez found, to his surprise, that he had no interest in his young female customers. All he could think about was Chloe and her progress in Connecticut.

When dreaming up the scheme, Dez had tried to prepare for every contingency, tried to imagine, in advance, every part of the plan and how it would play out. Up until now, everything had gone as he had hoped—indeed, better than he had hoped. It was as if he had foreseen every obstacle to success. And those for which he had not minutely preplanned (like Ames's removal)

had solved themselves like gifts from a well-disposed fate. What he had failed properly to foresee was the long stretch of silence that followed upon the custody hearing last month; the period he was living through now, when Chloe had moved into Ulrickson's home, there to begin, and complete, the seduction.

Dez had always understood, and strove to make Chloe understand, that this period's duration would be, by definition, indeterminate. It could not be planned to the minute, hour, day, week or even month. It would be contingent upon the state of Ulrickson's morals and the strength of his nervous system. What Dez had not anticipated was how excruciating this period would be for *him*.

His first inkling of the torments that awaited him came on the very day of the custody hearing, six weeks ago, when he felt the euphoria of knowing that the plan was finally under way—that his two principal players were finally meeting—but at the same time the frustration that he could not *be* there, in the courthouse, to witness that meeting. He had toyed with fantasies of donning a simple disguise (janitor's uniform, mop and pail), to lurk in the hallways in the hope of glimpsing the newly united "father" and "daughter" as they emerged from the hearing room. But he had quickly recognized the folly of such a plan. Courthouses, police stations, legal offices: these were places Dez was born to avoid. So in the end, he had resigned himself to letting his carefully crafted scenario play out beyond his witness and outside his control.

Consequently, he felt like old, deaf Beethoven who could know the glories of his Ninth Symphony only theoretically,

because the actual music was swallowed up into his deafness. Except that Beethoven, at least, could conduct the orchestra that performed his masterpiece, could see the bowing of the silent violins, the clashing of the noiseless cymbals, could, through the gesticulations of his baton, influence the pace and emphasis of the performance. Dez was forced to remain at a complete remove from *his* creation, blind to its unfolding, wholly unable to influence, affect or otherwise control its course.

To be sure, he had meticulously coached Chloe before her removal into foster care with the Gaitskills. He had attended to every detail, down to her wardrobe for the hearing, which he decreed should have a formality in keeping with the occasion, but with a subtle, though unmistakable, element of seductive sexuality. On a trip to the Burlington shopping mall, he had chosen for her the white blouse that was in unimpeachably "good taste," but with a decidedly body-conscious fit, the cunningly darted seams following closely the contour of her slim torso and the plump heft of her breasts; likewise, the dark skirt that hugged the outline of her hips and buttocks and allowed a generous glimpse of her firm, long thighs. The shoes were cheap Louboutin knockoffs, but they brought her high on her toes, throwing her body into a sinuous S-curve, accentuating the play of rounded forms and the long lyrical lines that ran from the nape of her neck to the curve of her Achilles tendons. These shoes, to whose height she was unaccustomed, also introduced a poignant teeter and tremble to her gait, which emblematized how her body was so precariously perched between foal-like childhood and the full, fecund effulgence of erotically charged womanhood.

For the seduction, he schooled her to work with deliberation, but not too quickly—to draw out the torment, the titillation and the torture, so that once the man succumbed, his capitulation would be that much more annihilating. Though the girl was an inveterate flirt hardly in need of tutelage from him or anyone (for that was what the plan hinged upon: her almost unknowing irresistibility, her flower-fresh erotic appeal that came, to paraphrase Keats on poetry, as naturally as leaves to the trees), Dez had yet thought it wise to remind her that she must play innocent, must never be the overt seductress. Their prey must not detect any conscious attempt to arouse. Their new life together as father and daughter must be one of half glimpses of an "accidentally" exposed leg or a glossy bare back (as she emerged perhaps from a shower or bath, the door left open a crack to allow a surreptitious glimpse by an unsuspecting father passing through the hallway), followed by a shy, embarrassed smile, or a dimpled blush and a soft giggle. Yet she must also slowly increase the glimpses and the amount revealed in a steady, ascending, unbroken curve while never seeming to rush the operation, never revealing her intent to excite. She must, in short, seem benignly chaste, even as she turned his entrails into a molten furnace of lust—a devilishly difficult equipoise to establish and maintain; and indeed, as the days went by and he tried to imagine the individual steps in the seduction, from initial half glimpses to full coital submission, he found that he kept encountering a blind spot.

Where was that turning point at which "unconscious," unintended arousal tipped into actual invitation? Trying to envision

this moment—this critical shift—he would encounter a gap, a hiatus, a blank. He would back up and play the imagined events over again in his mind, to get some forward momentum into the psychological sequence, but every time he would hit the same sticking place, the same cul-de-sac.

How easily he could imagine those opening gambits, those subtle flashes of skin, those freighted, silent glances, those curly half smiles that would set the fuse alight. An accidental look up her skirt to a shaded area of her inner thigh, or down her boat-neck shirt for a peek at a swaying, half-seen breast. Then slowly to move to affectionate hugs, spontaneous clasping of hands, and, in the evenings, after the invalided stepmother and the little sister had been taken off to bed, and father and teenaged daughter were alone—all alone!—a session of oh-so-innocent cuddling on the sofa as the television, only half noticed, burbled away to itself. Inklings, peeklings, ticklings . . . soft sudden kisses on the side of the neck . . . quivery, hot exhalations of breath into a flaming ear during a hug that goes on just a fraction of a second too long . . . shy peeks over the top of a magazine during hushed reading times and the eyes snatched away just a moment too late . . . tremulous exhalations . . .

Yes, yes, he could see how the man's fuse could be made to smolder toward the powder keg. But the words and touches and smiles and kisses that would take Ulrickson from those dulcet, tender-eyed, clinging glances, those moist-lipped smiles of innocent invitation, to actual, purposeful erotic caresses, to something criminal, to plunging penetration and the actual explosion? He could not see it!

2

Work, at first, seemed as if it might provide a useful distraction from what was turning into a mad and maddening obsession. The tavern's raucous talk and laughter, the jukebox tunes, those pretty young girls crowding up to his bar, guzzling their drinks, and slipping ever deeper into drunkenness—all of it should have helped him forget Chloe and Connecticut, at least for a few hours. But no. He remained indifferent to all distractions and enticements, blind to everything except that scenario that kept playing, over and over in his mind, without a resolution.

The problem was that every imagined seduction would, at a certain indefinable point, go from plausible, believable flirtation to something wildly, laughably unreal—as crude and coarse as

one of those online video clips that he was addicted to in the days when he could afford a computer. Those movies that purported to show "stepfather" and "stepdaughter" unable to contain their illicit passion for each other, the "teen" girl actually a battle-scarred veteran porn actress of twenty-nine summers grotesquely tattooed at the base of her spine with the wings of an eagle, and mimicking the lisping tones of a near child; the "stepfather," a reputed straitlaced middle-class professional man in boxy suit and garish tie, with a ridiculously incongruous ponytail and a porn industry goatee and (once his clothes came off) a prison-pumped body also writhing in tats. The illicit lovers flatly proclaiming their lines at each other. "Hey, Cyn*dee*, what the heck are you *do*ing?" "Don't worry. I won't tell my mom. If *you* don't." "But you're my stepdaughter!"

Incidentally, Dez asked himself, was there some reason that the porn purveyors always called those girls "stepdaughters" as opposed simply to "daughters"—some wrinkle in the federal pornography laws, perhaps, that forbade depiction of that final frontier of erotic fantasy? Or was this the result of some squeamishness on the part of the porn makers themselves? Were they all too traumatized by the actual parental abuses they had suffered as children (and that had driven them into sex work in the first place) to depict such events as fuel to erotic fantasy? Lord knows, they were willing to show just about anything else: acts whose memory could actually turn Dez's stomach, ten years later. Pee. Vomit. Poop! But to show a man, posing as a girl's father, engaged in an act of illicit love? *That* was too far?

Perhaps, he thought with a stab of terror, it *was* too far! Was

this why his attempts to envision the seduction kept running aground? Were there laws of biology and nature that protected the species against the impulse to inbreed? There were—there assuredly were. And yet the man *must* succumb! There must exist a point at which Ulrickson's natural revulsion at the idea of biblically knowing his daughter would meet the urgency of raw, untamed, biological need. Perhaps such surrender was not inevitable in *every* man. But a man in Ulrickson's uniquely vulnerable position? A man forced into celibacy by fate and his own puritanical determination to adhere to a set of silly vows? A man teased to the point of internal rupture, who is then subjected to the satiny charms of an eighteen-year-old seductress whom custom could allow to climb onto the sofa and curl up in his lap, snuggling against him with a warm, contented sigh, a slight squirm of her body against his, a gentle, loving, innocent caress of her hand on his thigh, a languid tilting up of her face to him and a murmured appeal for a kiss? A girl, furthermore, who did *not* share his DNA, who would thus fail to emit whatever scents or vibrations or emanations presumably help to protect the species against the dangers of inbreeding? Yes! Yes! It was more than possible that he would succumb. It was inevitable! That is what Dez, the artist, the plot-maker, needed to believe: that the capitulation would not be *forced* into being by clumsy acts of routine, clichéd seduction, but instead that it would flow out naturally, as a spontaneous organic outgrowth of their situation, as an act inevitable, a fait accompli. Yes! It was going to happen! He need only sit tight.

Then his doubts would rise again.

If only, he thought, he could *talk* to the girl. Get a progress report. But by Dez's own Draconian decree, they could not communicate with each other. Determined to leave no trace of connection between them, he had given her the express order not to phone him except in the direst emergency. Thus cut off, he was like a lone astronaut stranded in a disabled space capsule slowly orbiting the dark side of the moon and knowing that his return to Earth, his survival, depends on the actions of the engineers and scientists back home with whom radio contact has been severed. Were they getting anywhere in their invisible ministrations to return him to Earth? Were they even trying anymore to bring him home?

It was near the end of August, almost four weeks into this ordeal, when Dez was assailed with the paranoid conviction that the silence emanating from Connecticut had subtly changed in tone. An ominous note had entered into the vibration, like a dog whistle above human hearing but which Dez alone could detect, a flesh-crawling squeal with a subliminal hysterical edge. *Something had gone wrong with the plan.* But what? Detection? Chloe's arrest? Was she even now being held in a jail somewhere in Connecticut, bravely refusing to give up Dez's name as her accomplice? And more to the point, was she *about* to? He would work himself into a panic, then catch himself—and remember that this unbearable, inhuman silence was precisely what he had been hoping for; indeed, what he had demanded of her. This silence, this all-embracing nullity, meant that everything was going exactly to plan and all he had

to do was calm down and wait for the signal that it was time to spring the trap.

That signal would be a call from Chloe to Dez's cell phone. Using Ulrickson's home landline, she was to leave a voice mail saying, simply, "Sorry, wrong number"—then instantly hang up: at which point he would know that she had completed her mission and that they could embark on phase two. Such thoughts calmed him. But only momentarily. Soon he would be back to conjuring, from her silence, the darkest imaginings of failure, exposure, arrest and imprisonment.

Added to all his usual torments, he felt a stab of indignation. Of hurt. Did she not miss him? Did she not wonder about him, about his state of mind and heart? How could she so coldly obey his orders not to call? How could she leave him out in the interstellar darkness, orbiting alone? And, strangely, it was this question, as much as his concern for the progress of the plan, that finally prompted Dez, on a chilly, blue-bright morning at the beginning of September when the deciduous trees around his trailer had begun to turn orange at their tips like matches photographed at the precise moment they were struck, and the snowbirds in their neighboring RVs were already packing up to begin the long trek to Florida, chasing the sun—almost a month and a half after she had left Vermont—to realize that he could stand it no longer. He must make contact.

Telephoning was out of the question. He refused to leave, as a trail for the lawmen, any record of connection between their two cell phones. But neither could he, say, bike to the

pizza parlor and use the pay phone to call Ulrickson's landline. Even assuming that he could dream up a plausible pretext to get around the man and have Chloe summoned to the phone, he could too clearly imagine Ulrickson hovering in the background while she tried to talk, or (far worse) listening in on the call. To hope that he might happen to phone when Chloe was home alone was pure fantasy: Ulrickson was a writer, and thus a virtual shut-in.

No. There was one way, and one way only, to satisfy his gnawing, cancerous, killing curiosity. He would have to go to Connecticut. He would have to risk once again invading Ulrickson's home. He would have to *act*.

3

He rose the next day at dawn after a sleepless night of planning. At six, he phoned his boss and, pinching his nose between index finger and thumb, left a voice mail saying that he'd been laid low by flu and would not be able to make it into the bar tonight. Then he called jetBlue and loaded onto his already overburdened MasterCard the price of a return ticket from Burlington to JFK, departing at 10:50 that morning. He showered, then addressed his reflection in the misty postage stamp–sized mirror above the sink in the bathroom cubicle. He had not shaved in weeks. A dark, curly, unpleasantly pubic-looking growth now covered the lower half of his face. He dispensed a mound of shaving cream onto his palm and was about to

apply it to his wetted beard when he abruptly came to his senses. Peering at the unfamiliar face in the mirror—a gaunt, dark-bearded, hollow-eyed, pre-fame Dr. Freud—he realized that he had, unwittingly, prepared the perfect disguise for his planned exploit. No one would mistake this sensitive-looking, bearded intellectual for the overall-clad, peaked-capped furnace repairman whom Ulrickson had met back in May. Beard intact, he rinsed off his hand and set down his razor.

He donned the slightly out-of-date dark suit that had done duty in his role as Innocence Project lawyer at the G-Tek Clinic. Then he mounted his bicycle and rode into Sayer's Cliff, where he bought a fried egg sandwich and a Greyhound ticket to Burlington airport. It felt inexpressibly good to be on the move again, no longer passively waiting.

His flight (another blessedly uneventful passage) landed at JFK a little after noon. Driving a new rental car north into Connecticut, he watched the flow of oncoming traffic across the median and tried to imagine how he would be feeling when he was traveling along this stretch of highway back to the airport, mission accomplished. Would he be in despair over discovering that the plan had capsized, or in a state of exultant triumph?

He glided into Clay Cross's wealthy purlieus, swooshing smoothly along the well-tended, tree-lined streets. He felt the usual surge of preperformance anxiety and excitement, a fluttering in the stomach and a racing of the pulse. Turning onto Cherry Tree Lane, he progressed a quarter of a mile beneath the thinning canopy of turning, late summer leaves, until he saw

Ulrickson's house appear a few hundred yards ahead, on his left. Drawing closer, he noticed that there were two cars parked out front: Ulrickson's Jeep and a boxy black SUV—the retrofitted minivan that the home care worker used to ferry the stroked-out wife back and forth to the local hospital for her physiotherapy. He'd read about it in the memoir. There was also a bicycle lying on its side on the front lawn.

A red, adult-sized ten-speed.

Chloe's, he surmised. This boded well. If she'd been arrested, surely Ulrickson would not have left her bike out front.

He parked by the curb, got out and eased the door shut. The stealth of his mission made him reluctant to fling it shut with a neighborhood-rousing slam. He ran a nervous palm from back to front over his hair, straightened his tie, then walked up the flagstone path to the front door and pushed the bell. He could hear activity inside—a muffled female voice, with an Indian accent: "I will get it." Footsteps. Then the door opened and he was looking into the face of a short, plump, dark-skinned woman who smiled at him, clearly puzzled. This, he realized, must be the home care worker, Deepti. He had not had the pleasure on his last visit.

"Dr. Geld," Dez said in a lightly inflected Teutonic accent. He extended between two fingers a business card bearing the name and phone number of his old psychotherapist. The legendary sexologist had passed away a few years earlier. Dez, during his treatments, had had the foresight to steal a small stack of Geld's business cards, on the theory that they might be useful to him someday.

Deepti took the card, looked at it, then back at Dez, uncomprehending. "I'm sorry . . . ?" she said, handing the card back.

"I have a four o'clock meeting," Dez said, repocketing the card. "With Mr. Ulrickson's daughter. Vermont Department of Children and Families arranged it. A routine status follow-up."

"Mr. Ulrickson is expecting you?" she asked.

"I believe so," Dez said.

"He did not mention anything."

Dez pulled a notebook from his jacket pocket, glanced into it, then put it back. "Yes," he said. "Wednesday, four o'clock."

She asked him to step inside. "Your name again?"

"Dr. Geld."

She hastened away.

Dez consulted his reflection in the gilt-framed mirror that hung on the wall above a small crescent-shaped mail table. He admired his beard and modified Caesar hairdo (he had thought to finger-comb forward his thinning hair to mitigate the widow's peak that was such a distinctive feature of his face). He flexed his lips and tongue, like an actor before taking the stage. Gradually, as his nervous system calmed, he became aware of a sound emanating from a nearby recess of the house: a young woman's voice speaking in a gentle, incantatory manner. He had dismissed it as the murmur of a radio or television, but something in its familiar cadences made him realize that the voice belonged to Chloe.

He moved on silent tiptoe to the end of the vestibule, where he stopped and peered into the living space.

She was some ten feet or so down the room, seated, facing

him, on a beige sofa. The younger child, the one he had stolen the sample from—the brat Maddy—was on her lap. Chloe, with one hand, stroked the child's bobbed brown hair, and with the other she held a book from which she was reading aloud. Dez could just make out the title: *The Little Prince*. Directly in front of Chloe, with her back to him, sat Ulrickson's wife in her wheelchair, immobile, hunched.

It was a picture of happy, healthy domesticity—of family harmony—the likes of which Dez had, in all his nights of recent insomnias, never once conjured as a possibility. He could not have said what, exactly, he expected to find at the house on this visit of inspection, but this wholesome tableau was not it. What could it portend?

He was about to pull his head back around the corner of the door frame, to feint back into the foyer, when Chloe caught the shadow of his movement, looked up and saw him. The beard and suit could not for a moment disguise him. The shock jolted her whole body. Dez saw a deep blush flow upward from the neck of her baggy gray sweatshirt into her face. With her eyes locked on him, she shifted Maddy onto the sofa and rose quickly to her feet.

She was plumper, better fed than he had ever seen her, and if he was not hallucinating, those shorts she was wearing (her legs were, if anything, more beautifully sculpted for all their extra muscle mass) were *tennis* shorts, and she wore anklet socks with pom-poms and a pair of those revolting puffy running shoes with the thick molded soles and despicable bands of nylon and rubber and webbing and God knows what else forming a garish pattern from heel to toe. With her hair pulled back into

a ponytail, her lashes free of mascara and lids free of eyeliner, her mouth innocent of gloss or lipstick, she looked for all the world like a scrubbed and buffed upper-middle-class Connecticut preppie, a pampered daughter of the Northeast, jock-like, essentially sexless.

"What are you doing h—" she started to say, and then slapped a hand over her mouth. There was a sound of approaching footsteps. Her eyes flashed.

"Keep reading, Chloe!" Maddy cried.

Chloe sat down again and Maddy climbed back onto her lap. Dez retreated a half step into the foyer.

Deepti came around the corner from the hallway. "Mr. Jasper will be right with you," she said and went into the kitchen.

A few racking heartbeats later, Ulrickson appeared. Dez noticed instantly that, in contrast to Chloe, he had *lost* weight, his blue dress shirt standing out from his neck, the waistline of his khaki pants cinched in with his belt. His face looked narrowed, almost gaunt, his eye sockets shadowed. *Was this a product of overwork?* Dez wondered. He had said, during Dez's last visit, that he was writing a new novel—or was his emaciation the result of some other stress in his life?

"Can I help you?" Jasper said, stopping a couple of paces in front of Dez.

Dez explained that Vermont Child Services had arranged for him to do a psychological assessment of Chloe.

"I'm afraid that this is the first I've heard of it," Jasper said. "Chloe?" He turned. "Do you know anything about an appointment?"

Dez, rising on tiptoe and peering over Ulrickson's shoulder, caught Chloe's eye. He nodded vehemently.

"I forgot," she told Jasper. "They called a couple of days ago."

"Oh—well," Jasper said, turning back to Dez, who had dropped back onto his heels and rearranged his features into a bland smile, "it seems I owe you an apology."

"Not at all," Dez said. "Teenagers."

"The thing is," Jasper said, "Chloe saw a social worker just last week. We were told that she's adjusting well. Better than expected. So I wonder if it's really necessary—"

"A social work assessment is one thing," Dez interrupted. He smiled with just a hint of condescension. "As a psychiatrist—a *medical doctor*—my job is to make sure that various *deeper*, psychodynamic needs are being met."

Jasper nodded slowly. "I see," he said. "So would this be a private session? I mean, would you need me or my other daughter too? We've had some group work."

"Oh, no—purely one on one," Dez assured him. "We will need only a private room, away from the rest of the family—not, however, the child's bedchamber. A more neutral environment."

Jasper paused, thinking this over. "I suppose you can use my office," he said. "I was about to take a break anyway."

"That sounds perfectly perfect," said Dez.

Jasper led him into the living room to meet the "patient." At their approach, Chloe rose from the sofa. She shook Dez's extended hand but avoided his eye. *What*, he wondered, *has been going on here?*

"Does Chloe have to stop reading?" Maddy asked.

Dez smiled down at the little girl. "I promise not to keep her long," he said. Then he turned to Pauline. "And of course I know *you*. I've read your husband's magnificent memoir—which is already a classic in psychiatric circles." He bowed, bringing his face down to Pauline's level. He saw her eyes kindle. Was she *recognizing* him? He quickly straightened.

Jasper led them down the hall and into his office. Dez swept his gaze around the room. It was, to the last detail, the clichéd writer's den: Persian carpet underfoot, deep leather sofa and armchair, floor-to-ceiling bookcases, stout wooden desk upon which Dez half expected to see an old Remington typewriter. Instead, there was an iMac. A number of framed posters featuring the covers of Ulrickson's inane mystery novels were hung on the walls. Heavy curtains covered the one window. "Quite perfect," Dez said. "Thank you."

"And how long will you need?" Jasper asked, moving to the door.

"The standard therapeutic hour," Dez said. "Fifty minutes."

Jasper nodded, glanced at Chloe, smiled and then went out, closing the door behind him.

4

Dez waited until Jasper's footsteps had faded, then he stepped quickly to the door and twisted the small latch under the knob, locking them in. He turned to face Chloe, who was standing, frozen, in the middle of the room, watching him. He saw her eyes flash quickly around, as if she were searching for an escape route. Indeed, for a crazed moment, she imagined diving for the window, clawing the curtains aside and clambering out to freedom. Instead, she turned her eyes back to him. Her lips quivered into a feeble smile that quickly died. He couldn't help noticing that she did not run into his arms, as she would have done just a few short weeks ago.

"So," Dez said, also holding his ground. "Alone at last."

"Why are you here?" she almost shouted.

Dez shrugged, smiled. "Got lonesome. But let's keep it down. I'd hate for our host to get curious." He looked over at the leather sofa. "Come," he said. "Sit."

Without taking her eyes off him, she moved to the sofa and lowered herself onto its creaking leather. Dez sat on the armchair adjacent to her, assuming the position he would have taken if this were an actual therapy session, or a *New Yorker* cartoon. But Chloe, instead of lying on the sofa, remained sitting up alertly, her joined hands between her knees. (She felt ready, at any moment, to run, should he pounce on her.) Dez, unconsciously adopting the role of doctor of the mind, said nothing, simply regarded her with a quizzical expression.

"I thought you said we weren't supposed to be in touch," Chloe said. "I mean, until . . . well, *until.*"

"Correct," Dez said. "And I am quite naughty for breaking my own rule. But I got restless, back home. I was curious as to how the plan was proceeding. And," he added with a bitter little self-mocking smile, "I missed you."

She looked away. Her brow wrinkled and she began to work her mouth as if she were rolling something around inside it. Apparently, she was not going to tell Dez that she had missed *him*.

"So," he said, "can I assume, from this cool reception, that the plan has run into a snag?"

She continued to avoid his eyes. Almost a minute passed. Dez waited. Suddenly, she turned and looked at him with an expression of desperate, pleading appeal—an appeal for understanding,

for mercy. "Oh God, Dez," she burst out. "I'm sorry. I'm so sorry! I would have told you. I *should* have told you. Probably fifty times I picked up the phone to call you. But I couldn't. I just couldn't." She began to cry.

Dez, with all the cool dispassion of his former psychiatrist, said, "Take your time."

She swallowed her sobs, and then wiped her nose with the inside of her wrist. "I knew right away that it wasn't going to work," she said. She described how practically the second she laid eyes on Jasper, in that courthouse, she knew that it wasn't going to happen. His eyes were so warm and kind, and he looked at her with such love. A *father's* love. She had never seen that look before. Every other man stared at her with hunger, sneaky desire or open lust. Not Jasper. He looked at her as if he wanted to protect her, to teach her things, to be an example to her. She must have been waiting for such a thing all her life.

"Don't get me wrong," she said. "I tried."

On the long drive down from Vermont, she showed him her legs; she looked at him in that way that made men melt. But it had no effect. He didn't react the way other men did. He continued to look at her like a father. And she felt so grateful. Grateful and happy. To be looked at as a person, as someone lovable. Not just—just *fuckable*. It meant everything to her. Could Dez see that?

"Please," he said, "go on."

Well, she said, when they got home, here, to this house, and she saw Pauline—that poor woman—trapped in her wheelchair, in her silence, and the little girl, Maddy, who was so brave and

smart and funny and who was so happy to have a big sister—well, it made things even harder. Still, she tried! That first night, when the others had gone to bed, Chloe talked her way into his bedroom, sat on his bed, cried and got him to comfort her, and she climbed onto his lap and tried to make him kiss her. But he just held her and rocked her like a *baby*, and it was so nice, and that's when she started to be sure that he wasn't going to do anything bad, anything he shouldn't do. And then he took her to her own bedroom and showed her everything that he had bought for her—and it wasn't the things themselves, wasn't the *money* he had spent, it was the thoughtfulness, the idea that he had devoted days and maybe weeks to thinking about her, thinking about what she might want, and then assembling these things and surprising her with them—well, really, it was *then* that she just knew. Knew it was impossible. That was when she became his daughter, became part of the family.

She started helping Deepti with the grocery shopping and the cooking and the cleaning and with looking after Pauline. She began reading to Pauline every day and taking her on walks through the neighborhood, pushing her wheelchair along the sidewalk. And meanwhile, Dad—well, she called Ulrickson "Dad" now, and it didn't even seem strange—Dad got her a membership at the tennis club and she was learning how to play and she turned out to have a lot of natural talent for the game and she had made friends with some of the teenagers there—they weren't half as snobby as you would think, even though they went to private schools, but of course Chloe was going to be attending one of those schools in a few days herself, and

when she went for an orientation session last week, it wasn't nearly so scary as she had thought it would be. All the teachers and the principal were so nice, and they assured her that it would not be long at all before she was up to speed with the other students. So before she knew it, she had just fallen into life here, with Jasper as her dad and Pauline as her mom and Maddy as her little sister and sweet Deepti. It all just *happened*.

"I didn't want it to," she said. "I never saw it coming. But I'm happy, Dez. I can't help it, I'm happy. You know, I . . ." She paused, then went on in a near whisper: "What we had . . . it wasn't right. Wasn't normal. Now I can see what a normal life is. And it's funny. From all the social workers I've been talking to, I see how I always *wanted* a dad, but I didn't know it. I was messed up. I didn't think I deserved a father. So when I met *him*—" She paused, then looked at Dez pityingly. "I'm not saying I didn't love you, Dez. I did. I do. But it wasn't right. What we were doing was not right. The sex. My social worker told me that what I *really* wanted was a daddy. I was *sublimating*, she told me."

He felt an impulse to throw himself at her, to seize her with one strong claw around her tender throat; but he could not risk her crying out and, besides, there was the old problem of his aversion to violence. The thought of hurting her made his gorge rise. He choked out a question: "Are you saying you *can't* go through with it, or you *won't* go through with it?"

She gestured helplessly. "Both," she said. "I can't do it. He's my father! He is my father now, Dez. And girls don't sleep with their fathers! And I *won't* go through with it because it wouldn't work anyway. You don't understand. He would never *do* it; he's

not like that. He's *good.* A decent person. Not everyone is like—" She stopped, and pressed her lips together.

"Like me?" Dez said.

"I was going to say 'like us.'" Then her expression grew excited, animated, like a religious convert bent on bringing a sinner the good news. "But I've changed, Dez. And you can too. I swear. It's never too late. You just have to learn to see the good in people! And in yourself."

She talked on in this vein, this dithery, inane, ridiculous vein—for all the world like one of those morons on *Tovah*. But he was no longer listening. He was thinking. Thinking about how, in all his worst imaginings over the last five weeks, he had never pictured this turn of events, never admitted of its remotest possibility. How could he have been so blind? Really, he had no one to blame but himself. He could have—he *should* have—seen that the girl was not up to the task, that she was fatally afflicted with a conscience; all that weeping and wailing over the death of her despised mother should have been the tip-off. But he had not seen what was directly under his nose.

"Say something, Dez," Chloe begged. "Please say something."

"What can I say?" he managed, finally, to squeeze out through the strange constriction in his throat. "How could I possibly have anticipated how pathologically needy you are? How emotionally damaged and deficient?"

"Please, Dez," she said, "don't."

If Chloe had been a very different person, he might have suspected her of having planned this double cross: letting him go through the dangerous and difficult machinations that

established her as one of the rightful heirs to the fortune of a wealthy man, only to cut Dez loose and keep all the spoils to herself. But there was no question of Chloe being so duplicitous, so calculating. The problem was precisely the opposite: she was so fundamentally innocent, so malleable and impressionable, and that is why she had fallen in love with Ulrickson and his loathsome, freakish family—gone hopelessly native. A victim of Stockholm syndrome. *That* was why the plan had gone awry. There was, equally, no point in trying to force her back on track by issuing empty ultimatums, threatening to expose her to Ulrickson unless she continued with the plan. That would mean admitting his own role in the hoax, implicating himself. No. No, it was done. All done. He had lost. He would have to skulk back to the trailer park, tail between his legs, leave Chloe to the ideal life he had unwittingly bestowed upon her.

The sight of her sitting there, her face brimming with pitying compassion for him, was enraging. If he could do anything to disrupt the life that Chloe was imagining for herself, he would do it; he would do what it took to destroy both her and Ulrickson. But what?

An idea came to him—a sad compromise in comparison with the original plan. But better than nothing.

He jumped to his feet and hurried to the desk. He gingerly slid open the central drawer and peered inside. He carefully lifted a notebook and looked underneath it. He riffled through a small stack of papers. He moved aside pencils and bottles of ink, then replaced them in their exact positions.

"What are you doing?" Chloe said, having risen from the sofa. "Don't do that!"

Ignoring her, he slid open a deep drawer to the right of the kneehole. It contained a set of hanging file folders. He thumbed through the identification tabs: "Insurance," "Maddy's drawings," "Bannister contracts," "Royalty statements," "*Lessons from My Daughter* MS." He pushed in the drawer and opened another. Chloe appeared beside him. She reached out to stop him, but he gave her a murderous glare and she instantly stepped back.

"At least tell me what you're looking for," she said.

"Numbers," he said, paging through a ledger book he'd found in a bottom drawer. "Social Security, ATMs, bank accounts, investment accounts, PINs. If I can't take him down as planned, I'll do it this way. Cruder, less elegant. But better than nothing. I can probably empty two or three accounts—funnel them into a Swiss bank—before he notices a penny is missing."

"Dez, no. Please don't."

He pulled open a shallow drawer. It was filled with antiquarian ink bottles, crow quill pens, paper clip boxes and other vintage office supplies. He pushed it closed. "Fuck!" he said. His gaze fell on Ulrickson's computer. What he needed must be in there! Who used bankbooks and tellers anymore? He tapped the keyboard. An alert box popped up requesting the password to waken the computer. He looked at Chloe.

She held up her hands. "*I* don't know it," she said, quite honestly.

"Does he have a pet?" Dez asked. He'd read somewhere that everyone with a filthy animal used the pet's name for a password.

"No pets," she said with enraging satisfaction.

He cursed. Then he typed *m-a-d-d-y* and hit Return. The alert box wiggled back and forth, in one of those coy animations that mimicked a head shaking. He could have smashed the machine to pieces. He tried the wife's name. Then Chloe's. He looked at his watch. Eight minutes until the end of the session. A thought struck him. He wrenched open the middle drawer and grabbed up the passport he'd seen lying there. He turned to the page listing Jasper's birthdate. September 10, 1965. Forty-two years old as of two days ago.

He typed in *0-9-1-0-6-5*. The alert box wiggled. He tried *1-0-9-6-5*. Then he tried *s-e-p-t-1-0-6-5*. And several other variants. Nothing. He dropped back in the chair. He could spend the next hour coming up with variations on that date. And who knew if the man's birthdate was even the key to his password? Dez stared vacantly, his unseeing eyes directed at the wall opposite, where a framed poster for one of Ulrickson's detective novels, *Blind Man's Cuffs*, hung. It featured a painting of the sightless detective, Geoffrey Bannister, in a narrow hallway, one hand holding a set of handcuffs, the other grasping the harness of his faithful Seeing Eye dog. As the image came into focus for Dez, the epiphany was immediate: as if Dez, himself blind, could suddenly see. He shot forward in the chair, typed *s-m-o-k-e-y*, then hit Return. The hard disk revived with a muffled clunk, there was a humming sound, and the screen sprang to life, flooding his face with light.

"No!" Chloe said, reaching for his hands on the keyboard. He swung his elbow and hit the point of her pelvis. "Ow!" she

cried. She retreated, massaging her hip, backing toward the door. "If you don't stop right now," she said, "I'll tell him."

He ignored her. His eyes moved over the screen, darting back and forth as if he were watching a speeded-up tennis match. A look of disbelief on his face.

"What is it?" she said.

"My God," he whispered. His eyes continued moving side to side, his fingers on the mouse.

"Stop it!" she said. Her back came into contact with the door. She grasped the knob. "I'm serious. If you don't stop right now, I'll open this door. I'll call him. I swear!" That this was an empty threat, and that she had now been assailed with a terrible premonitory sense of doom over what Dez was seeing on that screen, was obvious to her when she failed to make a move, allowing Dez to continue his rapt study of whatever was on the computer. A full minute passed.

"You might want to take a look at this," he said at length. He looked up from the screen and lifted his hands from the keyboard and mouse and held them, palms outward, at shoulder height. He pushed the chair back, stood and stepped away from the desk. "See for yourself. You wouldn't believe me if I told you."

With a terrible foreboding, yet unable to resist, she came forward, came around the corner of the desk and bent close to the screen. She hoped to see a banking document or a spreadsheet. Figures, balances. Instead, she saw words—a text document, something Jasper had been writing. She assumed it was his novel, which he'd been working on relentlessly, eight hours a day. But why did Dez want her to read that?

She leaned closer. She saw the words: ". . . her unbearably lovely legs, her weepingly beautiful skin, her thrilling breasts." Her eyes skittered off to another part of the screen: ". . . consumed by guilt and shame but I cannot end this madness." She glanced down to the last phrase he had written: ". . . masturbate three times a day; still, the mere sight of her, the smell of her, the sound of her soft voice makes my tortured member rise again—"

She looked at Dez, who was standing beside her, his arms folded across his chest. "What is this?" she said.

Dez reached for the mouse and scrolled up. She saw the words: ". . . figure out why the merest movement of her hand does this to me? The sway of her walk? The sound of her laughter? My own child. My Chloe. This insane life-crippling lust that moves me to acts of vile degradation . . ."

"You wrote this!" she cried. "Just now—you wrote this! He never, he couldn't, he wouldn't . . ."

Dez continued to scroll, past entries written weeks ago, carefully dated. He paused so that, together, they could read: ". . . was getting ready for her bath and me like some insane fiend, trying not to look and yet unable to stop looking . . ." He scrolled higher: ". . . thank God has noticed nothing and must never notice anything. I will keep her inviolate, pure, innocent of my illness. With the aid of this diary, where I hope to purge and exorcise this madness, I pray that I can conquer . . ." He scrolled higher: ". . . I crept into her room after she went out to see friends and, to my shamed horror and disbelief, on the pretext of 'tidying up,' lifted from the floor the underwear that lay, like a figure eight, on the carpet, and raised it to my face . . ."

She clapped her hand over her mouth.

Dez began to pace ruminatively in front of the desk. "I confess, it's a shock—even for me," he said. "Given what you told me about his goodness. His virtue. The purity of his fatherly feelings." He halted and looked at her. "Of course, you know the worst of it."

She stared at him, uncomprehending.

"Why, poor Maddy, of course," he said, as if this were self-evident. "Well," he shrugged, "in a few years."

"Maddy?" she said. Then understanding dawned. "*Maddy!*"

"Certainly," Dez said. "These men all follow a pattern."

In reality, he felt certain that Ulrickson posed no threat to Maddy—or any other girl. It was Dez who had created the special circumstances necessary to waken the beast in Ulrickson, with Chloe as his instrument, his weapon. But there was no reason to point this out to her. Just the opposite. Indeed, now he began to wonder, aloud, about precisely *when* Ulrickson would start to interfere with the younger girl.

"Will he wait until she's a teenager, like you?" he mused. "Or will he get started earlier? At seven or eight? Or will it be tomorrow? Or later today?"

"Stop!" Chloe said, putting her hands over her ears.

Dez stepped nimbly around the corner of the desk. He crouched beside her chair. "But we can *stop* it," he said urgently. "If we go back to our plan. This"—he gestured at the computer—"this shows that he's *inches* from the edge. He just needs a little shove; a little encouragement. Then he can never hurt anyone again, never exploit or abandon anyone—the way

he abandoned your mother. The way he was planning to do with you. And, one day, Maddy."

Chloe was reeling from the revelations of the diary. Of how the man whom she had assumed loved her as a father had actually been seeing her. She felt the cathedral of love and trust that she had built, within herself, for Jasper crumble to dust; and she saw the truth of Dez's warnings about Maddy. Appalled at her own gullibility, and at Jasper's sickness, she clutched at Dez. "I'm sorry," she cried into his shoulder. "I'm sorry! He fooled me! He fooled me!"

"Yes, he did," Dez said soothingly. "Just like he fooled your mother. Just like he fooled all the readers of his book, and all the people who watched him on *Tovah*. They all think he's a saint. And they'll think he's a saint even when he's diddling Maddy." He took her head between his hands and lifted it from his shoulder. He looked into her eyes. "Unless we stop him," he said. "Unless *you* stop him."

Chloe stared, stricken, into his eyes. She knew, now, what he was suggesting, what he was urging her to do. To return to the plan, to continue on the path of destroying Ulrickson. She was revisited by the fear that had gripped her upon first entering this house: of how the plan would destroy the family, blow it apart as surely as a bomb planted under the living room sofa. But even as this thought formed, she saw how events would unfold if Ulrickson was *not* stopped—the sickening scenario that Dez had painted: Ulrickson's eventual molestation of Maddy. And that would be worse, far worse for the little girl, than the consequences of enacting Dez's plan. Indeed, it was only by returning

to the scheme that she could save Maddy. Dez was right. She was wrong ever to doubt him.

"Chloe," Dez said softly. He had seen the capitulation in her eyes. "Are we back on track?"

She stifled a sob, and nodded. Then a thought occurred to her. A terrible impediment. "But he says right here that he'd never *do* it," she said, pointing at the computer screen. "He says he'd never actually give in."

"Oh, that," he said. "All he needs is some enabling. Some . . ." He paused, looking for the right word. "Some *permission*."

5

Sitting silently on the sofa beside Maddy and Pauline as he waited for Chloe's therapy session to end, Jasper turned over and over in his mind the subject that had obsessed him for weeks, occupied his every thought to the exclusion of all other interests, preoccupations, duties or ambitions. His monstrous sickness. His vile lust. Specifically, he was thinking about the distance it had placed between him and the two people who sat next to him. For quite apart from the suicidal self-loathing that his lust gave rise to, it was this intergalactic gap between him and his family that caused him the greatest pain, the greatest grief.

His reaction to his grotesque secret had been to absent himself from the family, to skulk off to his office at every opportunity—

not to write his new Bannister mystery, as he would ostentatiously announce. *That* project, about an impersonating psychopathic trickster, was now as dead to him as everything else about his former life. He had not written a word of the novel since Chloe's arrival. Instead, he would sit at his computer and pour out feverish diary entries, confessing his shame and humiliation, his yearning and desire, his self-disgust, meanwhile cataloging every tiny aspect of her physical beauty, as if fixing these phenomena in words could expunge their effect on his soul. Yet no amount of written description, no amount of self-abasing confession, no amount of self-abuse, could dispel the insane desire. It only deepened, grew more obsessive. And he drifted further from everyone and everything he once loved.

When not writing diary entries, he searched the Internet for books and essays about incest, trying to understand his sickness. That he happened to fall into that category of male most at risk for transgressing—celibate middle-aged men who meet their daughters for the first time when the girls are in their teens or twenties—offered no comfort. Jasper believed all people to be masters of their own appetites and destinies: no excuse could exist for such feelings. He felt this with particular shame when reading the case histories of incest victims—and of the other family members affected by a parent's monstrous betrayal. The shattered trust, the broken spirits, the shame and self-blame of the victims—this was unbearable to read about. And yet, even knowing this, his desire for the child only grew! That pheromone-based fail-safe system about which he had mused on the drive down from Vermont apparently did not exist—or was powerless to check his fatal lust.

He looked at his wife and child. Like people glimpsed through the wrong end of a telescope, they seemed strangely diminished, distant figures. Pauline's gaze shifted to him, and he saw in it a desperate yearning to connect. He looked away, avoiding her beseeching gaze, pretending he did not see it, directing his eyes back to the unseen book open on his lap. This weasel-like evasiveness had been his strategy for weeks. Adopting a brittle tone of false normality, he would announce that he had reached a "difficult passage" in his novel and didn't want to "lose the momentum"—hence his need to retreat, to disappear to his office for a bout of supposed novel writing.

Sitting there now, on the sofa, he asked himself, *when* did healthy paternal love turn into this unspeakable sickness? In retrospect, it was obvious that the spark of obsession was immediate, from the moment his eyes first fell upon her in the courthouse. That instinct to hold her at arm's length—he recognized that reflex now as a subconscious reaction to the desire he knew he could not allow himself to feel or acknowledge. On the car ride from Vermont, he had willed himself to stop staring at her. Any erotic flickerings that he might have acknowledged were successfully dismissed as the action of memory—memories of Holly, whom Chloe so closely resembled. Then came that glimpse of her on the driveway; on the sofa as she showed him her yoga exercises; those moments when she sat on his lap in the semi-darkness of his bedroom and leaned her face so close to his, so close . . . yet still he had successfully fooled himself. Denied what was so obviously taking place within him, allowed himself to believe that the stirrings were only the wholesome surges

of normal fatherly love. That is, until the shattering moment of revelation: that dream he had had of Chloe spooning with him in bed, pressing her buttocks against him—after which he no longer was able to deny what had been silently breeding, incubating like a virus, within him. He had not been able to sleep or eat in the weeks since that vision. His life had become a waking nightmare.

Gone was his routine of reading with Pauline his daily fan letters; no longer did he sit with Maddy in his lap after preschool and ask about her day. He ate his meals hurriedly, eyes on his plate, evading Pauline's pleading stare and trying not to look at Chloe, with whom he adopted a pose of cool paternal reserve even as he engaged in the most revolting, unconscionable, unforgivable, surreptitious voyeurism; for despite all the chilly distance he attempted to put between them, despite his efforts not to feast upon her with his eyes, he could not keep his gaze from straying over when she was not aware, from trying to gulp down great stolen glimpses of her beauty on which he would later sustain himself. Thinking of this now, he was engulfed by a wave of agonizing guilt the more potent for the mocking libidinal excitement those memories of her awoke within him.

In a bid to arrest the dreadful tumescence, the humiliating hardening, he again turned his attention to his wife and daughter. Maddy was lightly chanting a song—the same song she had been singing now for days—the alphabet song she learned in preschool. She never sang it through to completion. Her habit was to chant a few bars, then abruptly break off, sometimes near the beginning, or middle, or near the end, only to begin

again from the start. A few weeks ago, he would have delighted in her singing, fetched his video camera to tape it. Now, he found inexpressibly irritating her unending repetition of this simple tune, its minor scale sung on a dying fall—incomplete, oddly joyless and dutiful. Unable to bear for a second longer the sound of her voice feeling its way cautiously along that melody, he turned and snapped at her, "Why do you keep *singing* that?"

She was scribbling with a crayon. She stopped and looked at him. "I learned it from the butterfly man," she said.

"Who?"

"You know. That man. The butterfly man."

He frowned and opened his mouth to ask what this could possibly mean—but at that moment, he heard the click and creak of his office door. His heart kicked in his chest and all thought of Maddy was driven from his mind. He turned and saw his obsession step into the hallway. Even in that baggy sweatshirt, those formless shorts and those terrible running shoes, she was a vision, a deadly virus of desire.

"Chloe!" Maddy cried, bouncing her bottom on the sofa. "Keep reading to us!"

"Of course," she said, approaching from down the hall.

Jasper stood and stepped quickly away from the sofa, to make room for Chloe to sit down again with Maddy. As was his habit, he kept his eyes directed down and away from her. But she veered over to where he stood and stopped in front of him, forcing him to look at her. She whispered: "The doctor wants to talk to you."

"Me?" Jasper said, startled. He looked down the hall. Dr. Geld

was standing in the office doorway, arms folded, one foot crossed jauntily over the opposite ankle. Watching them. Jasper turned back to Chloe. She had an unreadable look on her face. Her eyes were red, as if she had been crying. Panic bucked in his chest.

"He wants to talk to you about something I told him," she whispered. "Something . . . private. I hope you won't be mad."

His mouth went dry. What had she said to this man? What was going on? The doctor had expressly said that he did not need to speak to anyone but Chloe. He looked at Pauline. She stared at him with that inexplicable message of warning.

"He wants to talk to you *now*," Chloe said.

There was no escape. He could not very well refuse to meet with his daughter's court-ordered therapist. And so, with a deep sense of foreboding, like a man mounting the gallows, he turned and walked down the hall.

6

Dez, watching Jasper's approach, was struck now by the clear signs of psychological distress that he had, earlier, stupidly misread as overwork: the haggard face, the haunted stare, the weight loss, the hangdog, sheepish, guilty look in the eyes. This was a man in the end stages of acute sexual despair. How could he have failed to read the symptoms! In any case, he read them now, and they told him that his work would not be difficult.

"Thank you for taking the time to talk to me," Dez said, stepping aside to allow Jasper to enter the room. He followed his victim inside, then shut the door behind them.

"So what's this all about?" Jasper asked, turning to face Dez. He spoke in as casual a voice as he could muster. "I thought you said you needed to speak only to Chloe."

"If you wouldn't mind," Dez said, indicating with a wave of one hand the sofa that Chloe had recently vacated. "This won't take a minute. Something has come up. I think it best we nip it in the bud."

Jasper felt a fresh jolt of panic. Had he been less successful than he supposed in disguising his yearning for Chloe? Had she noticed something—and spoken of it to this man? She had seemed so happy, so well adjusted, so serenely untroubled by any of the evils her transitioning social worker had told him to look out for, and so unaware of his toxic lust. But was she? He tried to keep his features and voice neutral when he said as he sat down on the sofa, "I hope it's nothing—nothing serious."

"Well," Dez said, resuming his place in the armchair, "I'm afraid it could *become* serious if it is not attended to in a timely fashion."

Jasper studied Dr. Geld's face: a lean, handsome face, but one whose skull-like qualities were not much mitigated by the presence of the short dark beard that clung to his jaws and chin. The man was scrutinizing him with a slight smile, and Jasper was suddenly filled with the odd conviction that he *knew* this man, that he had seen him before, talked with him: something about the almost mocking, insolent frankness in his pale, colorless eyes. Jasper dismissed this as a play of nerves.

Dez, in turn, studied Jasper's face, cataloging the tics and twitches that made his victim's pale, perspiring cheek flicker and spasm and that pulled one corner of his mouth into a desperate attempt at a smile. This was sheer delight! He could have stared at it all day—but there was work to do.

"Mr. Ulrickson," he said at length, "would it surprise you to learn that your daughter has been harboring strong sexual desires for you?"

From thinking that Geld was going to ambush him with questions about his criminal lust for Chloe, he had been hit from a wholly unexpected direction—like the boxer who, feinting from the anticipated left jab, is all the more stunned by a strong right hook. He could do nothing but helplessly move his lower jaw up and down. He produced no sound.

"Your daughter," said Dez, "has volunteered to me, in her session, that she has an overwhelming desire to make love to you. She has, to be frank, alleviated these feelings, as best she can, through onanism—but such a palliative can be only so successful when true obsession is at work, and I'm afraid that that is what we have in this case. Obsession. Compulsive, neurotic, sexual obsession. Now, before you judge her too harshly—before you accuse her of deviancy—I think it is essential that you understand that these erotic reactions are, within the situational matrix in which she finds herself, not only quite predictable but quite normal."

"Normal," Jasper said in a parched whisper. He was dazed, dizzy, barely able to form the word.

"Quite normal," Dez reiterated. "How familiar are you with the tenets of Freudian psychotherapy?"

Jasper shook his head. "Not very."

Dez happened to be well versed in the subject. While in the care of Dr. Geld, he had received many lectures on Freud. And indeed, in his younger days, when struggling to understand and

curtail his compulsions, he had read widely in the Master and his followers—all to no avail, of course.

"Even in some psychoanalytic circles," Dez said ruefully, "Freud has lost favor, his theories replaced by belief in the all-powerful pharmaceutical. I reject such fashionable apostasy and profess myself to be a strict adherent to the urtexts, and to what they tell us of the invisible currents of motivation and desire that shape our minute-to-minute, second-to-second actions. To say nothing of the fundamental building blocks of identity, which is what concerns us at present." Dez scrutinized Jasper for a few silent seconds over his joined fingertips. "You are, undoubtedly, familiar with the term 'Oedipus complex'?" he went on. Jasper nodded weakly. "Most people are—at least in rough outline," Dez said. "Boys, Freud tells us, arrive at a healthy sexual identity by the successful working through of certain deep-seated urges. Namely, to remove the rival for his mother's affections, and thus consummate desire for her. Bluntly put, to kill the father and sleep with the mother. But I would wager that you are less familiar with Freud's theory of how *female* sexual identity is formed?"

"That's true," Jasper said.

"Oh, the casual male chauvinism of our sexist culture!" Dez lamented. "Well, in any case, as with boys, the process begins in earliest childhood and is activated by rivalry with the same-sex parent. Girls experience 'penis envy'—a syndrome stemming from the small child's conviction that the male sex organ, which she believes herself to have been born with, has been *stolen* from her in an act of parental castration—by the mother.

To regain the penis, the child looks to the man closest by, usually her father, literally to 'take back' the lost member. It is in this yearning for possession of the father's phallus that the daughter resolves her rage against the castrating mother and forms the underlying heterosexual erotic orientation which will, in later years, fuel her drive for marriage and procreation—a dynamic that Freud's colleague Jung dubbed the Electra Complex.

"The point I am trying to get to, Mr. Ulrickson, is that your Chloe is currently in the throes of a most severe Electra conflict. And little wonder! We have, in her, a girl who grew up never knowing her father, a girl whose adolescence was characterized by flagrant Electra struggles with her mother—the denying, rivalrous and increasingly jealous mother who happened, tragically, to die before any of these universal mother-daughter tensions could be resolved.

"Then, at the tender age of seventeen, the child bravely speaks up about the secret of her true father. At eighteen, she goes to live with that father, who proves to be a deeply understanding, loving and openhearted man: a *good* man. Well, Mr. Ulrickson, should it surprise any of us who are students of the mind—and you, sir, a writer and artist, are every inch an expert in the universal truths that I speak of; Freud himself admitted that everything he ever discovered about the mysteries of human nature was first said by Shakespeare—should it surprise us if a girl with the history of your Chloe should, once accepted into the secure embrace of her long-lost father, find awakened in her breast those very conflicts never worked through during the requisite phase, the critical window, of childhood? A century of psychoanalytic thought has

taught us nothing if not that those earliest childhood wounds do not magically heal themselves, but rather fester in the unconscious, distorting our growth and maturation, until they erupt in some form of neurotic, or worse, behavior. And that, Mr. Ulrickson, is what we see happening in your Chloe today."

"My God," Jasper whispered.

"I hasten to add," said Dez, "that she feels especially guilty because you have been such a good father—one deserving of nothing but her chaste devotion. Yet, instead, she burns with this terrible, ungovernable lust for you."

Jasper was dumbstruck.

"Do I understand, by your silence, that you had no knowledge of this?" said Dez.

"None," Jasper said weakly. "None whatsoever."

Or was this true? He suddenly recalled that doe-eyed, submissive, somehow come-hither look she gave him in the courthouse, when he first came into the small antechamber, and that charged, mischievous glance she pierced him with when she settled into the passenger seat of his car, tugging at the hem of her short skirt. The way she had displayed her legs on that car ride, and during her yoga stretches, and then, later, in his bedroom, how she had hiked herself onto his lap, crushed herself against him and stared into his eyes as if trying to hypnotize him into a kiss. Then her whispered request to sleep with him in his bed—a request that would, later (he now surmised), trigger that shattering dream.

"Perhaps . . ." Jasper said haltingly. "Perhaps there were some *small* signs, after all."

"Aah, so," said Dez.

"But tell me," Jasper said, "how did she tell *you*? About her feelings for me?"

"The truth," Dez said, "emerged quite without my prompting, in a spontaneous free association the revelatory power of which has left your daughter in a dangerous state of shame, confusion and embarrassment. What concerns me now is that we take proper action to neutralize, and *normalize*, Chloe's psychological situation. May I speak plainly? I think unvarnished frankness is imperative. You say that you 'never suspected.' But, Mr. Ulrickson, in my experience, few men in your position fail to notice what is going on inside their child, owing to the unconscious ways that we—all of us—communicate with one another. In psychoanalysis, we call it the transference and countertransference."

"I'm not sure I follow," Jasper said.

"It would be perfectly understandable, within the dynamics of the transference and countertransference, that you should, due to Chloe's invisible—and quite unconscious—machinations and projections, begin to feel an 'answering' response. Not because of any deliberate, cold-blooded or (to cast this in outmoded moral terms) *evil* effort on the part of your daughter to *seduce* you. We are speaking of purely subliminal, subconscious actions on her part to arouse in you a reciprocal erotic response—all in the interest of resolving her Electra complex, all in her bid to repossess the male organ stolen from her, and thus feel *whole*. Do you see?"

Jasper was beginning to—and the illumination filled him with dread.

"Mr. Ulrickson, what I am trying to say, in my albeit roundabout and jargon-filled manner, is that your daughter has been trying to provoke a *response* in you. May I prevail upon your admirable honesty and ask if you have experienced *any* such countertransferential reaction? Please understand that anything you say in this session is protected under patient–doctor confidentiality; nothing can or will be used to undermine your custodial rights—quite the opposite. I am groping to understand the dimensions of poor Chloe's complex in the service of *strengthening* the bond between the two of you and thus ensure that nothing occur that would lead to her forcible removal from the home."

Jasper began slowly to move his lips, but soundlessly.

"Take your time," Dez said.

"I—" Jasper said, then stopped. He felt an overwhelming urge to disburden himself. But could he reveal his terrible secret to this man? This stranger?

He could. Of course he could. Geld had come expressly to lay bare such subterranean drives and desires, to root them out and destroy them, not just in Chloe but in the rest of the family! If Jasper did not speak up *now*, when would he ever speak up?

"Yes," he said at length. "Yes—and the feeling of counter . . . counter . . . ?"

"Countertransference," Dez said.

"Those reactions have not been subtle. I've had horrible, monstrous feelings. It has been overwhelming. I hope you can help us!"

"I am here," Dez said, "to help you."

"I've bottled it up," Jasper said. "Trying to master myself.

Trying to get it out of my system by writing it down. By—if I may be completely honest—by abusing myself. Mercilessly. Repeatedly. Nothing—nothing helps."

"I must commend you for your wonderful, and quite rare, honesty," Dez said. "With many fathers, it takes far, far longer to hear the truth. But the truth is critical. Freud taught us that we must confront our demons and thus exorcise them. And make no mistake, Mr. Ulrickson, what I have heard and seen here today from your daughter—and now yourself—convinces me that this is a much more advanced case than I had feared. I see in both of you signs of acute neurosis."

"I haven't been sleeping," Jasper admitted. "And I cannot eat. *Working* has been out of the question."

"Yes," Dez said gravely. "A very advanced case. We cannot rule out the possibility that one or the other of you will do yourself harm, if the syndrome is allowed to advance unchecked."

Suicide, Jasper thought. The doctor was talking about suicide. He flashed on thoughts that had plagued him in recent weeks: images of himself stepping in front of a speeding Amtrak train, or washing down a bottle of painkillers with vodka. Never before had he indulged such thoughts, not when his parents died, not when Pauline had her stroke. But the shame and humiliation of his incestuous lust had been so terrible, death had seemed a welcome respite.

"*Have* you had suicidal thoughts?" Dez asked.

Jasper silently nodded.

"Yes . . ." Dez muttered. "And I heard clear evidence of suicidal ideation from the girl."

"Oh God," Jasper cried. "Is there anything you can do to help us?"

"I?" said Dez. "Mr. Ulrickson, I'm sure you're aware of the joke which asks: How many psychiatrists does it take to change a light bulb? Only one, but the bulb *really* has to want to change. That is, you and your daughter must do the work. You must both cease to blame yourselves for desires that society deems beyond the pale, but which psychoanalysis tells us are quite natural and even necessary. Freud often scoffed at society's pious restrictions against such perfectly normal Id-cravings. In his divine *Introductory Lectures on Psychoanalysis*, the Master, speaking to a learned audience of fellow mental healers about parent-child sexual intercourse, referred to the 'horror that is felt, or at least professed, in human society at such intercourse.' *Or at least professed!* Could he have been plainer? What hypocrisy it is to feign disgust at the powerful erotic attractions between parent and child, Freud tells us! For this delicate dance of family love is one played out in every household on Earth, where parents and children find themselves. 'The *nicest* father is but an anagram for the *incest* father,' as my training analyst in Zurich used to quip.

"But we get ahead of ourselves. We must take a proper history of the case. How have you behaved toward your daughter? Since recognizing these impulses?"

"I pulled away," Jasper said. "Physically. Emotionally. I retreated to my office. But I haven't been able to write my novel for weeks. Not since she arrived. Thank goodness she goes off to the club during the day, or sees friends. But still, she haunts me. We all have dinner together. I listen when she tells me about her

doings; I ask appropriate questions. But I minimize contact. For her own good! I'm horrified to think that she might catch even the slightest hint of the—the *urges* I am having."

"Rest assured," Dez said, "that there is nothing about your instinct for retreat that is surprising. But it is precisely the *wrong* reaction—the most damaging you could have. You must not be standoffish, rejecting, shunning. Mr. Ulrickson, we are talking about a girl deprived of a father-daughter relationship while growing up! A girl who now, at barely eighteen, is regressing and enacting all the stages of earliest infancy. Just when she is yearning for contact and connection, you stand back, you treat her coldly like the distanced, disapproving father of Victorian stereotype. I shudder to think what damage may already have been done with such a program of rejection.

"The prescription is for warmth, and expressed affection. You must break down the physical barriers you have erected, you must supply to her the touches, hugs, cuddles and kisses that she would have received from you when she was an infant, a babe in arms—what Freud and others have recognized as the sublimated sexual touching which, in fact, establishes the framework for later heterosexual responsiveness. Chloe missed all those stages with you, as infant, toddler and young child; hence her current neurosis—and your *own*. You must now make up for what was denied to her in her developmental stages. Mr. Ulrickson, you must feel no prohibition against physically expressed affection!"

"But she's almost an adult now," Jasper protested. "She's no longer in that childhood phase when—"

"Mr. Ulrickson," Dez interrupted. "Surely you, as a writer, know that this carapace of maturity that we all come cloaked in is merely that: a covering, a disguise—a shroud. Underneath, we remain frightened, needy children. Yes, your daughter has grown into a young woman. But this makes her no less a baby, *your* baby, who aches, with all her being, for your touch, for your caresses."

"But," Jasper persisted, "with all the feelings, the suppressed feelings, that we have for each other—"

"Do you suppose that pulling back, withdrawing, *withholding* is a better prescription for dispersing those yearnings?" Dez said. He smiled and dropped his voice. "Mr. Ulrickson, think of how you unhesitatingly soap up your younger daughter in the bathtub. Think of how you, without a worry in the world, take her onto your knee. Think of how you lie beside her in bed when she has a nightmare, how you stroke her hair and caress her cheeks, nuzzle her neck and kiss her bare belly. It is precisely such natural, loving touching with young Madeline that inoculates the two of you against future erotic acting out with each other! But you have missed that period of vaccination with Chloe; you have not been given that tiny bit of the disease that builds the antibodies against future illness, so to speak. You must vaccinate yourself, now, when there is still time, and before it is too late."

Jasper could see the doctor's reasoning. He could see why turning a cold shoulder to Chloe—"shunning" her, as the doctor put it—might have served only to exacerbate the problem, clouding the atmosphere with unspoken feelings that had

further curdled into perverse taboo desire. But the thought of adopting the kind of uninhibited displays of physical affection that the doctor was proposing struck Jasper dumb with terror—and for no better reason than that even the contemplation of such acts caused his mutinous body grotesquely to react.

"And of course," Dez went on, "you will be aided in your program of physically expressed affection by Chloe, who will be making every effort to curtail her unconscious efforts to arouse you. We have spoken of the possibility that you have been experiencing a countertransferential erotic desire for her, so she is alert to the dangers."

"I'm sorry," Jasper said, not sure he had understood. "You're saying that *Chloe* knows about my feelings for *her*?"

"I expressed to her the likelihood that she has stirred you to a symmetrical state of desire, yes. She came to the insightful conclusion that your standoffishness might reflect your efforts to deny incestuous urges. She is a sensitive child, quite alive to the undercurrents."

"Good Lord," Jasper said, mortified that she knew his horrendous secret. On the other hand, he now knew hers. Perhaps this state of mutual unmasking would serve to defuse the situation.

"Trust me," Dez said as if reading Jasper's mind, "it is far, far better to have things out in the open, to throw open the shutters, so to speak, on a house formerly cloaked in darkness. Sunlight, Mr. Ulrickson, is the best disinfectant! And I'm sure you will find that, by indulging in the very physicality that you fear will have an aphrodisiac effect, you have, paradoxically, neutralized that effect, robbed Eros of the strength it draws from secrecy

and hiding and denial, thus to enter that state of perfect asexual innocence enjoyed by middle-aged fathers and their budding teenaged daughters the world over!"

"Yes, I suppose so," said Jasper doubtfully.

"So you understand the prescription? Greater physical affection, greater expressed love. More cuddling, touching, kissing. Do you have any questions?"

"I do have a question," Jasper said.

Dez started, grew alert. He had not been expecting this. "Please," he said.

"It concerns my wife," Jasper said. "I'm accustomed to telling her about any and every momentous event in our lives. I was wondering if it would be appropriate for me to talk with her about what we've been dealing with here today? I've hated having secrets from her. Those secrets have caused me as much anguish almost as the feelings themselves. Now that everything's out in the open between me and Chloe, I'd like very much to be able to explain to Pauline what's going on. As you say, throwing open the shutters. Shouldn't that apply for all the adults in the house?"

Now it was Dez's turn to be blindsided. He had assumed that Ulrickson would do everything possible to keep his wife in the dark about the novel therapy he had been prescribed. But then, Dez had not accounted for the man's almost crazed virtue and transparency. At first, he thought that this unexpected development might impede his plan. But on reflection, he sensed an opportunity.

"Why, yes," he said at length. "I *do* think your wife should

be informed. And I was just about to suggest it. In situations like this, where a strong complex reigns, the whole family is drawn into the destructive dynamic, thus exacerbating it. Indeed, it would be my guess that Pauline has been less than accepting of Chloe? I would imagine that she has acted suspicious of her, rejecting—almost as if she believed Chloe not to be your legitimate daughter? Almost as if she believed the child were an impostor?"

"But that's it *exactly*!" Jasper cried, stunned at the doctor's perspicacity. He described Pauline's strange reversal, from initial, ready acceptance to outright rejection of Chloe overnight. "Things have thawed a little lately because Chloe is simply so loving and affectionate and solicitous with Pauline. But tensions remain."

"A classic case!" Dez cried. "Your wife recognizes the threat to her domain by the invasion of a competing daughter-figure. She has been pulled into the Electra dynamic. She *cuts off* the daughter—as she would an offending penis! She becomes the castrating mother and vies, as best she can in her state of paralysis, for ownership of your phallus. Your wife's helplessness makes it impossible for her to hang on to the organ, so she spurns Chloe, who aches to receive it. An extraordinarily volatile situation. We must bring her into the equation."

Jasper offered to go and fetch Pauline.

"Allow me," said Dez. "It is important that you remain, both physically and psychologically, in the session."

7

Outside, in the corridor, Dez mastered an urge to crow in triumph, and instead proceeded at a sober, thoughtful pace down to the living room, where Chloe had resumed reading to the brat and the cripple.

"Sorry to interrupt," he told her, "but I'm afraid I must borrow Mrs. Ulrickson for a few minutes. You may go on reading to the young one."

"Borrow her?" Chloe said doubtfully. He had said nothing about bringing Pauline into this. She did not like the sound of it.

"Her *husband* wishes her to join the session," Dez said, giving her a hard warning stare.

"Are—are you sure you need her?" Chloe said. She was determined that nothing be done to hurt Pauline. She was blameless.

Dez stepped behind the wheelchair and took the handles. "*Quite* sure," he said. "Do you object?"

"I'm just not sure that—"

"Is everything all right?" said Deepti, sticking her head out of the kitchen door.

"Everything is fine," Dez called out. "Mr. Ulrickson wishes for his wife to join the session. Young Chloe is not convinced that this is wise."

"Chloe," Deepti said in an admonishing tone. "Your mother is quite capable." She pulled her head back into the kitchen.

Chloe shifted Maddy off her lap and stood. "Can I speak to you?" she said to Dez.

"Certainly." He stepped out from behind the wheelchair and they retreated a few steps from the living area into the dining room. Dez left the wheelchair pointing toward the hallway, Pauline in profile to them, so that she could not watch their whispered colloquy.

"Why do you need her?" Chloe said.

"An inspired improvisation. She's become crucial to the plan. To *stopping* Ulrickson." He shot a glance into the living room at Maddy, who was now standing beside her mother, stroking her cheek. "Or have you forgotten?"

Chloe's eyes lingered for a moment on the little girl. She turned back to Dez. "Okay," she said. "But don't hurt Pauline. *He's* the one."

"Of course," Dez said soothingly. He started to move off, but Chloe grasped his forearm.

"I'm *serious*," she hissed. "Don't hurt *her.*" She looked again at Pauline and saw that Maddy, in climbing onto her mother's lap,

had turned the wheelchair in their direction. Chloe pulled her hand from Dez's arm. But too late. She saw Pauline's eyes widen.

"It's good of you to be concerned about the welfare of your stepmother," said Dez, who also saw that Pauline had witnessed that intimate, familiar touch. What did it matter? The woman could say nothing. "But as Deepti says," he went on, "there is really nothing to worry about."

Dez strolled back into the living room and shooed Maddy off Pauline's lap. "I'll bring your mommy right back," he told the child. He stepped behind the chair and seized the handles. Chloe watched helplessly as he rolled Pauline out of the room.

As Dez proceeded down the hallway, he suppressed an antic urge to lean on the handles of the wheelchair and pop it into a wheelie. He might have done so too if not for fear that Ulrickson, wondering what was delaying things, would stick his head out the door and spoil the fun.

Jasper, sitting in a pose of despondency, elbows on his knees, head hanging between his shoulders, looked up when Dez and Pauline entered the room. He greeted his wife with a smile that looked like a grimace. Dez parked her facing the sofa and then resumed his seat in the wingback armchair. Pauline's eyes darted nervously back and forth between the two men, who sat facing her.

"I think," Dez said to Jasper, "that it would be best if *you* were to explain to your wife what has come to light in the sessions."

"Me?" said Jasper.

"*You* must break the silence."

This seemed to make sense. Jasper cleared his throat. He began, haltingly, to tell Pauline about Chloe's "emotional confusion," her tendency toward regression "around issues relating to her lack of a father while growing up." He traced, as Dez had explained it to him, Freud's theory of erotic orientation and gender identity in females. Eventually, meanderingly, he arrived at the crux of the issue: Chloe's Electra complex; her desire to "repossess the male member stolen from her at birth." Pauline's face flooded scarlet. Jasper, alarmed, looked at Dez.

"Go on," Dez prompted him.

"So what this has resulted in," Jasper said carefully, "is a quite predictable state of compensation in Chloe. One in which she has deluded herself into thinking that she is experiencing a kind of, well, infatuation with me."

"There is no need to speak in euphemisms," Dez cut in. "Your wife is an intelligent woman, fully capable of understanding the psychodynamics. To speak in anything but direct terms is to condescend needlessly." Dez turned to Pauline. "Your husband is saying, or trying to say, that his daughter has formed a strong erotic desire for him. Furthermore, *her* unconscious desires have, predictably, awakened a countertransference response in your husband. In short, they strongly desire each other."

"I have never acted on these feelings," Jasper hastened to tell Pauline. "And I have made every effort to keep them hidden from Chloe. But, as Dr. Geld has made clear to me, the problem only continues to fester. I must stop sweeping all of this under the carpet. That's why I'm telling you this. You, who are the most important person in my life. I know it's difficult to hear,

and God knows it's difficult to speak about, but Dr. Geld is committed to helping all of us resolve this, and that's why you need to know."

He paused, waiting for a reaction. Pauline glared at him. The blush had drained from her face. Her pupils had dilated, crowding out the light brown of her irises and making all but the whites of her eyes into gaping black holes. He looked at Dez with concern.

Dez avoided his eye. "I have prescribed," Dez said to Pauline, "a regimen of physical closeness and expressed affection between father and daughter that would mimic, and thus make up for, the kisses, caresses and cuddling that Chloe missed from her father during the all-important childhood developmental stage. You might call it a form of regression therapy. The aim is to bring father and daughter closer together, to bring them, as it were, to the point of symbolic consummation."

Pauline began to blink rapidly.

"Hold on," Jasper said. "I think something's wrong."

"Yes—she's resisting," Dez said. "In denial. A not uncommon reaction."

Pauline continued to flutter her eyelids.

"I don't know if that's it—" Jasper started to say, but Dez cut him off.

"Mr. Ulrickson," he rapped out, "you alluded to a diary that you keep in an effort to exorcise your feelings toward your daughter. It would be beneficial for you to read some entries aloud, to impress upon Pauline the severity of your affliction and thus help her understand why I have prescribed such a course of treatment."

"Read from my diary?" Jasper said, incredulous.

"If you would."

Pauline stared at Jasper with a strangely glazed, empty expression.

Dez repeated, with an irritated emphasis, "If you would."

Jasper, surrendering his will to the doctor—believing him the only person who could extricate his family from the deadly trap it had fallen into—rose and walked, with the heavy tread of a sleepwalker, over to his desk. He sat and typed in the password. He stared for a moment at the screen, and then looked at Dez, who nodded.

Jasper began, stumblingly, to read aloud. "'No matter how I—I abuse myself, it is as if I cannot . . . cannot leech from my guts the poison that breeds there. It is Chloe's face, Chloe's limbs, Chloe's scent, Chloe's gestures and movements that stir this poison to life within me . . .'"

He read on in a robotic, stilted monotone, while Dez, his back to Jasper, grinned at Pauline. Oh, she recognized him all right: that was obvious from the look of freezing hatred that had come into her eyes. That touch on his arm from Chloe must have swept away any doubts.

"'It is as if Chloe,'" Jasper's voice read on, "'were a stranger to me, an erotically intoxicating stranger not of my flesh, not of my blood—'"

Dez, his back to Jasper, grinned at the helpless woman. Pauline closed her eyes. A terrible grating noise came from her throat.

Jasper jumped to his feet and hurried over.

"She appears to be having a seizure," Dez said coolly.

Her eyes had rolled up into her head. The grating noise continued to come from her throat. Jasper bellowed for Deepti—needlessly, since she had heard the sounds of Pauline's distress and was already rushing down the hall. She burst in through the closed door, ran to Pauline and pried open her mouth. "I don't see any obstruction," she said.

Another set of footsteps came rapidly down the hallway. Then Chloe stepped through the open door into the office. She gaped at Pauline, screamed and looked at Dez, who imperceptibly shrugged. "What have you done?" she began to ask, when she was interrupted by the patter of small feet advancing up the hall. Maddy's voice came from outside the office: "What's everybody *doin'* in there?"

"Take the little one outside," Deepti said. "She must not see this."

"Right," Chloe said, backing out of the room. She pulled the door closed behind her.

Deepti stood. "Call 911," she said.

Dez had already strolled over to the desk and punched in the number. He handed the ringing phone to Jasper, who, when he heard the operator's voice, began to wail, "It's my wife! She's dying! We need an ambulance." The operator asked for the address. His mind went blank. "Where are we?" he cried helplessly.

Deepti took the phone and Jasper stumbled back to the wheelchair. "It's my fault!" he cried, falling to his knees and putting his head in Pauline's lap. "I insisted on bringing her into the session! Oh God, Pauline, I'm sorry! Hang on, honey!"

Dez was starting to find the emotionality of the scene

tiresome, and he was also beginning to detect in his stomach ominous stirrings of nausea at the sight of the woman's white, upturned eyes and frothing lips. He announced his intention to venture out onto the front lawn so that he could direct the ambulance when it arrived.

"Good idea!" Jasper said. "Thank you!" He buried his face again in Pauline's lap.

Dez ambled to the front of the house, opened the door and stepped out into the cool tranquility of the autumn evening. No sign of Chloe and the little brat. They must have gone out back. He thought about nipping around the house, but something in the beauty and stillness of the evening held him. The sun, low in the sky, shone through the canopy of changing leaves, igniting them into a glowing membrane of yellow and plum and pumpkin. A powdered light seemed to hang in the air, shrouding the housefronts, opposite, behind their mauve lawns. Dez was not much for scenic splendors, but in his present state of relief over how beautifully his exploit had played out, he found himself strangely receptive to the delights of the waning day.

He had been standing for only a minute or two on the flagstone walk, inhaling deeply the perfumed air, a mix of sourly rotting leaves and fragrant wood smoke, when he saw, in the misty reaches at the end of the street, a blinking red light. Almost immediately, the sound of a siren reached his ears. As the ambulance drew nearer, he stepped along the front path and waved it down. The vehicle, boxy white with *Beckford Emergency Medical Services* emblazoned on the side, swerved into the driveway and

halted with a spray of gravel from under its tires. Four uniformed BEMS personnel jumped out, three men and a woman in dark blue uniforms, squawking walkie-talkies on their waists, and ran toward Dez. "End of the hall on your left," he said, pointing toward the open front door. They rushed inside, bearing a wheeled gurney and boxes of equipment. Dez did not follow.

Less than five minutes later, the emergency team emerged from the house. They rolled the gurney, upon which the woman lay. An L-shaped device was down her throat and a bag dripped liquid through a tube inserted into the crook of her arm. Jasper and Deepti followed behind. As Pauline was loaded into the back of the ambulance, one of the emergency personnel pointed Jasper toward the front passenger seat. He climbed in. "I'll phone when I know something," he told Deepti through the open passenger window. To Dez he added, "Please don't blame yourself—it was *my* idea to bring her into the session."

Dez bowed wordlessly. The engine caught, the siren wailed to hysterical life, and the vehicle swung off the driveway, then roared down the street.

"It is a terrible thing."

Dez turned toward the voice. The home care woman was standing at his elbow, looking at him closely.

"Can you tell me," she said, "what brought this on?"

"Search me," Dez said bluntly. "I'm a shrink, not a neurologist." Why coddle this woman?

Deepti stared at him in surprise, then said, "Well, it is in God's hands now."

Dez couldn't resist. "Whose?" he said with smiling interest,

as if he had heard rumors of this entity but could not quite place him.

Deepti, unable to tell if this was impudence, obtuseness or a misplaced effort at humor, could find no reply. She turned, went up the path and entered the house. Dez immediately hied it around the side of the building to the backyard. He found Chloe and Maddy crouching, in the descending dusk, next to a flower bed. Chloe was apparently distracting the little girl by teaching her about flowers. At his approach, Chloe jumped to her feet and rushed over to him. She grimaced and raised her fists as if to batter his chest. But he caught her frail wrists. "Whoa!" he laughed.

"You *said* you wouldn't hurt her!" she hissed.

"And I didn't," Dez said, feeling her cease to struggle in his grip. He released her. "It was *his* idea to bring her into the session."

"*His?*" she echoed. Then the full horror of the situation dawned on her, and she asked in a stricken voice, "What if she dies?"

"If she dies," Dez said, "he will be plunged into existential despair and guilt, and be ready for anything. And if she survives, he'll be euphoric, and equally at our mercy. *Your* mercy."

Chloe regarded him, incredulous. "So that's why you—"

"Like I said," Dez interrupted, "it was his idea to bring her into our session. I merely seized an opportunity. And don't forget why we're doing this." He turned his gaze to Maddy, who was squatting by the bed of white impatiens, singing lightly to herself as she delicately fingered a flower petal.

Chloe studied the girl for a long moment. She turned back to Dez.

"No more silly wavering?" he said. "No more fantasies about what a wonderful man Ulrickson is? You'll help that poor child?"

How could she say no? She nodded.

"That's my girl," he said, moving to take her in his arms. She retreated a step. "As you wish," he said, lifting his hands.

There was a movement on the edge of Dez's vision. Through the patio's glass doors, he saw the loathsome home care woman. She was inside the house, standing by the kitchen and looking out at them.

"So, please don't hesitate to call," he said to Chloe, at slightly louder than normal volume. "I, or one of my colleagues, will be happy to talk to you. And one of us will be back to check on your progress in a few weeks." He leaned in and whispered, "Good luck—not that you'll need it."

He patted her shoulder, waved to Deepti, and took his leave.

8

The ambulance sped through the twilit streets. Over the sound of the wailing siren, Jasper heard someone in the back of the vehicle say, "Start bagging her."

Bagging her?

He twisted round. But instead of being confronted with the sight of Pauline being zipped into a body bag, he saw one of the ambulance workers attaching an inflated, balloon-like device to the end of the tube in her throat. The man began rhythmically squeezing the bag, forcing air into her lungs. *Thank God*, he thought.

The ambulance, barely slowing at the intersections, took just three minutes to get from 10 Cherry Tree Lane to Beckford

General. Jasper then sat for an excruciating forty-five minutes in a downstairs waiting area. This was the very hospital where Pauline, while in labor with Maddy, had had her stroke. Sitting now in the molded plastic chair in that dismal emergency waiting area with its floor-to-ceiling window overlooking the ambulance bay, Jasper was visited with harrowing memories of that earlier ordeal. And yet this was worse, so much worse, since this time it was his own actions that had brought about the catastrophe.

It was close to eight o'clock when a nurse appeared and beckoned for him to follow. She led him through the set of double doors behind which Pauline had earlier vanished and brought him to an elevator that took them up to a hushed area on the third floor where, above a pentagonal reception desk, a sign hung saying Intensive Care Unit. She led him to the right, down a hallway to a private room.

And there she lay, unconscious, on a bed with incongruous aluminum guardrails on either side, as if she were in danger of rolling off. A tangle of tubes ran from everywhere on her body—nose and mouth and arms and ankles—connecting her to an array of beeping and blinking machines banked around her. A hose from a fridge-sized contraption with a bellows inside ran down her throat and rhythmically forced air into her, causing her body to jerk unnaturally with each forced lungful.

Dr. Carlucci was standing by the bed. He came forward and shook Jasper's hand. "We don't yet know if it's a stroke or a seizure," he said. "They present in very similar ways. We'll know more tomorrow, after some scans. But the situation is serious. I

don't want to paint too dark a picture, but I also don't want to give you false hope. You need to prepare for any eventuality, and that includes further severe impairment, or losing her. Or perhaps she will come out of the coma and be as she was before."

"Losing her . . ." Jasper echoed.

"Look," Carlucci said, touching Jasper's elbow, "we're going to do everything we can."

"Yes," Jasper said.

"You're welcome to sit with her," the doctor said. "I'm afraid I've got to keep on my rounds."

"No, of course."

"She's strong. Very strong." The doctor gave a tight-lipped smile. He turned and left.

Jasper lowered himself into a chair by Pauline's bedside. He wept convulsively. When he had finally emptied himself, he lifted one of her hands from the bedsheet, taking care not to dislodge the needle in the back of her wrist. Her hand felt unexpectedly warm, alive. He brought his face close to hers and whispered, "I love you, Paulie. Please, hold on. I'm sorry. I'm so sorry."

His cell phone vibrated in his pocket. Deepti. He hit Talk and told her what the doctor had said: that they could lose her.

"We must have hope," Deepti told him. "We must not despair."

Over the next hours, nurses came in and out and ministered to her, massaging her extremities, changing tubes, replenishing IV bags. Around ten-thirty, a kindly-looking middle-aged nurse with artificially colored bronze curls looked at him and said gently, "She's in good hands. You really don't *need* to stay—if you're tired."

The thought of climbing into his own bed, of stretching out under the cool sheets, of letting his head sink into a soft pillow filled him with desperate yearning.

"Nothing is going to happen tonight," the nurse added. "You can come back first thing."

He was wavering, trying to make up his mind, when his cell twitched. Deepti again. She told him that Maddy had asked to sleep with her in the guesthouse. "She said that it 'smells like Mommy.' Is it all right with you?"

"Of course," Jasper said.

He mentioned his indecision about whether to stay the night at the hospital. Deepti said that she was sure Maddy would wish for her father to be at home in the morning when she woke up. "To make things as normal as possible," she said. He thanked her for this wise advice and hung up. He rose and kissed Pauline's cold, moist forehead. He thanked the nurse, said he would be back in the morning and stumbled out.

9

His watch read 11:05 when the cab pulled up in front of the house. The night was pitch-black, and at some point it must have stormed, because the air was charged with a strange electricity and the humid maple overhead was still ticking with droplets from the downpour. He might have had difficulty seeing the flagstone path had not someone left the porch light on for him. An oily gleam lay on the dark stones. The rest of the lights in the house were out.

He opened the front door with his key. Stepping into the dark foyer, he saw that he was mistaken: the dull glow from a lamp illumined a part of the living room. He called out, "Hello?" No response. He moved across the unlit foyer, arriving at the

threshold of the living room just in time to see a fleet, spectral figure—Chloe—rise from the sofa and run off toward the arched door at the end of the room. He called out to her.

She stopped and slowly turned. Sniffling, dabbing at her nose with a balled-up tissue, she gazed at him. She was dressed in a pink teddy, its hem grazing the tops of her bare thighs. The low light of the lamp shone through the gauzy fabric and revealed her body within. What he at first mistook for the three white triangles of her undergarments were, he realized with a shock, the tender areas of naked, unbronzed flesh that had been covered by her bikini during her backyard sunbathing sessions. Her hair, damp from a shower, lay in shiny, ribbonlike coils around her shoulders, which were bare but for the thin straps of her nightie. She flushed at the sight of him and said in a small, halting voice, trembly with suppressed tears, "I couldn't sleep. I was worried about Mom . . ."

He took a few steps forward into the room, then stopped. They stared at each other, a long minute of charged eye contact. She said, in a voice barely above a whisper, "I poured you a drink." She glanced at the coffee table. His gaze followed hers. He saw a stubby glass with an inch of brown liquid in it. A nearly full bottle of Scotch stood beside it. "I thought you might need one," she said.

There followed another extended moment of unbearable eye contact. Then they moved toward each other, like combatants in a gladiatorial ring clashing for battle, but when they met in the center of the room, it was to cling to one another as if for solace, in their shared grief.

"Poor Mommy," Chloe said, in a hot rush of moist breath, into his ear. "Poor Mommy."

"I know, I know," he said.

He pulled back his head and looked into her face. She drew her lower lip under her two front teeth, biting a little at the tender flesh, pulling its delicate vertical creases smooth. She lowered her eyes. Then raised them again and stared searchingly into his. Her gaze, for all its softness, cut into him, into his soul, which, in his grief and guilt over Pauline, felt like a howling vacuum. She tilted her face back, allowing her mouth to fall open and her eyes to swoon closed. Suddenly he was kissing her, feverishly, hungrily. He greedily sucked her tongue into his mouth. He could taste the salt of her tears along with the toothpaste flavor of her saliva. With his hands, he molded her back, her tapering waist, sweeping his palms down over the sliding fabric of her nightie and cupping her buttocks. He felt one of her nimble hands snake down his flank, then slide between their bodies, over his twitching lower belly, her cool, tickling fingers blindly groping their way into his waistband, then finding and closing around his flaming member. She squeezed and he shouted "Oh God," his legs nearly giving way beneath him.

Her hand quickly withdrew. He opened his eyes. She had retreated a few steps across the carpet, and she was looking at him with wide eyes. "No!" she said. "No—we shouldn't."

He tried to say something but could produce only a garbled, guttural growl.

She turned and, legs flashing, ran off and disappeared through the arched doorway. He heard her bedroom door slam shut.

He stood panting, his chest heaving. "Oh, thank God," he gasped. "Thank God!"

He had been on the point of doing something that he would regret forever. She had brought him back to himself just in time. The wild momentum of insane desire had been arrested at the very point where it would have been impossible to turn back. But his body was still in a state of riot, his blood on fire, his tumescence agonizing, and he could smell and taste her saliva cooling on his mouth, feel the sliding sensation of the flimsy fabric on his palms, the smooth, firm muscles of her back, and the silken texture of her naked buttocks.

He stumbled across to the coffee table and snatched up the drink she had poured for him. He took a cautious sip—he was not a spirits drinker—and felt the liquid burn a scorching path down his esophagus to his stomach. It rebounded, rose in his bloodstream and blossomed in his head, an anesthetic as effective as morphine. He took another sip. Yes—she had saved them both, pulled them back from the brink.

He drank off the glass. Trembling, still panting lightly, he poured another, which he sipped slowly. He began to pace the living room carpet. Of course, Dr. Geld had told him that, according to Freud, his feelings for Chloe, and hers for him, were *not* criminal. Were not even *unusual*! With that thought, a new and wholly unfamiliar emotion awoke in him, an angry defiance—aimed at whom or what, he would not have been able to articulate. His thoughts were rushing around now, undirected, in circles, as if prodded by his thundering, wildly pumping heart.

He drained his glass, then went back to the coffee table. He

picked up the bottle and poured another half glass. He drank, and the liquid coursed down his throat like water.

He wiped his mouth with the back of his wrist. He had a sudden urge to apologize to Chloe, to tell her that he should *not* have kissed her that way, should *not* have groped at her body. Yes! He must do just that. And right away. Before another moment passed.

Setting out for her room, he stumbled into the coffee table, barking his shins painfully. He cursed. He set off again. He could hear his own breathing—thick, oddly rasping—as he moved his slow thighs and entered the short hallway that led to her closed bedroom door. The sight of that bland wooden rectangle awoke in him a thrill of terror and excitement. At some point he had put down his glass, but he still held the bottle. This he tipped to his lips and took a courage-inducing pull. He grasped the door knob, turned it and pushed the door open.

Her room was lit only by the pink-shaded bedside lamp. She was in bed, and lay on her side, bent in a Z-shape, as if asleep.

"Chloe . . . ?" he said, with a tongue that he now realized felt oddly uncooperative, slowed and thickened. "Naw sleep yet?"

He walked to the side of her bed and stood over her.

She stirred as if waking, then looked at him, pretending to be startled. She drew the duvet and sheet up over her breasts. "Daddy?" she said in a trembling whisper.

He took a slug from the bottle to steady himself, then tried to place it carefully on the bedside table, but he misjudged and banged it down hard. He turned back to her. "Were you a-sleeping?" he said. He corrected himself. "Asleep?"

She gazed up at him, and then slowly drew the covers up over her nose, hiding all but her huge, depthless eyes. "What are you doing in here, Daddy?" she said.

Something about the look of submission in her gaze, the coy way she had drawn up the sheet, the softness of her voice . . . the infantile use of the word *Daddy* and even the slight tremble of apparent fear in her tone . . . He felt something huge creak and teeter within him, then begin to give way, to dislodge or cleave off—like a great wall of ice from a calving glacier—something he had been holding up, holding *together*, for so long. He tried to fight the ecstatic, catastrophic plunge, to step away from the bed, to pull himself away. But at that moment, her body stirred languorously under the covers and he heard a comfortable moan come from the back of her throat. Her eyes seemed to twinkle up at him with a glint of mischief and challenge and smiling invitation. He gaped at her. An appalled apprehension filled him. Rage, as much as desire, seized him, and in a spasm of fury and lust he tore away his shirt. He bent and wrenched off his pants and underwear, liberating the smarting prong, which stood out from his body at an almost upright angle not achieved since he was, himself, Chloe's age.

"Daddy!" she cried.

With an animal bellow that combined plangent mourning and savage desire, he collapsed upon her.

10

He was curled in a fetal position, hugging Pauline.

He opened his eyes. The room was dark. He searched for the digital clock. Could not find it. He turned to the opposite side of the bed and, strangely, found the clock there: 6:17 a.m. He turned back to see if Pauline too had awakened.

It was not Pauline he was embracing, but a pillow. Alarmed, he raised himself on one elbow and felt an ax blade drop through his skull. A peal of pain in his head met a swirl of nausea in his stomach and he sagged back with a whimper onto the pillow. His brain made a sloshing movement within the bowl of his skull. His tongue was pasted to his dry, achingly dry, palate. Almost blinded by the steady tom-tom pulse behind his eyes, he squinted into the mottled darkness.

Through a misplaced window (why was it, too, on the wrong side of the bed?), a predawn grayness dully shone. He looked down at the bed—not his and Pauline's king-size, but a narrow single bed, the covers and sheets in disarray, pulled loose from the mattress's corners and wrapped around him like a serpent. Groping for a lamp, he became aware of a sensation of bruising and chafing in his groin. He gingerly pulled away the winding sheet. In the half-light, he saw his member lying curled, abashedly shriveled like a dead snail, against his thigh.

Then it came back. In strobe-like memory flashes. Chloe, eyes closed, mouth in a rictus of pleasurable agony as she tossed her head from side to side beneath him. His hands, curled into claws, roughly flipping her over. Chloe on all fours, her cello-shaped back and inverted-heart buttocks as if sprouting from his midsection, which pistoned back and forth, his fingers digging into the flesh of her hips while she whipped her hair like a horse trying to throw off flies. Chloe kneeling, facing him. Peering up, batting her lashes like a scolded child, his hands grasping either side of her head as she engulfed him.

He stifled a cry of horror and disbelief.

Another nightmare?

Ignoring the pain, he reared up and turned on the bedside lamp. The bottle of Scotch, empty, lay on its side on the floor. Stains, some dried, some still drying, covered the exposed satin of the mattress. A pink nightie, torn, hung from the edge of a framed poster askew on the wall. His clothes lay in separate corners of the room.

"My God," he said.

He crawled from the bed and, wrapping the sheet around his naked body, stumbled out into the living room calling Chloe's name, his voice like the barking of a dog: raw, rasped, guttural. Silence. He moved down the hall past Maddy's bedroom—and recalled (thank God!) that she and Deepti were sleeping in the guesthouse. He doubled back and pushed open Maddy's door. No one. He moved down the hall and shouldered his way into his bedroom. Empty. Sheets undisturbed.

He returned to Chloe's room. Head banging. Mouth a desert. Now he noticed, for the first time, that her closet stood open, the hangers free of clothes. Her dresser drawers pulled out. Emptied. He crouched, at great danger to his banging brain, and looked under the bed. Her carry-on was not there. Fled. Escaped her abuser, her attacker. Her rapist.

Him.

He clutched at the edge of her dresser.

He had gone insane. Morally, sexually, insane. Crossed a boundary from which there was no return. He had committed acts of unequaled evil, the most heinous a parent could commit. Never mind what Dr. Geld had told him. That was all theoretical, abstract, *symbolic.* He was not meant to *act* upon it. Yet he had. Had used the excuse of the doctor's words, and his own drunkenness, guilt and grief, to sanction acts of debased savagery. To murder one's daughter was at least to make her suffering finite; what he had done to Chloe would haunt her for the rest of her life, the ever-fresh, just-inflicted wound.

Unless, he suddenly thought with terror as he hastily pulled on a T-shirt and jeans, she chose to end that suffering *herself* . . .

His heart revved, raced. Toxic alcohol sweat prickled along his hairline and upper lip. His armpits flared. He pictured her shrieking in terror as she plummeted from an overpass into roaring traffic. Gouging open an artery in her wrist with a broken bottle in an alley where she had taken refuge—from him. Gurgling down a bottle of bleach, searing her entrails, trying to burn away forever the memory of the raping father—to whom she had turned for protection, for hope, for love, when she had no one else.

With an inarticulate cry, he ran to the telephone in the kitchen. He snatched up the receiver and punched in 911. "I'm reporting a rape," Jasper shouted at the operator. "A sexual assault. It's my daughter. I attacked her. She has run away. You must find her before she hurts herself!"

The operator, bewildered, asked him to repeat himself. He did. Clearly no closer to comprehending him ("*Who* did you say attacked her?"), she asked for his address, took down the details and said she would dispatch a car.

"Hurry," he bleated.

As he returned the phone to its charger, he heard someone pounding on the front door. A fist repeatedly slamming against the wood. He ran out to the foyer and put his eye to the peephole. Two uniformed police officers, one short and dark, the other tall and fair, were standing on the front stoop. How had they responded so quickly? He had only just hung up. Had they been patrolling the neighborhood and, while passing this very house, heard his emergency call on their police scanner?

"Just a sec," he said and turned the lock. The door flew open, nearly striking him in the face. The cops piled into the foyer and

backed him against the wall, hands hovering over their holstered guns.

"Name?" one of the cops barked at him.

"Ulrickson," he gasped out. "Jasper Ulrickson. I called 911. To report a rape."

"*You* reported a rape?"

"Yes," he said, looking back and forth between the police officers, who were staring at him in confusion.

"Who was raped?" the tall one asked, a note of suspicion in his voice.

"Daughter," Jasper said. "My daughter."

"What's your daughter's name?" the short one asked.

"Chloe. Chloe Dwight—or *Ulrickson*. She only recently came to live with me. I'm not sure which name she would use. Anyway, she's gone. I don't know where. You've got to find her. Before she—before she hurts herself."

"I see," the dark cop said, a strange note of sarcasm in his voice. "So you got no *clue* where she is?"

"That's why I called you," Jasper said. "You must find her. She could hurt herself."

Now the cop frowned, as if suddenly angry. "Hurt *herself*?" he echoed in a tone of incredulity. Incredulity mixed with menace. "Hurt *herself*?"

"Yes," Jasper said. "She might try anything. Suicide or—"

"Okay," the tall cop said. "I've had enough."

He grabbed Jasper's elbow, swung him around and pushed him hard, face-first, against the wall. Jasper heard behind him a swift grating sound and felt something close around one

wrist, then the other. Handcuffs. He had felt them before—while researching a Bannister novel. He had asked a cop of his acquaintance to cuff him. These were considerably tighter and bit painfully into his wrists.

The cop swung him around to face them.

The short, dark-haired cop told him that he had the right to remain silent and that anything he said could be used against him in court. Jasper had expected something like this, but only *after* he had explained to the police about how he had attacked Chloe. "Yes," he said when they had finished reading him his rights. "I understand."

The tall cop, pulling painfully at his arm, wrestled him across the foyer to the front door, where Jasper was allowed to pause just long enough to kick on a pair of Adidas running shoes that lay there. As they frog-marched him down the flagstone path, he saw lights come on in his neighbors' houses. Silhouetted figures appeared in windows all along the street. The tall cop pushed him into the backseat of the squad car. Jasper settled in awkwardly, elbows akimbo in his handcuffs, behind the metal mesh that separated front seat from back.

Just then, another police cruiser roared up the street and stopped in front of the house. A lean, rangy cop with graying hair shaved down to a military crew cut, like iron filings, got out. "We got a 911 call—missing child?" he said, speaking to the tall cop, who now stood with one foot in the cruiser.

"She's not missing," the tall cop said. He climbed into the driver's seat in front of Jasper. "She's with the DA. Been there all morning. Undergoing a rape test. She says this asshole did it." He jerked a thumb over his shoulder. "Her fucking *father.*"

11

They drove him to the Beckford Correctional Center, a long, low, gray stone pile on the city's northern fringe. There, they ushered him through institutional corridors of off-white cinder block and fluorescent ceiling lights to a large, bustling booking room where they took his fingerprints, then posed him against a backdrop marked off with feet and inches hash marks, and photographed him, front view and profile. Waiving his right to a lawyer, he sat with a detective in a small, windowless room and confessed his criminal attack. He was allowed one phone call. With a guard standing at his elbow, he called his sister in San Francisco. It was still early on the west coast—6 a.m.—and Laura had clearly been woken from a deep sleep. He explained that he had gone insane, raped Chloe and was under arrest. He would be

spending some significant amount of time behind bars—years—and she must come to Connecticut and begin proceedings for taking custody of Maddy. Laura, groping to comprehend the incomprehensible, tried to interrupt, but Jasper spoke over her, telling her to hurry, that Maddy was in Deepti's care but that she needed a family member, that she was without either parent.

"But where's *Pauline*?" Laura cried.

"Hospitalized—possibly a stroke," he said. "Also my doing."

"Good God!" Laura said. "I'll book a flight the minute we get off the phone."

He passed the night in an eight-by-seven-foot cell, on a hinged metal cot, shivering beneath a sandpapery gray blanket. At six the next morning, a pair of guards cuffed his hands and shackled his ankles, then led him, in shuffling baby steps, out to an idling van. He was driven into the city of Beckford, to the domed and pillared courts building. In a brightly lit hearing room, with the district attorney (a vulpine woman with a frozen wave of blond hair cresting her sharp profile), a court reporter and three armed guards present, he listened as the judge, a tiny, bespectacled man with a fuzzy fringe ringing a pate so bald as to appear waxed and polished, read in a slow, sepulchral baritone the charges against him, which included second-degree sexual assault, incest, oral sodomy and sex with a minor. "This last charge might require some explanation," the judge said. "At eighteen, the victim has passed the age of consent in Connecticut, but when the accused is in the role of guardian and responsible for her general supervision and welfare, the victim is classified as a minor. Do you understand?"

"I do," Jasper said in a cracked whisper.

The DA then laid out the probable cause for Jasper's arrest, which included not only a sworn affidavit from the victim but semen samples taken from her vagina and throat on the morning following the attack, and from the sheets and clothing recovered from the victim's bedroom. Search of a personal computer seized from the home revealed an extensive written record of the accused's unnatural obsession with his daughter. There existed, in addition, a digital video recording of the assault secretly made by the victim, who feared that, owing to her father's fame and reputation, no one would believe her claims of an attack. "On that digital video recording," the DA said, "the defendant's face and voice are clearly recognizable and the victim clearly refers to him as 'Daddy.'" The DA ended with a vehement appeal that bail be denied. "The defendant is a rich man and a significant flight risk."

The judge, peering at Jasper over his bifocals, asked if he wished to hire private counsel. Jasper said no. "I'm guilty, so I—"

The judge interrupted and said that this was not the time for him to enter a plea—that would come at his arraignment. "For the time being," the judge added, "I will appoint a public defender. I am in agreement with the district attorney and hereby deny bail. Defendant shall be remanded to custody."

Jasper was led out a back exit of the building and across a small parking lot seething now with a scrum of yelling, jostling reporters and paparazzi who, by whatever occult methods used by the press, had learned of his arrest. Voices shouted: "Where's your *other* daughter?" "Did you attack her too?" "What

happened to your wife?" "Will your publisher withdraw your memoir?" "Have you heard from Tovah?" He made no reply. A guard helped him step up into the police van, which then nosed its way through the scrum—flashes strobing the interior—until it finally broke free of the encircling herd and sped off.

That night, as he again lay shivering on his cot in the Correctional Center, he tried to keep at bay thoughts of Maddy facing the bewildering terror of the disappearance of both parents. Also prowling the edges of his consciousness were images of Chloe in her feverish abandon, images which, instead of waking desire in him, were like the memories a contrite killer might have of his victim as she succumbed to a murder committed when the subject was in a state of temporary, but florid, insanity. When he managed to push these visions from his mind, he was visited by memories of Pauline in the ICU, where his actions had put her: gray-faced, unconscious, jerking with the respirator, hovering between life and death. He had wrought this destruction on his entire family. He alone. It was unencompassable. Incomprehensible. A single act of moral weakness, a single night of poisoned pleasure, that had blighted four lives, forever.

The next morning, his court-appointed defense lawyer arrived. A stocky Irishman with a red face and wheezing breath, he introduced himself as Declan McInnis. He glanced around the tiny cell, rejected the option of sitting on the steel toilet and remained standing.

"I don't need a lawyer," Jasper said in a low monotone, "because I'm guilty and will be pleading that way."

McInnis tried to dissuade him. "But if you stick to that line, my advice would be to plead *nolo contendere*—no contest. You don't *deny* guilt, but you also don't *admit* to it. Leaves some wiggle room. When you plea-bargain, the judge might be inclined to knock some time off. While we're on that, you might start thinking of mitigating factors to bargain down your sentence. Not to steer you, but—purely as a 'for instance'—if there was a sense of your being seduced or entrapped—"

"No, no," Jasper said, turning his face away and staring at the putty-colored wall beside him. "Nothing like that. It was me, and me alone."

At his arraignment ten days later, Jasper, in orange prison jumpsuit, hands and ankles enchained, stood before the bench. The visitors' gallery was filled to capacity with reporters. "Guilty, your Honor," he said.

Loud whispers started up in the gallery. The judge banged his gavel and demanded order in the court. Then he moved on to the penalty phase. Ordinarily, the judge said, he might need some time to arrive at a sentence. "But I find myself in no great confusion about this case," he said.

He explained that he had taken into consideration the heinous nature of Jasper's actions. The accused had grotesquely abused his daughter's trust, in the most craven and despicable manner possible. That Jasper was lionized, throughout the country and world, as a model husband and father—owing to the widespread popularity of his best-selling memoir—only compounded his betrayal, for his daughter would have had

every reason to expect that Jasper would be an especially loving and caring parent. For these reasons, and to set an example in what had become an internationally known case, the judge was handing down the maximum term afforded by the federal guidelines: two years for each charge, served consecutively. Jasper would serve eight years, three years suspended with good behavior.

"I only wish, sir, that I could give you a far longer term of incarceration," the judge said, "but our sentencing guidelines fail to perceive in sex crimes such as this that the effect on the victim is at least as dreadful as murder, if not more so, since she is obliged to live with the scars from your crime forever."

The judge imposed a permanent restraining order preventing Jasper, upon his release, from coming within one hundred yards of Chloe, and barring him from seeing his younger daughter, Madeline, until she was eighteen years of age, at which point she could decide for herself what kind of relationship, if any, she wished to have with her father. His name and mug shot would be entered onto the state's sex offender registry and he would have to abide by the rules and regulations of the governing statutes, which included notifying his neighbors of his offender status, attending regular therapy, and meeting, thrice weekly, with his parole officer.

The judge asked if he would like to make a statement.

Jasper rose and, head hanging, spoke in a raspy, nearly inaudible whisper. He said that he wished to apologize to his family, his friends, his publisher, his readers and everyone who had ever

respected him. Most especially, he wanted to apologize to Chloe, upon whom he had inflicted irreparable psychic and emotional damage. "Although I recognize," he said, his voice breaking, "that it is far too late for apologies."

12

For his own safety, he was placed in the Administrative Segregation Program—solitary confinement—away from the other inmates, whose code dictated that they beat or kill those prisoners convicted of crimes against children.

He spent twenty-three hours a day in a seven-by-twelve-foot cell, with one hour for solo exercise, which he took by walking in a circle in a small yard bounded by high walls of gray brick, a postage stamp of sky visible overhead. His only other glimpse of sky was through a small barred window a few inches from the ceiling of his cell. He pored again and again over the letters that arrived, almost daily, from his sister, who told him of Maddy's adjustment to life in San Francisco. "She's

settling in well," Laura wrote. "She already feels like a member of the family, a twin sister to our Josie. She of course asks after you and Pauline, and we have told her that she will eventually be returning to Connecticut, but that at present you need to be able to devote all your time to Pauline." In a letter one month later, Laura wrote that Maddy's questions about her parents had dwindled almost to nothing—news which, for Jasper, was bittersweet: he was glad that the natural resilience of childhood had made Maddy bond so quickly and closely with her new family, but he was heartbroken to think that he and Pauline had already dimmed for her to ghostly presences, posthumous people.

Three months into his sentence, he received notification of Chloe's civil suit. As with the criminal trial, he refused to offer any defense. The judge entered a default judgment in Chloe's favor, and her lawyer (an aggressive New York attorney famous for winning record-setting cash awards, and recommended by Dez) argued strenuously for damages commensurate with the horrors of Jasper's crime and as a warning to abusers everywhere. The judge agreed and seized Jasper's bank accounts, securities, investments, cars and future royalties, as well as the Connecticut house. The property and possessions were sold at auction. The judge ordered the accumulated proceeds divided evenly between Jasper's dependents: Maddy's share put in trust until her eighteenth birthday; Pauline's held in escrow against the day she either revived or passed away (at which point her portion would be split between daughter and stepdaughter); the final third for Chloe, who would take immediate possession, having passed her eighteenth birthday.

News of his destitution was curiously comforting to Jasper, who felt that he had, in raping his daughter, abrogated all claims to humanity, including wealth and possessions. What character was it in the Bible who, stripped of everything, said that he came into this world naked and would leave it that way?

He refused all visitors—saying that he would not, could not, face anyone from his former life. Deepti, however, wrote to him regularly with news of Pauline, whose condition, she said, remained unchanged. MRIs and other scans showed that her brain was alive, but she remained unresponsive.

A daily, one-hour session of mandatory group therapy with a hangdog, mostly silent group of serial sex offenders—prison-pale, shifty-eyed men, with uniformly rounded shoulders and halting, whispery voices—was his sole human contact, save for the shouted orders of the guards ("Get back in there!") and the implied presence of whoever it was that slid open the small hatch on his cell door to push in his three meals a day, an array of rubbery eggs, cold toast, greasy stews, gristly meats and vegetables boiled to limp, pale flavorlessness. His nights were filled with despairing dreams of Maddy and Pauline, and also of Chloe—dreams steeped in helplessness, hopelessness and horror, as when, in one recurring nightmare, he came to her weeping, begging forgiveness, touching her cheek with one hand as she looked down with troubled, confused eyes and he, in following her gaze, saw that he was, with his free hand, working deep into her spilling entrails a rusty blade.

PART FIVE

1

There was, of course, the question of where they should live.

Chloe, now with a fortune at her disposal, faced the unaccustomed conundrum of too many choices—the dilemma of no monetary restrictions on her future. Dez, however, had ideas.

He pushed for a move to Manhattan, where he thought that the anonymity conferred by the biggest and busiest of American cities would aid him in maintaining a useful incognito. Chloe liked the idea because New York was a center of modeling and acting—careers she hoped, finally, to pursue (despite Dez's scoffing objections). On Dez's urging, they set out to find one of those soaring-ceilinged, sun-pervaded, floor-through lofts in Lower Manhattan. They looked first in

SoHo, but settled finally on a vast space—an entire floor—in a former sewing-machine factory in Tribeca, a neighborhood (the real estate agent explained) thick with movie stars, models, musicians and trust-funders, and which afforded to its inhabitants a paradoxical privacy, based on the blasé disregard the denizens studiously affected when glimpsing a fellow notable or scion in the street or elevator. The dreaded European and Asian tourist mobs rarely ventured into the area, as it was, deliberately, lacking in any of the amenities—clothing boutiques, Michelin three-star restaurants—designed to lure them. A matrix of treeless, rather forbidding streets lined in gray-façaded thirties-era high-rises, it was as close to a gated community as any Manhattan had to offer.

After the cramped, dim confines of the malodorous trailer, this oceanic twelfth-floor loft swimming in pure ether was almost too much for Dez's nervous system to absorb. At first, he felt a kind of vertiginous agoraphobia that made him frightened to leave the building. But he soon adapted, venturing out with Chloe for short walks in the narrow canyons of the streets, tentatively investigating the neighborhood. Soon, he was striding those sidewalks with confidence, and he found that he loved to explore all of Manhattan, going to and fro, from the East River to the Hudson, and walking up and down in it, from Battery Park to the Cloisters. He found himself infected by the spirit of louche creativity that animated so many of their wealthy, artist-manqué neighbors. Dez revived an old, adolescent ambition to "take photographs." He bought an array of vintage Hasselblads and made over a corner of the loft as a photography studio with

lights on adjustable stanchions, colored paper backdrops on great rolls, fancy tripods and a small walled-off darkroom. At first, he applied himself with some assiduousness to taking moody shots of city architecture, the jagged slices of sky between the buildings, stark girders silhouetted against a livid sunset on a construction site, gritty black-and-white shots of subway platforms. But he soon recognized these efforts for what they were—amateur visual clichés—and began to address matters closer to his own heart, training his long lens surreptitiously on the passing private schoolers in their short pleated skirts and starchy blouses, creating some pretty pictures that proved useful for fueling his solo sessions on those nights when Chloe proclaimed herself "not in the mood." (Which was happening, come to think of it, with increasing frequency.)

It was on a day in late June, three weeks after they moved in, when Dez, feeling frisky, ignored Chloe's objections and pulled her down onto one of the absurdly luxurious, semicircular Roche Bobois white leather sofas (together, they cost an unimaginable eighteen thousand dollars and had just been delivered by an army of sweating movers from a shop on Spring Street) and possessed her, twice. He was sprawled voluptuously on the glove-soft leather, regally naked, watching Chloe, also naked, clatter around in the vast open-plan kitchen at the opposite end of the space. She was searching for a rag with which to wipe up the mess he'd made on the upholstery. Propped on one elbow, he called out to her, "Forget it. So we buy another sofa. Or *two*."

He rolled onto his opposite side and looked out through the vast casement window, a wall-sized, fifteen-foot-long, eight-

foot-high expanse of wavery old glass panes between oxidized strips of greenish copper. It framed a stunning view of Manhattan, from the foot of the island, through the picturesque tenements of the East and West Villages, to the skyscrapers of Midtown, past the emerald green of the bucolic park with its amoeboid blue lakes and lagoons, straight up to the blocky, dirt-hued brick projects of Harlem, the graceful arches of bridges sprouting, at intervals, over the rivers, west and east, decorated here and there with white sails and powerboats pulling their frothing wakes, all of it under a summer sky of purest blue with only a few flat-bottomed puff clouds, as in an Old Master painting, to help point up the endless, receding perspective.

"So," he continued languidly, "only one more thing to do, in order to wrap things up."

"Wrap things up?" she said as she returned with a moistened dishcloth in her hand.

"Why, yes," he said, rolling over to look at her. "The *Tovah* show. *Obviously*."

That Chloe *would* appear as a guest on that program—to share with Tovah's audience the sordid details of the crime committed against her by her father—was more than an incidental sideline in Dez's plan. It was the plan's secret raison d'être—its pièce de résistance. More than any dreams of avarice, more than the sadistic fun of engineering an eminent man's fall, it was the denunciation of Ulrickson *on Tovah's show* that had so awakened Dez's artistic impulses over a year ago, when the scheme first burst into his consciousness. Chloe's visit to Tovah's show would be the symmetrical bookend to Ulrickson's triumphal

appearance to promote his saccharin memoir. Furthermore, Dez wanted—he *needed*—to see America's collective Puritan nose (in the person of Tovah's hypnotized audience of millions) rubbed in the reality of rank male desire. Fully to feel his *own* ascent from the ignominy, shame and poverty of the trailer park to his current position of easeful privilege in this ethereal loft, Dez needed to see Ulrickson vilified by the very people who had formerly raised him up. And now Chloe wanted to pretend that she didn't know what he was talking about?

Chloe did, in fact, know. He had talked of little else for weeks, months. But she had hoped that he would, over time, drop his strange insistence that she go on the show. She could not understand his obsession with it. It seemed, to *her*, that they had achieved their goals with Ulrickson: they had gotten him away from Maddy and had seen to it that he was punished for what he had done to Chloe's mother. The press had widely covered the criminal and civil cases, exposing the lie behind Ulrickson's saintly public image. Why was it so important that she appear on *Tovah* and further publicize his crime?

She had not admitted this to Dez, but she didn't *want* to go on the show. She wanted people to *forget* about that part of her life—*she* wanted to forget it, especially that final, horrible act of dissembling when she had lured Ulrickson, a man then so hateful to her, into her bed and submitted to the strenuous, repeated expression of his lust. She wanted to forget it all so that she could get on with her future. She had signed with a boutique downtown modeling agency and just last week had enrolled in an acting class in Greenwich Village—all of this over

Dez's angry objections. (He told her that she was rich now and should not be rubbing elbows with the penniless scroungers doing Off-Off Broadway and toting their modeling portfolios on the Q train from Brooklyn.) But she had to do *something* with her time. She couldn't just lie around the loft—like Dez wanted her to do. But that was another argument for another time. For now, she had to try to deflect him from his insistence that she go on the show.

Without looking at him, she said, quietly, as she dabbed at the stains on the leather, that maybe they'd already paid Ulrickson back and so maybe it wasn't necessary for her to go on *Tovah*.

Dez scrambled to his feet. He stood over her, his skinny chest heaving as if he had just run up a flight of stairs. He spoke through shaking lips, and his voice, thin and reedy and tight, sounded as though he were being strangled. He told her that he had stood by, *un*complaining, when she de*fied* him and enrolled in *act*ing classes; he made no protest when she signed on with the modeling agency; he did not complain when she disappeared for hours every day to run around with her ridiculous portfolio. But if she *ever* again attempted to break her promise about going on Tovah's show—for she *had* promised, he reminded her, all those months ago, when he had concocted the plan—if she ever again so much as breathed a *word* of defiance on this point, he would have no choice but to put her out on the *street*.

The loft and all other assets were Chloe's, but she was still so much in the habit of thinking of herself as Dez's dependent, so used to looking up to him for guidance, advice, direction—

so accustomed to being under his complete emotional and mental control—that she took with deadly seriousness his threat of throwing her out. Frightened, she relented a little, saying that maybe she could appear on the show if it really meant that much to Dez.

"Oh, it means nothing to *me*," he said airily. "I am entirely indifferent to what you do. But it should mean *everything* to you—to expose Ulrickson's sickness to as wide an audience as possible, so that people like him don't continue to get away with their sick perversions against children like *Maddy*. Your selfishness on this matter is beyond me. Just because *you* now enjoy a life of luxury, free from that man's clutches, does not mean that there are not hundreds—no, thousands—of girls, some younger than Maddy, who are suffering the most appalling and unthinkable abuses at the hands of men like him. I'm frankly amazed to learn of the heartlessness that this new life of ease has given rise to in you."

Dez, of course, was right; he was always right. She was forgetting about Maddy—and all the Maddys in the world. She was rich now and comfortable and free of any threat from men like Ulrickson. And so she had forgotten. She was letting her own ambition for a career as an actress or model drive thoughts of others out of her head. She had become like so many girls she had met in Manhattan, at cattle calls and auditions, thinking only of themselves, of success at any cost.

She began to cry. She told Dez that she was sorry. "I'll go on the show," she said. "I *want* to go on the show! I swear I want to go on the show!"

"As I say," Dez sniffed, "it's entirely up to you."

Nevertheless, he put in a call to Havot Productions that afternoon. Tovah's producers were ecstatic at the prospect of this world-exclusive journalistic "get." Tovah, told of the scoop, scrapped the week's taping schedule and told her senior producers, "Let's get this thing in the can by Friday, before she changes her mind."

And so it was that, two days later, Chloe, in an elegant dark sleeveless dress that stretched to mid-calf and a pair of black ballet flats, descended in the elevator from her loft, hurried across the sidewalk and climbed into the waiting limousine—a Havot Productions car dispatched by the show's producers. She was ferried from Tribeca, through the late morning traffic, uptown to Tovah's studios housed in a four-story converted carriage house in the far west Fifties. There, she was ushered past the dauntingly intense, airport-like security ("Tovah has a pretty serious stalker," the limo driver confided) to the greenroom, where a motherly woman patted antiglare makeup onto her face, smoothed her hair, then passed her off to a headset-wearing, clipboard-wielding production assistant (not much older than Chloe herself), who led her through a maze of corridors, past tool belt–wearing technicians, over thick cables snaking underfoot, to the edge of the brightly lit stage. On a hand signal cue from a man crouched in the opposite wings, the PA propelled Chloe with a light push at her back into a maelstrom of applause and cheering and music and lights, as Tovah, galvanizing in an olive green jumpsuit and flaming orange neck scarf, opened her arms wide, then enveloped Chloe in a bear hug. "Just relax," Tovah whispered into her ear over the cacophony of clapping. "It's just you and me talking."

Fighting down panic, Chloe recalled Dez's injunction simply to tell the truth of what had happened to her—or at least the *emotional* truth. Thus did she describe, sitting across from Tovah in a deep powder blue armchair, cameras looking on, how she had, in the wake of her mother's death, found her biological father, Jasper Ulrickson, the famous memoirist, and gone to live with him, and how everything had crumbled when this man whom the world held up as an inspiring model of family duty and sacrifice, and whom she revered as a father—the only father she had ever known—was revealed as a monster, a man boiling with lust for her. Tovah took her time parsing out every painful detail of the betrayal, eliciting from Chloe descriptions of how, precisely, she came to realize that her father harbored these unwholesome feelings. Chloe described the clinging glances, the surreptitious looks, the overt ogling that she had gradually become aware of—and then the discovery of the terrible diary.

"I don't want you to have to relive your whole ordeal," Tovah said. "But you've been brave enough to bring the video that you secretly shot of your father—and you have said that we can air a few minutes of it." Chloe wordlessly nodded.

Tovah turned and spoke directly into one of the cameras mounted on a dolly stage left. "Please believe me when I say that it is not with an air of sensationalism or exploitation that we show you the following video. It is in the earnest hope that its horrors bring fully home the nightmare that is incest and parental child abuse—crimes too often hidden in the shadows. I ask viewers who might find the following images too difficult to bear to please turn away and, of course, any children should be asked to leave the room."

The studio lights dimmed and the blue backdrop behind Chloe and Tovah faded to black. Then it was illuminated by a bright rectangle of light. This turned into a low-resolution shot of Chloe's bedroom at 10 Cherry Tree Lane, filmed with the camera in her laptop: a static shot of one wall containing her bookshelves, the bed and her bedside table. Chloe, onscreen, stepped into the foreground, close to the camera, bending over it. The room lights were low. She was wrapped in a duvet, which she held closed around her throat. Looking into the camera with an expression of furtive desperation (just as Dez had demonstrated to her all those months before), she whispered in an urgent undertone: "I don't know if he'll come again tonight." She cast a nervous glance to the left. "But he's been drinking, and that usually means bad things." She turned back to the camera. "I'll leave this on, just in case." She ran to the bed and climbed under the covers. She left the bedside lamp on. An excruciating half minute passed—during which not a sound was heard in Tovah's audience. Then came the crunching turn of a doorknob on the soundtrack—and someone in Tovah's audience screamed.

A man lurched into view from the left. He walked unsteadily, stumbling over to the bed. The profile against the lamp-lit wall behind him was clearly that of Jasper Ulrickson. In his right hand he carried a bottle. Chloe turned onto her back and pulled the covers up, in a protective gesture, to her chin. She could be heard on the video's muffled soundtrack saying, "Daddy?" Jasper asked, in a slurred voice, if she had been asleep. She asked what he was doing in her room. He raised the bottle, took a slug, then slammed it down onto the bedside table. He swayed a little.

She pulled the covers over her nose. Then he began to tear off his clothes. Tovah's producers pixelated the offending parts of his anatomy. He stood for a moment over her, and then, with a shout, he dropped, like a felled tree, onto the bed. The audience let out a collective cry of horror.

The video was paused, showing Ulrickson on top of Chloe. The lights in the studio came up and the image abruptly disappeared, replaced once again by the blue background with the word *Tovah!* in flowing off-white script.

Chloe was sitting, turned away from the screen, a tissue to her face. Tovah, holding Chloe's free hand, addressed the camera. "We cannot show you what takes place next on that video," she said gravely, "but it is gut-wrenching, and it offers solid proof of Jasper Ulrickson's guilt—as was determined in both a criminal and a civil trial." She turned to Chloe. "What do you think when you see that recording?"

"I can't look at it," Chloe said, quite truthfully.

"I don't think any of us blame you," Tovah said. "It's hard enough for me to imagine that that man sat across from me, in that chair, on this very stage—and that I praised him as a model husband and father!"

"He tricked everybody," Chloe said quietly.

"And yet *you* had the bravery to expose him," Tovah said. "To let us all know the truth. Girl, you *rock*!" The audience burst into wild applause. Chloe flushed and lowered her head. When the clapping died down, Tovah asked, "What will you do now?"

Chloe shook the hair off her face. "I'm nineteen now, so I don't have to live in foster care anymore. I found a place to live.

I don't want to say where. But a place where I can try to have a normal, private life."

"We made every effort," Tovah said, "to contact your father in prison, to notify him that we would be airing this interview with you, and to get comment from him. But we were not able to get through. If he is watching, what would you say to him?"

Dez had warned Chloe that this moment would be coming. He had told her simply to speak the truth, to speak from her heart. She looked into the camera. "I trusted you," she said. "You were the only father I ever knew. When I got to your house, I felt loved. For myself, as a person. I loved Pauline, and I loved Maddy. And I loved you. And none of this had to happen." She began to cry. "None of this."

The program, recorded live to tape, aired the following Monday. Chloe refused to watch it and fled to Crunch gym. Dez, however, would not allow her mutiny to dampen his spirit of celebration. He had prepared carefully, putting on ice a case of Veuve Clicquot and laying in, from Petrossian, eight ounces of beluga caviar, a tin of crème fraîche and a dozen of the restaurant's tender blini. Upon hearing the opening strains of Tovah's theme music, he popped a cork on the champagne and poured himself a flute. Installed on the Roche Bobois, in front of the seventy-eight-inch plasma high-definition screen mounted on one of the loft's huge white walls, he munched and sipped and watched, as Tovah exposed Ulrickson's perfidy. With the champagne coursing through his veins, the delicate caviar popping against his palate, he felt as if he were ascending, like a Renaissance angel on a ceiling painted by Raphael, into

the sun-suffused air, raised up into a state of glory and grace, of purest accomplishment and joy. He felt the completeness that comes with seeing a creative vision realized, to perfection, in all its parts. And when, toward the program's denouement, he felt a slight, inevitable diminishment in his joy, the first fading of the endorphins off his synapses, he dug from his wallet the little treat he had decided to indulge in, just for this occasion: a gram of very pure Colombian cocaine that he had bought from the building's doorman—a sly young fellow who had, almost immediately upon Dez's entry into the building four weeks ago, caught Dez's eye and given him a knowing lift of the eyebrow. Dez had not partaken in many years, not since his days at the law firm, and then only a few times in moderation, but he thought it the perfect way to celebrate his triumph. Chloe frowned on all drug use, *of course*, even a little light pot smoking. But with her out of the loft, there was no reason not to pour out a small mound on the top of the glass coffee table. He chopped it lovingly with his credit card, then laid out two thick lines. Through a rolled hundred, he sucked them deep and then sat back, smiling, restored to delirious ecstasy.

2

Jasper was not among the seven million Americans who watched Tovah's show that afternoon. Like his fellow sex offender inmates, he was forbidden from viewing any photographs, books, movies, television shows or Web sites that featured teenaged girls, and he was expressly barred from looking at images of the daughter he had violated. Many others at the Beckford Correctional Center, however, did watch—a cohort of murderers, muggers, robbers, wife beaters, drug sellers and other criminals who had long known that Jasper Ulrickson, the notorious daughter-rapist, dwelled within their walls. Now, galvanized by the outrage and horror that Tovah was so good at evoking (several prisoners were reduced to sobs), they resolved,

by whatever means necessary, to exact some jailhouse justice.

The day after the show, Jasper was taking his daily exercise, plodding around the perimeter of the yard, the looming prison walls around him, the taunting rectangle of sky above with its one tender, lone cloud. He had completed two circuits when he heard a noise that anyone who had not performed this routine day after day for weeks would have failed to register, but which to Jasper was as unusual, as unexpected, as the sudden striking up of a brass band. The sound was the muted click of the computer-controlled safety lock on the door that let him into and out of the yard. This door was always kept locked during his exercise hour, to protect him from the rest of the prison population. The lock was on a timer that could be manually overridden only by, say, a crooked guard bribed by, for instance, one of the well-heeled inmate drug dealers.

Jasper looked toward the door and saw two men—heavily muscled habitués of the weight room—approaching across the yard. They had eager grins on their faces and for a distorted moment he mistook their bright eyes and bared teeth for expressions of friendliness. He turned toward them. The first blow was to his chin, a roundhouse punch that made his teeth grind together and lifted him off his feet. He landed on his back on the ground. A stomping kick to his stomach knocked the breath from his lungs. A boot came down on the side of his head. Gasping, he curled into a fetal position, arms over his face. They beat and kicked and stomped—Jasper heard and felt things snapping and fracturing and splintering and tearing within him—until a guard not on the dealer's payroll noticed the commotion on a

security monitor and dispatched guards with cattle prods and Taser guns to halt the attack. The beating had lasted only thirty seconds, but it left Jasper with a fractured skull, two missing molars, a ruptured spleen, six broken ribs, a shattered pelvis and a broken scapula. His right eye had been kicked out of its socket and lay on his cheek.

He spent three months in the prison infirmary, his head bandaged, his torso tightly bound in restrictive bandages, his right leg in traction. His eye proved unsalvageable and was surgically removed. His remaining eye, already dimming because of an unusual sensitivity to the flickering fluorescent lights that illumined the prison's interior, had been further damaged in the attack. He could, if he squinted, make out objects at very close range—he could read print if he held it an inch from his face—but anything at arm's length or greater disappeared into a fog, a blurriness that reduced the world to indistinguishable soft-formed blobs of weak, watered-down color.

Discharged from the infirmary back to solitary, he was issued a pair of dark glasses to protect what remained of the sight in his left eye. For his trips to the exercise yard, he was given a retractable white cane with a ball-shaped tip for feeling his way around the yard's perimeter. He moved in halting half steps owing to his legal blindness, and to a shortened leg that gave him a pronounced limp.

Unable now to detect by sight the subtle changes in the light from the window of his cell, he ceased to be aware of the passage of day from morning through afternoon into evening. Gone, too, were those visual cues that told him of the progress of

the seasons from brightening spring through effulgently sunny summer into dimming fall and dark winter. Apart from the chill that brought up goose bumps on his flesh in the months from November through March, or the slick of sweat that covered his body when summer arrived, he had no outward sensations, for the twenty-three hours a day he spent in his cell, of time passing. In this state of solipsistic inward-turning blindness, a single minute might stretch to hours or days or weeks; a month might vanish in a blink.

Unlike his fellow prisoners, he did not secrete in his mattress a safety pin or paper clip with which to scratch out hash marks in the stone wall of his cell, to keep track of how many days he had spent in captivity—and how many more he would have to endure. He lived in the timeless moment. Tiredness came upon him, and he slept; signals sent to his brain by enzymes in his guts informed him that he must eat, and he duly masticated whatever matter was passed through to him on the tin plate from the small hatch on his cell door, chewing and swallowing, until the signal from his gut was appeased. And so he existed, without hopes, without goals, without desires, in the numb non-time of prison, in the dimmed, blurred world of his legal blindness.

Then one day a guard arrived in his cell, filling its small space with the sour reek of his sweat and meaty breath, and in a deafening voice, told Jasper to follow. Limping, tapping with his cane, trying to penetrate with his remaining eye the enveloping grayness, Jasper followed the sound of the guard's footsteps. He knew he was walking past his fellow inmates because of the sudden cacophony of shouted imprecations and threats, and the

ringing clangor of tin drinking cups banged against barred cell doors. He heard a door crash shut behind him with a sound of ringing steel and an after-echo of tombal finality. They had entered a room that he judged to be cavernous because of the way it returned the sound, slightly delayed, of their footsteps.

"Right here," the guard said, grasping his upper arm.

He could make out a wavery figure standing behind a low table. It pushed toward him a box. Jasper opened it. He brought his face close and could see that there were objects inside.

"Personal effects," the figure behind the table said.

He lifted each object from darkness into the weak light that issued from a buzzing overhead fluorescent tube. They were the items that had been in his pockets at the time of his arrest. He handled each like a precious talisman from a vanished civilization: four twenty-dollar bills; a limp brown leather wallet; a tube of ChapStick; three quarters; and a small tin of mints. Some clothes lay folded at the bottom of the box: the jeans and T-shirt he had hastily pulled on that morning after waking to discover his crime. They might as well have been impregnated with Chloe's dried blood, so repellent were they to him; yet he was told to remove his orange prison jumpsuit and put the clothes on. He did so. They hung loose on his emaciated frame. Only by cinching the belt to its last hole was he able to prevent the pants from sliding off his bony pelvis. He pulled on the Adidas that he found at the bottom of the box.

The guard growled at him to follow. They proceeded through a corridor where unfamiliar smells—aromas and scents that he had not experienced in five years, a particular

deodorant, a female's perfume, the complex aroma of inexpressibly delicious-smelling nachos, all cheese and vinegary jalapeños, tart tomato salsa and garlic-infused ground beef—filled his quivering, awakened nostrils.

They passed through another vague doorway into a large indoor space, and a burst of bright light hit Jasper, causing him to wince. A shadow man materialized beside him and handed over something that, when Jasper raised it to his face, he saw was a yellow and black plastic card. He told Jasper how to find the bus stop. He also handed Jasper a piece of paper upon which (Jasper saw when he brought it so close to his face that it brushed the tip of his nose) was written the address of the place where he would be living for the next six months, until he earned his complete freedom.

Some time ago—a month? two days? two hours?—he had been taken from his cell and brought before a murky tableau of four people, two men and two women (judging from their voices). They had spoken to him about the day of his release, about the residential rehabilitation center, about his reintegration into society. But he had promptly dismissed all thoughts of his discharge—of his freedom. Because, for him, there was no chance, ever, of freedom, no respite from the knowledge that he had destroyed his family and each and every member of it. His prison was not a physical state.

Nevertheless, he passed through one door and suddenly he was standing in a bewildering blind swirl of sensations. He felt, through the soles of his unfamiliar shoes, the yielding texture of grass (he had accidentally stepped off the cement path that

led to the prison's exit). He felt wind and the long-forgotten touch of sunlight on his face. The bright September sun, not yet drained of all its summer strength, jabbed painfully at his remaining retina. He closed his eyelids. Cautiously tapping, he moved off the grass verge and onto the invisible sidewalk. Eventually, his probing cane hit something and he opened his eyes. He was standing at the base of a gigantic stone archway, the outside gate of the prison. He stepped across onto the sidewalk, and into his dubious freedom.

As instructed, he turned left and squinted in search of the bus stop. He could make out, vaguely, some twenty or so yards up the street, a blurry but familiar pattern of blue and white that the city used for its public transit signs. He moved toward it.

A flurry of shapes lunged from the darkness around him and raucous voices, at close range, shouted his name, yelled at him—"This way, Jasper!" "Over here!" "Look at me!"—and for a moment he was reminded of the attack, four years ago, in the exercise yard. He lifted his cane, holding it out in front of him. Someone batted it away, and he heard laughter. He braced to feel a blow to his head or a kick to his groin. He held a hand over his crotch. Someone yelled, "That's good! That's good!" He heard a chattering sound of rapid-fire clicking. He squinted, looked around, realized that a crowd of men had encircled him, jostling for a clear view, elbowing one another out of the way. "Please," he said, trying to push through the scrum, which moved like a single elastic organism, surrounding him on all sides, continuing to snap away. "Please," he repeated.

He had taken only a few stumbling paces toward the bus

stop when he heard, through the tumult, a female voice calling out from behind him: "Here! Over here!" He turned. The voice repeated, "Over here!" He tried to look for the owner of that voice—that familiar voice!—but could see only the insect-eye lenses and hunched shoulders of the people surrounding him. The gunning mechanical chatter continued on all sides. Overwhelmed, he crouched and put his arms over his head.

The female voice was close by, shouting, "Leave him alone! Leave him alone!" He heard shoes scraping on the pavement and rustling clothing.

"Who the fuck is *that*?" someone shouted.

"Fuck knows—but I'm getting a shot."

"Away!" the voice screamed. "Go away!"

A hand closed around his arm. He was being dragged back down the street. The crowd followed, clacking, snapping, shouting. Jasper was pushed hard. He fell, but instead of hitting asphalt, he landed on a soft surface that he recognized, by its smell of leather, to be a car seat. He drew in his feet and heard a door slam. There was muffled shouting and more clicking, then another door slammed. An engine roared to life and a deep vibration ran through his body. His head jerked back.

3

Those horrible people!" Deepti said, glancing into her rear-view mirror as she accelerated away from the curb. The paparazzi were not giving chase. They were standing in a calm group, looking down into their camera viewfinders, checking their shots, laughing and chatting as if at a cocktail party. She eased up on the gas and looked at Mr. Jasper.

He sat mute, his eyes obscured behind dark glasses, his head shaved almost to baldness. His face was impassive, as if the ambush had not happened, or as if he had already forgotten about it. She was stunned by the changes in him. He was unrecognizable—hence her failure to intercept him when he first emerged from the prison gates. She had been expecting

a slightly older version of her tall, robust former boss. Instead, she had seen a wizened old man, stooped, shuffling, limping along in dark glasses. Until those horrible photographers began to attack him, she had had no idea that it was Mr. Jasper. And it was difficult to believe even now.

"Thank you for your help, Deepti," he said in a low growl.

"You are welcome, Mr. Jasper," she said.

His demeanor (head slumped forward, chin almost on his chest, mouth tightly closed) told her that he did not wish to speak. So she drove in silence. She had already apprised him, in her regular letters to the prison, of Pauline's and Maddy's progress, so there seemed little, in any case, to talk about. She had no intention of asking him about the scandal that had landed him in prison. Deepti had been as shocked as anyone by Mr. Jasper's acts—he had always seemed such a decent, good man. But she believed every person worthy of forgiveness, and capable of redemption, and that is why she was there for him, that is why she had phoned the prison, learned about his release date and come to pick him up.

She followed the GPS instructions that carried them to an address on Dunmore Road, in the city's gritty west end. Number 16 was a nondescript two-story house, vaguely institutional, with beige siding and white window trim behind a ten-foot-high chain-link fence, a coil of razor wire on top. She parked at the cracked curb in front, then helped him out of the car. He leaned heavily on her arm, tapping with his cane, as they went up the cement walk, past a leashed pit bull that growled but made no move to attack. There were two security cameras mounted on

either side of the door and a sign reading: All Visitors Must Buzz. Deepti pushed the intercom button, and after a moment a voice came through the crackly speaker. "Yup?"

"Mr. Jasper Ulrickson," she said.

A buzzer sounded and they pushed in through the door, into a bright, large room. Deepti saw, behind a reception counter, a tall man with a military-looking brushcut. He wore a starched, short-sleeved button-front shirt and a shoulder holster. Behind him were office machines—computers, printers, photocopiers—and a bank of small black-and-white screens, which showed ever-shifting views of the house's exterior and interior. In an area to the right of the desk were some tweedy brown chairs and sofas upon which a couple of men were seated. They looked up sharply at her, then just as quickly dismissed her as of no interest to them.

"This is Mr. Ulrickson," she said to the desk sergeant.

He looked at his computer screen, then at Jasper. "Okay," he said, "we'll get you processed."

Deepti handed Jasper a slip of paper. "You can call me anytime," she said. "And I will be back to visit." She also gave her name and number to the man behind the desk. "In case he needs me," she said. She silently squeezed Jasper's arm, then disappeared into the dim fog that surrounded him. He heard a buzz, and the door clanged shut behind her.

The man placed on the counter in front of Jasper a register book, and told him to sign in, giving Jasper the dislocated feeling that he was checking into a hotel. Then the desk sergeant—who

identified himself as Officer Dunwoody—told Jasper to stand with his arms extended at his sides. He patted Jasper down. He then explained the rules and regulations of life in the Turning Points Residential Rehabilitation Center. "And this *is* a rehabilitation center," he added. "We don't call them halfway houses anymore. And you *will* be rehabilitated, as long as you follow our rules."

The rules stated that Jasper would spend his first three weeks confined to the center. After which he would be permitted to come and go unsupervised, although his whereabouts would be monitored. "That is, upon leaving, you will give phone numbers and addresses for your destination, state the time of your return, and be subject to strict curfew. Any failure to abide by the curfew, or any deviation from the scheduled time and place of your trip, will result in sanctions up to and including reincarceration, depending on the severity of the infraction. You are required to meet, in person, with your parole officer daily. You are forbidden to use computers or the Internet. Regular drug tests will be administered. Unscheduled room searches will be in effect. All items brought into the center are subject to inspection. As a sex offender with a conviction for statutory rape and incest, you will not be permitted to see any material containing photographs of school-aged children or either of your daughters. After six months, if you have followed all the Turning Points rules and are deemed by our psychosocial team to have been rehabilitated, you will be released, fully free, into society."

Assigned a room on the second floor, he tapped his way

upstairs, then down a hall to his right, past several doors at whose numbers he peered closely, until he came to room six. The door was open. He stepped inside. Squinting, he made out two sets of bunk beds on either wall. There was no phone, no television set, no bookshelves.

There was, however, a man sitting on one of the beds. He identified himself as Chris and said that he had been released from Beckford Correctional two days earlier. He said that he'd heard Jasper was coming.

"You were on the *Tovah*," he said. "So you're famous."

Chris explained that he too was a sex offender—"All the guys are, in here; they keep us together"—and that he worked as a janitor at a fast-food place across town. He asked Jasper what job he would be doing. Jasper said that he did not know yet. Chris said that, so far, the center didn't seem too bad. "We gotta do group every evening at seven," he said. "It's okay. The facilitator does most of the talking." He added that their roommates were okay. One of them had done time for trading child porn on the Internet but hadn't actually "messed with any kids." Their other roommate had raped a girlfriend. "He's kind of an asshole," Chris said. "Hip-hop wigger."

Jasper sat and propped his cane against the bed, took off his dark glasses and rubbed his eyes.

"You blind or something?" Chris asked.

Jasper explained that he was indeed legally blind, but he could see blurry shapes and could read if he had good light and held the page close to his face.

"Bummer," Chris said. "But I guess that's better than, like,

totally blind." He stood. "Well, I've got to get to work. My shift starts at noon." Jasper now could make out that he was a tall, pear-shaped man. He went out.

So this now was his life: a room shared with three other sex offenders in a halfway house in a remote and bleak section of the city. No family. No money, except for the three thousand dollars he had made in prison gluing ornate nameplates into Bibles. But, then, did he need more? Not for any reason he could think of. In any case, he would not resume his writing career. He had not written a word in five years and had no urge to.

He ate, slept, went to group therapy. The sessions included the twenty other inmates in the center and were run by a psychologist named Dr. Jax, who encouraged each man to say something about what he had learned that day. He was constantly urging the participants to "call others out on their bullshit," insisting that this was the only effective method for making sex offenders face their illness and get around their practiced manipulations. Once, when Jasper spoke about his guilt over what he had done—his inability to understand his actions, his grief over the loss of his family and the impossibility of his ever forgiving himself for the lives he had destroyed—he was viciously verbally assaulted by an inmate who insisted that all such statements of guilt and remorse were a sham and a dodge, that Jasper in fact still harbored deep desires for his daughter, desires that he would act upon in an instant, given the chance. In his shame and disgrace, Jasper agreed, although he wondered if this was really true. The mere thought of Chloe caused him such anguish.

Three weeks passed. Then one morning Officer Dunwoody handed Jasper a map and a transit card and told him how to take the city bus to his place of employment, a large, windowless building on the city's far western fringe. There, Jasper sat in a tiny cubicle hardly wider than his shoulders and answered phones for a tech support line. He wore a hands-free headset and worked from a memorized script, directing callers to technicians depending on what model of computer the caller owned, what kinds of problems they were having with what kinds of devices. Equipped with a special large-print keyboard, he pushed buttons that directed the callers to the correct tech representative, in India, Pakistan or Malaysia.

After a month, he earned the privilege of making an unsupervised day trip from Turning Points. There was one place only where he dreamed of going: Beckford General Hospital, where Pauline remained in the intensive care unit, where Jasper had successfully appealed to have her treated, using funds freed up from the escrow account awarded to her after his incarceration. The hospital lay five miles east of the rehabilitation center, in the city's downtown core. Jasper caught a bus, then cut a careful swath with his tapping cane through the streaming, bumping, lurching crowds, across a broad avenue, to the hospital. He ascended the familiar stone stairs to the entrance, found his way across the vast lobby to the elevator bank and rode up to the third floor. There, he tapped his way to the nursing station, where he was greeted by a voice he recognized—that of a kindly middle-aged nurse with whom he used to chat, all those years

ago, when Pauline was first hospitalized after her stroke. "Friend or family?" she asked in a brusque, impersonal tone that revealed she did not recognize him.

Jasper identified himself and the woman inhaled sharply. "I'm sorry, Mr. Ulrickson," she said. "I didn't—that is, it has been so long . . ."

She bustled out from behind the pentangle-shaped desk and took his arm. "We were all very sorry to hear about your troubles," she murmured in an undertone as she led him down the hall. "But I'm very glad to see that you haven't forgotten your wife." At the end of the corridor, she turned left and guided him through a doorway into a private room. "Here she is," the nurse said, bringing him over to her bedside. "Take as long as you like." Her footsteps retreated down the hall.

Jasper leaned over the bed and brought his face close enough to make out Pauline's features. Her closed eyelids were motionless, her skin waxy and pale but with a faint glow of life. A smell, not unpleasant, arose from her, as of lightly heated milk. He propped his cane against the side of the bed and groped for one of her hands. It was warm. He wept, sobbing softly, a strange mixture of grief and joy. Joy to be reunited with her. Grief at his awareness of the state to which he had brought her. Finally, he was able to say, in a low rumble, "Pauline. It's me." There was no reaction. He said her name several more times. Her eyelids remained as motionless as those of a stone saint carved on a sarcophagus. Nevertheless, he continued to speak to her, telling her of his release from prison, of his determination to visit her every

day, of his conviction that she would one day wake up, and that he would never, ever abandon her.

He heard approaching footsteps. He straightened and wiped at his eyes. A figure stepped into the bright gap of the door.

"Mr. Ulrickson," said Dr. Carlucci's voice.

Jasper did not think he was imagining the slight hitch in the doctor's speech, that millisecond pause at the shock of how much he had changed. Or was that delay, that hiccup, the result of the awkwardness of addressing a man convicted of Jasper's unthinkable crimes? In any case, the doctor stepped forward, as if from a surrounding nimbus of gray smoke, into Jasper's range of focus, his dark, intense eyes and the pontoons of curly hair above his ears taking shape. He offered his hand. Jasper took it. Carlucci said, "I was sorry to hear about"—that pause again—"about your difficulties."

Jasper silently bowed his head.

Carlucci shifted into brisk professional mode, explaining that scans showed normal brain activity in Pauline's prefrontal cortex, suggesting cognition and awareness. "But she remains unresponsive, for reasons we don't understand. In some respects, she resembles victims of severe shock rendered blind, deaf or dumb through psychological trauma. At times, she seems to respond to verbal stimuli with movements of her eyes beneath the closed lids, but these minute twitches and tics could be haphazard, random reflexes. In any case, it certainly does no harm to talk to her—and it may even do some good.

"I wish I had better news," Dr. Carlucci added. "But there is

always hope." He paused as if expecting Jasper to say something. But what was there to say? "I'll leave you now," the doctor said finally. "Please feel free to get the nurses to page me, if any questions arise. Stay as long as you like. And it's good to see you."

4

The visit made Jasper the happiest he had been in years. He returned to the hospital every day after work, at 5 p.m., sitting with Pauline for a half hour before taking the bus back to Turning Points for dinner, then group. On Saturdays and Sundays, he spent all day at the hospital and often crossed paths with Deepti, who visited with Pauline each Sunday after church. It was on one of those Sunday visits that she said she had something for him—items she had salvaged from 10 Cherry Tree Lane before the house went on the auction block. "Just some small mementos that I think you might like to have," she said. "Nothing of great value." She promised to drop them at the rehabilitation center.

On a morning shortly after that, he was in his room, trying to write a letter to his sister, when he was buzzed from the front desk. He went downstairs and found Deepti in the lobby. When he drew close, he was able to make out a box sitting on the counter in front of Dunwoody, who was lifting out items and studying them. "The souvenirs I mentioned," said Deepti. "From the house."

"I've got to inspect everything before I hand it over to you," Dunwoody said. "These are all fine," he added, waving at the items he had already pulled out and put on the counter.

Jasper picked one up and raised it to his face. It was a framed photograph of his parents that had hung on his office wall. For a moment he was looking into his father's mild, gently smiling face, his mother's head, with its tousled mane of white-blond hair and her sun-toughened skin, resting on his shoulder. He put it down and groped for another object. He knew, the second his fingers closed around the smooth, glassy surface, that it was one of the glazed pottery sculptures Maddy had made in preschool—a dog—which Jasper once kept on his desk.

Dunwoody extracted a photograph of Chloe that had sat on Jasper's office bookshelf. It showed her at age fifteen, standing, in cutoff jean shorts and a halter top, on a dock in New Halcyon. "Confiscating *this*," Dunwoody said, placing the picture face down on the shelf behind him. He flipped through a drawing tablet filled with Maddy's crayon scribbling and placed it with the other approved objects. He inspected a box of carved chessmen. "These are fine," he said. He placed all the items back in the box. "You're good," he added.

Jasper thanked Deepti, but when he returned to his room with the box held awkwardly under one arm, he could not bring himself to unpack the objects. They stabbed at his heart too painfully. He stowed the box under the desk attached to his bed and told himself that there might, one day, be a time when he would feel strong enough to put the objects on display. But not now.

He did make progress. In group therapy, he began to understand how markedly he differed from his fellow inmates, who described daily struggles with the demons of their criminal lusts. Jasper felt no such struggle. When he thought about Chloe, it was with remorse, regret and guilt, even tenderness—but not the tenderness of erotic desire. Somehow, that single episode of horrendous violation, committed under the combined impetus of his grief and guilt over Pauline's hospitalization, Dr. Geld's therapeutic revelations, and the loosening effects of the alcohol, had purged Jasper of his twisted lust for Chloe, quenched it as thoroughly as a bucket of water dumped over a robustly burning campfire, turning it to cold ash. When he said this in group, he expected, as before, to be shouted down by the others and Dr. Jax. Instead, they agreed that he was, somehow, "different." Jasper's crime, they unanimously agreed, was "situational"—the result not of an inherent sexual sickness, but of the special circumstances he had found himself in. "None of which is to excuse your behavior," Dr. Jax told him. "And none of which is to say that you could not again find yourself in the kind of compromising situation that would make you vulnerable to acting out. But on the whole, I do not see you as a repeat offender."

Jasper began to hate himself less, and began to see a more defined, less dire, future for himself. He could never regain what he had lost, but he could, upon his discharge from Turning Points, find an apartment or room close to Pauline and see her every day. Perhaps he might even see Maddy again—after she turned eighteen; until then, he would dedicate his life to becoming the kind of person she would wish to know. And who knew? Perhaps even a rapprochement with Chloe was not too much to hope for?

It was in this mood of fledgling optimism that, one morning in early March, two weeks before his scheduled release from Turning Points, he remembered the box of souvenirs that Deepti had brought to him. He was suddenly eager to touch those enchanted objects, to look at those tokens of his former happiness. He groped under his desk, located the box, pulled it out and, sitting on the edge of his bed, opened it. On top was that photograph of his parents. He set it on his desk. He lifted out Maddy's dog sculpture and put it on the desk too.

He took from the box Maddy's drawing tablet and lovingly opened the cover. He tilted the page to the light from the window and moved his face to within an inch of the fragrant newsprint. Printed in crayon, in Maddy's wobbling, childish hand, were the letters of the alphabet, from *A* to *M.* He smiled, recalling her obsession with letters that long-ago summer. He moved his eye down the page. Beneath the alphabet, she had printed, in block capitals, *CHLOE.* The printing had a childish wobble and tilt, and the *E* was backward and had several extra crossbars in the middle, like a ladder. But the name was perfectly

legible. Jasper was puzzled. At four years old, Maddy had been too young to read or write—and he had not known her to have progressed from scribbling single letters to spelling out actual words or names. Chloe herself must have told Maddy how to write the name—spelling it out for her.

He turned the page and saw a drawing of what he took to be a horse, given its mane and long snout and the "bent-back" look of its hind legs. Beneath this, Maddy had written two more words—inexpertly formed, the spacing uncertain. Nevertheless, she had printed near the middle of the page the word *NOT* and near the bottom, *YOURS*. Again, he was mystified by her apparent ability to spell out words, but he again reasoned that Chloe or Deepti must have been dictating something to her—a full sentence, presumably—and become distracted, leaving the phrase incomplete. Or more likely Maddy, with her child's short attention span, had grown bored and simply stopped writing.

He turned to the next page, which contained random squiggles and lines. Near the bottom, he saw written, in that now-familiar printing: *MADDYS ONA*.

"Huh," he said aloud.

What could this sentence have been part of? What could she have been trying to write? Or, rather, what could Chloe or Deepti, who must have dictated it, been trying to tell her? He puzzled over this for almost a minute but could make no sense of it—even as a sentence fragment, an incomplete thought. Perhaps he would bring the drawing pad with him to the hospital on Sunday and see if Deepti could recall what this was. It

bothered him, obscurely, to think that the import of the phrase could be lost forever.

He turned the page and was surprised to discover still *more* words, again in that blocky, childish, ill-spaced hand, with the *P*s and *E*s backward, and the words running almost diagonally down the page: *ACE*; and a little lower, *CAP*; and below that, the almost-illegible word *TOOK*; and then near the bottom, as if it were an afterthought—it was in a different color of crayon, orange this time—the mysterious word fragment *ONA* again.

"What on earth . . . ?" he mumbled.

Chris came into the room. He stopped and stared at Jasper, who was squinting hard at the page. He held the pad so close to his face that his nose almost touched the paper. "Dude," Chris said, "what's up? Looks like you're *eating* that thing."

"I'm trying to read something," Jasper said. "But I can't see it properly. Tell me. What does this say?" He held the book out. "Just here," Jasper said, pointing at the words at the top of the page.

Chris bent over and looked. "It says, uh, 'ace . . . cap . . . took.'" He straightened up. "What's it mean?"

"I'm not sure," Jasper said. "What's this last bit? Does that say 'ona'?"

Chris bent over again. He nodded. "Yup, that's it. 'Ona.' No, wait," he said. "No, sorry, that's a *D*. It's—well, it's not a word. Just letters. *D-N-A*. Hey, is that like *DNA*?"

Jasper stared at Chris's blurry, indistinct outline. Then he pulled the book under his eyes. He brought his face close to the paper. "Yes," he said. "DNA."

The page was shaking now in his hands and it took him a

moment to steady himself. He reread all the words on that page, saying them aloud to himself in a whisper: "'Ace . . . cap . . . took . . . DNA.'"

"Dude," Chris said, "you okay?"

Jasper flipped back to the first page. His heart was hammering hard in his chest. "Help me here," he said. "What does this word say?" He held the first page up to Chris.

"Chloe," Chris said.

Jasper turned the page. "And this?"

Chris squinted. "Not," he read.

"And here at the bottom?"

"Yours," Chris read.

Jasper turned another page. "And what does *this* say?"

"'Maddy, uh, maddys ONA'—I mean, DNA," Chris said. "What the hell is this?"

Jasper spoke the words aloud, running them together and supplying what he gleaned must be the missing punctuation: "Chloe not yours. Maddy's DNA."

"Dude," Chris said admonishingly, "isn't Chloe your daughter? I mean, didn't Dr. Jax say you aren't supposed to talk about her out of group?"

Jasper lowered the tablet onto his knees. He could not breathe and his heart was convulsing wildly. He stared ahead of him into the indefinite gray, trying to calm himself.

"Man, you better talk about this in group," Chris said. "You look like *shit*."

Jasper was back at 10 Cherry Tree Lane. He saw himself ushering into the house the man with the ACE cap. A slim

man, eyes hidden behind aviator shades. Hollow cheeks. The man followed Jasper with a silent tread through the living room, down the hall to the kitchen, where Jasper showed him the back stairs leading down to the furnace. Had Jasper let him out of his sight? Yes—the man had gone down the stairs. And he had *stayed* down there. Maybe ten minutes later, Jasper heard him ascending from the basement. Jasper had gotten up from the sofa to escort the man out. He couldn't have stolen *anything*, let alone Maddy's DNA.

Then he remembered. The bathroom. The man asked to use the bathroom.

"Oh my God," he said.

"Damn," said Chris, who had moved off. He was sitting on the edge of his bed, taking off his shoes and socks. "You look bad. You want me to get Dunwoody?"

Jasper didn't answer. He was thinking about how the ACE man had spent several minutes, supposedly, in the bathroom. More than enough time for him actually to have tiptoed into Maddy's room. To bend over the sleeping child, to swab the inside of her cheeks. Had he not imagined precisely this scenario for his abortive Bannister novel? Yes. He had even written a detailed draft of the scene, as the basis for a story about a diabolical imposture, a fraud . . . It was beyond belief. It could not be. He had imagined this very crime. In just this way. It had been in front of his eyes all along. All the clues. He had *seen* it. Yet he had not seen it. Nor would he ever have seen it—if not for these words on the page.

"It's not possible," he whispered.

But of course, it *was* possible. After the man left, Jasper had gone to Maddy's bedroom to wake the child and fetch Pauline. And she had stared at him in horror. In distress. Trying to warn him.

Pauline had seen it all.

The words in Maddy's tablet were dictated not by Chloe or Deepti. They were dictated by *Pauline.* Somehow, in her horror and distress, she had managed to overcome that cognitive deficit that had, up until then, forbidden her from blinking out messages, letter by letter, with the help of an assistant who recited the alphabet. These were warnings, for him, painstakingly blinked out to Maddy, who had dutifully chanted the alphabet to Pauline, day after day. Maddy could have had no idea of the messages' meanings; she would have simply viewed the exercise as a game, a way to show off her prowess at recognizing, and writing, letters. The unwitting amanuensis. Jasper himself might have elicited these same messages from Pauline, thus averting the disaster, had he not, in his state of crazed lust, fallen off from the habit of trying to train Pauline in precisely this form of dictation, had he not retreated every evening to his office to pour out, into his computer, his stream of filthy fantasies.

Now he saw Maddy sitting with Pauline, singing the alphabet song, always incomplete, always breaking off, then returning to the beginning, only to sing it again—stopping at seemingly random points, then resuming from the start. Pauline staring raptly as the child sang and scribbled with her crayon. He had, on that last day, in his terrible blindness, asked Maddy *why* she

kept singing the song. She had said something about "the butterfly man." He had not understood, had been too bound up in his obsession with Chloe even to try to understand. He understood now. The butterfly man was Jean-Dominique Bauby, a locked-in patient who dictated a memoir to an assistant, letter by letter, by blinking at the appropriate time as the assistant recited the alphabet—blinking twice to indicate the space between words. A superhuman effort that had produced a book both beautiful and heartbreaking. Jasper had read it repeatedly in the days and weeks after Pauline's stroke. He later watched Julian Schnabel's masterful movie adaptation on DVD—Maddy sitting on the floor in front of the television, scribbling with her crayons. She had asked him what was going on in the movie. He had explained it to her. *The Diving Bell and the Butterfly.*

"The butterfly man," he said aloud.

"What's that?" Chris said.

There were no phones in the inmates' rooms. All calls had to be placed within earshot of the desk sergeant, on a pay phone in the reception area downstairs.

"Chris," Jasper said, struggling to rise from the bed. "Help me downstairs. I've got to make a phone call."

Chris looked up from the issue of *Popular Science* he had been paging through. "I don't know, man," he said. "You don't look so good. Maybe you should just lie down."

"*Now!*" Jasper yelled.

Chris tossed aside the magazine and sprang off his bed. He took Jasper's arm and led him downstairs. In the lobby, Chris brought Jasper over to the pay phone on the wall above the

seating area, then retreated upstairs. Jasper felt frantically in his pockets. He had no change.

He tapped over to the desk, took a twenty from his pocket and asked Dunwoody for change. Dunwoody counted it out slowly: three fives, four ones and four quarters. Jasper made his way back across the lobby to the phone. He fed a quarter into the maddeningly narrow slot and punched in a number from memory. After two rings, a crisp female voice rapped out: "Pollock, Munson and Kline." He croaked out his request and was put through to an assistant, who said that Mr. Pollock was in a meeting.

"No!" Jasper shouted. He said that he was a client, he was calling from a pay phone at a halfway house, that it was an emergency, and that he needed to speak to Mr. Pollock right away. The assistant told him to hold on. Almost a minute went by, then he heard a click and Pollock's voice said, on a note of wary surprise, "Mr. Ulrickson?" It was obvious from his tone that Pollock had never expected to hear from Jasper again, and was not overjoyed to do so now.

Jasper explained his discovery. It all spilled out: the words dictated by Pauline and transcribed by Maddy, the messages saying that Chloe was *not* his biological daughter, that it had all been a trick, a hoax to defraud him of his money, to destroy him, professionally and personally. "You—you even suspected such a thing, at first, when I called you up," Jasper reminded him. "You mentioned the scammers and con men who make false paternity claims! But I'm sure you've never encountered something this diabolical." To expose the scheme, Jasper said, Pollock need only dispatch someone to his sister's house in San Francisco,

take a DNA swab from Maddy and check that sample against the one submitted under Chloe's name. "They would still have Chloe's DNA sequence on file at DDS, right?" he added excitedly. "Well, it won't be hers! It will be Maddy's!"

Pollock greeted this news with a long silence. Then he said, in a low, quiet voice, "Where are you calling from?"

"A halfway house," Jasper said. "I mean, a residential rehabilitation center, they call them now. I was released six months ago. Sorry—I should have said that right at the start."

"Yes, I did hear about your release," Pollock said. "Tell me, are you attending psychiatric sessions? Therapy? To help you readjust to society?"

Jasper was puzzled by Pollock's desire to discuss this triviality, given the stunning news he had just relayed of the fraud. But he answered, "Yes—we have group therapy every evening. But about Maddy's DNA. Can we get that started right away? I don't want to lose any time. I think Pauline's health, even her survival, could depend on her hearing that the culprit or culprits have been—"

"Mr. Ulrickson," Pollock interrupted sharply.

"Yes?" Jasper said, startled by the other man's abrupt tone.

"I'm having a very busy day, and I need to get back to work. But let me just say that I understand how difficult it must be to reintegrate into society after long incarceration. The best advice I can give you is to continue your group sessions, but also to inquire into personal, one-on-one therapy, where you can address any problems you're having dealing with any lingering guilt about your daughter and—"

"No!" Jasper cried. "I'm not crazy. I have evidence. Maddy's drawing pad. She wrote the messages—in crayon. Pauline dictated them to her. I can show you. If you send a messenger—"

"Mr. Ulrickson," Pollock said. "I really must get back to work. I was very sorry to hear of your troubles. I hope you can make a successful reintegration and become a useful member of society." He hung up.

Jasper stood in mute astonishment, the phone at his ear. He hung up.

He had been a fool—gibbering incoherently about Maddy's drawing pad and secret messages in crayon. Unless he could physically *show* someone the evidence, they would never believe it.

He tapped his way back to the desk. "Officer Dunwoody," Jasper said. "I need your help." He held up the drawing tablet.

"Yeah," Dunwoody said. "I heard every word." Jasper could not see Dunwoody's expression—the desk sergeant was a murky pink and purple outline against the dull flicker of small TV screens—but he could hear the sarcasm in his voice.

"Please," Jasper said, "let me show you." He put the pad on the counter and began to open the cover. Dunwoody slapped it closed.

"Don't fuck with me," he said. "I don't know if you're trying to be funny. But I'm not laughing."

"It's my daughter's printing," Jasper persisted. "She was four at the time. How could she be writing messages about stolen DNA? It had to be my wife!"

"Okay," Dunwoody said, "get the fuck out of here." There was true threat in his tone now.

"Please—" Jasper started to say, but the man cut him off.

"You're due at work in thirty minutes," Dunwoody said. "If you're late, you lose outside privileges—for a *month*."

Jasper stood there, lost. He was still filled with exultation over his discovery, his mind racing, his heart drumming hard. But he was thwarted, blocked. Then he had a thought—a crucial realization. "Yes—okay," he said, snatching the drawing pad off the desk. "I'm going. I—I was only joking about the messages."

"No shit," Dunwoody said. He pushed the button to release the front door lock. "Now, get to work."

Jasper tapped across the lobby, pushed open the door and went out.

Cool air hit his face and body. It was mid-March, the keen cold of lingering winter stirred to tepid warmth by a brightening sun. He had not brought a coat, but it was too late to go back for it. Dragging his uncooperative leg behind him, feeling his way with his cane, he moved as quickly as he could up the street to the bus stop. But instead of joining his usual group waiting for the bus westbound to go to work, he proceeded to the curb, looked both ways, up and down Venice Street. He could hear the eastbound bus approaching some way off—perhaps a block away, the distinctive grind of its engine. There was no time to limp down to the lights at the intersection. Through the watery blur, he could not see any cars coming. Trusting to fate, he set out across the avenue, tapping, heaving his lame leg along with a jerking motion of his hips.

He got to the opposite side. Fifty yards up the sidewalk was the eastbound stop for people going downtown—toward the

hospital. He made it just as the bus pulled up. The doors opened with a sharp hydraulic hiss and he climbed aboard. As usual, he took a seat near the front.

"Fulton?" asked the driver, whose voice Jasper recognized.

"Yes, thank you," he said.

"Not your usual time," the driver said.

"No," Jasper said with finality.

Panting, heart hammering, he collapsed back against the seat and closed his eyes. He had suddenly known, in the lobby with Dunwoody, that more important even than alerting the authorities was the urgency of telling Pauline of his discovery. Whether she could hear him or not, whether she could process his words—whether anyone else ever believed him—he must tell *her* that her Herculean efforts to warn him about the fraud had not been in vain. Carlucci had said that Pauline's condition was not dissimilar to that of people suffering posttraumatic stress, her brain and body shut down in defense. Was it not possible that Pauline's state derived from the unimaginable frustration of having tried—and failed—to alert him to the hoax? He would not be able to forgive himself if she died before he had the chance to tell her that her messages had been heard; that she had *reached him*.

He asked the driver how close they were—surely they were almost there? The driver named a street ten long blocks from the hospital. Panicked, Jasper touched the face of his glassless watch. Noon. He should, right now, be stepping through the door at his workplace. How long before his boss called Dunwoody to alert him that he was AWOL? How long before Dunwoody put out a bulletin to have Jasper apprehended?

The bus moved with aching slowness through the clogged traffic, edging up, tentatively, to each stop to let people in and out. Sluggish passengers disembarked, and sluggish passengers climbed laboriously in. Then the driver sat for a seeming eternity before pulling the handle that caused the doors to shut with a wan sigh. Often he was obliged to open the doors again, to allow a passenger to yank his bag or elbow or coattail from between the doors' rubber gusset, before once again closing them. Then he would nudge the bus into gear and slowly pull away from the curb, only to lurch immediately to a stop in the unmoving traffic.

Jasper was seized suddenly with horror. Perhaps Pollock was right—perhaps he had imagined everything. He was overwrought. He had gone mad. He ripped the drawing tablet from under his arm, opened it and brought the page close to his face. Yes—yes, there they were, those words. *Chloe not yours. Maddy's DNA*. He had not imagined it. He was not insane. He paged ahead. Saw the ACE man message. Then he turned to the tablet's last page, where there was another set of shakily drawn letters and words—a message he had not yet seen:

DR GELD ACE M

The message was incomplete—but he knew its meaning, and even recalled when it must have been written. He was sitting beside Pauline and Maddy on the sofa, on that last day they were ever together as a family. Chloe was in her session with Dr. Geld. Maddy was softly singing the alphabet song as Pauline stared at her hypnotically. He had snapped irritably at Maddy, interrupting her in mid-song, interrupting Pauline (he now realized) in

mid-message. But he knew now what Pauline was trying to tell him: *Dr. Geld is the ACE man*. Had he known it, on some level, all along? Those pale eyes? That mocking smile and aura of amused insolence? A chill shivered his marrow.

"Here's Fulton," said the driver.

He stuck the tablet under his arm, struggled to his feet and then climbed down from the bus onto the sidewalk. He peered around helplessly through his dark glasses, suddenly disoriented in his excitement. A deep-voiced man said, "Can I help you?" Jasper felt a hand gently take his upper arm and he was enveloped in a comforting aroma of pipe smoke and leather. "On the way to the hospital?" the man asked in a kindly voice. Jasper said he was. "So am I," the man said. "I'll take you."

They crossed the busy avenue and together negotiated the stairs up to the hospital entrance. In the lobby, the man said that he had to see someone on the first floor. "You'll be okay?" he asked. Jasper said he was fine, thanked his invisible angel, and headed for the elevator bank. The whole time, he expected to hear a voice cry out, "There he is!" and to hear the hard-soled shoes of the hospital's security personnel scuff rapidly up to him over the polished marble floors. But the lobby remained a placid, sunlit aquarium where soft shapes swirled and swam like fish. He joined a large, vague crowd waiting for the elevator. He heard the musical ping followed by the oily swish of the doors. Carried forward like a cork on a wave, he stepped inside.

The nurses expressed surprise when he limped, tapping, out of the elevator and up to the reception desk. "We usually

see you at the *end* of the day," one of them sang out cheerfully.

"I have a little time off," he said, trying to sound breezy. "I thought I'd say a quick hello to Pauline."

"Be our guest!"

He moved down the hallway, expecting at any moment to hear a phone come to life in the nursing station behind him, then one of the nurses calling out, on a note of hysteria and surprise, "Mr. Ulrickson!" That did not happen. He made it to Pauline's room and stepped inside. He approached the bed. She lay, as usual, utterly still, eyes closed, face pointed toward the ceiling, inert. He felt for and took her hand. He brought his face close. "Pauline," he whispered.

Her closed eyelids remained still.

"Listen to me, honey," he said. "Deepti brought me Maddy's drawing tablet. I saw the messages. I read the warnings. I *know* the truth. I know that Chloe is *not* my daughter. I know it was a *trick*—a hoax."

He paused. He squinted at her face. He thought he saw Pauline's eyeballs stir beneath the thin flesh of the lids. But he could not be sure.

"I know about the man in the ACE cap," he continued. "I know he went to Maddy's bedroom when she was napping. He swabbed her. You saw it all. Honey, *I got your messages*."

Her closed eyelids compressed, once. This could not be a random reflex, Jasper felt sure.

"I know about *Geld*," he whispered. You managed to tell me *everything*, my love."

Her eyelids trembled. Then, tentatively, quiveringly, they cracked open. He glimpsed through the slits the moist brown of her irises.

"My God," Jasper said. "Oh my God." He filled his lungs to bellow for the nurses. But he quashed the impulse. He had something to ask her. Something of grave importance. "Honey," he said, "are you listening?"

Her eyelids fluttered. Opened wider. She was looking at the ceiling, her irises moving wildly, restlessly. Then, with her head rigidly immobile on the pillow, she turned her gaze in Jasper's direction. She stared into his face. He saw her pupils contract, as she focused on him. He snatched off his dark glasses so that she might better recognize him. Was she registering the changes in him? The weight loss, the empty eye socket, the silvered hair? He watched with disbelief as her eyes began to take on a glint of life, to fill with recognition, animation, that spark of vitality and awareness that had always brimmed within them, that had convinced Jasper of her fierce determination to live.

"In a minute, I'll tell the nurses you're awake," he whispered. "Everything is going to change. They'll start the physio again. You're going to improve. And I'm going to be with you. Forever. But first—I've got to ask you something. Something very important." He cocked his head, listening, to hear if anyone was coming who might interrupt them. The corridor outside was silent. He turned back to her. "Did *Chloe* know?" he asked. "Was *she* part of this?"

Pauline saw, in her mind's eye, the way Chloe had clutched

at the man's arm—then let go when aware that the touch had been witnessed. She blinked once.

"Good Lord," he said.

There had existed the possibility, however remote, that Chloe too had been the victim of his unknown adversary; she too might have been tricked into believing she was his biological daughter. He had, he realized, been clinging to this hope. But no. She knew. She was part of the conspiracy. Part of the plan to destroy him. Her every smile and batted eyelash a stratagem. That transparent pink nightie, and carefully prepared glass of Scotch, part of a coldly calculated trap. The revelation was nightmarish, unthinkable. The depth of her evil so much more chilling for being hidden behind that seeming innocence. But now, at least, he had a place to start, a thread to pull. He did not have long. By now, Dunwoody would know that Jasper had not arrived at work. That he had fled.

"I've got to go," he whispered to Pauline. "They're going to be looking for me. But please don't worry. Everything is going to be all right. I promise. You were not too late." He kissed her cheek. "You were *not* too late."

He stabbed his glasses back onto his face and tapped his way out the door.

Approaching the nursing station he tensed, preparing to try to run, even with his damaged hip, if they tried to accost him. But, miraculously, he heard the nurse at the desk call out, "See you soon!"

Jasper limped up to her. "My wife is conscious," he said,

addressing the indistinct shape. "She's blinking in response to questions. Get the doctor—hurry!"

He heard a rattle as the nurse snatched up the phone.

"Hurry!" he cried. "She is awake. She is aware!"

He heard the nurse slam down the phone. The sound of her shoes hurried off down the hall.

He went to the elevator and pushed the Down button. Behind him, one of the phones in the now-abandoned nursing station exploded to life, letting out ring after ring. He heard the nurse's shoes moving rapidly back up the corridor toward the phone. The elevator doors slid open. He stepped inside. He heard the plastic rattle of a receiver being lifted, then the nurse saying, "Hello?"

The doors closed.

The elevator swooshed downward. He felt the floor push up against the soles of his shoes, forcing his knees to flex. The doors slid open and two people surged at him out of the gray mist. But they were not the police—only a woman in a white lab coat and a doctor in green surgical scrubs. Jasper tapped out into the lobby. He made his way, heart pounding, to one end of the welcome desk, where there was a free public telephone—he had used it on his previous visits to notify Dunwoody that he was on his way back to the center. He took out his wallet, extracted a slip of paper, brought it to his face, squinted at the digits written upon it, then punched them into the phone. He turned his back on the brightness from the revolving doors at the entrance, hiding his face. He heard two rings, then a female voice said, "Hello?"

"Deepti," he said. "It's Mr. Ulrickson. I need your help." He told her to meet him at the diner across the street from the hospital. "Right away," he added. "And don't tell *anyone*."

5

Jasper arrived first and was shown to a booth near the back. His hypersensitive ears were assaulted by the din of crashing cutlery, waitresses calling out orders, frozen hamburgers clacked onto hissing grills and the roar of frozen french fries plunged into hot oil. A shadow fell over him. He waved away the menu and ordered a ham sandwich. He was not hungry but feared he would be asked to go if he tried to occupy a prime table without eating during the lunch rush.

He glanced up hopefully every time he heard the jingle of the bell over the door. In the wavering dimness, he could make out only the blurred silhouettes of people against the midday glare. He had been there for almost ten minutes and had seen

scores of people come and go before a figure entered the restaurant, hesitated, then rapidly approached.

"What is going on, Mr. Jasper?" Deepti said as she settled into the seat opposite him. "I was leaving to come here when that Officer Dunwoody phoned. He asked if you were with me. Or if I knew where you were." Jasper, unable to respond, waited. "I told him no."

His breathing and heartbeat resumed. "Thank you, Deepti," he said. He glanced out the window beside him, toward the gray monolith of the hospital. Any minute now, he thought, a cruiser would pull up.

The waitress appeared, placed Jasper's sandwich and coffee in front of him and offered Deepti a menu. "Just a coffee for me, please," she said. The waitress dissolved into the noisy blur.

"Look at this," he said, pushing his food aside and placing the drawing pad on the table between them. He opened the cover. "These are messages. From Pauline. Transcribed by Maddy. The alphabet game." He explained about the day when the man in the ACE cap came to the house, ostensibly to inspect the furnace. "You were in the guesthouse, phoning your daughter, so you didn't see him. But he went into Maddy's room and swabbed her cheeks. He used *Maddy's* DNA to establish that Chloe was my child. Pauline saw it all, and tried to warn me."

Deepti seemed to be struggling with doubts. Then he showed her the final message, the one about Dr. Geld being the man in the ACE cap. "He was an impostor," Jasper said. "He was no doctor."

The memory of Dr. Geld's insolent face flashed in Deepti's

mind. "I did not trust that man," she said. "There was something about him." She recalled those final moments, after Pauline had been taken by ambulance to the hospital, and she had been alone with that man on the front path. He had said something impossibly rude in reply to her questions. A few minutes later, she had seen him, through the sliding glass doors of the living room; he had shown a disturbing overfamiliarity with Chloe. Recalling this, a sickening suspicion arose in Deepti's mind. "Could Chloe have been part of this?" she asked.

Jasper nodded. He explained that he had confirmed this with Pauline.

"Pauline?" she said, incredulous.

He described how she had awakened from her coma when he told her that he had deciphered her warnings.

"Poor Miss Pauline!" Deepti said, when the full implications of this had sunk in. "Knowing the truth, and not being able to tell anyone!"

"Worse," Jasper said. "Trying to tell—and failing. It nearly killed her."

They sat for some time in silence. Then Deepti made a helpless gesture. "I would not have believed it of Chloe," she said. "Perhaps this man *forced* her?"

"Perhaps," Jasper said.

"In any case, we must now go to the police."

"No," he said. He told her about Pollock's and Dunwoody's reactions. "We need evidence. Solid evidence. Otherwise, it sounds like an insane fantasy."

"But what can we do?"

"I can talk to Chloe."

Deepti shook her head. She reminded him of the restraining order. "You cannot go near her. They will send you back to jail—for many, many years."

"There's no choice," he told her. "I need your help to find her. I *must* talk to her. Do you know where she is?"

Deepti turned and stared out the window at the late lunch crowds hurrying past. Just a few weeks ago, she had received a card from Chloe—quite out of the blue. *I hope you and your daughter are well,* she had written. *I think of you, Pauline and Maddy often.* Deepti had written back a short, polite note. She had not heard back. But, in her meticulous way, she had taken care to write Chloe's return address in her diary, which sat in the purse next to her on the leather banquette.

"Deepti," Jasper said. "You know how to get in touch with her."

She looked at him. He was hunched, leaning forward, peering at her through his dark glasses. Suddenly, he frowned and cocked his head. A look of alarm seized his features. "What is it?" Deepti said.

"Listen!"

It was several seconds before her ears were able to pick out what his sharpened hearing had easily detected over the diner's clash and clatter and shouted conversations: a distant, high-pitched wailing sound. A siren. It grew louder. They turned and looked out the window. To the accompaniment of a crescendoing siren scream, one of the city's blue-and-white squad cars streaked into view and pulled up at the curb across the street. A policeman got out of the passenger's side and went up the hospital steps. The driver stayed in the car, talking into his police radio.

"My God," Deepti said. "They are looking for you!" She glanced at the pad on the table in front of her. Written there, in crayon, were the words: *DR GELD ACE M.* She saw again that slyly insinuating, unsettlingly impudent face and shivered, as if a cold draft had played over her.

"My car is parked on the next side street," she said. "I will take you to her."

6

Traffic was light on the southbound I-95. Their destination, Deepti said, was an apartment building in Washington Heights—a Dominican enclave north of Harlem. "She lives there with two other girls. She is a student. She told me nothing else."

"Why is she living there—with roommates?" Jasper said. "She has the settlement money. Millions."

Deepti repeated, "She told me nothing else."

They drove in silence. In his side window, the fuzzed gray outline of Manhattan appeared out of the mists of his blindness. Striped shadows flicked stroboscopically in his vision as they rode beneath the girders of the bridge that he still knew as the Triborough but which, since his incarceration, had become the

RFK. They turned left and swept past sights of East Harlem that Jasper could no longer clearly make out but which he knew intimately from trips into the city when he still had his full vision: brown brick projects, cracked concrete basketball courts and chain-link fencing. They turned right and beat their way through stop-and-go cross-town traffic on 125th Street. Pedestrian crowds pushed past at the intersections, heedless of the lights, forcing Deepti to slow or stop altogether, yellow cabs swerving around them, horns blaring. At Broadway, Deepti turned north. Thumping hip-hop gave way, at 155th Street, to frenzied merengue and salsa. They drove through the shadow of looming Columbia Presbyterian Hospital, then turned left onto 172nd. "This is her street," Deepti said.

They crossed Fort Washington Avenue. Deepti guided her car up a steep grade, craning her head to see the numbers on the fronts of the soot-begrimed buildings, with their imitation Greek columns framing smeared glass doors.

"There it is," she said. "Number 710." She found a parking spot nearby and stopped. They got out. The aroma of roasting meat floated from an apartment window. Music, all clattering pot-and-pan percussion and shrill horns, issued from another window, and from somewhere an excited voice, in Spanish, was breathlessly announcing a soccer game.

Deepti took his arm and they went up the sidewalk. They pushed through a street door into a stuffy lobby, their shoes echoing against bare stone tile. Deepti found the buzzer and pushed it. An electronic crackle came from the speaker and a youthful-sounding female voice said, "Yup?" Deepti said that

she was looking for Chloe. "Just a sec." Then, after a short pause, Jasper heard from the speaker Chloe's familiar, featherlight voice, sounding just as it had that first day on the phone, when he called her at the Gaitskills'.

"Yes? Who is it?"

Jasper was stunned. To know, now, the malevolence that lay behind that voice!

"It is Deepti."

"Deepti!" she cried. "What a surprise. Come on up! Fifth floor—there's no elevator. Sorry."

There was a buzz. They pushed through the security door. In the weak light of the lobby, Jasper made out a row of brass mailboxes mounted to the mud-brown plaster wall. They came to a dark, narrow staircase and he could discern, through the haze, a set of white stone steps worn to a crescent shape in the middle. A cramped, collapsing tenement: *why was she living here?*

They climbed to the third-floor landing. He heard, over the sound of his own labored breathing and pounding heart, the shooting of a bolt above them and then footsteps padding along a hall. Chloe's voice called down: "Deepti! We're all the way up on—" She abruptly fell silent. She must have been hanging over the banister and caught sight of them. Of *him*. "Who's that with you?" she asked.

Deepti made no reply.

He listened. He did not hear feet retreating along the hall, nor the slam of the apartment door and its locking mechanism. They resumed their climb.

They reached the top, then stood for a moment, catching

their breath. Through the gray blur he could make out, over Deepti's shoulder, a shadow shape—Chloe's silhouette, slender, sylphlike—standing against a patch of light behind her. She made a sudden movement, a flinch of shock and surprise. "Oh my God," he heard her say. Then she asked, on a rising note of panic: "What are you doing here? Deepti—why did you bring him here?"

Just then other shapes appeared against the brightness of the apartment's open door.

"What's happening, Chloe?" said a female voice unfamiliar to him—slightly raspy, with a Latin tinge in the vowels and cadences. "Is everything okay?"

Then there was another female voice, this one higher-pitched, girlish, frightened: "Yeah, who's there?"

"Wait a sec," he heard the Latina say, and Jasper could tell from the clarity and direction of her voice that she was looking at him. "That's your *dad*!" she cried out. "He isn't supposed to be here! Hey, you sick fuck, you're not supposed to be here!"

"Call 911," the second girl said.

Deepti told them to calm down. "Mr. Jasper simply needs to have a word with Chloe. It is important. He is not here to hurt you, Chloe."

The Latina spoke up again. "He's not supposed to come near her! I know for a fact. My aunt had a restraining order against my uncle and one time he came with a gun and—"

"No one has a gun," Jasper interrupted. He placed his cane between his knees and reached into his pockets. He turned

them out, showing that he had only a few crumpled bills and a wallet. "I just need to speak to Chloe. Briefly. Alone."

"*Alone?*" said the Latina, incredulous. "Hey, listen up: you got no right to talk to nobody *alone*, you rapist fuck. C'mon, Clo, let's call the cops."

"It's okay," he heard Chloe say.

"Yeah, but—" her friend started to protest.

"I'm all right," Chloe said. "You and Misty—why don't you go to the coffee shop? For ten minutes."

"And leave you *alone* with him?"

"I'll call your cell if there's a problem."

"This fucker raped you! You want to be *alone* with him?"

"I'll be fine," Chloe said. "I mean," she added, and Jasper thought he heard some pity in her voice, "look at him."

He imagined that all three girls must now be staring at him, sizing up his sorry, wasted, crippled figure.

The Latina made a noncommittal grunt. Then she added, skeptically, grudgingly, "Well . . . okay. I'll get my laptop. And we *will* be back in ten minutes." She retreated down the hall. A minute later, she emerged from the apartment. "C'mon, Misty," she said. The two shapes moved up the hall toward him. Passing Jasper, the Latina thrust her face close to his, her dark eyes, sharp angular features and café au lait skin moving into his narrow range of focus. "*Sicko*," she hissed. She moved off. Another shadow moved past, although this girl shrank from him, sliding her body along the railing that enclosed the stairwell. The sound of their feet diminished down the stairs.

When silence returned, Chloe told him to come into the apartment. She flattened herself against the door frame. Passing within inches of her, he felt the radiating nimbus of her body warmth and was inundated by the remembered scent of ginger and vanilla. He was suddenly thankful that he could not see her, that she existed only as a shadow. Deepti stayed in the hallway.

He took a few halting paces into the apartment. He could make out little—a blurred grouping of chairs around what must be a coffee table, a bookshelf, a window overflowing with blinding white light. The air was hung with a smell of pizza and beer and cigarette smoke: the aromas of student life. He heard the door close and click behind him. He turned. He could make out her fuzzy-edged, wavery outline against the gray-white wall.

Facing him, about five feet across the bare tile floor, she was unable to believe that this was the same person she had first met in that courthouse antechamber, all those years ago: the tall, sturdily built blond man whose expression of seeming sympathy and love had stirred her to a surge of daughterly love, that misdirected devotion later dashed to dust by the words in his diary. Now, she saw a tiny, stooped figure in dark glasses, white stubble on his bowed head, cheeks hollowed—and this, coupled with her awareness of how her own actions had brought him to this state, stirred her to pity and horror. She tried to put some steel in her tone, but her voice carried a telltale tremor when she said, "Why are you here?"

"I think you know." He spoke in a low growl utterly unlike the kindly, clear voice she remembered. "To start with: you're not my daughter."

She could not speak, could not draw breath. How did he

know? Was it a bluff? The rush of blood in her ears drowned out everything.

"It was Maddy's DNA," he said.

Would she attack him? Run and collect a knife from the kitchen? Stab him? A mistake—it had been a terrible mistake to meet with her alone! But no. She made no move toward him. Instead, she moved with dreamlike slowness. Moved sideways across the room. Her blurry arm reached for the back of what he surmised was an armchair. She stepped around it and sagged down onto its cushions. Sensing that he was in no physical danger from her, he used his cane, groped in front of him, so that he could move a step closer to her.

"Pauline," he said. "She knew. She dictated it all to Maddy. Remember the alphabet game?"

"The alphabet game . . ." Chloe limply echoed. She recalled that first night in the house, when little Maddy had pulled at her arm, on the sofa, and mentioned the game. They had played it many times in the weeks that followed, Chloe saying a letter and Maddy having to write it down. Those happy weeks before the disaster. The disaster of his diary. Followed by the disaster she had visited upon him. Upon his family.

"Pauline saw everything," he went on. "The woman you called *mother*," he could not resist adding bitterly. "She figured out everything. Not just the DNA scam. But Dr. Geld."

At the mention of Dez's alter ego, her head shot up and she gaped at Jasper, stunned, terrified. He *did* know the truth. He had found out. Not only about the fraud, but about *Dez*. "Oh my God," she said.

He tapped forward. He was standing over her. He wanted

now to see her, to see her expression. But her face remained only a blurred oval, and he was afraid to move his own face closer in case she did throw off this strange, unexpected torpor and attack him. But she had no intention of attacking him, had no wish to hurt him further.

"I know the whole sick, disgusting game," he said. "But there are two questions I have for you. Why? I need to know why you did it. Why did you destroy my family?"

"I didn't want to destroy your family," she whispered.

"Then why?"

She pulled up, in memory, those rationales that Dez had drummed into her, rationales that now sounded so weak, so laughably lame. "We—to pay you back for my mother," she said in a barely audible voice.

"Your *mother*?" he said, mystified.

She felt a surge of defensiveness, felt the old certainties flare up, a final, desperate effort to convince, not so much him, but herself. "You took advantage of her!" she wailed. "You never called her! You thought you could just, just *sleep* with her—*seduce* her—then leave and—and—and—and never talk to her again!"

He was genuinely baffled. "But it was your *mother* who initiated everything. Your mother who pursued *me*—"

Yes, Chloe thought, that would be true of her poor mother. All those men she brought home from the bars every weekend, slept with and then kicked out. Of course she had pursued Jasper the same way back then, taken her pleasure and then moved on. Back to Hughie, her boyfriend, Chloe's father. Not

pined away, for years, in sadness for this man. Not waited by the phone for his call. Chloe had always known it, on some deeply buried level. So how could she have swallowed Dez's version? Dez's lies?

"And Maddy!" she now cried in desperation.

"Maddy?" he said, even more bewildered. "What are you talking about?"

Her hands flew to the sides of her head. She stopped up her ears, refusing to hear what he was saying. She had to silence any protest of his, any counterargument, just as she had had to silence, in herself, the terrible, stealthy doubts that had tried to seep into her mind over the years since his arrest and imprisonment. "You—you—you would abuse Maddy next," she cried. "Just like you abused *me*." Aware of some fatal flaw in this logic (after all, *she* had set out to seduce *him*; she had set his lust in motion), she changed tack. "I trusted you! I *loved* you. Like a daughter." She added, on a weak, helpless sob, "I never, ever—I didn't want to hurt you. I didn't want to hurt anyone."

He had not expected this. He had expected jeering, insults, threats, even gloating. Not tears. Not this obvious pain and remorse. It was worse, so much worse than any defiance or denial she might have retreated behind. "But surely you set out to seduce me?" he said. That pink nightie. The glass of Scotch. "Wasn't that your plan?" Had he somehow gotten everything wrong?

"At *first*," she said, woefully, weakly. "At first." She raised her eyes and peered at the pathetic creature before her, saw the look of confusion on his ravaged face, a confusion accentuated

by the round, owlish black glasses obscuring his eyes. She owed him at least some explanation. Some insight. "I did set out to seduce you, at the very beginning, when you came to get me. But then I didn't want to go through with it. I didn't think *you* would go through with it. I never believed you would have those feelings. I thought you liked me. I thought you *loved* me. Like a daughter."

"But—but I did," Jasper protested. Had he, though? Had he ever truly loved her with the purity of a real father? Yes—yes, in that first phone call, before he had ever seen her, when she had been only a detached, disembodied voice—a light, innocent, sweetly melodic voice—as now.

"Then I saw your diary," she said.

It took him a moment to process this. "My diary?"

"That's when I knew how you really felt about me."

He saw before him the words of the diary he had kept during that nightmare summer. His foul catalog of lust. The computer had been seized by prosecutors, the contents used in court against him, but he had never known, until now, that she had read those shameful entries while still living in his house. "Oh God," he said. That he now knew her not to be his actual daughter did nothing to soften his shame and horror and guilt. Those mortifying passages spelling out his degraded obsession.

"And if you could feel that way about *me*," she went on, "then what about Maddy?"

"Never," he objected weakly. "I would never—"

"But that's what *he* told me," Chloe burst out. "He told me you were bad. Sick. He said that you exploited my mother, and

that you were going to exploit me, then you were going to hurt *Maddy*." She had spoken herself into boldness. "He said the only way to stop you was to put you in jail. If I helped, I was doing the right thing. And I *believed* him. I did believe him! But then—" She stopped. He heard a gulping sound, heard her wipe at her face with something that made a soft crinkling noise—perhaps a napkin left over from the pizza. He waited, reeling at her revelations, but she remained silent.

"But then?" he prompted.

"But then I started to wonder," she said. "Things he said. The way he behaved. Especially when we got the money."

Should she be telling him this? Talking about this? But why shouldn't she—now? He already knew about the scam. Knew about *Dez*! And she had held it all in for so long. She had wanted to tell someone, so many times over the years. But there was no one to tell, no one she could trust—not even Misty or Gabriella—and she had no blood relations left to whom she could confide the story, the story of the scheme, and the nightmare that came after it. Strange to think, but this man standing in front of her was the closest thing to family she had left in the whole world.

"I mean, it was okay for a while," she said, her voice low and quiet, almost as if she were talking to herself. "We bought a place downtown. I thought I was in love with him. I *was* in love. But I also wanted to *do* something with my life. I tried acting and modeling—but it didn't work out. I stunk at it. He was happy about that. But it wasn't too late for me to try something else. I wanted to go back to school. Study psychology.

He said I was crazy. What did I need school for? But I got my GED, by correspondence. I wanted to go to college. He said no. He wanted me with *him*. Then he started with the drugs. Cocaine. Ecstasy. Other stuff. And girls. Young girls. Younger than me. Girls that made me feel old—and I was only *twenty*. He wanted me to be with them. I *was* with them a couple of times, because he—he—" She broke off.

There could be no question about her sincerity, Jasper realized. Really, she was no different from Jasper himself, a victim of this man who had destroyed her life, or tried to. Who had preyed on her innocence and vulnerability.

"I tried to kick him out," she went on. "He just laughed at me. He said, 'Kick me out? It's *my* apartment.' That's when I found out that he had put everything in his name: bank accounts, property, investments, royalties from your books—everything. I don't know how he did it. I mean, one day he had me sign a bunch of papers, but he said it was for *taxes*. One day he showed me. Everything was in his name. I didn't have a penny. I was completely dependent on him.

"I guess he thought he could keep me there with him, forever. He didn't expect me to run. But I did. He was passed out one night, with these girls we'd brought back from this club. I put some clothes in a bag and took off. Took three hundred dollars from his wallet. It wasn't stealing, really. It was mine anyway. Or, really, *yours*. I didn't care about the money. By that time, I didn't trust anything he said, and I didn't trust why I had done what I did. To you. To your family. Nothing made sense anymore. I just wanted to get away from him. To forget everything.

So I left. I stayed in a shelter. Applied to school, and I got a scholarship to NYU. I met Gabriella and Misty. We found this place. And—and everything has been really good."

She tried to smile, but her voice cracked on the word "good" and she began to sob. Jasper, his own chest roiling, took a tentative step forward, but he did not, could not, reach out and touch her: what if she were to misconstrue the nature of that touch? He longed now to tell her that he did not blame her for anything, to comfort her, as a father would, with a gentle hand on her shoulder or knee. But that was impossible. He had rendered it so by his violation of her all those years ago.

"You can believe me or not, but I always felt bad about you," she choked out. "About what we did to you. And your family. But I pushed it out of my mind—I had to, to survive. Then I saw the newspapers when you got out of jail. I read about how you were beaten in prison. I wrote a card to Deepti after seeing the newspaper. I wanted to see if she would tell me anything about you and Maddy and Mo—Pauline. When I heard Deepti on the intercom, I buzzed her in, because I thought she would tell me how you were doing. I saw you on the stairs . . . I almost called 911. But I guess I wanted to tell you that I'm sorry." She started crying again. "Because I am. I *am* sorry."

She ventured a look at him and saw a face utterly without a vestige of the lust that had distorted his features on that last night, when he had come home from the hospital and stared at her with a desire that looked almost like fear; and, later, when he had come into her bedroom and stood over her, his face twisted into a mask of terrible need, twitching and sweating,

his eyes boring into her. Now he was peering at her, blindly, two tear trails rolling out from under his dark lenses and down his desiccated cheeks. She was filled with that old sensation of yearning after him as a father, that instinct that had arisen in her in the courthouse and that had strengthened over the following days and weeks, when she had never felt so whole, so safe and so loved. She had never expected to feel that way again, about anyone. "I know you want to put me in jail," she said. "I deserve it. But I *am* sorry."

"No, Chloe," he said in a hoarse whisper. "I don't want to put you in jail." That was perfectly true, now. "And please don't apologize. *I'm* sorry. There's no excuse for what I did to you—none."

It struck him with unendurable force that her part in the conspiracy—her deliberate efforts to seduce him—did nothing to mitigate his crime of sleeping with her; if anything, her role as helpless puppet only magnified his guilt. In succumbing to his basest urges, he had in effect *joined* his nemesis in exploiting and victimizing her, the two adults whose only proper role would have been to keep her from such harm. That he could not now obey the instinct physically to comfort her was evidence of his vile kinship with the man who had directed her actions, and proof of how he himself, by raping her, had destroyed any chance of establishing with her a bond of trust or affection, the healthy bond that had moved him to tears that day on the phone, in his office, when he had first heard her featherlight voice. He might even now have become a kind of father to her, to alleviate their shared loneliness, to rebuild their mutually broken lives, had he not surrendered to that

urge for fleeting, meaningless physical pleasure and destroyed everything between them forever.

Thinking of this, he wondered, suddenly, if lust had even been his sole sin in regard to her. Hubris. Excessive pride. That, on reflection, was the catalyst, a kind of overconfidence in his own powers of self-control. He was visited with a memory of a comment he had made on that television show, all those years ago, when asked about his celibate life with Pauline. He had said something about the way straying men justified their infidelities by blaming the demands of their biology. "We *can* control ourselves," he had asserted. Would he have been as susceptible to temptation had he not suffered from such an unshakable, unwarranted confidence in his own higher nature; had he recognized, from the outset, before even meeting Chloe, the peril of bringing into his home an eighteen-year-old girl, daughter of a past lover, when he was so vulnerable to his thwarted, frustrated urges?

And when it came to that, how completely blind had he truly been to the danger? For one stubborn detail stuck in his mind, a detail that he had worried away at, and ruminated over, for days and weeks and months and years during his incarceration, a detail he had never been able to bring himself to mention to the prison therapist or in group sessions at the halfway house. He was thinking of one of the gifts that he had bought for Chloe during his shopping spree at Urban Outfitters, weeks before he ever laid eyes on her: that present purchased along with the shirts and jeans and sneakers—an item glimpsed, on a shelf near the back of the store, and which had somehow cried

out to be bought. He was thinking of that pretty pair of strappy silver sandals, identical to the pair worn by Holly at the closing dance, and for which he had left her forlornly searching, with a pointed toe, in the dark sand. Those sandals, flat-soled, with the Y-shaped, glittering cross straps that left most of the foot bare, and which sat in the center of his mind, like one of those clues he liked to hide in plain sight in his Bannister mysteries. Certainly, in surrendering to that seemingly innocent impulse purchase in the days before Chloe came to live with him, he had not been conscious of trying to retrieve a mislaid piece of the past, had not been conscious of drawing a fatal link between the girl with whom he had shared a moment of excruciatingly arrested passion on a moonlit beach and the girl he was slated, soon, to meet—but it is in the very nature of the subconscious mind that often its devious needs, and darkest desires, remain unknown to us, until it is too late.

"It was all my doing—I was in the wrong," he now said, "and I will have to live with that for the rest of my life."

She shook her head. "We were both in the wrong."

He was going to contest this, but thought better of it. "Perhaps," he allowed. "But there was someone *else* in the wrong too," he added, his voice quickening.

He was aware of how much time had gone by since he had arrived in this apartment. Her roommates would be back any minute. And he had yet to put to her the second of the two questions he had come here to ask. A crucial question that must be answered.

"This man you mentioned," he said. "The man who put you up to this." His shadow nemesis, his dark double. "What is his name?"

She began vigorously shaking her head. "No," she said. "I can't. Don't ask me that. I'll tell you what *I* did, but I can't give you *his* name. He would find me and kill me. I can't do it. I can't tell you."

"He must be locked up," Jasper said. "He'll hurt others. He's a dangerous person. A sadist."

"But I *can't*," she said, "I just can't tell—"

There was a noise in the hall, a sound like an army running rapidly up the stairs, a great clumping commotion that seemed to shake the frail building. Jasper heard shouts—female voices—crying out: "It's on the fifth floor!" and "Right at the top!" The pounding footsteps, growing louder, were mounting the final set of stairs. Before those footfalls reached the top landing, the apartment door burst open and Deepti ran in, screaming, "They have brought the police!"

Chloe jumped up, streaked to the door and tried to slam it closed. But it was pushed open powerfully from the outside. She backed up across the room. Jasper saw huge dark shapes pile into the room. A male voice barked: "Where is he?"

"There!" the Latina cried. "Right there!"

The cops rushed at him and grabbed him roughly by the arms. One of them turned to Chloe and demanded: "This your father?"

She hesitated.

Jasper could summon no words. He simply stared imploringly at the hunched, dark shape of the girl he had once believed to be his daughter.

"That's—" Her voice caught, and she fell silent.

"Who is it?" the cop barked at her.

"Come on, Chloe!" the Latina girl cried.

"That is my father," Chloe said.

The police spun him around. They disarmed him of his cane and pulled his hands behind him. The precious drawing tablet, which had been under his arm, fell to the floor. He felt the familiar sensation of handcuffs closing over his wrists. They tightened, biting into the flesh.

"Chloe!" Jasper cried as the police wrestled him toward the door.

Deepti stepped in front of the policemen. "Please," she entreated, "let me explain! You must let him go!"

Chloe's roommates crowded over and yelled, "Take him away! Take him!"

Chloe wailed, "Oh God! Oh God! Oh God!"

One of the policemen roared at everyone to *shut up*. The room went silent.

"This man is under arrest," the cop said. "There is an APB out on him in three states. He is a fugitive from justice. Now, stand aside."

They pulled him out the door. Jasper went limp in their arms. They half carried, half dragged him down the stairs. They would put him away for years. He thought about Pauline. Of how he would never see her again. She would never survive.

Maddy would be in her late twenties, her thirties, before he was free. Lost to him.

They had manhandled him as far as the second floor when he heard a noise from above. A door wrenched open. The sound of footfalls pounding along a corridor.

Chloe stopped in the hallway and, bending over the railing, looked down at Jasper's hopeful, upturned face on the landing below, his shriveled figure sandwiched between the two policemen. Her voice reverberated down the stairwell.

"Wait!"

7

On that day when she left him—a day not long after her twenty-first birthday—Dez woke around noon, as usual. Finding her not in the loft, he assumed that she had gone to one of her absurd modeling or acting classes (for all her natural grace and beauty, she had proved, thank God, peculiarly wooden when posing for photographs or trying to impersonate anyone but herself). Then he found the note, helpfully taped to the coffee machine, where he could not fail to see it. *I have left you,* it read. *I am not coming back.*

He did not believe it at first. She would soon return. After all, she had no money (he had not yet noticed the three hundred dollars missing from his wallet) and nowhere to stay. Besides

which, she loved him. It could only be a matter of time before she dragged in through the door of the loft, a bag over her shoulder, looking sheepish and apologetic. He even, that night, took the trouble (thoughtful Dez!) of ordering in one of her favorite dinner treats—a noxious Hawaiian pizza, with salty ham and virulently sweet pineapple slices. (Dez contented himself with a couple of garlic knots.) When she failed to return by nightfall, he slid the execrable pie into the garbage. So the little minx intended a more thorough punishment. Fine. He could wait her out.

A week passed. Then two more days. At which point he was forced to accept that she was well and truly gone. His reaction was one of puzzled indignation—the way a grand master chess player might respond when, through a massive oversight (owing to a too-deep calculation into an impossibly elegant thirty-move forced mate combination), his queen is captured by a patzer. The prankish inversion of the way things were meant to unfurl reduced him at first to a state of almost amused confusion, mouth slightly ajar, eyebrows up, an idiot smile trying to tug at the corners of his lips. Bitterness soon followed. Then rage. But a certain instinct for self-preservation made him decide that it was really *he* who had pushed *her* out, banished her to the streets—and under those circumstances, he could feel only glad that she was gone. After all, this is what he had long ago dreamed of—years before now, as she lay in the trailer's bedroom, sniveling and weeping for days on end after her mother's death. He recalled how he had fantasized about slipping out while she slept. Slipping out to freedom!

Well, he had that freedom now—and a great deal of money with which to enjoy it. Why, when you got right down to it, he had been insane to tie himself down to a domestic partnership with Chloe! Chloe—who, at twenty-two, was an *adult* now, a mature creature, with hips as wide as her ample bust and a wasp waist that only accentuated the distasteful *womanliness* of her voluptuous curves. How could he miss such a creature?

The answer was that he could not. He *would* not. Indeed, on the day when it was finally borne home to him that she was gone for good—the echo of her non-goodbye reverberating off the spare white walls of the suddenly vastly-too-big-feeling loft—Dez resolved that the last thing he would do would be to sit around listening to that mocking silence. Instead, he sprung from the sofa (where he had spent the better part of the afternoon and evening) and lit out for the downtown nightclubs and dance halls on the hunt for a teenaged beauty to soothe him. Only *now*, he would not have to listen to Chloe's endless whining about not wanting to "share" him, about how she didn't really *like* having sex with other girls. Now, he could flash his bankroll and entice back to his abode an entire *harem* of oh-so-young, oh-so-jaded teen beauties—and not have to answer to anyone.

He dismissed as sheer sentimentality—as a sign of his *own* woeful aging—those piercing moments when the image of Chloe, in all her wide-hipped womanly adultness, would flash before him and cause a kind of gulping sensation in his diaphragm, as if he'd been winded by a punch to the gut. At times—for instance, when he recalled the particular purring

softness of her speaking voice or the rough, burred sound of her laughter, or her way of waving helplessly a loose-wristed hand when Dez said something she deemed funny—he could even feel an aching sensation, like a bruise, in that part of his chest where he had reliably been told the heart resides.

All of this was too ridiculous to be true, of course, but on those occasions when he could not dismiss these maudlin reactions, he learned that he could douse them with a few tumblers of iced vodka; and when that failed to work, with the mounds of equally icy white powder supplied to him by his grinning doorman.

His reliance on both chemical prophylaxes increased sharply in the months following Chloe's departure. How was it that remembered images from their first year together—of her tenderly protruding pelvic bones or the girlish gap between her thighs—could grow *more* anguishing over time? More to the point, how was it possible that the memory of her broadened hips, her thickened legs, her increased breast size—all those manifestations of dreaded maturity—could cause him equal pain? A pain that only two thick lines laid out on the surface of his iPad, rinsed down with a tumbler of vodka, could numb?

On a night in December, six months after Chloe's vanishing act, Dez, wild-eyed and teeth-chattering on two large lines of a lightly saffron-tinged coke, found himself in an unmarked after-hours basement dance dungeon on the *extremely* Lower East Side, his ephebophile antenna twitching in his silk boxers, pointing him through the crowd like a dowsing rod. Through an atmosphere thickened by dance beats that seemed to convert

the air into a solid substance that pounded against his brain and body like oversized hammers swaddled in foam rubber, he spotted her through the DJ's strobing lights: a willowy young blonde in a shoulderless, second-skin spandex microdress, the concavity at the sides of her narrow nates, the folded-wing protrusions of her delicate scapulae and the telltale negative space between her slender thighs revealing that this was a sylph who had slipped into the club on a borrowed ID, one that misstated her age by at least two years, probably three. But more than these tender indices of illicit youth, it was a certain heart-lifting resemblance, a thrilling echo of gesture and outline, that made Dez halt, then circle in and gently interpose himself into the protective phalanx of girlfriends with which such beauties always surround themselves.

Up close, and in the flashing of the colored lights, the resemblance seemed uncanny—as if the years separating him from that day when he stood at the front of an eleventh-grade classroom in New Halcyon, Vermont, never took place. Dumbstruck, flustered, his heart trying to flee up and out through his esophagus like a panicked man escaping a fire, he could only extend, between quivering fingers, the business card he had had made for just such occasions, a card that stated his name (a pseudonym) and occupation (Professional Photographer, equally specious). He had little hope that she would call, but the very next day, when he was out on a coffee run to the corner bistro, he felt his iPhone stir in his pocket, vibrating against his flaccid member, soon stiffening in sweet anticipation. *Yes—yes, of course he remembered her. Certainly, he took model portfolio shots!*

Why, no—she did not need to have an agent. Yes, of course they could set up an appointment. How about later today? At his photographer's loft in Tribeca?

In stark daylight, and when Dez was relatively sober (he had drunk only a single vodka-spiked coffee and quickened his reflexes with a single, small key bump), he found the resemblance not as convincing—the skin less ethereally perfect, the features not as sculpturally pure, the hair a little dull, at least in comparison with the remembered gossamer, the movements devoid of that floating, fluid grace that haunted his memory almost more than any other aspect of her ghost—but she was a passable simulacrum and it was a stroke of pure genius when Dez, while snapping pictures against a blue paper background in his "studio," had the inspiration for her to "try on a few outfits." They visited Chloe's closet and for the next four hours, fueled by regular bumps of his yellowy powder, he found himself in an ecstatic dream state, as the increasingly convincing doppelgänger modeled his lost girl through the ages—not just in that period of prosperity following the civil suit, when Dez showered her with Prada and Lanvin, Burberry and Stella, but right back to that first glimpse, in that costume that he had never permitted her to throw out, the one in which he had first seen her: the faded, homemade denim skirt, cheap white halter top and grubby pink flip-flops.

Her name was Isabel and, like so many New Yorkers (Dez had come to notice), she conformed perfectly to the set of clichés and stereotypes assigned to her by the city: like the red-faced Irish bartenders; the bespectacled Ivy League journalists; the turbaned taxi drivers; the pin-striped, pig-faced bankers; and

the bearded artisanal cheese–making househusbands of Greenpoint, Isabel played her role as faithfully as if her words had been scripted for her, her clothes selected by a costumer, her pose and attitude shaped by an offstage director. She was an Upper East Side princess: the spoiled but neglected eldest daughter of a wealthy philandering restaurateur much in the society pages; a girl jaded, embittered; a sixteen-year-old-going-on-forty Brearley junior with daddy issues and a taste for any drug that could blunt the pain of her infinite, bottomless boredom. To Dez's initial naïve fears that someone would object to her being out all night, she rolled her eyes, then gave him a withering "You're kidding me" glance.

They holed up for days—weeks—at a time in the increasingly sordid loft and indulged their mutual appetite for what Dez's doorman cheerfully supplied. Isabel, who had connections of her own, introduced Dez to the dangerous delights of the speedball, and to an array of prescription medicines culled from the vast pharmacopoeia of her father's medicine cabinet. Isabel's own antidepressants and antianxiety pills also came in handy, as did the street Ritalin for which she bartered with her school pals, trading this or that frock bought (or stolen, just for the dangerous thrill of it) from Bergdorf's or Barneys.

Sex is also a drug of sorts, and, as with any drug, one builds up tolerances. So it was that the pair, around the one-year anniversary of their union, went in search of ever-greater novelty and began to bring home a parade of playthings: teen girls, of course (Isabel had exactly no restrictions against sapphic excursions), but also an increasingly eclectic array of men,

women and boys, a confused and confusing mass of random limbs such that Dez would often awake, at some unknown, ungodly hour, with the sky outside the window a predawn purple with a single bright red slash, like an incision, along the horizon of distant Queens, to find himself afloat on his king-size mattress like one of those half-dead survivors piled any which way in Géricault's painting *The Raft of the Medusa*, bodies hanging off the bed edge, with one lone figure, Dez, atop the pile and waving a grotesquely come-stained and -stiffened white T-shirt for rescue.

On one of those hungover, coke-jangled, OxyContin-numbed mornings, he surfaced to find himself in the spooning embrace of a reeking, white-bearded, tawny-toothed leprechaun—the amiable, if addled, outpatient who begged for change by holding open the door to the local Associated grocery store for patrons and who kept up a running commentary on everyone and everything in a squeaky voice like an unoiled wheel. Shouting in alarm, Dez leapt from the bed, which, he only then became aware, was peopled by three or four other entwined couples, including the floppy-haired Gallic-faced fruit seller who operated a stand at the corner of Morton Street, the apparently less-prim-than-Dez-thought female clerk (an exceptionally pretty black girl) at their local Tribeca branch of the New York Public Library, and Isabel herself, her ankle encircled by a chain looped through the nipple ring of the dreadlocked, white, trustfundian piercing enthusiast who lived one floor below them.

"We need to talk," Dez told her later that day, once their guests had been redistributed through the neighborhood.

"About what?" she asked, peering into the iPad propped on her knees. She was sitting on the begrimed and tattered Roche Bobois, smoking a menthol Benson & Hedges. As he contemplated her naked, monkey-thin body, breastless and smoothly tanned, her flat-ironed blonded hair, her affectless, empty-eyed, sad-mouthed dead end of a face, he realized, with a soft shock, that he was a little afraid of her.

"About us," he ventured. "About what we're doing. About last night. I think it's time—"

"Huh," she interrupted, dull eyes still on the screen. "That perv just got out of jail."

"What?"

"That guy—writer guy, whatever? Who was doing his daughter?" She held up her iPad for him to see. Dez, sitting opposite her on the matching white leather armchair, equally soiled, could make out only the bright red letters "TMZ.com" and a headline: Daughter Despoiler Free after Five-Year Stint. He jumped up and grabbed the device from her. "Hey," she stated tonelessly, "I was looking at that."

Dez ignored this limp protest and walked off to a far corner of the loft, peering into the screen, sweeping his fingertips with increasing speed across its smooth surface, flicking through the pictures. The first showed a stooped, impossibly aged, infirm, blind man, a white cane extended in front of him, stepping with obvious caution through a wide gate onto a stretch of sidewalk. Then a series of photographs, each at closer range, of this same man, confused, frightened, his mouth a black hole, waving his helpless cane, surrounded by paparazzi. Finally, a sequence that

showed the arrival on the scene of the home care worker—Padma? Deepak? (he could no longer recall)—pushing away the lensmen, waving her hands, shouting—and finally leading the halting old man down the sidewalk to a car, photographers in pursuit. The final shot was of the expressionless man, hair shaved down to a glinting white stubble, slumped into himself in the passenger seat, an explosion of reflected flashes bursting from the black lenses of his glasses.

Dez brought the iPad back to the living area. The photographs, to his surprise, had given him no pleasure.

"Funny, right?" she said as she took back the computer. "He looks like an owl. I saw his daughter on *Tovah*. What a low-rent skank."

Dez, who had begun walking toward the kitchen in search of some steadying vodka, stopped and turned. "What did you say?"

"This girl," she said, "his daughter, was on—whatever—*Tovah*? And like giving this whole big sob story about how her dad, like, fucked her or whatever and how she sued him and got him put in jail? And I mean, my friends and I were like, 'Uh, *yeah*, if we all went on *Tovah* and talked about our dads, every man on the Upper East Side would be in jail.' It's like, 'Uh, grow up, attention whore.'"

Dez stood contemplating her. She was flicking and clicking listlessly now on the iPad, probably on a shopping Web site. That the incident at the center of the disaster he had visited upon Ulrickson's family could be perceived—by this denizen of Manhattan's serenely untouchable, ultra-privileged money class—as simply a dreary, dull, quotidian occurrence hardly

worth mention; and that Chloe's emotional devastation could be seen merely as a sign of how hopelessly déclassé she was, how *poorly bred*—this brought him up short. Dez was hardly naïve or unworldly. But suddenly, and for the first time ever in his adult life, he felt the urge to go home to North Carolina.

He did not, of course, go home. Instead, he lived on, in the ruined loft, with Isabel, in that grim parody of his former relationship with Chloe. Their sex life, inevitably, dwindled to nothing, a casualty of overfamiliarity and rampant drug use. Other pursuits filled the void. They became habitués of the casinos in Atlantic City, staying in a succession of high-roller luxury suites in the hotels overlooking the bleak expanse of sandy swamp and watery wasteland that stretched to infinity around them. Buoyed by whatever concoction or combination of substances was their current favorite, sipping the free cocktails borne on serving trays by the miniskirted waitresses, they joined in the gloomy gaming halls the tobacco-tinged senior citizens bused in every day from their old folks' homes to play the computer poker machines, eat the Early Bird specials and ply the nickel slots. Desiccated Dez, with a spectral, hollow-eyed, skeletal Isabel draped upon him, started at the blackjack tables, placing heavy bets, and it took him a mere four months to work his way, with steady deliberation, through the fortune Chloe had been awarded.

Soon enough, he could not even afford the two round-trip bus tickets from Lower Manhattan to Atlantic City and they were reduced to playing online betting games on Isabel's iPad, gambling via PayPal. Meanwhile, each day's mail brought frightening threats from Dez's various creditors: MasterCard,

Visa, American Express. When the condo folks started to write to him, and then phone, about his nonpayment of the five-thousand-dollar monthly fee, he was obliged to admit that things were getting serious. Forced to switch from premium cocaine and the purest of heroin to cheap street meth and cough syrups to keep sickness at bay, they soon found that even these substitutes were beyond their means. (By now, they'd pawned everything pawnable.) Isabel, cut off by her family, was game to sell the only item left to them of any value, but Dez put his foot down, at first, insisting that he had more pride than that—not because he was especially averse to trading on the sexual allure of a girlfriend (what, after all, had his plot against Ulrickson hinged upon?), but because of the sheer lack of imagination—the inelegance—inherent in being a pimp. But when the illness became too acute (Dez spent a dreadful two days and two nights lying on the bathroom floor, hugging the toilet bowl between bouts of seizures), he let her go. She first raided Chloe's now almost empty clothes closet, and emerged dressed in the immortal denim skirt, white halter and pink flip-flops. "Not those," Dez weakly protested, "not those." But she had already slipped out, shivering, sniffling, into the cold March night.

When the phone rang less than an hour later, he pulled himself along the stained broadloom and answered it. She was phoning from the police station. Her first customer—or what she, in her illness and misery, took to be her first customer—turned out to be a pair of uniformed cops in a marked squad car. She was in the precinct house, under arrest, and she didn't know what to do.

"Call your father," he said, and hung up.

He dragged himself back to the bathroom for a fresh bout of vomiting and shaking. As he lay there, he was, for some reason, visited with a hallucinogenically vivid memory of *her* voice, from that day he masqueraded as Dr. Geld. She was trying to convince him that she was a changed person, that life with Ulrickson and his family had imbued her with goodness, purified her. "I've changed, Dez," he heard her saying in the bright cadences of one of Tovah's spiritual converts. "And you can too. I swear. It's never too late. You just have to learn to see the good in people! And in yourself."

The good in himself! Dez had to laugh, even as he lay, groaning, in agony, on the cold bathroom tiles. He had spent his whole life staring into the abyss of his own personality, had shivered in horror, even in childhood, at its impenetrable depths, and had set himself the task of sounding those depths, of taking the true measure of his malice and spite, his lust and cruelty. Where was the good? What good had ever existed in him? What good had he ever *known*? His mother? Yes—except that her slow, excruciating death from motor neuron disease, when he was fourteen, had only confirmed for him that "goodness," like white-bearded old God himself, was an illusion, a rumor, a jape played on credulous little boys and other innocents. Life was a sick prank that always ended in tears.

Suddenly, his fever broke. One minute he was dry-heaving into the spattered toilet bowl, the next he was rising to his feet, the pain in his guts—the slashing, knifing pain—turned off, as if by the flick of a switch. He had ceased to shiver, and his skin,

which had prickled with rough gooseflesh, had smoothed out, warmed, become that of a human being once again. Scarcely able to believe that the agonies of his cold turkey were over, he stepped to the sink, splashed his face with cold water, then straightened up and looked in the glass. If he had always been gaunt and pale, he was now a skull: bone white, fleshless, with eyes sunk deep into blackened sockets, his lips withered and receding, exposing his unmentionable teeth and gray gums. But he was alive, and the pain, the *pain*, was gone. He felt a rush of euphoria, of hope, more potent than any drug.

In the living room, he stood and surveyed the condition to which he and Isabel had managed to bring the loft. All of the furniture had been pawned or sold. For weeks, they had slept on old boxes smuggled from the garbage room. These torn pieces of corrugated cardboard lay strewn among the shreds of old clothes, broken dishes, empty pill bottles, bent syringes and pulverized coke vials. Evidence of the sickness of their withdrawal was splashed everywhere on the floor and on the walls.

He turned and saw the notices that had been shoved under his door by the condo company. Notices of pending eviction. Yes, he had certainly allowed himself to sink low. But he had been low before and dug himself out. And now, standing there in the detritus, he allowed himself to daydream about a new strategy for survival. It involved Ulrickson's daughter—the one from whom he had stolen the DNA sample. He smiled as he imagined how he would bide his time, patiently wait until the child, now nine or ten (and, according to Chloe, living in San Francisco with her aunt), turned a delectable fifteen, that

age Dez liked best, when the face still holds significant baby fat but the breasts have swollen almost to full size, the limbs gawkily sprouted to supermodel length, as if in sheer surprise at the pubertal changes taking place. He would travel to San Francisco, insinuate himself (somehow!) into Ulrickson's sister's home—perhaps as a tutor?—then woo and win the girl. When she turned eighteen, he (an elegant yet still Peter Pan–like forty-five-year-old) could wed her! And thus win access to the other third of her father's fortune.

He was amusing himself with these idle fancies when there was a knock on the door. He started. Visitors were not allowed up to a tenant's apartment unless announced by the security team in the lobby. Could it be the condo people coming to enforce an eviction order? No, their last notice still gave him three months to make good on his debt to the building. He crept on tiptoe across the living room toward the peephole, but halted several paces from the door when he heard a jingling sound in the hall, followed by the rattle of a key pushed into the lock. His heart rose on an irrational hope.

"Chloe?" he said.

The door swung open and into the apartment stepped Pete, the building's short, stocky, white-haired superintendent. In his hand was a key, attached to a massive ring of similar-looking keys. He had a strange look on his face. "These men," he said in his thick Bulgarian accent, "they need to see you."

Two men in long dark overcoats stepped into the loft from the hallway. Dez recognized them instantly, from their taciturn,

slablike faces, as lawmen. He turned, intent on making a run for the vast window, to hurl himself through its lucent membrane of glass and copper, to cast himself to the earth twelve stories below. But, enfeebled by his recent illness, he was able to hobble only a few paces before he felt hands grab at him and wrestle him facedown onto the filthy rug. A boulder-like knee pressed into his fragile spine as the cuffs tightened. He assumed that he was being arrested on a charge of aiding and abetting Isabel's hopeless attempt at prostitution. Only later, when he was in an interrogation room at the First Precinct House, on Varick Street, under questioning by the detectives, did he learn about the drawing tablet containing the messages Pauline dictated to Maddy; about Chloe's confession and the immunity that protected her from prosecution; about how Ulrickson, although nearly as blind as his absurd fictional detective, Geoffrey Bannister, had brought Dez's master plan to ruin.

Adding grotesque insult to unspeakable injury, the cops informed him of how the family, including little Maddy, had now been reunited in a house in Ulrickson's old neighborhood, Deepti once more caring for Pauline—and Chloe, having transferred to Jasper's nearby alma mater, Yale, happily ensconced in the house as helpmeet, friend and surrogate daughter to the man Dez had tried to destroy. An eye operation on Ulrickson had been a big success. He was writing again.

For those in the police station that day—cops and criminals alike—it was an unusual and eerie occurrence when, from behind the closed interrogation room door, there came a sound

rarely, if ever, heard in those dour purlieus: laughter. First quiet, then rising on an out-of-control note, on a pitch of hysteria that seemed to border on madness.

They drove him across town to Manhattan Central Booking, the grim gray stone edifice that housed the criminal courts and the subterranean holding cells known, colloquially, as the Tombs. In a ground-floor office, he was fingerprinted and photographed.

Quiet and cooperative, Dez (already plotting his escape, his return, his revenge) was led downstairs.

Acknowledgments

A number of people were instrumental to this novel's seeing the light of day, first as a manuscript, then as an actual published work.

I conceived the plot in 2001, but not until summer 2009 did I start writing—inspired, in part, by my friend Oivind Magnussun, who quit his job to start his own (successful) business, and who warned me that a life lived sailing close to shore in safe harbors was no real life. That I found a two-week stretch of quiet to begin a rough draft, I owe to my friends Chris and Erinn Deri, who happened to have invited my then ten-year-old son to Florida to visit with their daughter, Katie. My wife was visiting her parents in Canada, so I found myself alone in our Upper

East Side apartment, where I wrote some thirty thousand words in a two-week-long, round-the-clock marathon of scribbling.

My brother, Ted, a neurosurgeon, answered my many questions about locked-in syndrome (although all departures from fact, for poetic license, are my responsibility alone). I also found helpful the books *Look Up for Yes* by locked-in patient Julia Tavalaro and Jean-Dominque Bauby's *Diving Bell and the Butterfly*. For legal details, I'm hugely grateful to Susan E. Barnes, whom I happened to find as the first hit on a single, random Google search ("Family Lawyer, Vermont") and who proved extraordinarily helpful, faxing me, from her office in Stowe, sample paternity claim documents, talking me through the process by which courts vet prospective custodial parents in such cases, and describing to me the role of social workers and psychologists in easing the transfer of a child from one living situation to another—all vital to the workings of my book. (Again, all errors are my own.)

Some timely comments by my editor at the *New Yorker*, Nick Trautwein, some two years into the writing, revived for me a project I had all but abandoned as impossible. When I described to Nick what seemed the insurmountable task of making a good and decent man perform one of the most heinous acts imaginable, he said, "Given that we know she's not his real daughter, we might just forgive him one slip-up—but no more than that." (I had been imagining Jasper descending into a hellish period of violation of Chloe lasting weeks or months). Suddenly I was writing again.

My first reader, aside from my wife, was my agent Lisa Bankoff, to whom, for superstitious reasons, I had not even described the book. I was overjoyed by her enthusiastic reaction

(but also properly warned by her proviso that I would have to be as "ready for the hate mail as the honors.")

Indeed, given the current prevailing winds (social, economic, political), I suspected that *Undone* might have some difficulty getting into print at all in the U.S.A., but I could not have aniticpated its circuitous route to publication. It might never have happened had not Lisa, at the outset, retained as separate the rights for Canada (the country where I was born and still hold citizenship); thus the manuscript found its way to Iris Tupholme, executive publisher and editor-in-chief of HarperCollins Canada. It is to Iris that I owe the un-repayable debt of passing my manuscript to Patrick Crean, who had recently launched his own imprint at the house.

By then, some forty-one publishers in America and a comparable number across Europe had rejected *Undone* on grounds of its "risky" subject matter. Patrick felt no such fears. Published in Canada in spring 2015, *Undone* was named one of the best books of the year in the Globe and Mail, and the paper's literary editor, Mark Medley, wrote a story detailing the novel's vexed publishing history. A link to Mark's story appeared on the website LitHub and (thank goodness!) caught the eye of Counterpoint/Soft Skull's Executive Editor, Dan Smetanka. Only then, after two years of steady rejection, did the book find a U.S. home. I could not be happier or more proud than to appear at an imprint justly renowned for blending risk-taking edginess with literary quality.

The wonderful novelist Claudia Casper was an early reader and gave me excellent suggestions for how to improve the book;

authors Harlan Coben, Frank Delaney, and Diane Meier were also early readers and great champions. Likewise, Ron Bernstein, ICM's man in Los Angeles and Jesse Kornbluth who featured *Undone* on his culture blog, Headbutler, a full year before it secured U.S. publication. My friend, author Joe Hooper, gave the book a careful read, and I benefited greatly from his typically cogent and subtle insights.

Thank you to my wife, Donna, who regularly warned me of the landmines such a story strewed before the feet of an unwary (male) writer; and our son, Johnny, who along with his parents lived with the writing of this book longer than any of us thought we would have to (I said it would take a year; it took four).

Finally, I'd like to make special acknowledgment of my late mother, Carol, an avid reader (and, in her seventies, a published author). It was from my sense of the pleasure and solace she took from the written word that I myself wanted to try my hand at writing. Before embarking on *Undone*, I was sufficiently nervous about the challenges of its subject matter (the invidious nature of desire) that I spelled out the plot to her, over Skype, and felt relieved when she pooh-poohed my trepidation over reception of the novel's faux-incest theme. "All subjects are fair game in literature," she reminded me. I returned to the task with fresh courage, and was happy when she, then in the final stages of ALS, read the finished manuscript and gave it her blessing. Always bearing in mind my agent's warning about the inevitable angry mail, I hope most other readers will be as indulgent.

Author Photo: Donna Mehalko

JOHN COLAPINTO is an award-winning journalist, author, and staff writer at *The New Yorker*, where he has written about subjects as diverse as medicinal leeches, Sotheby's auctioneer Tobias Meyer, fashion designers Karl Lagerfeld and Rick Owens, and Paul McCartney. Prior to this, he wrote for *Vanity Fair*, *New York Magazine*, and the *New York Times Magazine*, and he was a contributing editor at *Rolling Stone*. His nonfiction book, *As Nature Made Him: The Boy Who Was Raised as a Girl*, was a New York Times bestseller and his debut novel, *About The Author*, was nominated for the International IMPAC Dublin Literary Award. He lives in New York City.

D0373468